TOGGENBURG – BOOK 1
Early Purple Orchid

Michaela Francis

TOGGENBURG – BOOK 1
Early Purple Orchid

Chapter One

Incredibly, Sarah's train was late. There'd been some technical problem with the line in Burgdorf and it had delayed the train by about fifteen minutes. It was an extraordinary occurrence. There'd been a murmur of outraged indignation among Sarah's fellow passengers on the 11.35 St Gallen express and the train's officials had been apologetic to the point of grovelling abjection. Sarah had been amused by the situation and not at all distressed by the trifling inconvenience. The previous summer, she had spent a holiday in Italy and travelled on the Italian railway system extensively. In Italy, a train turning up on time was an unprecedented event eliciting gasps of astonishment and rounds of applause. She had once been a witness to an early morning train leaving Milan station so punctually that it had stranded over fifty percent of its commuters, who were habituated to its customary tardiness, on the platform. There'd nearly been a riot. But this wasn't Italy. This was Switzerland and trains were *never* late in Switzerland.

Sarah gazed out of the window of the dining salon of the train at the glorious early summer radiance of the Swiss countryside and smiled to herself as she let her fantasy roam. Fifteen minutes late! Good God there would be high level boards of enquiry; repercussions among the executive echelons of the Schweizer Bundesbahn; recriminations among the engineering divisions. She giggled to herself. Maybe they'd even form a hollow square for the Burgdorf station master; ceremoniously cut off his epaulettes and badges, break his baton and drum him out of the service in disgrace.

Sarah was half Swiss and half English and the half of her that was English displayed a somewhat less than reverent respect for the sombre institutions of the Helvetic Republic. She lived in Switzerland and had done for most of her life. She loved the country for its beauty, its warm hospitality and civilised courtesy. She adored the land as a haven of sanity and humanity. There was no place else in the world she could ever want to live in yet there was a little rebellious streak in her that refused to take it entirely seriously.

When the train had finally left Burgdorf station and crossed the River Emmen, with the big sandstone bluffs towering over the river, Sarah ordered another glass of wine from the waiter in the dining car. It was disgraceful really. It was far too early in the day to be drinking. But Sarah was in a happy, almost holiday mood. Her three years at the university in Bern were at an end and finally, gloriously, she was going home. Every kilometre that the train headed east took her closer to the place in which her heart truly resided. Even three years at university had not dulled the aching homesickness she felt for her beautiful valley. Every summer's day that had necessitated her exile, she had yearned for the flowery meadows on the hillsides above Unterwasser and every hint of snow from the distant mountains had beckoned her to the crisp whiteness of the mountain flanks gleaming under the winter sun. But now she was going home and she vowed not to leave her valley again.

Sarah was beautiful. Anybody would have told you that. The young man pretending to read the Zuricher Zeitung at the table of the dining car across the aisle would have readily agreed with that sentiment as he admired her covertly from behind the defensive shield of his newspaper. He saw a warm beauty that was not entirely explained by the soft waves of her long chestnut brown hair, the heart shaped, exquisitely fine boned features of her face, the gentle brown eyes and generous mouth made for smiling. The beauty went further even than the slender yet neatly proportioned body to be discerned beneath the casual open necked blouse and well-fitting blue jeans. It was true that her breasts were high and firm and her stomach admirably flattened to her

6

slim waist. Her legs were long and the seat of her jeans were moulded around a firm perfectly proportioned behind that many a woman would have sold her soul to the devil for. Even her hands were long and slender; seemingly designed for elegance. Yet, even taking all her undoubtedly attractive physical characteristics into account, there was something else that defied description, almost, that set her apart from just being a very pretty girl.

Sarah's true beauty came from some inner lode within her. On a superficial level she was indeed a very beautiful girl just twenty-one years of age now and emerging slowly into full womanhood. Her age was a constant astonishment to Sarah because she had never really reconciled herself to it. It still amazed her that she was a young woman in her twenties now. Perhaps the three long years as a student had somewhat arrested her maturity in some way for she was, both by appearance and outlook, still a teenager. Indeed she had gone to university a rather gangling long legged eighteen-year-old but somehow, in the intervening years, her youthful awkwardness had transmuted itself into a warm maturing loveliness even as Sarah was the last person to recognise the fact.

Sarah dressed habitually in jeans and rarely donned a dress or even a skirt. She was not a girl to use make-up extensively or even to fashion her hair much although she enjoyed wearing it long, even when she was obliged to tie it back for convenience. In fact, Sarah often seemed indifferent to her appearance and in some way that was one of her greatest charms. Sarah was actually one of those very rare creatures; a beautiful girl almost totally lacking in vanity.

It was Sarah's apparent oblivion to her own attractiveness that made Sarah so irresistible. There was no sense, whilst talking to Sarah that here was a girl completely obsessed by her own appearance. Some people are interesting but Sarah was always *interested.* She never seemed to notice that people found her attractive. Indeed she would have been surprised to know of it. She simply didn't think that she was beautiful. Such a thought was almost alien to her. She could talk to a young man in the university bar about some intriguing point of academic interest and be quite oblivious to the fact that the young gentleman in question was starting to gibber and slobber into his beer glass. Her friends at university had been much amused by this trait of Sarah's and had occasionally poked gentle fun at it.

This warm-hearted and un-self-centred nature had earned Sarah many friends at university. She was popular and well-liked by all her female colleagues and the object of much heart break among the male students. There was a wholesomeness to her that transcended the normal predatory male instincts. This wasn't a girl to bed for transient gratification. This was girl to fall in love with.

Despite the extensive fan club of young men who would have gladly thrown themselves at her feet and made terrible vows of unwavering devotion for life to her at university, Sarah's academic career was very nearly blemishless. In fact, she had never dated a boy throughout her university life, although it certainly wasn't for lack of suitors. Sarah didn't think this unusual. For one thing, she already had a boyfriend. His name was Alan and, although she saw him seldom, they had been solidly attached to each other ever since she had been just seventeen.

Alan was the son of one of Sarah's father's business partners and there'd been an understanding between the two families that had weathered Sarah's sojourn at university. To all intents and purposes, Sarah and Alan were betrothed although there had not been, as yet, any formal declaration of that betrothal. It had been accepted that Sarah would first finish her university studies and then the long-standing arrangement would be formalised and a date set for a future wedding. It was a highly agreeable arrangement for the families involved. They were tied ever more closely in alliance through business and Sarah and Alan's wedding would cement that alliance with familial ties. It would be a perfect union. Alan was a dynamic upcoming junior partner in the business and destined for great things in his future career. He was well on his way to becoming a wealthy young man and his family had all the wealth and connections to ensure the future prosperity of Sarah's family. Sarah's future was firmly assured.

Chapter Two

The train was pulling into Zurich and Sarah grimaced in distaste. She disliked Zurich. She realised that she was probably doing the city less than justice. After all, it was by no means an unpleasant city with an agreeable location on the banks of Lake Zurich, with lovely waterfront views and chic pedestrian precincts. Nevertheless she disliked it. Partly this dislike was due to her aversion to big cities. Sarah was a country girl at heart and needed the free country wind in her hair and not the loathsome clatter and noisome fumes of automobiles. It could not be entirely that, however, for she had taken to Bern with its old-world charm perched up on the hills above the River Aare. Zurich was different though. There was a clamour and bustle to the great city and its sprawling suburbs that Sarah found disagreeable. It lacked Bern's charm to her. It was a thoroughly modern sort of city; chaotic and restless and she never enjoyed any visit there even though Alan's business took him there often. She had dutifully accompanied or visited him there, on several occasions, but she had always breathed a sigh of relief upon leaving its boundaries behind. Alan was not in Zurich now however. He was away in America and would be for some weeks or months to come.

There was one part of Zurich to which she had no objection however. After the stop at Zurich Hauptbahnhof, the train plunged into a tunnel and, after a couple of minutes, emerged into the underground railway station that served the airport. Airports fascinated Sarah. On the occasions when she had been obliged to visit Zurich she had sometimes come out to the airport just to spend an afternoon drinking in the atmosphere of the place. She'd sit at a café bar in the terminal and just watch the holiday makers and travellers, lugging their baggage through the airport and looking worriedly at the information boards, and wonder where they were headed. Or she'd take a window seat, at one of the upstairs restaurants, and just watch the aeroplanes landing and taking off, still amazed how such enormous machines could take so gracefully to the air. Airports to her were gateways to exotic and strange fairy lands, she only knew from books and television. In all her twenty-one years of life, Sarah had never flown in an aeroplane. She dreamed of it sometimes. Alan had promised that, when she finished university, he would take some time off work and they would fly away for a holiday somewhere.

Perhaps they would fly to England. Sarah had been five years old when her family had left England. She could barely remember it anymore. Sarah's mother came from the small town of Beverly in Northern England and had met her father whilst on a skiing holiday in St Moritz. He'd been a young rising businessman then and his business had brought him often to England. The holiday romance he had forged with Sarah's mother then had bloomed and he had frequently visited her on his business trips. A few years before Sarah was born, her father's business had offered him the opportunity to take over their offices in England and the besmitten young man had leaped at the opportunity. He'd moved to Beverly and, within six months, he had married Sarah's mother in the lovely old parish church of St Mary's.

The marriage had been a happy one. Indeed it still was, Sarah realised with a fond affection not unmarked by anxiety over her own forthcoming nuptials. Sarah's parents were still hopelessly devoted to each other and still, after twenty-six years of marriage, demonstrably in love with each other. The marriage had been both prosperous and fruitful too, for they'd been comfortably well off and, in those early years, decidedly fertile. Sarah's elder sister, Jessica, had been born soon enough after the marriage to raise eyebrows and invite a certain degree of amused consultation of the calendar. Her brother, John, had followed within two years and then there'd been a gap of nearly three years before Sarah, the baby of the family, had graced the family with her presence to her doting father's everlasting delight. Sarah's connection to Switzerland went further than her father's nationality for, although she had been born in Beverly, her mother had always insisted that she had been conceived in front of a log fire one night whilst the family had been on holiday in Zermatt.

In spite of that, Sarah had spent the first five years of life in England before her father's business had wrapped up their English concerns and the whole family had moved to Switzerland. She could barely remember anything about Beverly now other than some vague impressions of an old quaint little market town and the images of the big garden they had had there and the huge minster that had dominated the town. She knew that she had still some relations there but she knew them hardly at all. Her English grandfather had died very young and her grandmother had married again and that to an American who had whisked her away to California, where she still resided. Sarah had only ever met her once since.

Her English roots fascinated Sarah and she had often looked up Beverly on the internet or in books. Most people in Switzerland had never heard of the place for it was a small town of less than thirty thousand inhabitants set in a rural area of East Yorkshire but Sarah had been astonished to learn that it had once been one of the most important cities in England and had a rich history dating back to the seventh century. Sarah was deeply interested in history, as evidenced by the fact that she had just spent three years at university studying it. It was an ambition of hers to one day visit the town in which she had been born.

Sarah had grown up in Eastern Switzerland but, although she was a thoroughly Swiss girl by now, she still regarded herself as English. She spoke English as fluently as Swiss German; a condition encouraged by her mother who, even after sixteen years in Switzerland, still struggled with the language. Her mother had new language problems now, of course, for, some three years ago, as her children had left the nest, she and her husband had moved to the Ticino; the southern Italian speaking region of Switzerland. She had nagged Sarah ever since to move to Ticino with them but Sarah had resisted claiming that it was too far from university. It was a transparent excuse. Her parents had a lovely home in a beautiful region near to Ascona but Sarah's heart was firmly wedded to the valley, in which she had spent her childhood, and the thought of living anywhere else filled her with horror.

Her excitement grew as the train emerged from the subterranean world beneath Zurich airport and sped once more out into the countryside. There was a brief stop in the funny little industrial town of Winterthur, for which Sarah had a strange affection, and then the final hop to the small town of Wil where Sarah was obliged to change trains. Her heart was fluttering as the PA system in the train announced the approach to Wil and she started to remove her luggage from the racks. She had two suitcases and a large shoulder bag. Most of her belongings had been transported back by her brother in his van over a week ago. John lived with his girlfriend in Appenzell in the next Canton and Sarah had solicited his assistance to move. It was incredible how much stuff you could acquire in three years in university digs.

The big intercity express slowed to a halt at Wil station and Sarah struggled to the Platform with her heavy luggage, worrying that the delay may have made her miss her connection. It was a needless worry. All Swiss trains connected to each other, late or otherwise, and her connection was waiting patiently on platform five. Sarah grabbed a convenient luggage trolley and, loading her bags aboard, set off in some haste for the ramp leading to the tunnel beneath the line, for the express had deposited her on platform one. It was hard pushing the heavy trolley up the long sloping ramp to platform five and she had a sudden dread that the train would depart before she had negotiated it. Her haste was irrational, she knew. Even if she did miss the train, there would be another within an hour and there was a perfectly congenial buffet at the station to while away the time in. But, now that she was so close, she found herself in a hurry. She wanted to be home.

In the event, the train was still waiting although she was the last person to board and the platform controller was tapping his baton impatiently against his leg as she muscled her bags onto the train. She had barely heaved herself aboard before the automatic doors clattered shut, the whistle blew and the local train gave a lurch and ground its way out of the station. It was to be the most frustrating part of the journey. The local train stopped at every village to cross its path and its progress was painfully slow. Sarah sighed and found a seat, before rummaging in her handbag for her mobile telephone. With a smile, she keyed Nicole's number.

Nicole was Sarah's best friend and housemate. They'd shared the tiny little old farmhouse up at Alpli for nearly four years now although Sarah had been absent for much of the time. Nicole was English too and it was that shared heritage that had brought them together at school where they had become inseparable. Their friendship was the source of much amusement in the valley for Sarah and Nicole were the classic example of the attraction of opposites. Sarah was the quiet, well mannered, serious girl of modesty, restraint, good sense and pleasant manner tinged with a touch of shyness. Nicole was none of the above! She was a flamboyant, muddle-headed, devil take the hindmost little extrovert with a penchant for finding trouble with alacrity and whose escapades and misdemeanours were of legendary status in the valley. She was a mad-cap little lunatic who apparently left chaos in her wake wherever she walked and Sarah adored her.

Nicole answered the phone immediately with a booming shout. "Hiya! That you Sarah?"

"Yes It's me and there's no need to shout Nicky dearest. We have modern electronic technology for amplifying and projecting our voices over the telephone."

"What's that Sarah? You'll have to speak up. Your signal's breaking up."

Sarah sighed and raised her voice. "I said it's me and I just got on the train in Wil. Where are you?"

"I'm in the car just driving down to pick you up. I should be there in about ten minutes or I would if this fat Dutch bastard with his caravan in front of me would get a move on or shift out of the way."

Sarah smiled. Nicole was not noted for her patience behind a steering wheel. "Don't be in too much of a hurry Nicky. My train got held up in Burgdorf and I'm running late."

Nicole's response was a few choice vulgarities in a mix of English and Swiss German which Sarah presumed was directed at Nicole's fellow motorists rather than at herself. "Sorry honey what was that?" Nicole enquired after venting her spleen.

"I said I'm running late. There's no need to knock yourself out getting there on time."

"Ok. I'll see you then." Nicole hung up and Sarah reflected that no advice urging caution or lack of urgency was liable to ease Nicole's foot pressure on the accelerator. Nicole considered herself a good driver; a boast sadly contradicted by her sorry past record of minor accidents and speeding tickets. Nicole steered a car along the roads of Switzerland in much the same way as she steered her own way through life; at high speed and with little regard for the consequences.

Finally the train pulled into the station at Nesslau. The little town was the final stop on the line. From here, the only connection to the upper valley was by post bus or, in Sarah's case, at the mercy of Nicole's erratic driving. Sarah had barely hefted her luggage out of the train when a piercing whistle startled her fellow passengers on the platform and started an old lady's little dog barking. Nicole was dashing along the platform towards her; her scandalously short mini-skirt whipping perilously high about her upper thighs. Above her mini-skirt she wore a T-shirt bearing the debatable slogan that bad girls do it better but it was not this that outraged Sarah's somewhat conservative sensibilities. She stared in horror at the head of her irrepressible young friend. Crowning Nicole's impish grinning face was a tousled mane of shocking pink.

With a squeal of delight Nicole launched herself into Sarah's arms in an effusive hug but Sarah refused to be mollified by the warm welcome. She held her friend at arms' length and regarded her with icy disapproval. "Nicole Richardson! What the bloody hell have you done to your hair?"

Nicole grinned. "What's up? Don't you like it?"

"No I do *not*! You look like a badly coiffed stick of candy floss."

"Oh don't start Sarah. You're as bad as my mother. Come on let's grab your bags and get out of here. I'm parked on a double line and if I get another parking ticket my dad will go ape shit with me."

Sarah groaned and shook her head. "I don't know why we just don't use all your traffic violations on the lavatory wall. We'd save on wallpaper."

"Well unless you want to cover the damp patch over the cistern today let's go."

Gladly Nicole's unauthorised parking location had not yet attracted the disapproval of officialdom and Nicole's battered old Renault 5 stood proudly, ticket free, outside the station as the two girls squeezed Sarah's luggage into its not particularly capacious interior. Sarah noticed a new scratch in the car's already somewhat degraded bodywork. "Er shall I drive?" she volunteered hopefully.

"Nah! Can't have you driving on your first day back. Let me drive and you just sit back and relax."

Sarah pulled a face. "I can think of a few emotional states that come to mind whilst being a passenger in any car that you're in charge of Nicky but relaxation is not one of them."

"You're an old mother hen Sarah. What's wrong with my driving?"

"Nothing I suppose if you happen to have a death wish."

"Oh stop moaning and get in."

Nesslau was a bit of a bottleneck on the valley's road system and it took them a few minutes of erratic manoeuvring and some frenzied swearing from Nicole before they finally clawed their way clear of its traffic. But Nesslau was the gateway to the upper valley and Sarah's pleasure grew with every kilometre of the road that passed beneath their wheels. This was the Upper Toggenburg; the mountain fringed heartland of Sarah's domain. To the south lay the teeth like chain of the Churfirsten mountains and as they came into view Sarah rolled their familiar names off her tongue; Selun, Frumsel, Brisi, Zuestoll, Schibenstoll, Hinterugg and Chaserugg. To the north the Toggenburg was bounded by the grandiose vastness of the Santis massif with its peaks of Silberplatten, Altman, Schafberg and, dominating them all, the gleaming peak of Mount Santis itself. There was late snow still clinging to the peaks of the mountains and they glistened like ice encrusted jewels in the pure blue sky of early summer as they welcomed their adopted daughter back to the valley that had taken her for its own.

Sarah never lost the thrill she felt upon re-entering this world of hers. It was, to her, a tiny enclave of sanctuary with its few villages of Alt St Johann, Unterwasser, Lisighaus and up to Wildhaus, and the scattered hamlets and farming communities clinging to the valley sides. It was a piece of paradise, this hidden little valley, in the East of Switzerland. Sarah had seen it in every mood and revelled in its every season. She loved it when the valley lay under the thick carpet of winter snow and the spruce trees of the great forests sparkled with their sugar coating of ice. When night fell in December, the fairy lights on the trees around the farmhouses, hotels and chalets reflected in the snow and turned the valley to a Christmas fantasy land.

But it was the summer months she adored the most, when the pastures turned to riotous colour with flowers and the clanging of cowbells provided a fitting harmony to the valley's rural loveliness. Every old and elaborately decorated wooden farmhouse was adorned with flowers in its window boxes and there was a neatness and comforting assuredness to the human habitations that clung so tenaciously to the few patches of level ground among the alpine grandeur of the surroundings.

In common with many an alpine valley the Toggenburg had been scarred by the demands of tourism but, in the Toggenburg's case, the scars were fairly superficial. The winter skiing was not particularly obtrusive and the ski-slopes confined largely to the slopes of the Chaserugg and Gamserugg. The summer tourist scene was mostly low key and mainly targeted at the hikers that came to the valley for the many kilometres of hiking trails among the magnificent peaks and the forests that gripped their feet. The modest tourist industry provided a welcome boost to the valley's economy but there was still a large pastoral community and sheep and dairy cattle roamed high and wide on the alps and meadows in the summer, around the little alpine huts occupied by the herdsmen in their lofty positions high above the valley floor. There was still a sense of old tradition that never faded in the valley's embracement of the modern age and Sarah loved it for its continuity and the stubborn resistance of its community. It was her home.

Chapter Three

Sarah was so entranced by the scenery around her, as they approached Alt St Johann, that she was barely listening to the flood of gossip flowing out freely from Nicole's lips. Nicole was an incessant chatterbox and she seemed to think that Sarah would be hopelessly at a loss unless brought fully up to date with all the local scandal and rumour. Nicole paused in exasperation. "Are you listening to a damn word I'm saying?" she asked testily.

Sarah tore her eyes from the window. "I'm sorry Nicky. It's just good to be home. What were you saying about Frau Heinzl?"

"I said the old battleaxe is threatening to put the rent up again."

Sarah laughed. "She's been saying she's going to put the rent up for the last three years Nicky. Nothing's happened yet."

"Yes but she sounds serious this time. Says that the cost of things is rising so sharply that she's on the edge of ruin. Edge of ruin! Her? The tight fisted old vixen's got millions stashed away and never spends a penny if she can help it. You'll have to talk to her. You're her favourite. Just give her that little Miss butter wouldn't melt in her mouth routine and maybe we can put her off for a few months."

Sarah sighed. "Ok I'll have a word with her. What's up with the telephone anyway? I tried to call you on the land line yesterday but I couldn't get through."

"Oh we've been cut off."

"Cut off! Why?" Sarah demanded furiously.

"No panic I was just a bit late with the bill."

"Oh bloody hell Nicky! How much was the bill?"

"Two hundred and eighty-five francs."

"WHAT?"

"Don't worry Sarah. It's payday on Friday I'll sort it out then."

"How the hell have you racked up a bill for 285 francs?"

"Just a few calls to the boyfriend that's all."

"For God's sake Nicky! I ought to slap you."

"I'm sorry. It won't happen again."

"It better not. What if my mum calls me and finds us cut off? She'll go loopy. I hope to hell Alan hasn't phoned up."

"It's only been a few days. I'll sort it."

"How is the boyfriend anyway? What was this one called? Roget wasn't it?"

Nicole snorted loudly. "Don't mention the foul pestilential low-life bacterial scum to me! I hope his balls turn into bicycle wheels and back pedal up his arse!"

Sarah grinned. "Do I take it that this outburst indicates that all is not well on the domestic front?"

"The bastard dumped me. Can you believe it? He dumped me!"

"Was this before or after the new hairstyle?"

"After. Why? What's that got to do with it?"

"Oh nothing."

"Yes anyway he's dumped me for some blond tart in Buchs. The bloody excrescence! The next time I want to get intimate with a nasty little invertebrate form of pond life I'll go drown myself in the Schwendisee."

"Well look on the bright side honey." Sarah told her. "It was quite an improvement on your usual form in relationships wasn't it? I mean he must have lasted all of three months."

"It's all right for you Sarah." noted Nicole resentfully. "We can't all be engaged to some good-looking bloke from a rich family in Zurich you know. It's pretty thin pickings around here."

"I'm not engaged."

"Not yet you're not. You will be soon though. Now you've finished uni Alan's bound to pop the question."

"I don't know if I *have* finished with university. My tutor wants me to go on to do my masters."

"What the hell for? It's not as if you're going to be making a career out of it. I mean with all the money Alan's got behind him you'd never have to work again."

"There's more to a career than just money Nicky. Maybe I've got other ambitions than just being a rich housewife."

"I'd like to see you tell your parents that. They'll never go for it."

Sarah sighed ruefully. "No you're right... they probably won't."

"What's the matter with you anyway? I thought that marrying Alan was the be all and end all of all your ambitions. God knows you've waited long enough for him."

"Well I thought it was. Now I'm not so sure."

"What on earth are you on about honey? Surely you're not having second thoughts."

"I don't know Nicky. I just don't see me as the perfect little housewife and hostess in a city somewhere. Alan will want to move to Zurich permanently. I can't live in Zurich. I'd be miserable there."

"What's wrong with Zurich? It's got more bloody life than this place."

"I'm a country girl Nicky. I'd wither away in the city."

"Christ Sarah! Have you got PMTs or something? It's not like you to talk like this. You've been with the guy for four years. You can't possibly be thinking of backing out of it. What the hell would your parents say? They got you and Alan all lined up for a nice cosy family dynasty. They've done everything but book the bloody church. You two are the match of the decade. You can't back down now."

"Maybe that's the problem Nicky. Everybody's got me and Alan all married up in their plans, nice little family understanding, all sorted and arranged. All I have to do is turn up obediently at church and get pedalled off like a prize cow. Nobody's actually asked me what *I* want. My compliance is taken for granted."

"I thought you loved him."

"So did I once. Now I don't know any more. He's been away abroad so much I've hardly seen him this past winter. I know he had to be away and I don't blame him for that but what really worries me is the fact that I didn't miss him. In fact I felt quite liberated. All I really missed was the Toggenburg and if I marry Alan I'd have to move away from here anyway. Every time I think about it my stomach turns over. This is my home. This is where I live."

"Sarah darling Alan's not only drop dead gorgeous but loaded as well; or at least his family is and he will be in due course. Where the hell else are you going to find a catch like that?"

"Perhaps it's not enough Nicky."

"Well for fuck's sake keep me out of it. If you split with Alan your mother is bound to blame me for influencing you. You know she will."

Sarah pulled a face. "I'm not saying I'm splitting with him. I just need some time to think is all."

"Well think fast Sarah sweetheart. Alan will be back from the States this summer and then he'll be wanting to make the engagement formal, sure as death and taxes. You'd better make up your mind what you *do* want."

Sarah groaned. "I know." She stared out of the window in quiet despair. They were just approaching Unterwasser and the turn off for the little country lane that led up to Alpli where their rented house lay. "Look Nicky let's go for a drink at the Alpli before we go home shall we? It's a gorgeous day and I don't feel like unpacking yet."

23

"Suits me. I'm thirsty."

The steep road up to the hanging valley, that was an offshoot to the main valley to the north, was normally free of traffic but, today, there was an obstruction. As they rounded a bend, there was the sonorous clanking of bells in front of them and Nicole swore in frustration. "That's all we bloody need!" In front of them was a solid mass of bovine backsides ambling along the road and being chivvied by cowherds dressed in bright traditional costumes. One of the docile Swiss Brown cows turned to look over its shoulder at Nicole's Renault behind it and stoically lifted its tail to deposit a large dollop of dung in the road in front of the car. "And the same to you!" Nicole riposted.

Sarah giggled. "God I've missed this." she remarked.

"Oh great! So you want to give up a life of wealth and luxury for a backwater dump like this and a liberal sprinkling of cow shit."

"Look let's drop the subject for the moment hey Nicky? I don't want to talk about it right now."

"Ok. Suit yourself. What are you going to do for the summer anyway?"

"I don't know. Get a job I suppose. I can't live off my dad forever."

"They're looking for waitresses at the Sternen for the summer if you're interested."

"I might be. I might see if they'll give me my old job at the Hotel Toggenburg back as well."

"That's right on the other side of the valley up at Schwendi Sarah. It's a sodding long walk back from there at night after you finish work."

"Well my dad was talking about getting me a little car after I finished uni."

"That'll be good. This old banger's had its day. We could do with a new car."

"You can forget the "we" Nicky. If my dad buys me a car it'll be a cold day in hell before I let you get your mitts on it. You'd trash it in no time."

"Oh ye of little faith." Nicole tapped the steering wheel impatiently. "These cows are doing my head in. We'll not get past them until we get to the top of the hill."

Sarah grinned. "Well I'm in no hurry." In truth, Sarah enjoyed the rustic scene as they dawdled behind the herd. It was the time of the year for the cowherds to drive their cattle up on to the high alpine pastures and the drives were accompanied by all the traditional trappings of the event. The cowherds were dressed in bright red tunics and bright scarves over blue and white shirts decorated with Edelweiss flower patterns. Their black hats were garnished with flowers and their brown trousers held at the waist by ornate black leather belts decorated with brass cows and stars. Some of the cowherds were even smoking the traditional funny little, upside down mountain pipes that were characteristic of the region. Even the cows were dressed up for the occasion with flowers about their necks and horns and the big ornamented festive cow bells called Treicheln hung around their necks. They were a colourful part of rural Switzerland's folk heritage, these processions, and Sarah was amused to note a small group of tourists in hiking gear by the side of the road taking photographs.

At last they came to a part of the road where the cowherds could wield their sticks on their beasts behinds to clear a path for the car and, a minute or two later, they pulled up at the little car park before the Alpli restaurant and guest house. It was the closest restaurant to Sarah and Nicole's house and they were familiar visitors to it. Being off the beaten track, it was a little on the rustic side but charming for all that while the sunny terrace in front of the restaurant afforded magnificent views across the alp to the foreboding presence of the towering

25

Schafberg mountain and, higher up the alp, the land climbed up to the great peak of the Santis itself; the highest mountain of the region at just over two and a half thousand metres.

As Sarah and Nicole dismounted from the car, there was a strange encounter. There was the toot of a car's horn and Nicole waved gaily. Sarah spun around to see a bright red Ferrari coupé cruising past with its hood down. Seated behind the wheel, smiling and waving in a friendly fashion was one of the most spectacularly beautiful young women Sarah had ever seen. Her glorious mane of golden blond hair crowned an exquisitely lovely face and the soft fabric of her clearly expensive rose and white summer dress clung to her perfect curves in a sensual grasp. With a final wave, the girl was gone the red car growling smoothly away toward the descent down into the lower valley. Sarah blinked in astonishment. The glamorous vision seemed almost ludicrously out of place in the rustic setting of the alp. "Who the hell was that?" Sarah demanded in amazement.

"That," began Nicole with a degree of smugness, "was Daniela Devin! Didn't you recognise her?"

"Who the devil is Daniela Devin?"

"Oh come on Sarah! Even *you* must have heard of Daniela Devin."

"Never seen her before. She isn't local surely."

"Oh really Sarah! You really have to get out more. Daniela Devin's a singer; a pop-singer. She's famous."

"Never heard of her."

"Oh God help us! She's only one of the biggest stars in Switzerland at the moment or Europe for that matter. She's English; well part English part American and part Swiss. You must have heard her new single "Blue Stone Lady". It's being played all the time and top of the charts. She's got half a dozen hit singles and three top-selling albums to her name."

Sarah frowned. "Blue Stone Lady sounds familiar. I think I've heard it somewhere. A bit west coast American style with a guitar solo in the middle isn't it?"

"That's the one. It's not her best though. I really like her music. I'm quite a fan of hers."

"Well what the hell is she doing in the Toggenburg?"

"She lives here."

"You're kidding me."

"Seriously. She moved here last summer and took a big villa over near Oberdorf. Apparently her grandma came from the Toggenburg and she used to visit her here when she was a kid and fell in love with the place so she's come here to live."

"Wow! That's a touch of glamour for the old valley isn't it?"

Nicole laughed. "Oh hell yes! She's had every man in the valley drooling over her from the moment she arrived." Nicole grabbed Sarah's arm. "Come on let's get a drink."

On the terrace of the Alpli restaurant a young waitress in a white pinafore came out to greet them warmly. "Hoi Gabi!" enthused Sarah and rose to embrace the girl fondly. Gabriela was an old friend.

"Hi Sarah! Welcome home!"

"It's good to be back Gabi!"

"What are you drinking then?"

Sarah turned to Nicole. "Let's have some wine Nicky. Bring us a half litre of Fendant Gabi."

"Of course. Good to see you back Sarah."

Sarah smiled at the little brunette waiter and she and Nicole settled onto a table at the front of the terrace overlooking the road. "So you know this Daniela Devin do you?" she asked Nicole.

"Sure! I see her about quite a bit. She's always friendly and nice."

"What on earth made a woman like that want to live in the Toggenburg?"

"Privacy I would guess. At least she can keep out of the public eye up here."

"Well she certainly catches the eye."

"Yes she does! She's drop dead gorgeous, famous and got more money than she knows what to do with... blast her."

"Does she get out a lot then?"

"No not really. Keeps herself to herself generally."

"A bit standoffish then?"

Nicole shook her head. "No not really. She's actually really nice; always takes the time to stop and chat when you bump into her. I guess she's just a pretty private sort of person and enjoys her privacy. God knows she's enough in the camera headlights when she's on tour or whatever."

Sarah smiled. "Well I think it's exciting. It's not often the Toggenburg gets to host a real live pop diva."

"Maybe she's come up here to get away from things." Nicole mused. "There was a lot of talk in the tabloids that she'd been in some sort of love triangle with the other members of her band."

Sarah gave a snort of laughter. "I wouldn't believe everything you read in the Blick Nicky."

Gabriela emerged from the interior of the pub with a tray bearing a carafe of white wine and two tiny glasses. The glasses were so small you could have taken them for shot glasses rather than wine glasses but that was the way people drank white wine in rural Switzerland. "We were just talking about Daniela Devin Gabi." Nicole told her. "Have you met her?"

"Oh yes a few times. She comes in here from time to time for a bite to eat or a coffee. She was in only last week."

"What's she like?" asked Sarah interestedly.

"She's a sweetheart; really lovely and friendly. She never stays long or drinks much but she always leaves a big tip. Haven't you met her then Sarah?"

Sarah shook her head. "No. I've never seen her until just now."

"She just drove past in her Ferrari Gabi." Nicole explained.

"Well I'm surprised Sarah." Gabriela remarked. "I mean she's been living here for over a year now. Didn't you see her last summer?"

"I wasn't home much last summer. I spent most of the time in Italy or at my parents in Ticino."

"Well you'll like her. She's a nice girl. Quite the celebrity around here as well."

"Blimey do we have paparazzi sniffing around the valley now then?"

Gabriela laughed. "Oh there were a few reporters around when she first came but they fizzled out. Danny's not the kind of celebrity that provides much in the way of colourful footage as it were. She just lives quietly alone with her cats and a cleaning lady that comes in twice a week. I suppose she's quite boring like that. There're only so many photographs you can take of a person pushing a shopping trolley around Migros before the public loses interest."

Nicole nodded in agreement. "Yeah. When she first came, I hoped it might spice the valley up a bit and we'd have loads of visiting stars and scandalous parties being thrown, and what have you, but she's been a bit of a dead loss. About the only interesting thing she's done, so far, is to have a row with Heinz Hartman when he took a chunk off her garden fence with his tractor. These modern rock stars are a waste of space. Whatever happened to the good old traditions of sex and drugs and rock and roll?"

Gabriela laughed. "Well you won't find Danny doing that Nicky. She's squeaky clean when it comes to drugs. She hardly even drinks. As to sex well rumour has it that she hasn't so much as looked at another person ever since her lead guitarist ran off with one of the backing vocalists."

"Well uninteresting or not she's obviously providing some material for gossip." noted Sarah with amusement.

"Anyway I have to see to my customers." Gabriela told them. "Prost girls and it's good to have you back Sarah."

As Gabriela departed Nicole picked up the carafe and poured out two thimbleful glasses of wine. "Cheers Sarah. Good to have you back."

"It's good to *be* back." Sarah picked up her glass. "Cheers."

Nicole sipped her wine and looked at Sarah mischievously. "By the way Peter was asking about you."

"Oh?" said Sarah non-committally, but her heart was fluttering and Nicole knew it.

"Yes he was wondering how you were."

"Really?" Peter was an old friend of Sarah's but she had long harboured a secret fondness for him that went some way beyond the limits of platonic friendship.

Nicole laid down her glass and looked at Sarah straight in the eye. "These... er… these second thoughts you're having about Alan wouldn't have anything to do with Peter would they?"

"Don't be ridiculous Nicky!"

"Who's being ridiculous? I know for a fact you've been sweet on him for ages. Don't deny it. I know you too well."

"I would like to point out Nicky that as you have already remarked today I already have a boyfriend and a pretty serious one too."

"That doesn't stop you thinking does it? Or looking for that matter. Peter's a hunk. He's worth looking at."

"Well whether he is or isn't there's nothing between us. He's never shown the slightest interest in me other than as a friend."

"Hmmph! As if you'd know anyway. Half the blokes in this valley have been lusting after you ever since school and you've never seemed to notice. It's not as if you've given the lad any encouragement either. I mean the last time you met him you bored him rigid telling him all about the trip you took to Italy with Alan. If you're thinking of dumping Alan and making a move on Peter I'd start being a little less sisterly with him and start showing him a bit more feminine guile if I were you."

"That's a monstrous suggestion Nicky."

"Well don't tell me that you haven't thought about it because I won't believe you."

"This conversation is at an end Nicky!"

Nicole held up her hands. "Ok, ok! Just trying to give you some advice."

"Advice from somebody who hasn't been able to hold on to a fellah for more than three months ever since I've known her? Thanks very much!"

Nicole picked up her wineglass. "Ok I'll shut up."

Instantly Sarah was contrite. "Oh I'm sorry Nicky! That was a bitchy thing to say. I'm sorry. I.... I'm just going through a bit of a patch over Alan for the moment and my head's a bit screwed up about it. I don't want to talk about it just now. Let's not argue honey. It's just good to be home. Let's talk about something else."

Nicole grinned. "Ok Sarah. I won't rattle your cage anymore. Here's to your return."

They clinked glasses together and there was peace between them. A speck in the air above the mountain to the east caught Sarah's attention. "Oh Nicky look! An eagle!"

"What? Where?"

"There soaring up over the side of the Schafberg. You must be able to see it."

Nicole peered at the distant speck uncertainly. "Is that an eagle?"

"Yes. There's always a pair around the Schafberg. I used to see them nearly every day when I was shepherding for the Bauerman's." Sarah gazed at the distant raptor circling effortlessly on the thermal over the mountainside. There were two pairs of Golden Eagles that nested regularly around the Toggenburg and a sight of them always thrilled Sarah. She watched the bird climb higher and higher on the thermal and felt a fitting sense of rightness at the spectacle. "God!" she said, "It's good to be home!"

Chapter Four

It took Sarah three days to unpack. This was not particularly a reflection on the amount of work involved in that particular chore. There was, it is true, quite a lot to unpack for there were all the boxes and cartons of things that her brother had transported for her the previous week in addition to the baggage she had brought herself. All of this had to be carefully unpacked and meticulously stowed away in the little farmhouse cottage she shared with Nicole. Sarah was fastidiously tidy and ordered; a great believer in the virtues of consigning possessions to their allotted place. This was a trait that brought her frequently into conflict with her much more unruly housemate who seemed to regard open areas of floor unadorned by personal articles as space wasted and tended to undress by force of gravity.

Sarah had expected to return to the house and find it in a state that suggested that some theoretical physicist was conducting experiments in chaos theory in it. She'd been pleasantly surprised to find the house reasonably tidy. The last time she'd come home for summer. the place had been an unholy mess and she'd had a fearful row with Nicole over it. Presumably a suitably chastened Nicole had made the effort and tidied up before her arrival this time. It wasn't perfect of course. Sarah opened one cupboard to find it stuffed to the gills with completely random miscellaneous articles that had quite obviously been thrown in there, in some haste, to get them out of the way before she'd arrived home. Still it was a start and Sarah was pleased to note some degree of reform in her woefully disordered and adorable housemate. In any case, Sarah was not in a position to criticise Nicole's lack of domestic thoroughness on this occasion for, as has been noted, it took her three days to unpack when she could, in all conscience, with due industriousness, have completed the task in one.

Sarah's lack of application was not a result of laziness but more that, now she was back home in her beloved Toggenburg, she resented any moment indoors wasted in domestic activity whilst the sun shone outside on the glory of the valley. She would do some unpacking in the morning and perhaps a little as evening fell but the lure of the sunshine on the alp would prove too much for her resolution and the chores became neglected as she rushed out of the house in joyous anticipation.

This sad state of affairs was not helped by the fact that one of the first things that Sarah unpacked was her favourite pair of footwear. Sarah, uncommonly for a woman, was not big on shoes. She spent more time in a pair of trainers than anything else and, in her whole wardrobe, she possessed only three pairs of suitably elegant feminine shoes and two of those were presents from her mother. The other pair, probably her best, she'd bought reluctantly the year before in order to attend a wedding. It was the only time she had ever worn them. There was one pair of footwear, however, that held a siren's call to her imagination and she lifted them reverently from the depths of her rucksack with deep pleasure. They were scuffed and somewhat battered and there were the traces of mud encrusted in the treads on the soles but they were her favourites. They were hardly designer shoes but they had a well-respected name attached to them for they were Raichle mountain boots; durable but comfortable quality boots for hiking in the high mountains.

Mountain hiking was Sarah's passion. In her years in the Toggenburg she had become familiar with nearly every trail that wound its way up the assorted peaks of the region. It was her proud claim that she had ascended every mountain in the Churfirsten chain although they were not her favourites. Most of the mountains of that line had only a single route to the summit and necessitated returning by the same path. The best of them was the Chaserugg for it gave the hiker more options by way of variety in its routes. But Sarah found the Churfirsten mostly quite tame. For her, the real thrills were on the other side of the valley and the vast expanse of the Santis massif.

Sarah knew the Santis and all its adjoining peaks like the back of her hand. She had first climbed to the summit when she was just seven years, old accompanied by her father, and had loved the mountain ever since. Since that first conquest, she had climbed the mountain more times than she could recall and she'd explored every marked trail that covered the whole complex of peaks for the Santis was not just one mountain but simply the highest peak in a complex of associated mountains, ridges, passes and valleys with deep glacial lakes sitting in the arms of the great up-thrusting limestone pinnacles. Sarah knew every mountain hut, every hostel, every nail biting arête, every fixed cable climb. Sarah was truly expert on the Santis Massif and even seasoned mountain guides and local shepherds respected her encyclopaedic knowledge of the mountain.

It was not just familiarity with the actually physical nature of the mountains of the Toggenburg and its surroundings that set Sarah apart however. In her hiking rucksack Sarah kept a number of well-thumbed and battered nature field guides. A pride of place was given to her tattered copy of Collin's guide to the Alpine Flowers of Britain and Europe. It was not enough for Sarah simply to enjoy the sight of all the extraordinary flowers that bedecked the high mountain pastures or nestled in the rock crevices at high altitude. She needed to know the names of them too and as much of their biology as she could learn from her reference books at home. Without trying Sarah could instantly identify well over five hundred species of flowering plant and she had logged in her field notebooks close on a thousand assorted flowers both lowland and alpine. If you wanted to know the location of the beautiful and scarce Martagnon Lilies Sarah was the person to ask. She could tell you to the inch the place to find the Yellow Bellflowers, the elusive fragile Edelweiss, the colonies of Alpine Larkspur, the strange looking Queen of the Alps or the tiny little Snow Gentians. They were all old friends to Sarah.

Her knowledge of botany was remarkable for one so young and it was just the tip of her extraordinary knowledge of the wildlife of the mountains. She was an authority on the Lepidoptera of the Toggenburg. She could tell you to the yard the colonies of rare butterflies on the mountains, where to find the lovely Apollos, the rare Mnestra's Ringlet or spot the difference between a Queen of Spain's Fritillary and a Niobe Fritillary from fifty metres. She carefully noted down the details of these in her notebooks and over the years her notes had added up to a remarkable record of the wildlife on the local mountains. She had probably the most comprehensive record of the altitudinal ranges of day flying moths for instance that had ever been recorded in the Toggenburg. She knew virtually every species of dragonfly and damselfly to be found and where it was to be found in the Toggenburg. She had a large-scale map in her collection that pinpointed every known Toggenburg colony of Alpine Marmots; the big mountain ground squirrels that lived in burrows on the high mountain pastures. She could point out any bird on the mountains and identify it or tell you the identity of a grasshopper just by its song alone. She knew the pools where the Alpine Newts gathered in spring and early summer to breed or the marshy meadows where you could find the Agile Frogs. Her knowledge was an enormous well and the source of that well lay in her profound love of the mountains in which she had spent all the days of her youth.

It was small wonder then that, newly returned to the land that gave her so much joy, her domestic obligations lay so wantonly neglected. Each day, as she ate breakfast with Nicole in the tiny kitchen of their little house, Sarah looked wistfully out of the window at the Santis. Regretfully there was still too much snow clinging to the mountain for her to contemplate an excursion up it just yet. Another couple of weeks or so she promised herself each day. But there was still much to be explored. The lower valley was gorgeous with the pastures awash in meadow flowers and the valley's birds were in full song at nesting. There was a Black Redstart singing from the roof of the house each day with its funny scratchy phrases and the White Wagtails were everywhere in the meadows and around the barns.

So, each day of her first week home, Sarah was out in the open air. She knew she should be looking for a job but her funds were still holding out and her doting father was usually generous to his youngest daughter upon her pleas of poverty should they run low before she had found meaningful employment for the summer. There were people to meet as well, for Sarah's return was already well known in the valley. She was a well-liked girl. Other girls took to her warm friendship immediately and, whilst she was beautiful, her lack of vanity and the way in which she seemed oblivious to her own beauty negated any sense of rivalry that other aspiring young ladies, more fond of their own appearance, might have felt. Young men of course cursed their luck that the lovely Sarah was spoken for. She'd been pretty enough when she'd gone to university but she'd seemingly blossomed since then and a smile from her was enough to take your breath away. That Sarah was experiencing her first pangs of doubt over her long-anticipated betrothal was not yet known or it would have electrified the long suffering, covert fan club she boasted among the unattached young men of the valley. The elder people were fond of Sarah too for she was both courteous and respectful and always ready to stop on the street to exchange greetings and inquiries about the other's family.

For the first three days then, whilst her unpacking proceeded so slowly, Sarah confined herself to wandering about in the lower valley. She revisited her old friend the Thurwasserfall; the hidden waterfall located in a steep gorge behind Unterwasser before taking lunch on the sunny terrace of the Sternen hotel without making enquiries as to job opportunities. She walked up the steep hill on the far side of the valley to the hamlet of Schwendi and walked around the two little lakes; the Schwendiseen before saying hello to friends that owned the little restaurant there. She visited an old favourite restaurant the Gade built from a converted barn on the descent back down to the valley floor. She took the post bus up to Wildhaus and from there she took the little cable car up to Gamplut where after a drink and a chat with the proprietors she walked across the meadow beneath the feet of the towering Schafberg, looking out for parties of Ibex, up on the mountainside before descending down through the forest to Alpli. It was gloomy in the damaged forest on the way down but she heard the loud yelping call of a Black Woodpecker and, better yet, the whistling of a Hazelhen.

She saw little of Nicole during these days for Nicole had a new job waiting on tables at the Hotel Hirschen in Wildhaus. Sarah hoped it would last. Nicole didn't have an exemplary record in holding down jobs. Sarah was not short of company however. If the people she met on her forays were not enough, then the numerous calls on her mobile certainly compensated for them. Sarah's older sister Jessica called her up to congratulate her on finishing university. Sarah loved her sister and she liked Jessica's husband as well, which somewhat set her apart from other family members. Jessica's husband, Damien, was a sore subject in Sarah's family because Jessica had married him without her parent's consent and her rebelliousness had been a bone of contention ever since.

Damien was an artist and, at the time he had met Jessica, he had not been either a particularly wealthy or successful one. This had filled Sarah's mother with abject horror and she had refused whatsoever to condone the relationship. Jessica had wilfully defied her parents and married him anyway. The rift had lasted nearly two years and Sarah had found herself in the impossible situation of acting as an intermediary between her sister and her parents who had barely been on talking terms with each other. Time had done much to heal the rift and, even more so, Damien's artistic talent had proved Jessica's mother's fears ungrounded for, after two years of abject marital poverty in a bedsitter in Luzern, Damien had achieved commercial breakthrough with his art work and illustrations and now he and Jessica lived comfortably in a converted farmhouse close to Luzern. Sarah's mother had reluctantly forgiven her daughter and peace reigned once more although there was always a tension between the domineering matriarch of the family and her strong-willed daughter.

Sarah often thought about Jessica's marriage. It was an exultantly happy one. Jessica and Damien had been married some five years now and they were still like a pair of love-struck teenagers with each other. She had visited them early in their marriage when times had been hard and she'd been struck at how closely bonded and happy they were; even when they were living off spaghetti and potatoes in a tiny bedsitter and worrying where next month's rent was coming from. It was an idealistic marriage to Sarah; a true marriage of love that no hardship seemed able to break. The little furniture they'd had they'd begged or salvaged from other people and they'd slept together in a single bed that Damien had rescued from a refuge skip. Jessica had cycled into town every day to work part time in a shop while Damien had helped to make ends meet by working as a kitchen porter in a hotel. They'd had no television and they'd spent their evenings together in their little bedsitter just enjoying each other's company. Sarah possessed a portrait of Jessica from this period that Damien had painted on their long evenings together in the flat. Sarah was always struck by how radiant her sister looked in the portrait. Perhaps it was because Jessica was truly deeply content that she shone so vividly in the portrait or perhaps it was because Damien's loving eye had seen her that way. Sarah suspected that it was both of those reasons. Sarah's mother had vehemently declared that she would never allow Sarah to make the same mistake her sister had. Sarah would look at her smiling sister's, shining face in that portrait and wonder just how much of a mistake it really could have been.

Sarah's father called her as well. Sarah adored her father. Whenever she talked to him it seemed as if she shed the growing burden of adulthood and reverted back to being a little girl. That was hardly surprising she realised because she knew that, in his heart of hearts, that was exactly how her father saw her. She was his youngest daughter and still secretly his favourite. To him she always was and probably always would be the captivating little child that had played on his knee and run to him for comfort whenever she had grazed her knee. His eyes were rose tinted and time distorted as far as she was concerned. Had Sarah been a different person she might have been terribly spoiled by his indulgence of her and ruthlessly exploited his softness toward her. He had hardly ever spanked her and rarely chastised her in any way. Her mother had assumed most of the responsibility for her daughter's discipline and perhaps that had been no bad thing for Sarah could have grown up pampered and spoiled had her father had anything to do with it. To his credit her father had never taken Sarah's side when her mother had chastised her and had made it plain that he agreed with his wife that it was necessary to spank her if she had been naughty. If she had been naughty he would be disappointed in her and his disappointment would always hurt far more than the wooden spoon her mother would use to paddle her bottom. If there was one thing that had always been important to Sarah it was the fear of disappointing her father. She wanted him to be proud of her.

The telephone call from him promised to be gratifying therefore. Able to report that her studies were successfully completed and that she had high hopes of a good mark in her final exams, there was nothing in her recent history to let down his good opinion of her. His praise was warm and heartfelt and Sarah quivered in pleasure as he told her of his pride in her. She mentioned her current lack of transport to him casually and he took the bait admirably. He would look into getting a little car for her. Sarah's pleasure grew. She had never owned her own car although she had borrowed one of her family's more or less exclusively until it had developed some mysterious and apparently incurable malaise and been sold for scrap. Her father was definitive however. She would have a car upon graduation. Sarah was disappointed. Graduation wasn't for some months. She began to plot how to wheedle her new automobile in advance. Her father generally let her have her own way if she babied up to him.

The conversation ended up on a rather worrying note however. "So what are your plans now?" her father asked.

"Oh I don't know immediately Daddy." Sarah's father was always "Daddy" never Father or even Dad. "The first thing I suppose is to get a summer job. There's usually plenty of work around here for the summer."

Her father hummed and haa-ed uncertainly. "If you came to stay here for the summer you wouldn't need a job." He pointed out.

Sarah's heart jumped in anxiety. "But Daddy I can't come to live on your charity!" she protested. "I've got my own place here."

"It would only be for a short time Sarah honey. After all Alan will be back this summer and I should imagine you'll have other plans by then."

"I... I don't really know when he's going to be back Daddy."

"I talked to his father the day before yesterday Sarah. He's expected to return around the end of July so maybe he could come down then. We were thinking of throwing a little party for the two of you."

Her mother would be behind that Sarah knew. Her social events were always large and significant dates on the calendar and Sarah was not fooled by the seeming casualness of the proposition.

"Yes your mother and I had a long talk with Alan's parents. They're of the opinion that now that you've finished at university there's nothing stopping you two from becoming formally engaged. In fact they went further than that and said that they didn't see any necessity for a long engagement. If you're married before the end of the year then you'll be able to take advantage of your married status on next year's tax returns they say. They suggested that we set a date by the end of summer or early Autumn. We've talked about where you'd live and so forth and I've told Bruno and Alan that you will inherit the property in Zurich upon marriage so you won't be out on the street. According to them, there's absolutely no reason why you can't be married by the end of August if we start planning now."

Sarah's throat was suddenly dry. "I... I see. And what did you say?"

"Well we told them we'd have to confer with you of course. It grieves me to let my little Sarah go but you've been patient up to now and it's the least we can do to reward your forbearance. Your mother thinks it's a splendid idea. She wanted you to marry here in Ticino but most of the nicest churches are Catholic so we might have to think again there."

Sarah's heart was hammering in her breast. "I... I always wanted to marry in the Toggenburg Daddy."

"Well we'll have to get together and talk it all through Sarah which is why it would be a good idea for you to stay here for the summer. That way we can all start planning together. It will be lovely to have you home for one last summer before you marry off."

"But Daddy I only just got back. I can't just up and move to Ticino now. I've Nicole to think about. I pay half the rent."

"I'm sure Nicole can find another house mate Sarah. If necessary we can help her with the rent until she finds someone new."

I.. I don't know Daddy. It's all a bit sudden."

"You don't sound very happy sweetheart. I thought you'd be pleased. God knows you've waited long enough to marry Alan. There's no point in dragging it out any further."

Sarah thought furiously feeling the walls of the trap closing about her. She only had one card to play but it was a devastating one if played carefully. "Daddy," she murmured in her best little girl voice. "I've only just finished my final exams and I was looking forward to relaxing for the summer. It's been three long hard years and I need a break. Then I've had all the stress of moving and everything. I just don't feel up to moving again just yet. I haven't even finished unpacking yet! Now you want me to start immediately planning for a wedding. If I come to Ticino mum will be all over me with guest lists, dress fittings and God knows what else.

I can't do it Daddy! I need some time to myself; to chill out and not think about the future too much. This is just too quick. It stresses me out." She managed a little sob at the end of the outburst.

Her father's voice became more concerned. Sarah's use of the word "stress" had been masterful. When she'd been at school studying for her final exams Sarah had become seriously ill from the stress and it had frightened her father badly. He had since been sensitive to his youngest daughter's vulnerability to the condition. "That's all right honey. Hush now. Nobody's trying to pressurise you into anything that you're not ready for. I can understand you wanting to take a little holiday. God knows you've worked hard enough. I'll tell them that you need a few weeks to get your head together. Maybe you could come down here next month and we can talk it out. We ought to know what we're doing before Alan comes home in any case."

"Daddy there's something else."

"What honey?"

"Well I mean isn't it a little premature to start planning for a wedding before we're even formally engaged? Alan's not even proposed to me yet."

Her father chuckled. "I think we can take that part of the proceedings as a formality honey. Don't say I said so because it's supposed to be a surprise but a little dicky bird whispered to me that Alan's already got the engagement ring."

Sarah started and she was glad that her father couldn't see the expression on her face. "Oh!" was all she managed to say.

"Yes darling so I wouldn't have any worries on that score. Anyway we'll leave it for the time being until you've had time to get your head around things." He paused for a short laugh. "I don't know what your mother's going to say though. She's already made up the short list for the bridesmaids."

Sarah groaned. "I thought the bride was supposed to choose her *own* bridesmaids!"

"You try telling your mother that. She's gone off to Milan for a few days to look at wedding dresses."

"Daddy! Who's damn wedding is this supposed to be? I'm the bloody *bride* not mum's personal Barbie doll for the day."

"Sarah, Sarah." said her father placatingly. He was a little shocked. It was uncharacteristic of Sarah to swear in front of her father. "You know what she's like. She's just so excited about your wedding. She's like a kid at Christmas. You can't blame her for wanting to be so proud of you."

"I can blame her for wanting to hi-jack *my* day. *I* am the bride and *I'll* choose my own bridesmaids thank you very much and I'll pick out my own wedding dress too."

"She just wants to help honey."

"No she doesn't Daddy! She just wants to be in control. This is my bloody wedding so tell her to butt out!"

"Sarah, Sarah," he repeated soothingly. "I'm sure your mother will defer to your wishes. I'll talk to her when she gets back from Milan. Now just don't worry about a thing for the moment. Look I have to go now. I'll talk to you again at the weekend. Love you!"

"Love you too Daddy."

After her father had hung up Sarah flopped into an armchair with a frown of anxiety. She was pretty sure that she had managed to obtain a stay of execution as far as her father was concerned but her mother promised to be a far more formidable adversary. She was still sat in agonies of indecision as the door crashed open and Nicole entered in her working uniform with her usual flamboyance. "Hi Sarah! God what a bloody day! We've had two coach loads of German tourists in and they've had us running about like blue arsed flies after them. My feet are killing me." Sarah grunted and Nicole looked at her sharply. "Uh oh! Had a bad one have we? What's up hun? You've got a face like a slapped arse."

"Just had a torrid phone call from my dad." Sarah regarded Nicole's less than unobtrusive hair colour with distaste. "You'd better change that flipping hair Nicky. I'm damned if one of my bridesmaids is going to accompany me down the aisle looking like a mentally deranged cockatoo."

"Bridesmaid? Bridesmaid? What's all this about?"

"My bloody parents have got together with Alan's folks and started planning my wedding already. They're all after shoving me off into marital bliss by the end of August at the latest."

"Oh brilliant!" Nicole clapped her hands in glee. "Wow! We've got some planning to do."

"Don't *you* bloody start Nicky! I'm not ready to get married yet. God I didn't even expect to be formally affianced until this summer and then I thought I'd have at least a year or two before we actually got down to the bloody logistics of the thing. Now they want me all packaged up and shipped out within three months. I can't do it."

Nicole frowned. "Well just tell them then."

"Oh Great Nicky! Have you ever tried telling my mother that something she's got her heart set on isn't going to happen?"

"Well it's your wedding after all."

Sarah snorted. "I think my mother would beg to differ. Dad says she's gone off to Milan to pick out a wedding dress for me! If she's got the bit in her teeth to that extent I'm never going to shift her. She'll Shanghai the whole bloody affair and that's me filed and receipted."

Nicole looked at her friend compassionately. "Poor Sarah. Come on hun grab a jacket and we'll walk over to the Alpli for a drink. It's my treat. I'm flush with cash. I made a load in tips today."

Chapter Five

Over a drink in their local restaurant, Sarah began to relax although she poured out her woes to her friend in somewhat bitter detail. "I'm just not ready for all this!" she ground out at last.

Nicole took her hand. "Look honey it's not my business maybe but this is your life you're talking about. If you're not ready then you just have to say it. Talk to Alan. Tell him that you need a bit more time. If he thinks enough about you he'll be prepared to wait."

"Alan wouldn't understand Nicky. He always does as his parents want him to do and he'll never understand me not doing the same. Anyway he's already waited for over three years."

"Well surely your family will understand if you need a little more time."

"Oh Nicky you know what it's like. My dad and Alan's dad are business partners. Our families are very nearly joined at the hip. Marrying me into Alan's family is a matter of formalising the bond between the two families; merging us into a common dynasty if you like. We've been groomed for each other for the better part of five years."

"I thought you'd only been an item for three and a half."

"We have but our parents had it in mind a lot earlier. When Alan finished university our parents introduced us to each other and more or less pushed us into each other's company. Right from the start we were left in no doubt that this was a relationship our families approved of."

"But you were in love with him weren't you?"

"Nicky I didn't know what love was. I was seventeen years old. I was still a virgin and knew nothing about men. Along comes this tall handsome man four years older than me and my hormones went into overdrive. I'd hardly ever even had any boyfriends and now this good-looking guy is calling to see me all the time. Of course I was infatuated. I had teenage illusions of romantic love. I was frustrated too. I couldn't tell the difference between sexual fantasy and love."

Nicole laughed shortly. "Well I can identify with that. You wouldn't be the first teenage girl to think she was madly in love when all she really needed was a good shagging."

"I lost my virginity with Alan Nicky. That was really important to me. I always thought that you only gave yourself for the first time with a man you truly loved."

Nicole snorted delightedly. "Oh God you were a real little innocent weren't you? Sod me! I lost my cherry by a campfire up at Grappelensee when I was fifteen; some lad from school; buggered if I can remember his name any more."

"I was nineteen Nicky. I'd been seeing Alan for over a year before we made love."

"How was it?"

Sarah frowned. "Not what I expected. It hurt a bit and it was over so quickly. I'd always thought it was going to be something special but in the end it just turned out to be a bit furtive and inconclusive. I remember feeling really disappointed."

"So is Alan any good in bed?"

"How the blazes would I know Nicky? It's not as if I've had much experience to draw comparisons with."

"You've never slept with another man? Never?" Nicole sounded shocked.

"Of course not! I don't sleep around Nicky. I wouldn't be unfaithful."

"Come on Sarah! What about at uni? Haven't you even bedded down another student?"

"No! I wouldn't have dreamed of it."

Nicole raised an eyebrow. "Really? Not even dreamed about it?"

Sarah blushed and smiled in embarrassment. "Well all right I *dreamed* about it I suppose but I never *did* anything about it."

"My God! A real little puritan. Alan doesn't know what he's got. There's not many fellahs that could trust their girlfriend to keep her drawers on throughout three years at university. Did your family furnish you with a chastity belt or something before shipping you off to uni?"

"Stop making fun of me!"

"I'm sorry Sarah. You've got to admit though it sounds loopy. I mean here you are one of the best-looking tarts in the valley by a long head and you've never had but the one guy in your life."

"To be honest Nicky it doesn't really bother me. I think that there's something wrong with me to be honest. I mean the girls at uni were always talking about the things they got up to with their boyfriends. They seemed to have sex on their minds but I seem to be able to take it or leave it. Oh of course when Alan wants to do it then I will comply but if he isn't in the mood then it doesn't really worry me. Maybe I don't have much sex drive. Maybe I'm frigid."

"Bullshit!"

"Nicky! Your language is appalling."

"Perfectly apt under the circumstances Sarah. Bullshit I said and bullshit I mean. I've lived with you for nearly four years now and if you're frigid then I'm a fucking nun! I know what you keep in your bedside cabinet."

Sarah gaped at Nicole appalled. "Have you been going through my private things?"

Nicole grinned. "Sarah darling if you don't want people to know about your private hobbies then you should live in a bigger house with thicker walls and not leave your toys lying around on the bed when your housemate pops in to borrow one of your tops."

"I don't believe this. This is an invasion of my privacy."

"Relax Sarah. I *am* private. So you play with yourself. So what? Did you think I didn't know? For crying out loud Sarah, it's not as if you're especially quiet about it."

Sarah blushed crimson and lifted a hand to her mouth. "Oh God! Am I so loud?"

"For fucks sake you started half the dogs between here and Unterwasser barking last night."

"Oh God! What must you have thought about me?"

"Just that I wish the bitch would hurry up and finish so I could get some shut eye."

Sarah hung her head shamefully. "Oh God this is awful!"

"Oh stop being such a prude Sarah. Do you honestly believe that I'd think that a normal healthy woman wouldn't play with herself. You know that I do for heaven's sake. You once even caught me at it on the sofa in the living room red-handed. Maybe I'm not as noisy as you but then I've got the sense to bite the pillow when my fantasy football team is violating me in their imaginary pre-match warm up."

"You fantasise about *football teams*?"

"Hell honey that's one of my milder sexual fantasies! You wouldn't believe some of the things I fantasise about and I'm buggered if I'm going to tell you about them."

"God! Why are we even talking about this?"

"I'm trying to make some sense out of this Sarah. You masturbate a lot don't you?"

"I wouldn't say a lot..... "

"In fact practically every day."

"Can we change the subject?"

"No we can't change the subject. I'm trying to establish a point here."

"And what point is that pray?" demanded Sarah indignantly.

"That you are in fact, in spite of your protestations to the contrary, a horny bitch who's well overdue for a damn good rogering."

"That'll *do* Nicky!" Sarah glanced around nervously at the other occupants of the restaurant. "Someone might hear!"

"Give over Sarah. The only person within audible range is old Herr Metzger and he's as deaf as a doorpost."

"Well let's discuss something else. I thought we were talking about my forthcoming nuptials not my personal habits."

"As if the two things were separate. Come on Sarah I'm trying to get to the bottom of these sudden misgivings of yours regarding your marriage and whilst we might not have reached it so far I think I can see some reflections off the basement floor."

"Well you'd be the person for plumbing the depths right enough."

"Do you actually enjoy sex with Alan?"

"I have done yes."

"Have done?"

"A couple of times sure."

"A couple!"

"Well we don't see each other very often Nicky. We don't get that much opportunity."

"Have you ever actually had an orgasm with him?"

"I once did."

"*Once*! Just once! Are you telling me that after three years of sleeping with this guy you've only managed to have the single orgasm with him?"

"I told you. We don't get to see each other very often."

"Ok so when he came back last Christmas you hadn't seen him for what over three months. How was it then?"

"Oh he was ever so sweet. He brought me a big box of chocolates and a gold bracelet for Christmas."

"Yes but did he give you what you really wanted; to whit a good solid drilling? Did he pick you up and throw you on the bed and tell you to say goodbye to the floor because you would only be looking at the ceiling for the next three days? Did he spend a few hundred francs of his not inconsiderable income on a flimsy little silk negligee and a pair of frilly knickers for you only to squander his investment by tearing them into shreds in his haste to divest you of it? Was there in other words an instant rapport of fire and passion?"

"Well he'd been working very hard and he was awfully tired and...."

"We'll take that as a no then shall we?"

"Sex isn't the only thing in a relationship you know Nicky."

"No it isn't. There's all the other things you have in common with Alan; your deep abiding interest in corporate finance for instance; your passion for golf; your infatuation with automobile engineering; your complete commitment to the joys of Zurich social life. No wonder you two are inseparable."

"All right! All right! A person is allowed to have interests outside of the relationship."

"Yes assuming there are some interests *within* the relationship too. Right now I'm having a hard time deciding what they are since we have more or less established that your sex life is pants."

"I didn't say it's pants. It's just.. well it's just..."

"Not enough?"

"I didn't say that! I'm not some sort of nymphomaniac you know."

"Wanting sex more than about three times a year isn't nymphomania Sarah."

"It's not Alan's fault Nicky. I mean he's not that sexually experienced himself I don't think. If he doesn't always satisfy me it's not his fault. He doesn't really know how... I mean the best things to do or where to touch me or anything."

"You mean you haven't *shown* him?" Nicole sounded shocked.

"No I haven't "shown" him! What do you think I am?"

"A bloody moron sometimes! How the hell is he ever going to learn your hot spots if you don't show him? Haven't you ever shown him how you do it to yourself?"

"Nicky you are barking mad if you think I've masturbated in front of Alan for his personal instruction."

"Good God! Why not Sarah? Not only would it provide him with much needed information but most men love watching a girl play with herself! Don't you know anything about sex?"

"It would seem not." replied Sarah in a huff. "I obviously lack your extensive experience."

Nicole pushed her glass to one side and tapped on the table. "Listen Sarah. This is important. You're *marrying* this guy. If there's no spark in the bedroom your marriage is dead on its feet. Surely you must know that."

"Well what do you suggest I do? Buy him a bloody instruction manual or something?"

"It would be a start! There's a new edition of Alex Comfort's "*The Joy of Sex*" out that is a pretty good standard or then there's Paul Joannides "*The Guide to Getting it on*" for a more in-depth look. Then of course there are the classical texts such as "*The Kama Sutra*" of *Vatsyayana*" but you might find that heavy going because most of it isn't about sexual instruction at all.

53

"*The Perfumed Garden of Sensual Delight*" by the author Muhammad ibn Muhammad al-Natzawi would be interesting if you happened to be a 15th century Arab courtesan shagging in a harem somewhere. For a more advanced modern text you might take a look at Steve and Vera Bodansky's "*The Illustrated Guide to Extended Massive Orgasm*" which you'll find has some good stuff in it or then there's ....."

"Nicky! Will you *shut up*!"

"I'm only trying to be helpful."

"You are suffering from extensive and acute marble deficiency if you think that I'm going to start providing my boyfriend with an encyclopaedic collection of dirty books just to spice up our love life."

"It sounds like it's about time you did something. It sounds as if the average Trappist monk gets up to more fun and games down the cloisters than you manage in your relationship."

Sarah blushed. "I'm sure it will come in time."

"You've been with the guy for over three years Sarah and you've only come the once so far." Nicole shook her head. "I don't get this Sarah. I always thought that Alan was the love of your life. This isn't a love match though is it? It's a bloody arranged marriage."

Sarah nodded sombrely. "Yes. Yes I suppose it is."

"How did that happen Sarah? I mean when we were at school together you had all these notions of romantic love; marrying up with some shining prince who would steal your heart and everything."

"So I was very naive." Sarah shook her head sadly. "You believe in a lot of things when you're a teenager I suppose."

"Oh right so you're a seasoned veteran now huh? You're only twenty-one for fuck's sake Sarah! It's a bit early for the jaded and world-weary outlook on life don't you think?"

"I'm just saying that I've grown up a bit since then."

"Grown up sufficiently for you to abandon your dreams of happiness and obey your parent's wishes?"

"It's not quite as bad as that!"

"Isn't it?"

"No! Yes I know that it's an arranged marriage to all intents and purposes but marrying for love isn't a guarantee of happiness is it? Look at Petra Fischer! She married that guy from Rapperswil; big love affair, all roses and candy; this was her soul partner and look what happened. Two years later she's in a safe house for battered women and filing divorce papers!"

"Ok then if you want to give examples what about Heiki Wolfe? She married under parental pressure."

"Well she *was* three months pregnant Nicky."

"Which at least sounds as if she was getting it more than you do."

"Anyway what's your point? Heiki's still married."

"Yes. I met Heiki about a month ago in the English pub in Winterthur. She was drunk."

"Ok so she was drunk. You can hardly moralise about that! You've been known to have the odd one too many yourself you know."

"It was eleven thirty in the morning Sarah. Heiki's drunk all the time these days; well drunk or addled out of her brain on prescription pills and anti-depressives."

"Oh God! Really?" Sarah was shocked. "I liked Heiki. What happened? She never used to be that way."

"No but then she wasn't trapped in a loveless marriage before."

"Oh poor Heiki. It's a rotten world isn't it?"

"It's not a rotten world Sarah but people make some rotten decisions. I just hope that you're not going to." Nicole picked up the carafe and replenished their glasses. "You know Sarah before Alan came along I always thought that you and Peter would become an item. You used to spend half your time with him."

Sarah picked up her drink thoughtfully. "So did I at one time. I like Peter. I always have done but we've never been more than just really good friends. We used to go hiking together a lot and I always enjoyed his company."

"Did he never intimate that he wanted to be more than just friends?"

"Not really. I mean he's so shy about things like that."

Nicole was watching her friend closely. "Not really? Sarah sweetheart there's a hole in that "not really" I could throw a cow through."

"Well ok there was one time..."

"Oh yes? Do tell Sarah darling."

Sarah grimaced ruefully. "All right but if you dare tell anyone I'll bloody murder you!"

"Something on our conscience have we?"

"Yes because it was after I started seeing Alan."

"Whoo! This sounds intriguing."

"I wasn't sleeping much with Alan at the time but I was pretty much attached to him and I suppose I was a bit frustrated. It was silly really. I suppose my hormones were getting the better of me. I should have known better. It was just that it was spring time and I guess that I was just feeling the spring a little and...."

"Look can we cut the background information short and get down to the sordid details?"

"Well all right. We were hiking down from the Rotsteinpass one day. It was late May and there was still a fair bit of snow and the weather wasn't great. We got caught in a heavy thunderstorm; it absolutely pissed it down and we got drenched. Well the bloody hut at Schafboden was closed so we had to take shelter in an old cow shed. We both had dry clothes in our rucksacks so we stripped down to our undies to change. Well the next thing we knew we were.... we were...."

"Rolling around among the cow pats?"

"We were *not* rolling around among the cow pats. We were.... well kissing each other."

"In your undies? Hmm a bit more than platonic friendship then?"

"Look do you want me to tell you this story or not?"

"Pray continue. I don't want to stop you just as things are getting interesting."

"Well I got really.... well quite excited. Stop giggling."

"I can't help it! Only Sarah would choose a smelly old cow shed for a romantic tryst."

"I didn't exactly plan it Nicky."

"Well carry on. What happened next? Did he get his wicked way with you?"

"No. Well not really."

"Aha! We're back to one of those conditional "not really" s"

"Well we just petted I suppose. I mean he er put his hand inside my knickers and...." Sarah paused blushing in embarrassment. "I.... I really wanted him. I wanted him right then and there. I must have been crazy."

"So you reciprocated his advances then?"

"Yes. I took hold of him and started to stroke him."

"I presume we are not talking about a sisterly caress to the side of the face here."

"No I took hold of his... his...."

"Let's just refer to it as his family virtues shall we?"

"Well I took hold of it and..... Oh God! This is embarrassing."

"Why what happened?"

"Not a lot as far as I was concerned. He sort of gave a funny snort and shivered and then he... he..."

"Oh Christ! He didn't shoot his load did he?"

Sarah nodded miserably. "Yes! All over my hand!"

"Oh my! Still it was to be expected I suppose. He was how old then?"

"Just eighteen."

Nicole nodded. "Poor lad. No control, teenage lads. I bet he'd had the hots for you for years and as soon as he finally gets his hand inside your drawers he goes and blows it by coming too soon. He must have been mortified."

"He was really ashamed of himself Nicky. I mean he thought he'd been taking advantage of me and me already spoken for too. He begged me to forgive him and swore it would never happen again."

"Much to your disgust I would hazard to guess."

Sarah pulled a wry face. "Well my recollections of that afternoon are a bit hazy Nicky but, as far as I can remember, it was more a case of *me* taking advantage rather than the reverse. I'm pretty sure I started the whole thing. Didn't make any difference. He was racked with guilt and ever so sorry."

"Would you have? I mean if it hadn't gone tits up on you would you have gone the whole way?"

Sarah nodded. "Yes. I was pretty right now about things. I was ever so disappointed. Peter told me that he'd never been with a girl before. I suppose I nearly took his virginity. I think there was a lot of shame attached to that memory for him for he's never mentioned it again."

Nicole pondered thoughtfully for a moment. "No Sarah but I'll bet he *thought* about it. You're the only girl I've ever known Peter get close to. He never seems to have a girlfriend. It's not because the girls aren't interested either. I mean he's one of the best-looking blokes in the valley."

"He's very shy Nicky."

"Yes I know. He doesn't get out much either. If you do see him out it's only for a few beers down the Post or that little pub near the chairlift up to Gamplut. He keeps himself pretty much to himself. I wonder sometimes."

"About what?"

"Well when you went away to university he seemed to go into a decline for a while and he was certainly devastated when it became apparent that you were serious about Alan."

"Oh really Nicky! You're imagining things."

"Including the photograph of you he keeps on the table in his bedroom?"

"Now you *are* fantasising. You've never been in his bedroom."

"No but his sister has. She told me he keeps a framed photograph taken of you at the school prom dance in his bedroom. She reckons that he's always had a thing about you. You realise that you might have broken his heart?"

"Oh God! You're joking."

Nicole shook her head emphatically. "No Sarah. A few people have commented on it. Peter seemed to lose all interest in other girls once you'd left the scene."

"Have you ever discussed me with him?"

"Only in the most general way honey. He always asks about you. I think he's pining for you."

Sarah regarded her glass sadly. "Oh damn! Life's not fair is it? Poor Peter."

"You were very fond of him once upon a day Sarah."

"I still am Nicky. He's one of my oldest and dearest friends but I never imagined, since that day, that he had other feelings for me. I don't know what to do."

"Well I couldn't imagine Peter gaining your family's approval Nicky. I mean he's a sound lad and all that but he's just a glorified shepherd and casual farm labourer, to all intents and purposes. Your mother wouldn't let him in the house."

59

Sarah sighed in agreement. "Yes. You're right. My mother's an insufferable snob. It makes you wonder what might have been though."

"Yes it does. And it makes me wonder if this forthcoming marriage is entirely the best idea honey."

"So what do you suggest I do?"

"Stall! Play for time. Your parents and Alan's parents are after marrying you off by the end of summer. You've got to assert your own rights on this honey or you'll never be your own woman again. You've got to lay down the line Sarah; this is your marriage, your future, your life. If you just let yourself get bullied into marrying now, before you're ready for it, you're just conceding the high ground. In the final analysis it has to be you and only you who decides your own future. That's why you have to buy time; time enough to think this thing through."

"Alan's coming home at the end of July or beginning of August Nicky. I'm going to have to be ready with some sort of answer by then."

"Tell him that you want more time. If he doesn't accept that then you have to ask yourself if you seriously want to spend the rest of your life with a man that couldn't give a monkey's toss about what you want."

"It's not just Alan I have to come up with answers for Nicky."

"No it's your family; and his as well. But honey, seriously, you're a grown woman now. Your family has to accept that you have to make your own decisions. They tried to have it their own way with your sister and damn well near ended up losing her for good."

"I can't go against my parents like Jess did Nicky. It would tear my family apart."

"Better that than you spend the rest of your life regretting that you didn't have the balls to assert your own right to determine your destiny Sarah."

Sarah sighed. "Maybe you're right." She paused to sip her drink. "Where is Peter working now for the moment now anyway?"

"Oh he's helping out for a couple of weeks with the cows up on the side of the Gamserugg I heard."

Sarah thought for a moment. "I might hike up there tomorrow. I'd like to see Peter again."

Chapter Six

Early next morning, on her fourth day back in the valley and with her unpacking finally completed, Sarah determined to hike up to the high pastures where Peter was employed in herding the mountain cattle. Nicole was already away at this early hour, having the breakfast shift at the hotel in Wildhaus, and Sarah was alone in the house. It was not entirely an unwelcome moment of solitude for Sarah was in a curiously titillated mood. She wasn't a girl that normally talked openly about sex and the somewhat frank discussion she'd had with Nicole the night before had been oddly liberating. Nicole's uninhibited bluntness had quite stimulated her and the one and a half litres of wine they had consumed had gone a long way to assisting this stimulation. Doubtless, under normal circumstances, she would have acted upon this stimulation in the privacy of her own bedroom the night before but Nicole's remarks had somewhat inhibited her and she'd not dared to fuel Nicole's speculations regarding her private habits by succumbing to the temptation to stroke herself to the point of sexual pleasure.

As a result, Sarah had woken up in the dangerously heightened mood of sexual tension that could lead one into indiscretions. The conversation with Nicole had given her a lot to think about and she was reluctantly forced to concede that masturbation was about her only current form of sexual gratification. She couldn't decide if that was shameful or just sad. What was plain was that Nicole had been uncomfortably close to the mark by suggesting that Sarah's relationship with Alan was certainly not one that afforded her much in the way of personal satisfaction. If she was honest with herself she had to admit that sex with Alan was a somewhat clumsy affair and had more to do with relieving Alan's immediate needs than it had to do with mutual pleasure and gratification.

Alan was not a man comfortable with the trappings of seduction and foreplay and seemingly oblivious to any sort of notion of post-coital tenderness. He certainly didn't match the fanciful ideals of sensitivity and loving with which Sarah endowed the imaginary lovers she played with alone in her bed. She sometimes felt as if Alan had an attitude toward sex akin to that of any other domestic or bodily requirement, such as brushing his teeth. She wondered if, in their new marriage, Alan would lay down specific timetables for sexual activity to be fitted in between attending to the kitchen plumbing and perusing the financial papers to determine the day's fluctuations in the Dow's index. Perhaps she ought to give him some sort of scoring method for his sexual performance so he could work on it like his golf handicap.

Sarah lay in bed with the early morning sun filtering through the curtains and wondered why she had never felt so dissatisfied with her sex life before. She knew that there was something seriously amiss with it. More and more these days, her mind turned to the subject and it was becoming increasingly difficult to subdue her own sexuality. Sarah in fact was a walking time bomb of repressed sexual tension at this time and it was a volatile state that threatened to undermine the fragile foundations of her security. Probably, of anybody, Nicole would have noticed the mounting storms in Sarah's libido for she knew her well and she had a certain shrewdness when it came to matters of passion. "It's always the quiet ones." Nicole would say to herself and there was truth in the observation that such a bomb often lurked beneath the outwardly calm exterior of such apparently innocuous people as Sarah. Even Nicole however might have been surprised to know just how close to detonation the bomb was or in what manner it would finally explode.

Sarah found her hands wandering languorously over her body as she lay abed but, before she could take their caresses to their logical conclusion, she thought of Peter and the day in the cow shed below the Rotsteinpass that she had related to Nicole. In sudden decision she leapt from bed and padded through into the bathroom. Dropping her nightdress on a stool she stepped under the shower and luxuriated in the stream of hot water over her body, soaping herself lavishly and shampooing her hair until it squeaked. Emerging from the shower she dried herself thoroughly before wrapping a towel about her and drying her hair with a the drier; loving the feel of it as she brushed it in the warm current of air. Her long dark hair was her greatest vanity. Finally, when her toiletry was complete, she stepped in front of the long bathroom mirror. There she did something curious that she rarely ever did. She unfastened the towel about her and let it slip to the ground and stood there to peruse her naked body in the mirror. Sarah was not a girl that spent a great deal of time admiring herself in a mirror and such a long critical appraisal of herself was uncharacteristic. In fact at her university digs she'd only had a very small mirror and it had been long since she'd had the opportunity at all to see herself in such panoramic detail.

She was pleasantly surprised at the spectacle. In the last year she had bloomed in admirable fashion. She had finally lost the somewhat gangling features of teenage adolescence and had ripened into full womanhood almost without her having noticed the fact. The legs were long but well formed with healthy muscles to attest to her many hours upon the hiking trails of her homeland. The stomach above her little bush of pubic hair was flat and firm and the breasts were high and ripe, crowned with pert nipples. Her shoulders too were well formed and square and her long neck a suitably graceful extension above them. Turning around, she carefully examined the round curvature of her buttocks and the long arch of her blemishless back with pleasure. The body was the firm one of a girl that exercises a lot and eats prudently and there was not the hint of excess fat upon it although it could not have been described as emaciated. It was simply the perfectly formed body of a startlingly lovely young woman. Sarah was not the most narcissistic of people but she found herself modestly enjoying the sight of herself naked. A less self-critical viewer would have found the sight exquisite.

Picking up her nightgown and returning to her bedroom, Sarah opened her wardrobe and pondered over her choice of dress for the day. Normally this would have been a simple and straightforward decision to make. She had the inclination to spend a day up the mountains and there was nothing in that programme to suggest anything other than her customary pair of old jeans and a top or blouse to complement her grubby hiking boots. She drew aside the curtains of her bedroom and looked out. The sky was a vivid blue and the day promised to be hot. Indeed the weather forecast on the television the night before had predicted the hottest day of the year so far. It was only partly this that determined her choice however.

As has been noted, Sarah was in a state of heightened sexual awareness and there was a little devil inside of her that urged her to a more frivolous decision. Among her wardrobe, was a little white tennis outfit with a short pleated skirt and sleeveless top that had the virtue of being both sporty and sexy. Sarah giggled as she pulled the outfit out. The skirt was short enough to be mildly outrageous and a downright hazard in anything other than a soft breeze. It was however extremely comfortable and just the thing for a hike on a hot day when too many clothes would be a wearisome burden and you wanted to feel the wind on your legs. Also tennis clothes were designed to be worn over socks and tennis pumps and the ensemble wouldn't look too out of place over hiking boots.

She pulled on underwear and then the tennis skirt and top before pulling a pair of white hiking socks on and finally lacing her mountain boots up. Friskily she dashed back to the bathroom mirror to admire herself. Her resolve nearly left her at this point because she hadn't exposed this much thigh since the day she'd turned out for the college hockey team against her better judgement. But the little devil was in a persuasive mood and she quickly convinced herself that it was an eminently practical ensemble for hot weather hiking. The fact that she was hoping to bump into Peter up on the alp was entirely coincidental to this consideration she told herself.

Sarah had not entirely abandoned good sense, however, for she packed warm and dry clothes into her rucksack for the mountain climate was notoriously fickle and could change in minutes. She also remained aware of the hazards of exposing so much skin to the intense ultra-violet light of the high mountains and packed a tube of alpine strength sunscreen into her pack. She tied her hair back in a pony tail, donned a white baseball cap to keep the sun from her face, slipped some money into her pack, shouldered her rucksack and, picking up an aluminium extendable walking stick in the hallway, stepped out into the daylight. It was to be a momentous day in her life.

Chapter Seven

She felt carefree and happy as she walked down the alp and descended the hill to Unterwasser. There was a little breeze in the air that wafted about her thighs deliciously and carried the scent of the lower meadow flowers to her nostrils and she almost skipped along, feeling almost as if she had slipped the growing pains of adulthood and reverted to the golden days of her childhood when she would take to the mountain slopes in her shorts at her father's side. She crossed the broad flat bottom of the main valley and made her way to the funicular station. A little cable drawn funicular railway rose up from the valley floor here to the restaurant and ski station at Iltios and Sarah climbed aboard the rickety old wagon to be hauled up though the lower forests to the terrace upon which the Iltios station stood. Iltios was a busy place in the winter months for it lay right at the end of the major ski slopes of the Chaserugg mountain. It was quieter now though, in early summer, and so Sarah took a while to say hello to friends and acquaintances that worked in the station. Outside the cable car station to the Chaserugg, an old friend, Wilhelm, who counted himself solidly among the ranks of Sarah's fan club, worked on the cable car at Iltios and he welcomed Sarah warmly and with a soft wolf whistle. "Whee Sarah! Legs!"

"I do *have* legs you know Willy."

"Well we don't get to see them too often Sarah."

"That's no reason to be staring at them Willy. They're perfectly normal anatomical appendages you know."

"It's going to be hot Sarah. Are you sure you wouldn't like me to smear lotion all over your legs? I'd hate you to get burned."

"Stop flirting Willy. When's the next car up to the summit?"

"In about twenty-five minutes."

"Well I suppose I'll get a cup of coffee and say hello to everyone in the restaurant."

"I've got a better idea. Why don't you come into the machinery room with me and rest your weary feet in my lap while I'll tickle your ankles and tell you how gorgeous you are."

"Get along with you! Bloody men! One glimpse of a pair of perfectly ordinary female legs and your brains go on holiday and reduce you to slobbering imbeciles."

"There's nothing ordinary about *your* legs Sarah. They're divine!"

"Well you can worship them at a distance then. Haven't you got some work to do?"

"Yes! In my capacity as the Chaserugg cable car public relations officer it is my solemn duty to offer all help and physical assistance to beautiful unaccompanied young ladies. It's a bit muddy around here. May I offer to carry you?"

"You can keep your greasy, machine oil stained hands to yourself."

"You misunderstand my honourable intentions." said Wilhelm rolling his eyes in exaggerated indignation.

"Look Willy go and do something unsavoury with a grease gun will you. I'm going for a coffee." Sarah tossed her head contemptuously and stalked away feeling quite pleased.

After exchanging courtesies with her acquaintances in the Iltios station Sarah mounted the gondola for the cable car trip to the summit of the mountain. She loved rides in cable cars and as the car swung high on its cable above the great circular basin to the north of the mountain summit she scoured the mountain flanks for the chamois that often grazed on the edges of the cliffs that formed the walls of the basin. Sarah thought that, in some remote geographical past, this basin must have been the root of a glacier; a so-called cirque-glacier that had been an icy tributary to the main glacier that had carved out the Toggenburg valley. In these warmer climes however the Chaserugg was not high enough to maintain a permanent ice cap for it was just 2,262 metres in altitude. It was high enough however to be appreciably cooler than the valley below however and Sarah began to wonder if her choice of dress had been altogether wise for the temperature dropped markedly as the cable car neared the summit. On the summit of the mountain Sarah stepped out of the gondola and reassured herself however. It was decidedly fresher up here but the sun was shining on the mountain and it was not uncomfortably cold.

Sarah had other friends that worked in the mountain restaurant at the cable car station at the summit of the Chaserugg but, by now, she was eager to be away and, adjusting her rucksack more comfortably she set off across the mountain. The top of the Chaserugg was peculiar because it was a broad gently curved great shoulder. To the south the mountain plunged away in a series of awesome cliffs down to the deep glacial lake; the Walensee, reputedly one of the deepest lakes in Switzerland. To the west the broad shoulder of the mountain rose gradually to the adjoining peak of the Hinterugg and to the north the main ski slopes of the mountain descended down a broad flank to the east of the old glacial basin. Eastwards the mountain top was nearly flat apart from a single step in the shoulder and Sarah took that route. It was a perfect place for tourists in the high summer months for the gentle terrain on the mountain top was perfect for strolling and pick-nicking. There were only a few patches of snow left scattered around the mountain top and some muddy patches just showing the first alpine snowbells poking through to indicate that the snow had only just melted in these parts.

Mostly however, the great grassy shoulder was dry and already ablaze with early flowers; Spring Gentians, Heartsease pansies, Alpine Birdsfoot Trefoil, the lovely Auricula Primroses and many more besides. There were few people on the mountain this early in the season and the undisturbed solitude was reflected as a pair of Ptarmigan, moulting into their summer plumage, flushed from beneath Sarah's boots as she crossed the mountain.

At the edge of the broad grassy plateau Sarah paused at the edge of a low cliff and looked down with some trepidation. Her hike this day was not a particularly challenging one or very dangerous but this stage of the descent promised to be the most taxing of all. The steep descent down to a large flat terrace a hundred or so metres below was one of the few places on the mountain that the snow clung tenaciously to for much of the summer. This early the snowfield was a forbidding great sweep that would task her abilities. Fortunately the steepest parts of the descent were facilitated by a fixed cable between posts to serve as hand grips and Sarah was able to negotiate the snowfield carefully. She didn't want to fall. It was not dangerous in a life-threatening fashion but a slide down a snow field whilst wearing such inadequate clothing would have been uncomfortable at least and old compacted snow can be surprisingly abrasive, causing nasty grazing.

At the foot of the snow field Sarah found herself on a series of large stepped terraces across which the trail wound to the north east toward the foot of the Gamserugg. This was one of Sarah's favourite sections for there was a deep peace and solitude in this sunny sheltered col between the two mountains. There were little pools of water standing on the terraces for this was a large outcropping of sandstone layered into the limestone of the mountain. You hardly ever found standing water on limestone for it seeped down into the rock and vanished underground. Limestone mountains were dry. Even springs and streams only bubbled to the surface where the water came upon a layer of insoluble rock. Sarah wound her way around the little pools and searched them for alpine newts which you sometimes found here, glorying at being alone in her mountains. She felt vividly alive. Her marriage seemed a distant unreal nightmare here and the only sounds to break her revelry were the chirruping calls of the Alpine Choughs about the summit, the gruff croak of a raven and the shrill whistling of the marmots from the limestone karst landscape to the west of the Gamserugg.

Jutting up ahead of her was the rounded peak of the Gamserugg and Sarah had the choice of two routes around this mountain. To the west was a fairly direct route above the nightmare of potholes and alpenrose scrub that lay below the Chaserugg whilst the eastern flank was a sunny, longer route overlooking the richer pastures that were grazed by cattle in the alp below. This was Sarah's choice for, according to Nicole, this was the area where she was most likely come across Peter who was herding the cattle up here. She came up to the little fence that closed the gap for the cattle between the two mountains and, wondering herself why she did it, she paused to take stock of her appearance. Her long exposed legs, she noted with some irritation, had gathered a couple of specks of mud on them and, dampening a finger, she hastily rubbed them away. "This is crazy!" she thought to herself. "Since when have I ever been worried about what I look like on a bloody mountainside?" She had the grace and humour to laugh at herself.

She climbed the stile that afforded passage over the fence and giggled as a puff of breeze caught at her skirt and lifted it perilously high on her thighs. She was thankfully alone or the momentary failure of her ensemble would have exposed her underwear scandalously. She smiled at her own daring and just beyond the stile she twirled rapidly just for devilment and imagined somebody possibly concealed in the cliffs above might be goggling at the spectacle she afforded. The exposure of her more private regions seemed to remind her of a pressing urgency as well. The coffee she had consumed at Iltios was coming back to haunt her and she turned aside where the nitrate enriched grasses of these grazed slopes were longer and slipped her knickers down to squat and urinate. She thought with some amusement that, whereas her dress for the day may have had many shortcomings as regards practicality, it had at least the virtue of facilitating this particular necessary function. Re-adjusting her dress, she pressed on around the mountainside.

The alp lay in a great sweep below her narrow path on the steep side of the mountain and the harmonious chime of cowbells rose up to her from the grazing cattle below. Sarah loved the sound of cowbells for they were always evocative of summer days on the mountains of the Toggenburg. The bells were the large Triechel bells made of hammered sheet metal that gave a more clanking tone than the clearer toned bells. They were larger than pure bells but lighter and more easy for the cattle to carry around their necks. Not all the cows wore them of course but only the matriarchs of the herd which the younger cattle would follow in any case. In her bedroom at home Sarah had a large Triechel with an ornate decorated leather strap mounted on her wall. That was one of the fancy versions, of course, used for the ceremonial trappings of the traditional summer procession of the cattle up on to the alps. Whilst up here the cattle generally wore more basic bells and their use was of a practical as well as traditional nature. It was easy to understand the practical purpose for the bells, as Sarah stood overlooking the vastness of the alp below her. The clanking of the bells pinpointed the locations of elements of the herd from every corner. An experienced cowherd could tell the exact location of nearly every one of his charges to within a few yards just by the sound of their bells across the alp.

As Sarah rounded the mountainside, virtually the whole alp came into view below her and she could see small groups of cattle peacefully grazing. The vegetation in the alp was much ranker and richer than the delicate little alpine plants and flowers of high altitudes. The grazing cattle were the reason for this, for cattle deposited their faeces liberally over the alp and these were rich in nitrates which allowed vegetation from lower altitudes to penetrate into these high regions where the thin poor soil would previously have denied them a foothold. Sarah had once hiked for a week in the Swiss National Park in the Engadine where no cattle had been grazed for over ninety years yet it was still possible to spot the locations where the cows had once roamed by the incursion of nitrate rich vegetation.

Sarah decided to take a break and scan the alp assiduously for the sight of Peter. It was not an easy task to accomplish for she became suddenly aware that simply slumping down on a dirty rock or patch of dry soil was not an option in her pristine white tennis skirt. Finding one slab of relatively clean stone she experimented by lifting her skirt and planting her knickers clad bottom onto it gingerly. She rose again quite sharply. The stone was in shadow and icy cold. Frowning she made a sensible decision and took her pullover from her rucksack and placed it on the rock to sit on. Once seated comfortably she took out the sandwiches and an apple she had had the foresight to pack before leaving and ate with pleasure. The repast was as basic as you could get; nutty Emmentaler cheese between slabs of good Swiss bread and overlaid with slices of raw onions and a crisp Granny Smith's apple; green and tart. In the fresh clear air of the alp it felt like a feast.

Sarah watched the cattle below in deep contentment. She had made something of a study of cow herding in the Alps for it had interested her. There was a big English word for the seasonal relocation of the cattle from their winter quarters to the high alpine pastures she knew. It was "transhumance" and transhumance was a major part of the agricultural economy of Switzerland. She knew that some 380,000 cattle including about 120,000 milk cows were grazed on the alpine pastures in Switzerland during the summer months as well as over 200,000 sheep and goats. She had read somewhere that some 35% of all the land devoted to agriculture in Switzerland was made up of alpine pasture land. But it was not a labour-intensive part of the agricultural life in the country for less than 15% of all the Swiss farming population was involved in mountain herding. Peter was part of a diminishing breed too for there were only some 160,000 people involved in the practice. At the beginning of the twentieth century the number had been closer to 450,000.

Sarah smiled wryly to think that Peter was an increasingly obsolescent figure on these mountains. He was also, as far as she could see, a conspicuously absent one for, scour the alp as she may through her binoculars, she could see nary the sight of him. She took her plastic bottle of Evian mineral water from her rucksack and took a pull to assuage her thirst and, putting her binoculars to her eyes, sought out the little hut that the cowherds stayed in whilst tending the cattle. Almost at once she spotted him. He was apparently doing some repairs for he was nailing a board to the roof of the hut. Sarah sprang to her feet and inflated her lungs to yodel at the top of her voice.

Yodelling was part of traditional Swiss music and a mastery of the skill was by no means easy for it involved a bridge between the tonal ranges of the higher head tones and the deeper chest vocalisations at high volume.

Once mastered however it useful skill to have in the high mountains for its origins lay not in aesthetic musicality but in the necessity for people to communicate to each other across the huge distances between mountains. With the backdrop of the cliffs of the Gamserugg behind her Sarah had a perfect echo trap to project her yodel across the Alp and Peter lifted his head to search out the source of the clear ringing voice. Sarah waved her arms expansively, reflecting that her costume for the day held another surprise advantage. The white of her tennis outfit made her conspicuous against the background of the mountain. She saw Peter wave in return although he seemed to hesitate before setting off to walk toward her. "He probably can't recognise me at this distance." Sarah thought to herself as she waited patiently. It took Peter several minutes to negotiate the terrain but as he began to scale the slope toward her lofty position he looked up and Sarah saw him smile as he finally realised the identity of the strange woman hailing him from the mountain.

Sarah grinned. Perhaps she should have brought him the Triechel on her wall she thought. There was an old Swiss fairy story, from the Simmental, about a young cowherd who finds himself confronted by a beautiful fairy maiden in a mountain cave. She offers him the choice of golden coins, a golden Triechel or herself and the young cowherd, with what Sarah could only consider remarkable perversity, chooses the Triechel. She wondered what Peter's choice would be. With a wry grin she thought that perhaps it might be better not to put him to the test.

Peter negotiated the last few metres in an easy lope and planting his boots firmly on the track smiled broadly at her. "Sarah! Well this is a surprise. What are *you* doing up here?"

Sarah's heart fluttered a little and she grinned and stepped forward to kiss him. Sarah was quite a tall girl but she had to stand on tip toes to peck Peter on both cheeks in the customary courtesy of good friends. Peter stood well over one metre eighty although he was not lanky in appearance for he had a well-built muscled frame and was broad across the shoulders. "I came up to see you." Sarah told him. "Nicole told me you were up here for the summer."

Peter shook his head. "No not for the whole summer. Just a couple of weeks. I'm filling in for the regular herder because his mother's ill."

"Well if you're not too busy come and sit awhile and tell me your news."

Peter smiled slowly and Sarah eyed him with pleasure. He was certainly a fine-looking man. He was dressed in an old pair of dark trousers and an open necked white and pale blue shirt decorated with Edelweiss that had seen better days but the physical manhood of him was by no means detracted from by his shabby clothing. Tall and strongly built, he had a shock of unruly blond hair above a well-tanned face whose rugged features were softened by the smoky grey eyes that always seemed to hold some of the quality of a dreamer about them. Sarah always felt that Peter was staring away into some far distance only he could see. It gave him a peculiarly unworldly aura as if part of his mind was always in some fantasy land from which the rest of the world was excluded. It also enhanced his own natural shyness for he was awkward in his social dealings with other people perhaps because his mind dwelt in other regions. Sarah knew he was a hard man to get to know for he rarely displayed his feelings or allowed anyone into his secret thoughts. Outside of his personal family Sarah probably knew him as well as anybody for Peter had known her and trusted her as far as that was possible for him since childhood. Even despite the friendship between them however Sarah knew that the walls of his reserve were difficult to break down and there would always be parts of his soul from which she was excluded.

"You're looking well Sarah." He told her.

Sarah felt slightly disappointed. She had hoped he might say that she was looking very pretty or even beautiful. "Looking well" was just a bit too neutral; more a comment on her health than a compliment. Nevertheless she thanked him and returned to her perch on the rock patting the surface of the stone beside her. "Come and sit for a while Pete. Are you hungry? I brought some sandwiches."

Peter took a seat uncertainly and accepted a sandwich with a smile of thanks. "I heard you were back." he said, "Pauli was up here yesterday and he said you were back in the valley."

"Yes I got back on Saturday." She looked at him searchingly. "You're looking good too Pete. How's life been treating you?"

"Just the usual." He told her non-committally. "I did some work on the ski-slopes for the winter and now I'm just pottering around doing odd jobs here and there."

"So you're only up here for a couple of weeks? What are you planning to do after that?"

Peter scratched his head thoughtfully. "Not sure. There's talk that they want me to do some reparation work up on the hiking trails on the Santis-Gebiet; replacing some of the markers and mending the fixed lines. I suppose half of it will just be walking over the trails with pots of red and white paint."

Sarah nodded. The mountain hiking trails were always marked out in stripes of red and white on rocks and boulders to guide tourists along the surveyed routes. "No further thoughts of going to college?" she asked him.

Peter shook his head ruefully. "Not really. I guess I'm just not the academic sort."

Nor was he much the ambitious sort thought Sarah glumly. Peter seemed perfectly happy just to muddle along in life, pottering about doing odd jobs and, if he never made much money at it, then as long as he was able to walk abroad on his beloved mountains, he counted himself rich and was completely contented. He wouldn't change, thought Sarah with a flash of insight. There was something in Peter that was hidden from her; hidden from everyone. These mountains were his solitude; his way of coming to terms with that which he concealed from all who knew him. This was where he could be himself. Sarah realised that the bond between them was due to her own love of these mountains. Peter saw her as a kindred spirit. Perhaps he thought that she too had some inner soul that could only find its expression in these heart-breakingly lovely peaks. The question in her mind though was whether Peter ever saw her as a woman. She decided to test him gently. "What do you think of my outfit?" She asked innocently. "I wore it for that tennis contest in Nesslau the summer before last."

Peter nodded. "I remember. You were good. You got up to the semi-final didn't you?"

"Yes but I got murdered in the semis in two straight sets. I haven't played since but I thought I'd wear it today." ("*Come on Peter*" she thought, "*I'm telling you that I put something short and sexy on for you*") She lifted one leg to place her foot on the rock and the skirt slipped away to reveal a long length of calf in a manner she hoped was seductive.

Peter took a bite of his sandwich. "Good idea. It's a warm day."

"Yes I suppose it is." ("*No bites so far!*") She brushed some imaginary speck of dust from her leg. "You don't think it's too revealing?"

"Well nobody's going to see you up here."

"I suppose not." ("*Apart from you, you brainless idiot and that was the whole object of the exercise in the first place!*") "I hope I haven't shocked you."

Peter shrugged. "I've seen you partly dressed before Sarah. We went swimming at the Schonenbodensee together once."

"Yes of course." ("*And I was twelve years old for fuck's sake Peter!*") She allowed her voice to deepen huskily. "Anyway you saw me more or less naked that day we got caught in that thunderstorm up near Schafboden."

Peter squirmed uncomfortably. "I've said that I'm sorry about that Sarah."

Sarah forced herself to look steadily at him. "Peter it was my fault not yours." She reached out to touch him on the arm but he recoiled.

"No Sarah! It was my fault. You were just.... just an innocent girl and.... I.... I took advantage."

"Oh Pete come on! You were more innocent than *I* was."

"I'm sorry Sarah. I told you it wouldn't happen again."

"Yes you did." ("*Blast you!*") "But Peter you did nothing wrong. It was nobody's fault really."

"It was wrong Sarah. You have Alan. What I did was wrong; wrong for all sorts of reasons."

Sarah looked at him, puzzled. "What sorts of reasons?"

"I don't want to talk about it Sarah. I don't want to lose you as my friend."

Sarah blinked in surprise. "Whatever do you mean Pete?"

"Look just forget it Sarah. What happened, happened. There's no point in dragging up the past. I'm just glad that Alan doesn't know about it and it jeopardises your engagement. I hear that you're going to be married soon."

Sarah took a deep breath. "So I'm told." ("*Jesus! This is hard work!*")

Peter glanced at her with a puzzled expression. "So you are told? What do you mean?"

"I mean Peter that I have been recently informed by my family that I am to be married off in the near future."

"You don't sound pleased."

"It would have been nice to have been asked."

"But I thought you would have been delighted. Alan is a fine man Sarah."

Sarah felt a flash of anger. "I'm a bit fed up of hearing how fine Alan is Pete. Maybe people think he's too good for me and that I'm lucky that he's considered me at all. Why does everybody assume my automatic consent? Does everyone think that I couldn't possibly do better and I'd better snatch the offer up whilst my luck's in?"

Peter looked at her seriously. "Sarah! You're in love with him."

"Really? On whose authority do you base that judgement?"

"Everybody knows that Sarah."

"Everybody but the person who most needs to apparently." replied Sarah bitterly.

"What are you talking about?"

Sarah shook her head. "Never mind Pete. You're right. Let's talk about something else." They exchanged small talk for a few more minutes until Peter's eyes started to wander nervously back to the unfinished chores around his cabin. Sarah took that as a signal to stand up and leave. She kissed him politely and picked up her rucksack. "I'll see you when you get back down off the alp then Peter."

"Yes we'll have a drink together. I've missed you." It was as close as Peter had come to expressing any feeling for her in the entire conversation.

She turned to go but hesitated and turned half back towards him. "Peter, do you know why I came up here today?"

"To say hello I guess."

Sarah shook her head sadly. "Not completely Peter. I came up here because when I was a young girl the person I always wanted to marry was *you*. I was foolish I suppose."

Peter stared at her dumbfounded. "Sarah I...." He paused not knowing how to continue.

"Never mind Peter. I understand."

"Do you Sarah? Do you really?"

Sarah shook her head. "No not really. Everybody's right I suppose. I'm lucky that Alan even looks at me. I'd best get going Peter." She turned to go.

Sarah!"

She turned again and eyed him quizzically. "Yes?"

Peter swallowed, his face a picture of tragedy. "Will we.... I mean will we still be friends.... I mean after you're married?"

Sarah smiled sadly. "I don't know how much we'll see of each other Pete. I mean I'll probably have to move to Zurich with Alan but yes.... yes we'll always be friends whatever happens."

Peter looked pathetically grateful and, with an awkward smile, she turned and set off along the trail. Just once she looked back. He was still watching her walk away; rooted to the spot. After a few hundred metres more, she had turned around the flank of the mountain and he was lost to view. In an uncharacteristically petulant fit of pique, she kicked a stone savagely over the cliff edge at her feet. She felt tears in her eyes and hated herself for them.

Chapter Eight

Soon she was descending through the Gamsalp. Normally this lovely garden like alp was her favourite part of this hike for it was a bewitching little miniature landscape of limestone outcroppings, little short grass meadows and alpenrose shrubs and dwarf pines and mountain willows just above the tree line. It was an enchanting, quiet corner, rich in alpine flowers where you often came upon grazing chamois; the Gams in German that gave the alp its name. The trees that abutted this small paradise were unusual in the Toggenburg for they were Arollo pines which were very uncommon in the spruce dominated forests around the valley. Because of these pines, this was the best place in the Toggenburg to find the garrulous little brown and pale freckled crows called Nutcrackers for they loved Arollo pines. It was a good place too to look for the little green mountain finches called Citril Finches or the Lesser White Throats that were mountain birds in the alps. Sometimes you were lucky enough to see a Redpoll, or even a Crossbill and there was often a Sparrowhawk hunting along the edge of the tree line.

But for once Sarah had no eye for the beauty of the alp today. She walked moodily, picking her way around the crevices and potholes in the limestone, her mind in turmoil. Suddenly she was startled by a loud eruptive clatter from nearly under her feet and a large black bird, with a lyre shaped tail, exploded from beneath a dwarf willow and took to the air noisily. She jumped and stared wildly as the Black Grouse towered once and then dropped quickly down into dense shrub cover in a hollow to her right. It was a long time since she had last seen a Blackcock but the sight afforded her little pleasure. Instead it shook her out of her dazed stupor and she sat down on the edge of a little exquisite patch of verdant green grass, as smooth as a putting green on a golf course and studded with gentians, and burst into tears.

Finally she pulled a tissue from her rucksack, dried her eyes and blew her nose. "Well" she thought to herself. "You made a right royal cock-up of that Sarah old girl!" Whatever had she been thinking of? She'd dressed provocatively to go and see Peter and he'd scarcely even registered the fact. If he *had* done he must have thought she was a forward slut and was too polite to tell her so. She suddenly felt cheap and as bad as the girls at college she so frequently turned her nose up for flaunting themselves before men. And why oh why had she left that parting sally about her always wanting to marry him? She must have been mad. Whatever must Peter think of her? She cringed with embarrassment at every recollection of the recent conversation. Her earlier frivolity had left her and now the skimpy clothes she'd donned were deeply embarrassing to her. Sniffing wretchedly she delved into her rucksack for her spare pair of jeans only to discover a new disaster. She'd packed a bar of chocolate with her lunch and it had lain forgotten in her pack, slowly melting. Her jeans were covered in sticky brown chocolate. She tried to scrape the mess off but it was hopeless. She couldn't possibly walk back down into the valley wearing them. In disgust she tossed them to one side and squatted on the grass clasping her knees feeling sorry for herself. She just wanted to get back home now. She thought how gently Peter had reminded her of her engagement to Alan. It was like being spanked for being a naughty girl. He must think her so immature that she could so brazenly flirt with other men possibly just weeks away from her marriage and how self-centredly she'd bleated about nobody asking her and not a thought for her duty and obligations. He had pointed out in the kindest way possible that she was very nearly a serious married woman: not a silly little teenager anymore and it was time to grow up.

Miserably she thought about how to get home quickly. She would take the chairlift down from the Gamsalp restaurant she decided. It would cut at least an hour off her homeward journey. As soon as she thought of the idea she groaned in despair as she realised it was not an option. There might be people in the meadows below the cable car on the way down and she was damned if she was going to hover in the air above them in a skirt that barely covered her rump with any degree of decency. It was no good. She was going to have to hike down through the forest. Coming to a decision she shouldered her rucksack once more and set off to the restaurant.

It was not her intention to stop at the mountain restaurant for she had little inclination to talk to anybody else today but, as she attempted to skirt it, she was hailed from the terrace of the establishment. Another friend of hers, Rosalie Gruner was waving to her. "Hoi! Sarahli!"

Rosalie's family ran the restaurant and as Sarah wearily approached she saw Rosalie's mother and brother emerge from the interior to greet her. Sarah blushed at her choice in clothing but had no polite option other than to walk over and exchange greetings. Roslie's mother called out and her husband emerged from the restaurant kitchen wiping his hands on his apron. His smile of welcome was a warm benediction to Sarah's troubled soul. "Gruezi mitternand." She intoned politely to the assembled family and Rosalie's mother regarded her in great pleasure.

"Sarah!" she declared delightedly. "God in heaven it must be two years or more since I last saw you! My hasn't she *blossomed* Albert? Why you look lovely Sarah."

Rosalie's father chuckled. "She was always a pretty girl." He declared firmly.

"Yes but just look at her now!" She clasped Sarah to her bosom in great hug. "You're a sight for sore eyes Schatzli!" She turned to her son. "Rudi! Run and fetch Sarah a bottle of beer. She must be thirsty out hiking on a hot day like today." With a huge smile she held Sarah at arms' length. "Let me look at you." She shook her head in wonder. "Why that young man of yours ought to count his blessings. He doesn't know how lucky he is. Come sit awhile girl and tell us all your news."

Blushing furiously under all the praise Sarah managed a smile. "Danke Frau Gruner. I will sit down for a little while." She took a place at a bench by a table on the terrace while the stout Frau Gruner hastened indoors to see to some necessary snacks apparently under the impression that Sarah was verging on the brink of collapse from starvation.

Rosalie took a seat at Sarah's side. "Hey!" she said, "You're dressed to kill today. Been to see someone nice?" She winked at Sarah. Rosalie belonged firmly in the Nicole school of "more is better" when it came to relationships with the opposite sex. She was a happy little extrovert, two years Sarah's junior.

"No I just popped up to see Peter. He's working up on the alp."

"I know that silly! He comes in here every evening for a beer!" Rosalie giggled. "I bet you had him yodelling around the alp dressed like that."

Sarah winced. It was not a subject upon which she wished to dwell. "Er not exactly." She murmured. She was saved from further enlargement on the topic by the sight of Rudi reappearing with a tray bearing a bottle of Appenzell beer and a glass followed closely by Frau Gruner carrying a platter so full of cheeses, smoked sausage, pickles and wholemeal bread that it suggested that she had decided that immediate and drastic action was required to save Sarah from imminent demise through malnutrition. Sarah wasn't very hungry anymore but she managed some of the food out of politeness whilst fielding an endless stream of questions from the gathered family and protesting feebly against Frau Gruner's apparent dissatisfaction with her appetite. It was a merry meeting for all that and Sarah's spirits revived under the warm hospitality of the Gruner family. Eventually she persuaded the family that no harm would come to her on the descent down to Oberdorf, and was able to take her leave although not before Frau Gruner, who was regarding her worriedly, had insisted upon wrapping up the considerable remnants of her repast for the trip down and pushing another bottle of beer into her rucksack. Sarah turned to wave as she set off and began her descent with a greatly improved morale.

This was her least favourite part of this trail for it was mostly in thick and quite gloomy forest and the track was steep and slippery in places. Sarah's legs and knees were starting to ache and it was a reminder to her that she'd been getting soft at university and needed to fitten up if she were to spend more time hiking. Finally the forests thinned out and gave way to patches of secondary growth and under-shrub where the Ring Ousels were nesting and she was out onto the lower meadows on the valley side at Oberdorf perched high above the drop to Wildhaus. She turned left onto the little tarmac road that led her toward Schwendi and the drop to Unterwasser. It was hot, by now, in these lower altitudes and she paused often to wipe the perspiration from her brow. Her feet ached. A tarmac road is purgatory on the feet after a long hike over rough mountain trails. She knew that her chances of passing through the hamlet of Schwendi without being obliged to socialise with some of her many acquaintances there was effectively zero but, with her reviving spirits, she wasn't too bothered and in any case she was ready for another rest after the gruelling drop from Gamsalp. There was one meeting to come this day that she didn't anticipate at all however and, in every way, it was the most curious and momentous of them all.

Chapter Nine

When one reflects back on one's life, it often strikes one how that life changes around entirely incidental occurrences as if life itself was just a random collection of entirely fortuitous or otherwise events. It might be a chance encounter in a public house, an impulsive decision to walk a different way home, an advertisement in a newspaper catching one's eye or any seemingly irrelevant, chance happening, upon which one's life seems suddenly to pivot. Certainly Sarah had no inclination that day that she was about to meet one of the most important and influential people in her life or that her life would change unrecognisably as a result. All she was truly concerned about as she approached Schwendi was an increasingly irritating physical discomfort. She was suffering an affliction which is the bane of the mountain hiker's life. A small pebble had insinuated itself into her right boot and was stabbing into the sole of her heel with every step.

Eventually the niggling discomfort became intolerable, forcing her to pause and sit on an old stone trough by the side of the little road to begin the laborious task of unlacing her boot with a view to eradicating the object of the outrage. Gingerly, she eased the boot off. This was always an unpleasant moment. Even the most shapely and alluring of female feet tended to acquire an odour of ripe cheese after a hot day's hike enclosed in woollen sock and mountain boot. She shook out the boot over her hand and a minute fragment of some sedimentary base rock material dropped into her palm. It was astonishing how tiny it was. It brought back a childhood recollection to her. She remembered her father once reading her a fairy story about a beautiful Princess who was forced to endure an uncomfortable night because a scheming queen had placed a pea in her bed.

The princess found herself unable to sleep even in spite of the help of twenty mattresses. The story had quite frightened Sarah as a little girl and she had been known to examine her bed meticulously in case some wicked person had concealed a pea within it. Later in life she had learned that the story was a retelling of an old Swedish folklore tale by Hans Christian Andersen and it sounded impossibly fanciful then. Nevertheless, as she regarded the miniscule fragment of stone in her hand, it was evident that even the most insignificant little fragments of chance material could inflict a suffering upon one quite out of proportion to their actual physical importance.

Her heel was sore and she eased her sock off and raised her foot to examine it. She had evidently left the elimination of the irritation too long for the continual abrasion of the pebble had caused a blister to form on her heel which, given that she still had a long walk home, promised to be an uncomfortable inconvenience at the least. She was examining the damage sourly when a car suddenly appeared around the corner, catching her by surprise. It was at this moment that it occurred to Sarah that, in her current seated position with her legs apart and one held high to be examined for physical damage, her short skirt was performing an absolute minimal function in concealing those items of her underwear which she had no intention of exposing to the public domain.

With a gasp she leapt off the trough and her eyes registered further surprise as the car pulled up sharply beside her. It was the same sleek red, open topped sports car she had last seen outside the Alpli restaurant with Nicole on her first day back in the Toggenburg and the driver the same sensationally beautiful woman she had caught a glimpse of on that occasion. Sarah would later ruefully consider that she had made better entrances into somebody's acquaintance for, if there was anybody in the Toggenburg she would have first liked to meet whilst hopping up and down foolishly on one leg, whilst clutching a hiking boot in one hand and a sock in the other, then this spectacular, exquisitely dressed beauty was about the last she would have chosen. The girl was perhaps a few years older than Sarah she thought and dressed in a short halter summer dress of warm pinks and lavenders. The plunging neckline of the dress revealed the soft curvature of perfect breasts and the dress clung sensuously to a figure of such masterfully crafted lines and contours that it would have outraged the sense of fairness in any women. The bare shoulders and arms were slender; the smooth skin blemishless. The hands that rested on the steering wheel and the sandal clad feet upon the pedals were shapely and elegant and her neck was long and graceful. The girl's hair was preposterously lovely; a great mane of wavy golden locks that shone in the sunlight and cascaded over her shoulders exuberantly. It was impossible not to desire to stroke those golden locks.

But it was the face that was the most striking for Sarah had never seen such exquisitely moulded features to a woman. The bones were delicate yet well formed with high cheek bones and a lovely shapely nose. The eyebrows arched high over a pair of huge azure eyes, that shone with warmth and gentleness, and the generously wide mouth was framed with perfect ruby lips. It was a girl to take your breath away; one with whom God had been lavish with his gifts as if He had created her in a holiday mood and been inclined to come up with something truly special to mark the occasion.

The girl was looking at Sarah in friendliness and with a touch of gentle amusement dancing in her beautiful eyes. "Hello there. You seem to be having a little trouble." The voice was a joy to hear; soft and musical; very English but with a hint of American in it. Nicole had said this woman was a singer. Sarah could believe it. She had rarely ever heard such a beautifully modulated voice.

Sarah blushed, suddenly realising how idiotic she must look standing on one leg. Gingerly she lowered her bare foot to the ground and tried to remember the name of this exotic women that Nicole had told her. It began with a D she was sure. "Oh er hello. Yes I just got a pea... I mean a stone in my er boot. I... I've been out hiking and I well I got er picked up this stone and I... was er just getting rid of it and...." Sarah tailed off aware that she was starting to babble.

The girl inclined her head and smiled, examining Sarah frankly. "You're Sarah aren't you? Nicole's friend?"

"Er yes that's right. I... I'm afraid you have the advantage of me Miss. I don't believe we've been introduced. Nicole did tell me your name but I'm afraid I've forgotten it."

The girl smiled hugely. It seemed to please her that there was somebody in the Toggenburg who hadn't the faintest idea of her identity. "I'm Daniela Sarah, Daniela Devin."

"I'm pleased to meet you Miss Devin."

"Oh please call me Daniela or better yet Danny."

"Thank you Daniela. Please, how do you know my name?"

Daniela laughed and it was like a musical charm. "Oh no great surprise there Sarah. I'm no Hercules Poirot. I've heard a lot about you. A lot of people have talked about you. You're well-loved in this valley. Well when I saw you with Nicole outside that restaurant the other day I put two and two together; long dark hair, big brown eyes; the prettiest girl in the Toggenburg.... well it had to be you."

Sarah blushed furiously. "I think that might be a bit of an exaggeration."

Daniela tossed back her hair and laughed warmly. "I think you might find yourself outvoted. The local populace seems pretty unanimous on that score and I must say I agree with the general consensus." Sarah blinked in confusion. Being told that she was the prettiest girl in the Toggenburg by the most beautiful woman she had ever met was bizarre to the point of unreality. Daniela regarded her with a smile. "Look I can't leave the Toggenburg's favourite damsel here in distress can I? May I offer you a lift somewhere?"

Sarah was torn between protesting that she wouldn't dream of inconveniencing the young lady and the temptation to accept. In the end the thought of hobbling all the way home with a blister was decisive and in any case there was a part of any girl that wasn't going to easily turn down the chance of a ride in a spectacular, open topped Ferrari. "Thank you Daniela that's very kind of you."

"Do call me Danny. Only my mother calls me Daniela."

"Thank you Danny. Just a moment while I put my boot back on."

Daniela waited patiently while Sarah struggled to pull her hiking boot back on and Sarah cursed the fact that she was apparently doomed to look so inelegant in front of this glamorous female. Daniela opened the car door and Sarah eased carefully onto the white leather upholstery alongside her, frightened of leaving muddy footprints on the immaculate interior. "So where were you heading Sarah" Daniela asked.

"Well I live over in the Alpli on the other side of the valley but, for the moment, my ambitions weren't any greater than getting over to Schwendi and taking a break and something to drink."

Daniela grinned. "I think that's an excellent idea. May I join you? We could have a drink and maybe a bite to eat at that lovely little restaurant by the lake there. I could drive you over to Alpli afterwards."

Sarah smiled, liking this warm friendly girl more by the second. "Yes thank you. I'd love to share a drink with you."

"Well come along then." Daniela released the clutch and eased the powerful car away. She drove carefully Sarah noted; even tentatively for someone in possession of such a thoroughbred racer.

Sarah stroked the upholstery with pleasure. "This is some car." she observed.

Daniela grimaced. "Yes it's horrible isn't it?"

"*Horrible*?"

Daniela nodded with a wry smile. "Yes. Between you and me I can't stand the bloody thing. The band bought it as a present for me to thank me for the success of our big European tour last year. I used to drive around in a little Citroen which was just fine as far as I was concerned but half way through the tour some idiot in a dirty great truck barged into it while it was parked and trashed it so the band pooled together and bought me this. Well since they'd been so sweet about it I didn't dare get rid of it and I've been lumbered with it ever since. The guys in the band say that it makes me look like a proper rock and roll star at last." Daniela laughed in amusement. "I still can't get used to it. I was scared to death of it for the first three months!"

Sarah laughed and looked at Daniela more closely. It was an interesting insight to this woman she realised. There was more than just a glamorous rock star. This woman had hidden depths. Behind the lovely smiling face and the gentle hint of perfume was a genuinely warm-hearted person. "Well it was quite a present." she noted.

"Yes it was although to be truthful it was a very successful time for us. We sold out in every venue we played and our CD sales topped the ten million mark worldwide. Then there were television appearances, radio airtime and all sorts of new deals." Daniela smiled gently. "We weren't exactly hurting for money. So I ended up stuck with a car out of the bands' best intentions and no way of divesting myself of it. I keep hoping somebody will steal it or something." She laughed shortly. "Fat chance in Switzerland! It's too damn law-abiding this country. You know what happened the other day? I went down to Buchs to do some shopping and I parked the car, with the hood down, just off the main drag and, like an idiot, forgot to take the keys out of the ignition. I came back two hours later and found an envelope under the windscreen wiper. It was a note from a shopkeeper, over the road, telling me that they'd noticed my keys in the ignition so they'd taken them out for safe keeping and I could collect them at the shop at my convenience. I was gob-smacked! In England the bloody car would have gone."

Sarah laughed and congratulated herself that she lived in one of the safest lands in Europe. "Well I think your car will be safe enough here in the Toggenburg."

Daniela nodded. "Yes. That I can believe. Look we're coming up to the restaurant. Where should I park?"

"There's a little car park just by the lane that goes down to the lake just off to the left." They parked the car easily and dismounted. Sarah experienced what she took to be the advantages of basking in the reflected glory of accompanying such a stunning companion, as a group of young men making their way down to the lake stopped in open admiration to gaze at them. Of course she wasn't aware that Daniela and she together, the one blond and the other brunette, were a strikingly arresting combination and as spectacular a pair of lovelies together as it was possible to desire.

The meadows by the car park were awash in flowers and one caught Daniela's attention. "Oh how lovely!" she exclaimed bending down to examine the little pyramidal head of deep purple red flowers. "I wonder what it is."

Sarah smiled. "It's an Early Purple Orchid Danny; *Orchis mascula* if you want the scientific name. You find lots of them in the meadows around here. They're quite common."

Daniela looked up her quizzically. You seem to be quite informed Sarah. Do you know much about flowers?"

"Er a bit." Sarah hedged carefully.

Daniela regarded the flower in pleasure and sighed. "I wish I did. Since I came to live in this valley I've never seen so many flowers in my life. I haven't the foggiest notion for the names of all of them. I guess I'm just a city girl. I ought to buy a book on them or something."

"Well I've plenty of books covering the flora of the Toggenburg if you're interested Danny."

"Why thank you Sarah. That's a sweet offer. I really do have to learn more about the place if I'm going to live here."

Sarah smiled and enjoyed looking at the radiant new inhabitant of the Toggenburg outside of her car for the first time. To Sarah's surprise Daniela was shorter than her and without her high heeled sandals the difference would have been noticeable. Revealed standing up for the first time Daniela seemed more beautiful than ever and she glowed against the backdrop of the little meadow in front of the lake. Sarah had never really taken much notice of female beauty before but Daniela was one of those women who was so lovely that it was simply a pleasure to look at her. Sarah found herself mesmerised by the vision.

"Shall we go for that drink Sarah?" Daniela was looking at her, the expression in her gentle smile unreadable, and Sarah was suddenly aware that she'd been starting to stare.

"Yes. Yes of course."

Daniela grinned although for what purpose Sarah couldn't tell. "Come along then Sarah." She said gaily and to Sarah's surprise she took her hand and led her toward the restaurant. Sarah was unused to holding a girl's hand and she felt a little strange about it. She never even held Nicole's hand much although Nicole was her best friend. She found, after she had adjusted to the unfamiliarity of it however, she quite enjoyed it. It made for a sisterly bonding and somehow forged an immediate friendship with Daniela even after only a few minutes acquaintance. She guessed that Daniela was far more comfortable with affectionate physical contact than she was.

Their arrival in the restaurant was suitably dramatic. Sarah, of course, was well known in the Schwendi restaurant and any appearance by her was always warmly greeted. Today, however, apparently leading the new, much talked about local celebrity in by the hand, the entrance was a sensation. The few clients in the restaurant found themselves neglected as the two waitresses rushed over to greet their spectacular new customers. The lads from the kitchen came to the kitchen door to ogle the arrivals until the proprietress of the establishment shooed them away and monopolised her VIP guests, ushering them to a table in the back garden overlooking the lake. Sarah felt much the ugly sister in the company of Daniela and she was aware that she was not a match for her companion's feminine elegance in her hiking boots and the inevitable dirty marks from a day's hiking on her once pristine tennis outfit. The proprietress was suitably fawning as she asked them what they would like to drink. Sarah was thirsty so she ordered a bottle of beer. To her surprise Daniela asked for the same and the proprietress walked away looking mildly disappointed as if she'd expected to be serving them nothing less than Dom Perignon.

Daniela's sophisticated beauty contrasted incongruously with the bottle of beer in front of her and Sarah giggled at the sight. Daniela looked at her inquiringly. "What's so funny Sarah?"

"I'm sorry Danny. I just didn't imagine you drinking beer."

Daniela pulled a look of mock indignation. "Nothing wrong with beer! I think I drank nothing but beer when I was at drama school."

"You went to drama school?"

"Oh yes. I'm not only a drama queen, I'm a seriously qualified one."

Sarah laughed enjoying the camaraderie with her new friend for already that was how Daniela felt to her. She wanted to know more about her. Her life sounded exciting.

"So what made you come to live in the Toggenburg Danny?" she asked.

"Oh my grandmother was from around here and I visited her a few times when I was young. I always remembered how beautiful the valley was and I harboured a secret dream that I'd like to live here one day. I'm Swiss on my father's side but I've lived most of my life in England or the States. Four years ago I came to Switzerland to do some recording and I fell in love with the country. I met up with some musicians and formed the band and we went straight ahead and recorded our first album."

"Your band are Swiss?"

"A bit of everything Sarah. My guitarist is American, my keyboards player is an English girl, my drummer is Swiss and my bass player is Italian. My two backing vocalists are English and French. We're a bit of an international set-up and that doesn't include all the guest musicians we have on tour or the session musicians in the studio, let alone the road crew."

"I'm sorry Danny. I interrupted you."

"Please don't apologise. Well the album took off and it seemed that we spent the next couple of years constantly on the road or in the studio. After recording our second and third albums we took a little break and I looked for somewhere more permanent to live and naturally I came up to the Toggenburg to look for property. I was lucky. There was a lovely place going near Oberdorf. I didn't live there much to begin with because it needed a lot of work but last summer I moved in. I still didn't get much use of it last year because no sooner had I settled in than we were back on the road for another tour. I hadn't really lived here continuously until last March when our last tour finished."

"Will you be touring again soon?"

Daniela pulled a face. "Not for a while. Our agents want us to but we're taking a break. I have nothing on all summer bar one television appearance some time or other and some time in studio to finish off our new album."

"Oh you'll have a relaxed summer then?"

"I hope so. I'm under doctor's orders to do so."

"Oh I'm sorry. Have you been ill?"

"I collapsed on our last tour Sarah. We had to cancel our last two gigs."

Sarah clapped a hand to her mouth. "Oh God! I'm sorry Danny. I hope it wasn't anything serious."

Daniela ran a finger around the rim of her beer glass thoughtfully. "Oh it wasn't anything that a good break won't put right. It was overwork and stress mostly; sheer nervous exhaustion. You've no idea how much a major tour can take it out of you. Fortunately most of the media were sympathetic although one paper did suggest I was being a bit of a prima donna and another rag had the nerve to insinuate that it was drugs related! Drugs! Me?

I've never touched drugs in my life. Anyway it frightened the guys in the band. I'd always been the rock; the one that held things together whenever they threatened to fall apart and so when I came apart at the seams it scared everybody shitless. They're always very protective of me and, when the quack wagged his finger and told me that I had to take things easy for a while for my health, they all started clucking like mother hens, cancelled all our engagements for the summer and packed me off to my country home to recuperate. I get concerned telephone calls every other day inquiring about my health. Actually I've never felt better. Maybe that quack knew what he was talking about."

"Sarah laughed. "Well you'll get plenty of relaxation around here. This is the sort of place that somebody losing their cat causes a local sensation."

Daniela grinned. "Yes! It's heavenly isn't it? Anyway that's enough about me. I want to learn about you. I've been looking forward to meeting the famous Sarah."

Sarah blushed. "There's nothing famous about me!"

Daniela shook her head. "Fame is a relative condition Sarah. You might not make it into the tabloid papers but you can take it from me; you're a celebrity in this valley. Everybody I've talked to has a good word to say about you. Your friend Nicole can't shut up about you. She worships you."

Sarah was shocked. "Has Nicole been talking about me?"

"Only in the nicest possible way Sarah. You seem to have quite an impact on people."

Sarah shook her head in confusion. "But I don't do anything."

Daniela smiled, "You know some people do extraordinary things and some people are just extraordinary people. I'd guess you fall into the latter category. You know I have millions of fans around the world but I'd swap them all just for the love and affection you seem to excite in people just for being yourself. I envy you."

Sarah looked at Daniela bemusedly. Daniela's words were odd to her because strangely she had been starting to think the same thing about Daniela. If she had millions of fans thought Sarah it was largely because she was so unpretentious and so warmly natural. Could it be possibly true that this astonishing woman didn't actually realise the extent of her own charm? And if it was true that she, Sarah herself, was guilty of the same thing was this then a case of two women staring at each other and admiring in the other the very qualities that they failed to see in themselves? Sarah shivered, suddenly feeling very close to some basic truth. Before she could find a sensible reply, they were interrupted. A group of young girls in their teens were sat at a table on the other side of the garden and they'd been observing Daniela and Sarah covertly for some time and whispering behind their hands. Eventually one of them had plucked up the courage to walk over with a request. "Excuse me." she said, addressing Daniela, "You're Danny Devin aren't you? My friends and I are all big fans of you. We were wondering if you'd let us take your photograph Miss Devin."

Daniela turned on a smile of dazzling brilliance for the young girl. "Of course. Thank you for having the courtesy to ask. Of course you may take my photograph."

The young girl almost danced with glee and within seconds she and her friends had produced cameras as Daniela posed demurely for them. They thanked her with profusion and returned to their table excitedly. Sarah shook her head. "I know those girls Danny. They're from Wildhaus. I should have told them to back off and not bother you."

"They're not bothering me Sarah."

"But isn't it an imposition? I mean you must get this sort of thing all the time."

"Sarah young people like them go out and spend their money on my music and make me a very rich woman. It is the least I can do to express my thanks for their support."

Sarah felt pleased with Daniela's answer. Here was a woman who despite all her fame and wealth realised that she owed it all to the people who bought her music. She was in some fundamental way connected to her fans. She found she liked this gracious woman more and more.

Daniela fanned herself with a menu from the table. "My word it's hot. I'm almost tempted to go and jump in that lake." The larger of the two little lakes at Schwendi had a large platform moored in the middle and there was a group of young boys cavorting on it and leaping in to swim in the lake.

Sarah frowned. "I wouldn't like you to do that Daniela. The lake looks deceptively inviting but it's icy cold and it has an evil reputation locally. Several people have drowned in it."

Daniela gave Sarah a curiously serious look. "Then, for you, I shall studiously avoid it Sarah." Then she laughed and addressed Sarah more mischievously. "Tell me what you've done today. You say you've been hiking. When I first saw you by the road, I thought you must have been playing tennis."

Sarah laughed in embarrassment. "Oh no! I just decided to wear something light to go hiking today because the weather was going to be so hot."

"Well I must say it's far nicer than what I usually associate with hiking gear. You look gorgeous. If your fan club had known you were abroad on the mountainside looking so fetching you'd have been beating them off with your walking stick."

Sarah grinned sheepishly. "Really Danny! I'm sure you're exaggerating. People around here don't think the sun shines out of my backside."

Daniela gave a low chuckle. "What's wrong with your backside? It looks pretty radiant from where I'm sitting."

Sarah pulled her inadequate skirt down as far as she could and sighed. "I should have worn something not quite so short."

Daniela took a long appraisal of Sarah's legs without embarrassment. "If you've got them honey, then flaunt them. You have the nicest pair of pins I've seen in many a long day. A woman's beauty is a gift of God. Surely you wouldn't deny honest God-fearing folk the blessings of his benevolence."

Sarah laughed. "Stop flattering me! I'm not beautiful. I look like a jaded old bag lady next to you."

Daniela shook her head seriously. "Sarah honey, I work in show business and I get to meet fabulously beautiful women all the time. You could hold your head up with the best of them. You are truly a lovely girl." Daniela suddenly reached over and laid her hand on Sarah's gently. "I mean that Sarah. Just because you don't realise how lovely you are doesn't alter the fact. In fact, it makes you even more lovely because it's a beauty without vanity." For a second Daniela held Sarah's eyes with her own and Sarah felt suddenly flustered, feeling that she was missing something but Daniela released her hand and picked up the menu again with a disarming laugh. "Come on I'm hungry. Let's order something to eat."

Sarah's appetite was sadly diminished by Frau Gruner's efforts up at Gamsalp but she decided to try something small out of politeness. She ordered a salad. Daniela, she observed, certainly didn't owe her admirably slender figure to self-starvation for her new friend ordered a hearty rosti; a mound of Swiss style, hash brown potatoes fried in butter with onions and pieces of bacon, topped with melted raclette cheese and a fried egg. "It's really fattening Danny." Sarah warned her of her choice.

Daniela grinned wickedly. "I know! It's one of my favourites. I don't eat it too often though; just as a treat on a special occasion."

"Oh what's the occasion?"

"Why meeting you of course. Don't worry about my figure honey I'm a pretty active person and I never seem to put on the pounds. You'd be surprised how physically demanding it can be performing live. I can drop half a kilo during a two-hour show. Even when I'm not touring I keep fit; a lot of dance training and that sort of thing." She paused for a moment. "What I'd really like to do is a bit of mountain hiking myself around here but I haven't the foggiest idea how to go about it. They tell me around here that it is criminal folly for an inexperienced person to go gallivanting off into the mountains on their own without a guide."

"Well yes, it can be dangerous if you don't know what you're doing."

"You're very brave hiking all alone."

Sarah laughed at Daniela's seriousness. "Oh I've been walking around in these mountains ever since I was a little kid Daniela. I know every inch of them."

"Including that one over there?" asked Daniela pointing beyond the restaurant to the looming bulk of the Santis hazy in the far distance.

"The Santis? Of course! I've been up it more times than I can remember. It's my favourite."

"I'd love to go to the top of it. Is it hard?"

"Only moderately so. It depends on which route you take. I wouldn't recommend you trying it on your own for a first attempt though. It can be a funny mountain." Sarah paused and smiled. "If you like I'll take you up one day."

"Oh would you? That's kind of you. I'd love to go. I'm probably not as fit as you but I hope I won't disgrace myself by not being able to keep up."

"Well I need to toughen up myself again Danny. I've been at university all winter and I've got soft. I noticed today that my legs were aching and that was an easy hike. I'd be delighted to be your mountain guide for the day though. I'm trained too. I completed a first-year course in aspiring mountain guiding when I was sixteen and I've often assisted on official guided tours."

"So you're a professional?"

Sarah shook her head with a smile. "No not really, just an aspirant. You have to have three years training and pass a tough exam before you can call yourself a professional guide."

"I'd be willing to pay you nevertheless."

"Nonsense! I wouldn't dream of accepting anything for it. It would be my pleasure. I get a thrill out of introducing people to the mountains for the first time."

"This sounds like it could be fun. Let's make a date."

Sarah held up her hand. "We'll have to wait a few weeks yet. There's still a lot of snow up on the mountain. You'll need proper boots as well."

"Oh I've got mountain boots. I bought them last summer when I first moved here. I've walked about in them a bit and they seem comfortable enough."

Sarah smiled to herself at the thought of this delicate beauty clad in mountain boots. "You'll find new style boots are usually comfortable Danny. In the old days they were big heavy leather things that were torment to wear until you'd broken them in but, with modern lightweight materials, you can nearly pick them off the shelf and take them straight out onto the mountain."

"I can't wait. There's a song on the new album about a lover's quest to find their beloved on top of a mountain and I've never climbed one in my life. I might have to rework the lyrics when I find out what it's really like."

Sarah laughed. "I can't imagine you finding much in the way of romantic love on top of the Santis Danny."

"Can't you? I can! Oh look the waitress is coming out with knives and forks. Our food must be nearly ready."

The waitress laid their table with ill-concealed excitement and it was plain that she was nearly obsessed with curiosity. Daniela watched her with a gentle smile and thanked her warmly. "It's my pleasure Miss." The young waitress replied.

Sarah grinned. She knew Monika well. The girl was a young German who had been working the summer and winter seasons in the Toggenburg for the last four years. She was a nice girl but a hopelessly inquisitive gossip. She was obviously dying to know what brought Sarah into the restaurant with such a famous and striking companion. The necessity to curb her curiosity out of deferential professional politeness must have been torment for the young lady.

Sarah and Daniela chatted easily as they ate. Daniela was a delicate and fastidiously tidy eater, Sarah noted. A plateful of Swiss farmhouse mountain rosti was not the kind of repast you might have associated with haute cuisine and elegant surroundings but Daniela managed to eat daintily and with beautifully studied poise. Everything this girl seemed to do was laced with harmonious elegance, it seemed. Her simplest actions were balletic and graceful, as if Daniela were continuously aware of the aesthetic qualities of her movement and pose. Perhaps it was the drama training Sarah supposed; or perhaps then again it was just natural grace and uninhibited femininity. Whatever it was, it enhanced the beauty of the lovely young woman; endowed her with charm and was a joy to watch. Sarah nibbled at her salad self-consciously, knowing that she was no match for the stylish etiquette of her companion.

Daniela's manners might have been ladylike but they certainly didn't detract from her enjoyment of her food for she finished her meal with alacrity and pushed her plate aside with satisfaction, dabbing at the corner of her mouth with a napkin. "So," she said, continuing their conversation, "Now that you've finished university, what are your plans?"

Sarah shrugged hopelessly. "I don't really know Danny." she confessed. "I'm in a bit of a flux for the moment. I was hoping for a nice relaxed summer but that seems to be falling by the wayside. I'm supposed to be getting married at the end of summer."

Daniela's eyes opened wide in surprise. "You're getting married?"

Sarah nodded sheepishly. "Yes that's right. It's a bit of a shock really. I didn't expect to get married until next year at the earliest but my family are quite keen for me to marry before the autumn."

"Well congratulations!" Daniela's felicitations were warm and heartfelt.

Sarah grimaced guiltily. "Thank you."

"Your fiancée is a very lucky man Sarah." Daniela told her with genuine warmth. "I do hope he appreciates his good fortune."

Sarah bit her lip not wishing to continue this line of discussion. "Oh I... I think it's me who should be appreciative Danny. He's very good looking and his family are very rich."

Daniela frowned. "You don't strike me as the sort of person who would be particularly impressed by a man's wealth Sarah."

Sarah felt uncomfortable. "No... no I'm not... well not really. I mean there's more to a person than how much money they have isn't there?"

"There is indeed. I meet millionaires every day in my line of business Sarah. You can take it from me; money doesn't preclude a person from being an insufferable bore."

Sarah smiled. "No I suppose not. But then not all poor people are interesting either."

Daniela laughed easily. "You're right Sarah. The only way to judge a person is through the riches they carry about between their ears." She stopped abruptly and regarded Sarah closely. "So do you love him?"

Sarah blinked, caught by surprise by the suddenly frank question. "Why.... well yes... I mean I.... well of course I do."

Daniela smiled enigmatically. "I'm pleased to hear it Sarah." She paused to brush a lock of her hair aside. "Forgive me for asking. I should have known that a girl like you would never think of marrying someone you didn't love completely." Sarah swallowed and felt the heat rush into her face. She knew that she must be displaying the doubts in her mind with every expression and suddenly she felt wretched. Daniela either didn't notice her discomfort or was too polite to remark upon it for she changed the subject easily and began to ask Sarah about her studies at university.

On the more secure ground, Sarah found herself discussing her studies with enthusiasm. She had enjoyed the academic life at university and her chosen subject was one which she was passionate about. Daniela asked her what aspects of history most interested her and Sarah hesitated. "Well I never really specialised in any one topic Danny but I've always been interested in the history of the town in England where I was born, although I can't remember much about it. I left England when I was just a little girl and I've not been back since."

"Where were you born?"

"Oh you've probably never heard of it. It's a little town in North England called Beverly."

"Beverly!" Daniela seemed delightedly surprised. "Of course I know Beverly. It's a lovely little town."

It was Sarah's turn to be surprised. "You know it?"

"Yes of course! I was born in York about forty miles away. I've been to Beverly many a time. I played at the Beverly folk festival one year." Daniela laughed in pleasure. "My word you're a fellow Yorkshire girl Sarah. Who would have thought it?"

Sarah was pleasantly surprised. She had hardly ever met anyone who had ever even heard of the town of her birth let alone someone intimately acquainted with it. "I... I hardly remember Beverly Danny." She said. "I was only very small when we moved to Switzerland. What's it like?"

"It's a charming little market town Sarah; all old houses and little streets around the minster which is a gorgeous old Gothic church that dominates the whole town. There's an old canal that runs from the town down to the river Hull and a big market square in the town centre. It's a wealthy little town; quite posh with lots of leafy suburbs of seriously big houses and a little race course abutting a large area of common land on the outskirts. It used to be a walled town in medieval times but there's little of the walls left apart from one of the old gates. It's a cosy little place and it possesses one of the most famous old pubs in Yorkshire; an amazing old place, all lit by gas lamps and a regular warren of snug little back rooms."

"It sounds lovely. I've always wanted to go back and visit the place."

"You'd like it. Yorkshire isn't Switzerland by any means but it has a charm all of its own."

"Really? I've always been under the impression that it was mostly an industrial region; all mill towns and coal mining and so on."

Daniela shook her head. "It's a common misconception Sarah. Most of the coal mines are closed now and, in any case, the industrial areas of the county are confined mainly to the West Riding. Most of Yorkshire is very rural and very beautiful. There are the Pennines which are a chain of low mountains running along the western edge of the county and intersected with lovely valleys in a region called the Dales. Then there's the Yorkshire Moors which are a forty-odd mile wide swathe of heather clad, high moorland along the north eastern coast; the chalk hills of the Yorkshire Wolds and the broad flat plain of the Vale of York and the coastal flats of Holderness. It's a county of many different contrasts Sarah from gorgeous little fishing villages to wild open places. Yes, there are some seriously big industrial towns but there are some of the most picturesque villages and towns to be found anywhere in England as well. The capital city, York, is one of the most beautiful cities in the country."

Sarah sighed. "I've never really travelled very much Danny I'm afraid."

Daniela grinned. "Well if you are going to be a person that sticks in one place Sarah then you'd be hard pushed to find a better one than this. I wake up every morning and can't believe the view from my bedroom window."

"Oh yes." Sarah agreed. "I love the Toggenburg. I often wonder if I could live anywhere else."

Daniela looked at her quizzically. "Are you marrying a local boy then?"

Sarah pulled a wry face. "No. He comes from Zurich. I don't see him very often."

"Why ever not? Zurich's not that far away. You can drive it in an hour and a half."

"Yes, but he spends a lot of time abroad, on business and, when he is in Switzerland, he prefers to be in Zurich. He's not really into the country life I'm afraid."

"And where will you live when you're married then?"

"In Zurich probably. His work is in Zurich so he'll need to be close to it."

"Is he a bit of a career man then?"

Sarah nodded. "Oh yes! He's an upcoming businessman in his father's business. He's very successful."

"He'll have to be. Zurich's a bloody expensive place to live."

"Well we're lucky in that respect. My family owns a property in Zurich which we'll be moving into I suppose."

"A property? You mean a house or something?"

"Yes. I've never actually seen it but it's supposed to be a big place; six bedrooms or something and with a large garden and a big garage."

Daniela whistled softly. "So you're a rich girl then Sarah!"

Sarah laughed. "Good God no! I'm not rich."

"Sweetheart, if you own a house in Zurich you are. Have you ever checked out the property prices in Zurich?"

"Well I suppose they're quite expensive but I've never really looked."

"They're expensive all right. If you own a house in Zurich you are, de facto, a millionaire. So you are taking possession of this house when you marry then?"

"Yes my parents are bequeathing it to me they say."

"That's quite a dowry Sarah. Your fiancée is not only marrying one of the most gorgeous girls in eastern Switzerland but he's also gaining the marital rights to a property worth millions on the market. No wonder he's in a rush to get you down the aisle."

Sarah found herself uncomfortable at the thought. It had never really occurred to her that she was not only a potential bride to Alan but also a sound business investment as well. The thought made her feel sordid. "I don't think he's marrying me for my money Danny." She protested. "After all his family are rich too."

Daniela laughed disarmingly. "Of course he's not marrying you for your money Sarah. Good God! Any warm-blooded man would have you in a shot if he found you penniless on the street in your petticoats. The fact that you're an heiress is just icing on the cake."

"Have you never thought of marrying Danny?"

"Once Sarah. It never worked out." Daniela didn't elaborate and Sarah didn't press for details out of deference to Daniela's privacy. She remembered something Nicole had said about some love triangle that Daniela had lost out on that had been reported in the papers and she guessed that it was not a subject that her new friend would like to discuss publicly.

They talked easily of other things and Sarah found herself relaxed and enjoying her glamorous friend's companionship. Daniela, she found, was an easy person to talk to. There was a natural charm to her that put you instantly at your ease. Daniela was an interesting person to be sure but she was that rare species of human that is more concerned in being interested in you than they are in being interesting to you. It was, paradoxically, a trait she shared with Sarah herself. A neutral observer would have concluded that the two young women were fascinated by each other. Sarah never quite grasped this however. She put Daniela's interest in her down to the naturally modest grace and deferential charm of her companion. It was an interest born of refined good manners and selflessness; politeness taken to a level of high level of courtesy, she believed. It never occurred to her that Daniela's interest was genuine and deep rooted.

At last Daniela glanced at her watch. "Good heavens! Look at the time. I promised to drive you home and I've kept you gossiping here for over two hours. That was very selfish of me."

"I don't mind at all Danny. I enjoyed our conversation."

Daniela smiled and her smile was gloriously radiant. "I enjoyed it too Sarah; so much so that I can't wait to continue it in the near future sometime. Perhaps you'd like to join me for dinner sometime. I'll leave the choice of restaurant up to you. You'll know more about the best places to eat around here than I do."

"Yes I'd like that."

"Well we'll have to make a date. I'm afraid it won't be this week though. I have a lot to do in the studio and we've got a video to make for our new single. Perhaps sometime after the weekend?"

"I don't know my plans Danny but it sounds fine to me."

"Great. Well we'd better pay our bill I suppose." The bill for their food and drinks came to a little over thirty francs and Daniela refused point blank to allow Sarah to contribute so much as a single rappen. "No Sarah!" she said. "Let me pay it. It's the least I can do for being so greedy and monopolising your company for two and a half hours." Daniela took out a hundred franc note and folded it neatly into the bill on the little plate at their table before rising to leave.

Sarah was shocked. "Really Danny! You're not leaving all that as a tip are you? I mean that's more than three times what we spent."

Daniela looked momentarily uncomfortable. "Oh! Do you think it's too much?"

"Well a bit. I mean ten francs would have been generous."

"Do you think I'm being patronising?"

Sarah smiled. Daniela seemed to be concerned. She guessed that Daniela was not comfortable with her wealth. It worried her that people might believe that she had no notion of the value of money and just cast it away as if it was meaningless to her. Of course a hundred francs was meaningless to Daniela but she was uncomfortable pushing her wealth in poorer people's faces. Sarah looked at Daniela who was biting her lip in indecision. "No Danny. I don't think you're being patronising. It's a very generous tip and I'm sure the girls will appreciate it."

Daniela nodded, still uncertain before coming to a decision. "I know!" She reached into her handbag and pulled out a slim CD case in a blank cover. "It's one of the demo CDs for our new single." She explained. With a fibre tipped pen she wrote on the blank cover. "**Thank you for a wonderful afternoon.**" and, signing it, placed the CD on the plate alongside the hundred francs. "There now!" she declared. "Now it's not a tip. It's a thank you present for a magical day."

Sarah stared at her bewildered. "A bottle of beer and a plate of rosti is a magical day?"

Daniela looked her straight in the eyes in the frank open way that Sarah was beginning to realise was characteristic of her. "Oh yes! Come along. Let me drive you home."

Daniela seemed happy and distracted by their conversation as they set off down the hill toward the valley bottom in the red Ferrari. Sarah was an incorrigible back seat driver and felt nervous about Daniela's wandering attention as she turned her eyes frequently from the road to address Sarah. About half way down the hill she found herself unable to prevent herself from issuing a warning to her companion. "Be careful Danny!" she admonished, "This bend here is dangerous. There's been a lot of accidents here."

113

Daniela slowed the car obediently to Sarah's concerns on the sharp bend on the decline. The hillside fell away steeply down some marshy meadows by the side of the road. Daniela glanced at the meadows in pleasure. "Oh look Sarah! There're some more of those pretty flowers; early Purple Orchids weren't they?"

Sarah smiled pleased that Daniela had remembered the name. "That's right." She confirmed.

Suddenly Daniela stopped the car and nudged Sarah's arm. "Sarah! Look! A deer."

Sarah followed Daniela's pointed finger to see a small deer grazing at the side of a little copse close to the road. The animal raised its head in alarm at their approach and with a couple of swift bounds disappeared into the woods. Sarah wrinkled her brow. "That's unusual." She noted. "You don't often see deer down in these lower meadows this late in the day."

"What sort of deer was it?" asked Daniela entranced by the view of the animal.

"Oh it was a Roe deer Danny. They're usually more or less confined to the forests in the middle of the day although you might see them out in the open very early in the morning. We occasionally get Red deer as well but they tend to be quite scarce locally."

Daniela's eyes were shining. "It was lovely!" she declared in a thrilled voice. "I love animals. It's always a pleasure to me to see wild animals. When I lived in the city I hardly ever saw any so it's fantastic in the country to see animals in the wild. I have squirrels in the trees of my garden here that are really tame and come right up to you to be fed. I don't know what kind of squirrels they are though. They're black. I've never heard of black squirrels before."

Sarah laughed delightedly at Daniela's city girl ignorance. "You won't have done Danny. There's no such thing as a black squirrel. They are Red squirrels."

Daniela looked unconvinced. "But they're not red Sarah. They're nearly all black with a bit of white on them."

Sarah nodded. "Oh I believe you Danny. Most of the Red squirrels locally are the dark phase of the animal. It's actually quite uncommon to see one of the real russet red examples. I have a theory that it's because most of the forests around here are coniferous. The dark phase is best for camouflage in gloomy dense coniferous forest. You only see the red phase a lot in deciduous woodland. Nevertheless they are the same animal; just different colour variations."

Daniela sighed theatrically. "I've got a lot to learn." She remarked wistfully. "I wish I knew as much about the fauna and flora around here as you seem to do."

"Well I grew up around here Danny."

Daniela looked at Sarah seriously. "Well I want you to teach me all you know Sarah. Would you do that?"

Sarah stared at Daniela feeling suddenly strange. For some unfathomable reason the unexpected encounter with the deer had brought an odd sensation of foreboding to her. "I... I'd be delighted to Danny." She croaked at last.

"Great." Daniela put the car back into gear and they moved off down the hillside with Sarah trying to understand the unsettling thrill of fear in her.

At last Daniela pulled the spectacular red automobile up outside Sarah's house and turned to smile at her. "Well here you are."

"Yes.... yes thank you. Thanks for the lift and the meal Danny."

"It was entirely my pleasure Sarah." Daniela reached out to touch Sarah's hand. "Are we still on for that dinner?"

"Why of course."

"And that trip up the mountain?"

"Yes of course."

"Good! I'm looking forward to it. I haven't enjoyed an afternoon so much in a long time. How will I get in touch with you?"

"Oh I'll give you my telephone number if you like."

"Thank you. Just a moment. I have a piece of paper and a pen in the glove compartment."

After Sarah had written down her house telephone number Daniela folded it reverently into her handbag. "I'll know more about my schedule next week tomorrow." She told Sarah, "Can I give you a call then?"

"Sure. If I'm not in then leave a message with my housemate."

"Thank you." Daniela took Sarah's hand and gripped it affectionately. "It was lovely to meet you Sarah. I can't wait until our next meeting."

Sarah felt the warmth of Daniela's hand and felt suddenly confused; her heart beating quickly in anxiety, as if sensing that this chance meeting with the beautiful girl held some significance to her future beyond the superficial pleasantries of polite conversation. Daniela she realised was an intensely emotional person and was not a person merely to brush one's life lightly. This was a woman that lived by the dictates of her heart. Daniela was not a person with whom to enjoy a casual acquaintance. She would impact powerfully on every person she touched. For a brief moment Sarah felt almost frightened of her. This was a woman with consequences.

The curious feeling stayed with Sarah as she waved goodbye and watched the red car drive away down the road away from the cottage and disappear around the bend, as it made its way out of the Alpli. It was only as the car finally vanished from view that she remembered that Nicole hadn't paid the telephone bill. Daniela would call in vain. The phone was cut off.

Chapter Ten

When Nicole returned home from work late that evening she found Sarah, newly emerged from the bath, clad in a somewhat tattered bathrobe, and examining the household bills over the coffee table in the living room with an expression that augured poorly for the maintenance of domestic harmony. Sarah was looking vexed. Nicole's neglect of the telephone bill was by no means the end to the story. The electricity bill was also in arrears and they were, apparently, also watching television illegally since the licence fee had not been paid for some months. The annual television fee alone came to nearly three hundred francs and with the substantial telephone bill and assorted other unpaid utility charges Sarah had discovered that the household was indebted to the tune of close on eight hundred francs even without the month's rent to pay. It had been the realisation that she had given Daniela a worthless telephone number that had led Sarah to an in-depth study into the household finances and she was clearly unhappy about them.

Nicole swallowed nervously as Sarah glanced up from her calculations with a glare. "Er hi Sarah honey. Got a few bills have we?"

Sarah slapped down the document she was perusing in exasperation. "Really Nicole! How could you have let things slip to this extent? Are you trying to bankrupt us? Why didn't you tell me that things had got this bad? You haven't even paid the television licence. I sent you half the money for the licence in March. Why haven't you paid it?"

"I... I was broke Sarah sweetheart."

"Don't sweetheart me! It's too bad of you. If we get controlled we'll have a bloody fine to pay. What did you do with the money I sent you?"

117

"Don't be mad Sarah. I didn't have a job. I had to eat didn't I?"

"So you blew it?"

"Come on Sarah. You know there's little enough work going out of season. What was I supposed to do? I thought that as soon as I got a job for the summer I could square things up."

"It's about time you thought of getting a proper job Nicky. One that lasts all year round. I can't keep bailing you out of these messes. For God's sake Nicky I'm getting married at the end of summer. I won't be around to pick up the tabs after that. I'm not exactly rolling in money either Nicky. I was saving up to pay for my masters' degree. You can't expect me to continuously dip into my savings just to keep this household running."

"You won't have to Sarah. I'm back earning now. I'll make up the difference."

"Nicky you're clearing about two thousand three hundred francs a month at the hotel. The rent and the bills alone this month are going to take over half of that and you're not the most frugal of spenders you know."

"I can get some extra cash from somewhere maybe."

"Yes and pigs might fly. It'll be a miracle if you even keep this job for the whole of summer. Your record in keeping a job is hardly exemplary. Look at what happened when you had that job in Buchs."

"That wasn't my fault."

"Or the job you had in the supermarket in Nesslau."

"Well all right but that could have happened to anyone."

"Or your sorry, short lived career as a chamber-maid in the Santis Hotel."

"Ok so maybe that could have turned out a bit better. How was I to know that that guy was the bloody owner's fiancée?"

Sarah tossed the bill onto the table in frustration. "Nicole I love you to bits but you're a bloody nightmare when it comes to practicalities. I'm fed up of coming home to find us once more on the verge of bankruptcy."

"You've still got money coming from your parents."

"I'm not going to rely on my parents Nicky. That was while I was studying. I can hardly keep tapping up my Dad now I've finished uni. We have to stand on our own two feet. I had hoped that I'd have enough money to see me through the summer without having to take a full-time job. Now it looks like I'll have to go out job hunting after all."

"What are you worried about? Once you're married you won't have to worry about money again."

"My money is my last hope of independence Nicky. I'm not about to marry as a pauper and depend for my pocket money on my husband's patronage. I'll not sacrifice every last vestige of my freedom."

Nicole flopped down into an armchair. "Hmm! For a woman about to be joined in blissful matrimony you sure as hell don't sound happy about the prospect."

"Don't change the subject."

"I'm not changing the subject. This guff about not wanting to marry as a pauper is bullshit isn't it? What you're really worried about is that fact that you might not marry at all and you don't know how you'll get by as a single woman."

"Rubbish!" Sarah blushed crimson. Nicole's shrewd guesses were close to the mark.

"It isn't rubbish and you know it. Ever since you got back you've been hedging about this marriage. Everything was all rosy when you were looking to marry into a comfortably rich family. Now you're not sure you want to and the future is all about electricity bills and whether our foul landlady is going to put the rent up. You say I haven't got a proper job. Well neither have you if your future career as a wealthy housewife goes tits up on you have you?"

"Nicky I'm just trying to keep my options open."

"Talking of options did you get to see Peter?"

"He's not an option Nicky."

"Tell it to the marines Sarah. You've been loopy about him since time out of mind. You are not going to tell me that all these sudden doubts about Alan have got nothing to do with the fact that Peter, despite being one of the best-looking blokes in the valley, is still seriously unattached and available."

"I said it wasn't an option and I meant it Nicky. Peter isn't interested in me."

"Bullshit!"

"It isn't bullshit Nicky. I saw him today and I think one of his bloody cows excited more interest in him than my presence."

"I don't believe that."

"It's true. I made a complete fool of myself. I flirted with him and even told him that I always wanted to marry him when I was a young girl. God I even reminded him about that bloody day up at Schafboden and let him know that I wouldn't be completely uninterested in a return bout."

"Oh hell! What happened?"

"He looked at me as if one of his heifers had developed foot and mouth disease, got all noble and turned me down like a bedspread. Said he still wanted to be my friend and I crawled away with my tail between my legs."

"Oh poor Sarah!"

"Yes. When it comes to moments of intense personal humiliation it was right up there with the best of them." Sarah took a deep breath. "God I felt awful! I even dressed up a little bit sexy to entice him and I might as well have turned up in a nun's habit. I must have looked a complete idiot!" To Nicole's incredulity Sarah burst into tears.

In an instance Nicole had joined her on the sofa and wrapped her arms around her. Sarah hardly ever cried. Nicole was shocked by the display of emotion from her usually such composed friend. "Come on Sarah. Don't cry honey. It's probably not as bad as you think. Pete's just shy with girls. You know that."

Sarah shook her head miserably and sobbed. "No Nicky. It wasn't just shyness. He really isn't interested in me other than as a friend. I could see it in his face. Oh God! How could I have been so stupid. I don't know what's happening to me. I'm damn near engaged to all intents and purposes and here I am snivelling over another man. For God's sake don't tell anyone."

Nicole comforted Sarah as best she could, worried about this sudden volatility in her. Normally these kind of emotional turmoils were Nicole's prerogative in the household. It seemed to turn the stability of the house on its head for Sarah to be the one breaking down. "Hush honey. Come on stop crying and dry your eyes. I'll go and get that bottle of Kirsch we've got in the kitchen and make us a couple of liqueur coffees and you can tell me all about it."

Clutching a rich hot liqueur coffee topped with cream Sarah poured out her story of her meeting with Peter to a sympathetic Nicole. To say that Nicole's compassion for Sarah was based partly in relief at not being in the firing line for her fiscal misdemeanours would be to do Nicole less than justice. Whilst it is true that she was not averse to having the subject changed to one of less immediate embarrassment to herself, she was nevertheless seriously concerned about Sarah. Her friend had always been the sensible one; the one who remained calm in the troubled maelstrom that frequently accompanied Nicole's journey through life. Nicole was honest enough to herself to realise that she had long depended on her friend's calming stability. Sarah had been the bedrock of common sense, certainty and measured consideration.

Sarah's life had seemed to run to the dictates of a strictly ordered plan in which everything was in its place and the future mapped out along a clearly defined route. Even Sarah's forthcoming marriage conformed to the pattern. Sarah's marriage had never been questioned. She would marry Alan according to a long agreed upon scenario, as cast in stone as her tightly choreographed life had been until now. Sarah's world was one of certainties. Nicole had long envied Sarah for her tranquil acceptance of fate, as if every tribulation was but a punctuation mark in the greater script defining her existence. It was as if that script had been written for her at birth and Sarah had followed the play of her life meticulously and never questioned her lines within the mundane drama to which she was committed.

Listening to Sarah's story, Nicole guessed that even Peter had been shocked at this sudden air of uncertainty in Sarah's life. Nicole was a shrewd girl in spite of her apparent muddle-headedness and she sensed that being confronted with a Sarah doubting the certainty of her future must have appeared to Peter to have been rather as if some fundamental law of reality had suddenly been violated and existence destabilised. Nicole rather suspected that what Sarah took for a rejection of herself was, in fact, little more than a Peter attempting to come to terms with drastic change in the ordering of the universe. Peter himself was not a person comfortable with all-encompassing change and Nicole could well imagine him making a hash of dealing with a newly revealed Sarah struggling with emotional turmoil.

Sarah was being overly dramatic. That, in itself, was telling because there were few people, of Nicole's acquaintance, less likely to be a drama queen than Sarah. Nicole well-remembered their school days together.

Sarah had never dated boys to the same extent as Nicole or any of her friends; had never suffered the hormonal fluctuations of teenage infatuation. Sarah had never cried on a friend's shoulder over some boy at school; had never walked around for days mooning over some juvenile adulation. She'd never written silly love letters, made a fool of herself over some young man at the school dance, made immature gestures of affection or in any way involved herself in the richly comic dramas of adolescent love. Sarah had always seemed to be mature beyond her years. Sarah had been the one you went to with your troubles. It never occurred to you that she would have troubles of her own. She never wore make-up at school, never spent hours in the day texting her newest boyfriend or neglected her studies over some contrived romance. The exaggerations of teenage sexuality, that could turn a flirtation into a life or death threatening obsession, had passed Sarah by. Whilst all the other girls at school had been carried along in a whirlwind of switched on hormones and confused emotions, Sarah had simply walked through the passage of adolescence with characteristic tranquillity, unmoved by the chaos of her schoolmates' convoluted love lives. She would simply grow to adulthood, marry some fine man approved by her parents, have children and live happily ever after. You just knew that; everybody did.

Nicole considered that Sarah's untroubled passage through adolescence was in fact a bad thing. She was of the opinion that it was a necessary rite of passage to battle with your hormones during your teenage years. It was part of growing up. In that sense Sarah had never truly grown up. The recent evidence of her instability was evidence of that. Here she was, a grown woman of twenty-one on the eve of her marriage, suddenly confronted with all the nonsense she should have got out of her system by the time she'd turned eighteen. A Sarah confronting her with unpaid bills, Nicole could have taken in her stride. A Sarah apparently experiencing delayed adolescence at the very moment in her life that she needed to be at her most mature and level headed was an entirely different matter.

Actually, when Nicole thought about it, she considered that Peter would have made the perfect mate for Sarah. It wasn't just the innate conservatism the two shared or even their mutual love of their homeland. There was something about them that suggested soul mates. Peter hadn't done much in the way of growing up either Nicole believed. He was still the big soft kid he always had been; the shy one; the gently reserved boy that all the girls had adored but had never managed to coax from his inner self. Peter had never realised that half the girls in school had had a crush on him. Girls had always been strange; alien and volatile creatures full of disturbing passions and desires and they had frankly scared him to death. If only he had finally seen that the lovely but undemanding Sarah had been the person virtually tailor made for him then all this drama might have been resolved years ago, Nicole believed. They would have been the perfect couple.

In fact, until the advent of Alan on the scene, Nicole had always thought it inevitable that somehow, in their own unhurried way, Sarah and Peter would find each other and everything would be right with the world. It was not a view likely to be shared by Sarah's mother however and that, reflected Nicole ruefully, was the fly in the ointment. If Sarah's mother would only have butted out of Sarah's life then such a seemingly preordained scenario would surely have come to pass. Now, though, another route was determined for Sarah and she was starting to finally rebel against it. It was late in the day for teenage rebellion however.

Sarah was calmer now as she finished her story. It had helped her to talk and, she realised with only a twinge of vexation, Nicole's medicinal therapy had swayed a little on the side of overkill and she had been overly generous in the application of strong alcohol in the coffee. The pungent fumes of the powerful cherry schnapps were overwhelming. "Look Sarah honey." Nicole said at last. "About the bills. If you're really worried about the hole we're in well I'm twenty-one in July and I can use some of the money my granddad left me."

Sarah wouldn't hear of it. "No!" she declared firmly. "We've discussed this before Nicky. I won't have it. That money is for your future. You have to start to think about finishing your education Nicky. You were going to use that money only to go to college. You promised me."

"But if we really need to Sarah...."

"We're not ruined yet Nicky. I'll go into town tomorrow and take a look at the finances. I don't think things are that bad yet. I'll sort out all the bills while I'm in town." Sarah raised her finger, "But," she warned sternly. "I want it paying back and I want you to promise me that you won't let things get this behind again. I've got enough on my mind as it is without worrying about bloody phone bills."

"I'm sorry Sarah. I've let you down again haven't I?"

"Oh forget it Nicky. I'll sort it out. Just, for heaven's sake, try to keep a lid on things." Sarah sighed mightily. "Take no notice of me if I was angry before. I'm just dramatising today. I don't know what's come over me."

"You just had a bad day Sarah."

Sarah managed a watery smile. "Actually that's the crazy thing. It wasn't such a bad day. In fact I had a really nice thing happen to me today."

"Oh yes?"

"Yes! Something right out of the blue. The last thing I would have expected."

"Come on Sarah. Don't tease. What happened?"

Sarah looked at her empty mug. "Go and pour us some more coffee and I'll tell you all about it. And for heaven's sake try not to experience an acute attack of premature Parkinson's disease when you're wielding the schnapps bottle this time. There was enough bloody juice in that last one to get a good-sized party under way."

Nicole grinned. "Ok. I'm on it."

With their mugs refilled Nicole joined Sarah on the sofa again. "Come on then. Out with it. We could do with some good news today."

"Well guess who I met when I came off the mountain this afternoon."

"Osama Bin Laden? Four Norwegian sailors singing sea shanties? Snow White and the Seven dwarves? How the fuck should I know?"

"Daniela Devin!"

"Wow! Seriously?"

"Yes. I met her on the road between Oberdorf and Schwendi."

"Of course she lives up that way. Hey did you speak to her?"

"Speak to her? Hell I had a bite to eat and a couple of drinks with her at the Schwendisee. I talked to her for over two hours. She even gave me a lift home."

"Brilliant! I've only met her briefly a few times. She's nice isn't she?"

"Oh yes she's lovely. She's a really nice person. It was weird though. I don't think I've met anybody as famous as that before. We got the full VIP treatment at the Schwendi. We even had people coming up and asking her for autographs and photos."

"Oh wow!" Nicole folded her legs under her and sat cross legged on the sofa her eyes bright with interest. "Come on then tell me all about what you talked about." It took a long time. Nicole wanted to hear everything no matter how minute. She wanted an exact description of

126

what Daniela had been wearing, what she had said, what she had eaten, what she had drunk, who she had met, everything: no detail too trivial. She plied Sarah with questions long after they had exhausted their second mugs of schnapps laden coffee. Her enthusiasm was infectious and Sarah found herself enjoying recounting the minutiae of her meeting with the Toggenburg's most glamorous resident.

When Sarah's account touched upon Daniela's personal life, Nicole had all the air of a truffle pig on a hot scent and she delved deep for further clarification. Sarah held up her hands in exasperation. "I don't know Nicky." she protested. "She only said that she'd been ill with nervous exhaustion on her last tour and she'd collapsed and they'd had to cut the last two concerts."

"Did she say what brought the collapse on?"

"No just that it was exhaustion."

"There were stories that she had a bust up with the guitar player in the band and that's why she lost it."

"I don't know Nicky and I was too polite to enquire into her private life."

"Oh you're hopeless Sarah. What kind of paparazzi do you call yourself?"

"I *don't* call myself a paparazzi. I wasn't about to rummage about in her private life."

"Well did she mention her backing vocalist?"

"She said she had two backing singers; a French girl and an English girl."

"Well which was the one that was involved in her bust up?"

"She didn't mention any such thing Nicky. Look I hope I'm not rude enough to say "Oh by the way Miss Devin I hear that your boyfriend has just run off with your backing vocalist. Would you care to confirm or deny that rumour?" Get real Nicky. You just don't ask people things like that."

"You could have wheedled it out of her subtly."

"Perhaps I could of if I'd been remotely interested in it. But I'm not. I just had a nice time talking to a very special lady and I wasn't about to spoil that with obtrusive enquiries into things that are none of my bloody business." Sarah shrugged. "If you want gossip column stuff I suggest you read it in the Blick or somewhere. Actually she didn't talk much about herself. She seemed more interested in asking about me. God knows why. Just being polite probably."

Nicole thumped Sarah on the shoulder. "Hey maybe she's looking for a new backing vocalist. You're a good singer and you've got the looks and it sure sounds as if there's a vacancy in the band."

"Oh don't be ridiculous Nicky. You're descending into the realms of fantasy now."

"Well you said she wanted to meet you again."

"Well yes. She asked if I'd like to go out for dinner sometime next week."

"Well there you are. It's more than just polite interest isn't it? Daniela Devin is known for this Sarah. Apparently she recruited most of her current band just by scouring clubs and pubs in Geneva and Montreaux."

"Well she's not recruiting *me* Nicky. Why would she? She has absolutely no inclination that I have any musical talent whatsoever; and I don't other than a reasonable voice that I used to have in the school choir."

"So why's she so keen to see you again?"

"Just friendship Nicky. I don't think she knows many people locally. It doesn't sound as if she gets out much; which is understandable if everywhere you go people are staring at you and wanting to take your photo. I think she just likes the idea of having a friend locally to show her around. I couldn't remember her name when she pulled up by me on the road. I think she liked that. I was the only person in the Toggenburg who didn't know who she was."

"God! What are you like?"

"Well even famous people must get tired of being in the public eye all the time. I think she enjoyed meeting someone who didn't know a thing about her." Sarah grimaced ruefully. "Actually she'd heard more about me than I had about her."

"Hmmph!" Nicole seemed unconvinced. "Well we'll see what she wants to talk about when you meet her next week."

"Well actually we won't since she was going to phone me tomorrow morning to confirm and I happened to momentarily forget that my brainless housemate hasn't paid the sodding telephone bill and we've been cut off."

"Didn't you give her your mobile number?"

"I didn't have my mobile on me and I can never remember my number without looking it up on my phone's directory."

"Oh you muppet Sarah."

"It's not me that got the flaming telephone cut off Nicky."

"Haven't you got *her* number?"

"No I haven't. I shouldn't imagine it'll be in the phone book either."

Nicole nodded. "No it'll be ex-directory sure as hell. Still all is not lost. We know where she lives. You could go round."

"Have you lost your marbles? I can't just go round to her place banging on the door without invitation."

"Well all right then why don't you just drop a note in her letterbox apologising that your phone's been cut off and giving her your mobile number."

Sarah furrowed her brow thoughtfully. "I don't know Nicky. It still seems a bit pushy."

"Hell! She invited you... out not the other way round."

"Well I suppose so. I'll give it some thought." Sarah stretched. "Anyway that schnapps is going to my head and if I'm going into town first thing tomorrow to do battle with the bureaucracy I need to get some sleep."

"Yeah I'd better get some shut eye too. I'm on the breakfast shift in the morning."

Later, dressed in the shorts and T-shirt she habitually wore to bed Sarah, nestled down beneath her duvet and reflected on a strange day. Her thoughts turned to Alan and to Peter and she frowned as she made inevitable comparisons between the two. It was not a mental exercise to assist relaxation into slumber and she lay awake for some time in worry. Finally she did find some harmonious thoughts. Before she drifted into sleep, her last thoughts were of her spectacular new friend; Daniela Devin.

Chapter Eleven

It was a good day to go into town the following morning for the weather had turned overnight and the day dawned dull and drizzly with rain. Nicole was away very early to work her breakfast shift at the hotel and Sarah was gratified to note that her house mate's punctuality in the workplace had improved somewhat of late. Nicole had enjoyed a certain notoriety for her inability to get up in a morning in her previous employments and, given the current financial situation, her newfound sense of responsibility to the necessities of earning a living was admirable. Sarah herself rose a little later and spent some time gathering all the necessary documentation into a slim briefcase before donning a jacket over her blouse, fleece and jeans to walk down to Unterwasser to catch the post bus.

The Toggenburg, in common with most of rural Switzerland, was possessed of an excellent, regular bus service, compliments of the national postal system, and the valley was served every hour by a bus. Unfortunately Sarah happened to be a few minutes late for the bus to Buchs and, since there seemed no point in cowering from the rain at the post office in Unterwasser, she idled away the time in the Hotel Post, next to the post office, over a coffee and the morning paper. Finally the post bus arrived, its livery of yellow and black a splash of colour in the grey damp day, and Sarah mounted for the journey to Buchs. It took around fifty minutes for the journey but this was more a measure of the large area serviced by the bus rather than an indication of the distance. The bus climbed first through Lisighaus and up to Wildhaus, stopping frequently for passengers, before cresting the highest point of the valley's main road and beginning the descent, through a narrow tree lined gap, down to the wide expanse of the Rhine valley far below.

Sarah normally enjoyed this trip, for the view, as the bus emerged from the forests, out across the huge flat plain of the upper Rhine valley, a great chasm between the mountains of the Toggenburg and the Voralp of Austria and Lichtenstein across the river, was magnificent. Today the view was misty and vague, however, and the windows of the bus streaked with rain. It matched the impending sense of gloom beginning to grip Sarah. Going to town to attend to business was not one of her favourite occupations and she was not fond of Buchs in any case. It was a rather functional and ugly little town with little to recommend it in the way of pleasant diversion. The bus journey seemed interminable, as the bus halted at every little hamlet, as it wound its way down the valley side and out across the river plain below. Travellers boarding the bus did so sodden with rain and shaking out their umbrellas while the interior of the bus took on the slightly stale odour of damp humanity and wet clothes.

Down on the valley floor, the rain did stop for a while however and Sarah, beginning to grow weary of the journey, decided to dismount short of Buchs at Werdenberg. From Werdenberg it was an easy walk into Buchs, and the little group of houses clustered beneath the old castle and alongside the duck pond had all the characteristics that Buchs itself lacked; charm and quaint aesthetic beauty. Sarah loved the little settlement. It was an extraordinary collection of ancient wooden houses, astride a single cobbled street, around the foot of the old rôche moutonnée upon which the little castle perched. Werdenberg had a population of less than one hundred people and, incredibly, it had civic status making it the smallest city in Switzerland. It was this quirkiness that Sarah loved and it was a much-needed boost to her morale.

She took a walk around the big duck pond watching the coots squabble with each other, the moorhens flitting nervously among the marginal bushes and the rafts of mallards and swans. To her great pleasure, she found a pair of old friends in one corner of the big pond; a pair of Mandarin Ducks that had been present for at least the last two years. Despite the inclement weather there were a few people feeding the ducks and Sarah watched with amusement the frantic efforts of the ducks to secure their crusts of bread. The ducks on the Werdenbergersee had serious competition for their daily bread for, not only did they have to fight among each other for it, but also with the hordes of large, greedy rainbow trout with which the little lake was stocked. A duck would make a desperate lunge for a piece of bread only to have it snatched from its bill by a grey green torpedo from the water below. Sometimes the trout would boil so furiously at the free offerings on the water's surface that you were reminded of awful horror films of mass shoals of rapacious piranhas from the Amazon basin.

With time on her hands and with her flagging morale somewhat restored, Sarah paused for a coffee at the little cafe on the edge of the main road before steeling herself to her task and walking into town. It was to be a day of mixed blessings and fortunes for Sarah but she had as yet little inclination of the oddly confusing collection of events the day would have in store. Her first task was to visit the banks for, before anything else, she had to ascertain her exact financial position. Sarah was a sensible girl who kept generally close ties on her finances and was usually fairly sure exactly how much she would find in her bank accounts but she did have some uncertainties today. Banks, by their avaricious nature, are apt to nibble away at one's accounts unless a very close eye was kept on them and there was a further undetermined random factor to take into account as well.

For the past three years Sarah had enjoyed a degree of financial security that might have been the envy of many a student in countries lacking the wealth of

Switzerland. Even by Swiss standards, Sarah's father had been generous in supporting his daughter's academic career. Each month for the past three years he had debited a monthly allowance of some two thousand francs into Sarah's current bank account. Since he had also picked up the bills for Sarah's accommodation at university this was a more than ample largesse to maintain Sarah in a comfortable position. Nicole had also been an indirect benefice of Sarah's father's generosity since the allowance had allowed Sarah to continue to pay half the rent of their shared house; a financial burden that Nicole would never have been able to afford alone.

Even with this extra cost, Sarah had rarely utilised her monthly allowance to the full. As has been noted before, Sarah was not a girl of expensive requirements. Unlike many another young woman, she was not a shopaholic. It was rare for Sarah to spend much time in boutiques and stores. Sarah rarely shopped on impulse. She tended to determine exactly what she wanted before visiting a shop and ruthlessly budgeted herself to that which she could comfortably afford. Most women would have been horrified at the paucity of Sarah's wardrobe as a result but many of them would shamefacedly confess themselves envious of her financial prudence.

Sarah had had little need for a large and costly wardrobe at university. She had spent such disposal income as she felt was necessary on matters of basic requirements and the necessities of serious study. She had certainly spent more on books at university than she had on shoes and was a more frequent visitor to the library than she was to the chic boutiques of Bern. Sarah's diligence in her studies had been rewarded by not only a first-class honours degree but also a healthy bank balance. Her father had even further assisted her by relieving her of major budget items, such as her desk top computer and her laptop and Sarah herself had ably contributed to her own security by taking temporary jobs during university breaks and with a part time job in a city coffee house during term time. As a result of this admirably cautious husbanding of her resources Sarah had finished university with still a solid balance of a little over seven thousand francs in her bank account. It might even be more, she realised. The latest direct payment into her bank had been due only in the past week. Sarah was unsure if it had been paid. On the one hand she had now finished university and, theoretically, her father's commitment to her financial safety was now at an end. On the other hand, she had received no word that her allowance was now terminated. It was eminently possible that her father was continuing to support her. If, therefore, he had paid her this week then her current account now held over nine thousand francs and possibly closer to ten.

To a person of Sarah's simple needs a sum close to ten thousand francs was more than enough to see her comfortably through the summer without the necessity of earning a living. Sarah, of course, didn't see it that way. She hated to see her resources dwindling. She wasn't mean with her money just careful and there was always a side to her that feared such a time as may arrive when she would have need of whatever financial backing she had managed to accumulate. Sarah was a bit of a squirrel in this regard. She tended to hoard things. She hated throwing anything away that may one day prove to be useful. This tendency was not always an advantage as the crowded room she occupied in the house was testimony to. Her room was always tidy but there was no doubt that, clothing apart, it was far too full of things that had no discernible justification for being there. To Sarah her collections of pressed flowers, her mineral and fossil collections, her voluminous photo albums, her many nature diaries, her collection of Appenzell naive artworks, her impressive book collection and such were priceless possessions that she could not bear to be parted from and they competed for wall and shelf space with such things as a full size Alpenhorn, a collection of ornamented hiking sticks, her microscope and other optical instruments and even a rather battered looking stuffed ptarmigan. If you had opened one of Sarah's drawers you would have been just as likely to find a Swiss army knife, a collection of microscope slides, a telephoto camera lens, half a dozen collecting jars, a moth-eaten guide to European Lepidoptera, a couple of climbing crampons and Burkhardt's history of the Renaissance as you would a collection of feminine lingerie.

There was even a box under her bed containing all her university papers and essays. After all the effort she had spent in composing them Sarah couldn't bear to throw them away. In this respect Sarah's money was much the same thing. She hoarded money in her bank account because of the private satisfaction it gave her to look over her statements and see a steady and sound increase. It was not a policy liable to make her rich quickly, for she was, by nature, not the sort of person to gamble with her assets, but for the positive, incremental accumulation of means it worked admirably. It was to Sarah, therefore, perfectly sound sense to take a job for the summer even though she was in a position, financially, not to have to do so.

There were other, more subtle reasons, for wishing to take a job as well. To begin with a job meant, not only increased security, but also greater liberty. Sarah was very conscious of the fact that she had, to all intents and purposes, been dependent on her father during her university career. She was certainly not alone in this regard for many of her friends at university had relied heavily on their parents' generosity to see them through their student years. Sarah was more acutely aware of this than many however. She had tended to regard her monthly allowance not so much as a gift from her father but rather as an investment; a loan to her given on trust and which carried with it a burden of responsibility. Sarah's dedication to her studies was a direct consequence of this sense of responsibility. If her father was paying her so selflessly to aid her studies then it was incumbent on her to work hard and diligently upon those studies. Nobody could accuse Sarah of shirking that responsibility for few students at the university had worked harder than Sarah. She was unique in her year class of having a one hundred percent attendance record for all her lectures and seminars. In three years she had never missed a deadline for any set work and her marks had been consistently high. She had been somewhat fanatical about her research and few people had spent longer hours in the library or carried such extensive bibliographies on their written essays. Sarah had knuckled down to her studies with a sense of purpose and would have considered herself criminally irresponsible if she had betrayed her father's trust and investment in her by failing to achieve all that she was capable of. This had had a markedly negative impact on Sarah's social life, whilst at university, but it had served the greater purpose excellently. Sarah had been the star student of her year class in her chosen subject and the only one to have achieved a first-class degree in that year. There was nothing in her academic achievement to have made her father dissatisfied with her efforts.

Now however Sarah was no longer at university. If her father continued to pay Sarah then she truly was merely a dependent on him and with no tangible way of demonstrating any value for her father's money. It was important to her, therefore, to become independent of her father at the earliest opportunity. A job represented freedom from dependency. There was perhaps an unworthy thought lurking within this consideration too. Whilst depending on her father for her living Sarah was also at the mercy of her parents' wishes. Sarah knew that it was likely that she was going to come under increasing pressure from her family to move to the Ticino for the summer until her marriage and, unless she had independent means, she was vulnerable to any threat to cut off her allowance as a means of forcing her to acquiesce in their wishes. Sarah didn't have any illusions about the fact that her father had modified his position in this regard and, at least, given her a breathing spell in the Toggenburg. The far more direct attack would come from her mother and it would be, Sarah knew, the decisive showdown. If her mother made up her mind that she required her youngest daughter's presence at home for the summer then she would pursue that aim single-mindedly and ruthlessly. This was a battle yet to be joined and Sarah knew the urgency of furnishing herself with some ammunition for the forthcoming conflict. A job would not only free her from financial blackmail either. The responsibility to an employer would also be a powerful card to play whilst arguing the necessity of remaining in the Toggenburg.

Sarah had also a financial obligation to Nicole although this was an argument that would likely hold little authority in any dispute with her mother. In crass material terms, Sarah owed Nicole nothing. On the contrary, she had been propping up her friend's precarious financial situation for years. Nevertheless she had a responsibility. It was a Chinese obligation; one whose roots were in the duties and rights demanded of friendship. Nicole was not yet in any fit state, financially, to live independently of her friend. Sarah maintained a half share in the rent on the house and had done all the way through university. Nicole frankly wasn't able to meet that obligation alone. It was unthinkable to Sarah simply to pull the rug from under her friend. At the least they would have to find Nicole a new housemate before

Sarah was obliged to leave and housemates as reliable and dependable as Sarah were hard to come by.

This is not to say that Nicole was a complete burden on Sarah. She was, it is true, by far the more volatile of the two and the least stable. Nicole was much the more profligate spender and by far the more likely of the two to mishandle her finances to the point of ruin. Nevertheless she had improved markedly over the years. In fact, when it came to money (as indeed in many things between them) there was a complex and complimentary relationship between the two girls. In her years as Sarah's housemate Nicole had absorbed much of Sarah's work ethic and her habits of prudence when it came to money. It was not a one-sided influence however for Sarah had also benefited from exposure to Nicole's more indulgent habits. Sarah was not a mean girl but her caution had tended sometimes towards pusillanimity. From Nicole Sarah had learned to put money into perspective. Nicole was not a girl frightened of being broke. She had suffered that affliction enough times to understand that a temporary lack of funds was not the end of the world and that, in the long run, there were more important things than money. Sarah had learned from Nicole that there were times when it was both right and necessary to be a little more free with your money; times to say, "Oh the hell with it!" and splash out. To draw an analogy, if money was blood then Nicole had learned from Sarah that to let it flow too freely was to bleed to death but Sarah had equally learned that to not let it flow at all was to risk it clotting. Between the two of them they had reached some middle ground that kept the heart of their relationship beating healthily.

One area where Sarah's money flowed little if at all was in her savings account. This was an entirely different account from her current account in a different bank and represented Sarah's personal fortune. It was not an earth-shaking fortune but it was a comfortably reassuring lump sum that was the result of certain inheritances from close relations. Sarah had long nurtured this account and it came to a little over fifty thousand francs. It was the last thing that Sarah wanted to draw upon for it represented her future. Sarah had once been inclined to refer to this as her "rainy day money" but Nicole had coined an earthier and more positive title for it. It was, she declared, Sarah's "fuck you fund!". Despite Nicole's unfortunate vocabulary there was a much more aggressively, active philosophy behind this terminology. A "fuck you fund" was the body of money that you hoped that one day would be big enough to enable you to turn to the rest of the world and say, "fuck you". It was the pot of money to make you free forever; to allow you to thumb your nose at the dangers of the world about you and control your own destiny. You never gambled with your "fuck you fund". You never risked it. It was your future; your hope. Sarah's "fuck you fund" was alive and well and steadily increasing at a rate of interest that would double it within twelve years. It might soon be augmented too. There were certain promises of inheritances to be claimed upon her successful graduation from university to take into account that could well swell the fund to close on one hundred thousand francs.

Sarah therefore first visited the bank that housed her jealously hoarded "fuck you fund". There was little practical reason for this since Sarah, more or less, knew to the last franc how much was in the account. It gave her satisfaction to do so, however, and reassurance that whatever else she was, she was not yet a pauper. It was another measure of her freedom. Much was made of the fact that she was marrying into a rich family and to a man that already commanded a high income and would surely rise to even greater wealth. There was a kernel of pride in Sarah that felt that, however much her own finances might be swallowed under the greater wealth of her husband, she would yet possess her own money. She would not enter into marriage a supplicant pauper and her husband would know that ultimately she did not need him for his money for she had the wherewithal to stand alone. She would not have it said of her that she married money.

It was an even more keen determination in her that demanded she hold on to her savings come what may today. Although she had not admitted it at the time, Daniela's observation that the house in Zurich was a large dowry to take into marriage had curiously disturbed her. Hitherto she had always thought of herself as the person marrying into riches. The thought that Alan was actually making quite a shrewd business deal by marrying her and thus gaining half share in a valuable property in Zurich was a disquieting notion. She knew Alan well enough to know that it would certainly have come to his attention. Alan delighted in the machinations of business. That morning Sarah had perused property prices in Zurich in the newspaper out of interest and she had been shocked. Even modest properties sold for millions. The large, six bed-roomed, house, with its own garden and large garage in a coveted neighbourhood, would be worth a fortune. She could well imagine Alan's avaricious glee at the thought of acquiring it. More than ever she felt like the prize cow at auction.

It was not that she wanted the house herself. Indeed it didn't belong to her. It was the gift of her family in the marriage; her dowry. Personally she wouldn't have cared two hoots if the place burned to the ground. It gave her no pleasure to consider that it would become half hers upon marriage to Alan. She didn't want to live in Zurich anyway let alone as humble housewife in a house far too big for her needs in a fashionably wealthy urban neighbourhood with which she had little in common. Alan would almost certainly control the destiny of the house in any case. He understood things like the property market. He might wish to sell it if it was financially advantageous to do so. It would be merely a chess piece in his business transactions. Instinctively Sarah knew that it would never feel like her own home.

Having satisfied herself that all was well with her savings account, Sarah walked down the main street of Buchs to the bank which held her current account and asked for a statement. This document proved to be the major bombshell in her day. Looking over the figures on the statement, Sarah at first refused to believe the evidence of her own eyes. She sat down heavily on a couch in the bank and subjected it to a thorough grilling. The numbers remained the same. She had expected at least seven and a half thousand or so francs in the account and perhaps around two thousand more if her father was continuing to pay her allowance. To her utter shock however her balance had suddenly bloomed and augmented itself to the tune of an extra twenty thousand francs! In shock Sarah found herself back at the teller's window. The pretty girl behind the counter, who had provided her with the statement, smiled warmly. "Hello again. Is there something wrong with your statement?"

"Yes! Yes there is. There seems to be some mistake. There's about twenty thousand francs more in my account than there should be."

"Just a minute and I'll take a look." the girl told her. She accessed Sarah's bank details on her computer screen and perused it for a second. "Everything seems to be in order Miss. You had a direct payment of twenty thousand francs into your account yesterday which accounts for the increase. Would you like me to print out the details?"

"Yes. Yes please."

"Just one moment." A few seconds later the girl handed Sarah a slip of paper. "There you are Miss."

Sarah regarded the paper in bafflement. She recognised the source of the payment of course. It was from her father's account. "This can't be right!" she protested. "I was expecting two thousand francs, not twenty."

"I'm sorry Miss but the payment seems to be correct. Everything seems to be correct from our point of view. If you think you've been overpaid perhaps you'd better talk to the person who's debited the sum."

"Yes. Yes I will. Er thank you."

"My pleasure Miss."

Sarah reeled away from the counter and walked outside in a daze. It was raining again so Sarah dashed over to a cafe on the other side of the street. Once inside she ordered a cappuccino and sat down at a table and stared at the statement. With a grim face she keyed in her father's work number on her mobile phone. He sounded delighted to hear her. "Sarah honey! How are you?"

"Er fine Daddy. Are you busy?"

"Never too busy to talk to my little Sarah."

"Daddy there's been a cock-up at the bank."

"Oh? In what way honey?"

"Well your direct debit for my allowance hasn't been discontinued and they've made a real mess of it. They must have added an extra nought on the figures somewhere because my statement says that you've paid twenty thousand francs into my account."

"Oh good! So it went through alright then?"

"What?"

"Yes I transferred the sum yesterday. I'm pleased to hear that it's arrived safely in your account."

"Daddy! Are you seriously telling me that you deliberately sent me twenty thousand francs?"

"Yes of course honey."

"Are you completely off your rocker Daddy? What the hell for?"

"Your mother and I have discussed it Sarah. You've got some money coming to you on graduation so we've advanced some of it now to cover your expenses. What with your marriage coming up you'll need all sorts of things; new clothes, personal items and so forth so we thought it best if you had some funds available. I just hope it'll be enough."

"Daddy I don't need twenty thousand francs for God's sake!"

"You need to have some money Sarah. Getting married is a big step. There're all sorts of things to think about. Your mother particularly wants you to get some nice clothes. She's planning all sorts of parties and so on for you to attend and to announce your engagement and you know how she's always telling you to dress a bit more like a lady."

"I don't need twenty thousand francs just to parade around at my mother's soirées like an overdressed Barbie doll Daddy."

"Try telling your mother that Sarah. She'd consider twenty thousand a miserly sum for the accumulation of even the most basic of wardrobes."

"I can't accept this money from you Daddy."

"Of course you can Sarah. Come on splash out a bit. Treat yourself a little. God knows you've earned it for all your hard work at university."

"It's too much Daddy! I don't need it."

"Now Sarah. Be a good girl and do as you're told. You were just telling me the other day that you'd have to take a job for the summer. Well you've got far too much on your plate thinking about getting married without that headache. Now you've got a bit of money, you don't need to get a job. You've earned yourself a bit of a break. God knows you'll be busy enough soon with all the preparations for your marriage so there's no point knocking yourself out in some menial work in a hotel or something."

144

"Was this Mum's idea Daddy?"

"It was both of us Sarah. We discussed it between us and we think it's for the best. We're just trying to make things a little easier for you."

"This is too bad of you Daddy."

"Not at all Sarah. I just want to take away your cares for a while. You can't stop me wanting to pamper my little baby Sarah so stop griping or Daddy will have to put you over his knee and spank your bottom." Sarah blushed crimson. The last time her father had spanked her was when she'd been twelve years old. She still had guilty erotic dreams about it.

Realising she had been brilliantly outmanoeuvred, Sarah conceded. "All right Daddy but it's too much you know."

"Of course it isn't. Nothing's too much for my baby girl."

"Well thank you anyway."

"It's my pleasure. Anyway business calls. I must ring off. Now go out and buy yourself something nice."

"Yes Daddy. Love you."

"I love you too honey. Bye, bye."

Once her father had signed off Sarah regarded her coffee sourly. It was growing cold and tasted bitter. She paid her bill and stepped back out onto the street in irritation. For several minutes she walked aimlessly along the street with her brow creased in a frown. She was furious at her naivety. She had feared the possibility of being held to ransom by the possibility of having her allowance terminated but she had not seen the greater danger. The twenty thousand francs had trapped her far more effectively than any threat to cut off her funds. She couldn't take a job now. The card of employment responsibility had been decisively trumped. Instead she was now tied directly to her mother's wishes. She would be expected to spend money on a new bride's ensemble and she had no doubts that her mother's opinions on her

145

new wardrobe would be both forthright and difficult to evade.

Sarah's dress sense had long been the source of friction between her and her mother. Sarah's mother was an ex fashion model and well known for her dedication to high fashion and haut couture. Sarah's mother had been a great beauty at Sarah's age and she was still a strikingly fine-looking woman in her late forties who dressed elegantly and in exquisite taste. Sarah had inherited her mother's natural beauty but little of her vanity and the casualness with which she regarded the birthright of her beauty was a major bone of contention for her mother. In her more reflective and honest moments, Sarah could concede that her rejection of the trappings of feminine vanity were rooted in rebellion. Sarah's mother lived in a world of high street fashion boutiques, hairdressers, manicurists, beauty salons, spas and the pages of women's magazines. She considered it unthinkable to step out of the house looking anything less than perfectly coiffed and becomingly attired in the latest mode. Sarah had once joked to Nicole that her mother would remain unaware of the fact that World War Three had broken out unless they happened to mention it that week in "Cosmopolitan". All her life Sarah had been subjected to her mother's continual attempts to transform her into a fashion icon.

Sarah hated to go shopping with her mother. It was an operation liable to take up most of a working day and Sarah would invariably find herself beating off her mother's insistence on sundry items of feminine attire. The last time her mother had visited her in Bern, she had bullied Sarah into buying a pair of expensive high heeled shoes that had proved to be quite the most excruciatingly uncomfortable items of footwear that she had ever inflicted on her feet. Sarah had given them away to a university friend with rather more fashion aspirations than respect for orthopaedic foot care. The friend had been delighted. Sarah's life was a paper trail of discarded items that she had been coerced into buying against her better judgement by her mother. Every time that Sarah stepped from the house in a faded pair of jeans, an old shirt and with her hair tied back in a pony tail and without make up on, it was an act of rebellion against the regime that her mother had so assiduously attempted to impose upon her and naturally this rejection of her mother's lifestyle rankled. Sarah's mother was outspokenly condemnatory about Sarah's dress sense and there were few occasions that Sarah and her mother had shared together that had not descended into bickering about the subject. Now, with Sarah's marriage impending, her mother would be even more vocal about it. Sarah could well imagine the barrage of social events her mother would be planning in celebration of her youngest daughter's forthcoming nuptials; shopping trips, soirées, afternoon teas with her mother's socialite acquaintances, house visits, garden parties and the Lord alone knew what else. It was, Sarah realised glumly, the real reason her mother wanted her in the Ticino. She wanted to parade her affianced daughter; a daughter about to be wed into fashionable society. Sarah quailed at the very thought. In the Ticino she would be at her mother's mercy and dressed up in some grotesque caricature of her mother's image to be publicly and triumphantly displayed. The twenty thousand francs was a whip crack to bring her rebellion to order.

Sarah swore under her breath and racked her brain to think of some way out of the trap. Now she needed a job more than ever as a declaration of independence but now she had even less reason than ever to justify it. Somehow she had to find some way to tie her firmly to the Toggenburg; some wall of obduracy; a defining line of resolution to erect against the inevitable assault of her mother's will. A battle was about to commence and Sarah had no illusions about the decisive nature of that battle. It would be a battle for her soul. Her status as a free woman within her marriage depended on the outcome. She could walk the aisle proud and free; her own woman or she could allow her marriage to be hijacked by her mother's social ambition and be waved down the aisle as her mother's ultimate fashion statement. Whatever else, she realised, Sarah had to regain control over her own marriage; had to wrestle that control out of the hands of her mother. If she failed to repossess her own marriage then, Sarah realised instinctively, she would have surrendered control over her future and condemned herself to a joyless subservience in a marriage that had ceased to be about her at all.

Shaking her head clear of all the disturbing thoughts Sarah turned her attention to her duties. There were bills to be paid. In a dark depression, ill-becoming somebody who had just discovered them self to be twenty thousand francs richer, Sarah busied herself about the town for the next two hours, correcting the arrears in the household budget. By the time lunchtime arrived, her newly swollen bank account had taken a minor setback but at least the household was now firmly back in the black. Sarah took a light luncheon at a small restaurant and wondered idly what to do with the rest of her day.

She had half a mind to take a walk along the banks of the River Rhine that lay to the east of the town and formed the border between Switzerland and Lichtenstein. On a bright sunny day this would have been an excellent balm to her troubled spirit for the grassy levees and buddleia bushes along the banks were a favourite hunting ground for her. It was a rich area for butterflies. It was one of the most reliable places locally to find the beautiful and spectacular Swallowtail butterflies and there was always the chance to see the big brown and curiously lovely Dryads too. There was even a little nature reserve, close by, where you could find a lovely and rare species of dragonfly; a precious little jewel of an insect with a red body and dark banded wings. Sarah had never read an English name for this creature but she knew its Latin name; *Sympetrum pedemontanum*. So on a sunny day there were joys in abundance to be found along the Rhine banks. But it wasn't a sunny day. The rain had at least stopped for the moment but there were enough dark scudding clouds in the sky above to intimate that this was a purely temporary state of affairs. In the end, Sarah went shopping instead.

Chapter Twelve

Given Sarah's general aversion to shopping, this may come as a surprise and indeed it was a surprise even to Sarah. Many a troubled young woman would have not have been so surprised at Sarah's sudden urge to go shopping. It was a tried and trusted balm to the feminine spirit whilst under stress. There was even a name for it; retail therapy. This was not the reason that suddenly propelled Sarah into a shopping spree, however. There was, inside of Sarah, a little rebellious demon that held the opinion that the solution to the latest crisis was to simply go out and blow every last franc her father had sent her; go absolutely loopy and phone her father to say, "sorry Daddy I spent all my money so I've had to take a job". It would have been a radical and brutally effective trump card to her father's ace and one which would have immediately recommended itself to Nicole. But Sarah was not her housemate and the idea of squandering the money, even in the cause of freedom, was anathema to her. Instead Sarah's little shopping trip was born of a completely different notion; one which started as an incidental happen chance and ballooned into something quite strange. It happened by way of a completely new influence in her life; a strangely disturbing chance encounter with a beautiful woman called Daniela Devin.

Throughout the day Sarah had thought of Daniela and the thought gave her pleasure. She had so enjoyed meeting the glamorous new star in the Toggenburg that she was utterly determined to renew their acquaintance. It was an odd feeling for Sarah, for she was not a girl liable to have her head turned by celebrity and star status. Indeed, Sarah mildly pitied people who spent their lives in the hopeless quest for celebrity. The pages of women's gossip magazines were alien territory to Sarah and the seemingly endless discussion of the stars of film, fashion, music and television bored her rigid. It would have surprised nobody who knew Sarah well that she had never heard of Daniela Devin or that she would not have instantly known her name upon meeting her. Sarah had once been introduced by her mother to one of Switzerland's most famous television personalities and disgraced herself by politely asking the bemused gentleman what he did for a living. Her mother had been mortified but it was typical of Sarah. She rarely watched television; despised it for its triviality and had no time for people who glued themselves to it and subjugated their existence to the artificial ideals of television personalities to the detriment of their own characters.

So Sarah's reaction to Daniela was not one of the star-struck young woman meeting some famous and glittering personality, well known from the screen of a television set. In fact Sarah had never seen Daniela on television and had never even really listened to one of her songs. Daniela wasn't a singing superstar to her but simply the lovely and captivating woman she had shared a light meal with and an hour or two of conversation. The entrancingly beautiful woman had touched Sarah in a very simple and fundamental way. She was a person that Sarah wanted to meet again for reasons that Sarah was unable to fathom. It had just been such an interesting encounter. There are just people you meet with whom you find an instant rapport; that certain chemistry that sets them apart and tells you that they could be very special to you. Daniela possessed that quality in magnitude and, most curiously of all, she seemed to feel the same about Sarah. There is something irresistible about someone who, upon meeting you, gives the impression that they have waited half a lifetime to meet you. It was perhaps, Sarah thought, merely a trick of the woman's charm. Perhaps Daniela possessed that magic touch to make anybody she met feel special. Perhaps, in fact, that was the secret of Daniela's reputed success. Whatever it was it left a warm glow in any person fortunate enough to meet her. That was her charisma. Sarah guessed that Daniela was a woman that was well loved both by her fans and those who knew her personally. It felt like a privilege to be included within the circle of people graced by the woman's magnetic personality even when you were just some obscure country girl from a rustic backwater like the Toggenburg. It made you feel important whether or not that feeling was just an illusion created by the woman's delicate touch.

So Sarah went shopping for Daniela. She certainly didn't plan it that way. It happened quite by accident. She was wandering down the main street in Buchs in a curiously lackadaisical mood wondering what to do with herself and with her mind still troubled by the crisis precipitated by an extra twenty thousand francs in her bank account when she passed a little music store. Sarah generally did not frequent music stores. She was not a great lover of contemporary pop music. Sarah's musical tastes tended towards folk music and a little classical but her own CD collection was thin indeed compared with that of Nicole who was by far the more musical of the two of them. Unless there was some piece of music that she was particularly looking for, therefore, Sarah would never have walked into a music shop. There were a hundred things she would rather have done than browse among shelves of popular music. She certainly would never have stepped inside this shop had it not been for Daniela.

The shop was exhibiting a promotional display of Daniela's last CD in the window. It was a display to arrest anybody's attention and Sarah stopped to look in astonishment. The front cover of Daniela's CD and the posters that accompanied their display in the window had a photograph of Daniela on them. It was a stunning picture not least because of which that it displayed

Daniela completely naked. It was not a nudity to offend the sensibilities of anybody but the most conservative of observers for the legs were strategically placed to conceal anything that might attract the notice of censors and Daniela held her arm demurely across her breasts. Nevertheless it was a stunningly daring picture and in the most exquisite of artistic taste, with her posed gently against a backdrop of a glittering waterfall, like some nymph of the stream caught unawares by the photographer. She smiled from the picture with that same easy warmth and natural beauty Sarah had found so entrancing in her and her golden wavy locks fell in a glorious cascade about her naked shoulders. In an instant Sarah wanted to possess that picture.

Within ten minutes Sarah was possessed of Daniela's complete portfolio of commercially released music, for she had not only bought the CD whose cover had taken her fancy but also the previous two CDs and the accompanying extended play singles of her top hits. It was crazy really for Sarah had not the slightest inkling of the music on the CDs. She was amazed in the shop to observe that Daniela not only held top place on the Swiss music charts for her latest single but was also solidly in first place for her album release as well. Daniela, it seemed, was carrying all before her in her musical career and Sarah was slightly ashamed that this meteoric success ride had passed her completely by.

She loved the album covers. Daniela had evidently discovered a photographer of rare talent to portray her on the covers for they had captured her remarkably. The second album showed her leaning against a railing by the side of Lake Geneva in a simple summer dress; the epitome of innocence and yet with just a touch of allure; a nice girl who might just be tempted to be naughty. The first album held a far more erotic image of her. It was an interior shot by a fireplace; her hair more tousled and the strap of her gown slipping from her shoulder enticingly and her eyes huge with promise and invitation. Feeling almost guilty Sarah had even bought one of the posters to accompany the last CD and worried about the decorum of having a nude portrait of her new friend on the wall of her bedroom.

It was well into the afternoon, by now, and Sarah hurried to a congenial cafe to drink a glass of wine and gloat over her new possessions. Over her glass of wine Sarah examined the CDs more carefully. The first thing she noted was that Daniela was more than just a popular singer and photogenic cover girl. Virtually every song on the three albums was credited to Daniela. Daniela was apparently her own songwriter too. On the internal cover of the second CD was a picture of Daniela surrounded by her band and it was evident that this was most definitely Daniela's band. She wasn't just the front for a band; she led them in every way. The band existed to support her and yet there pervaded, through the picture and accompanying text, a pride and affection for the musicians that had attached themselves to her wagon. Her tributes to the musicians in the album notes had the feeling of genuine admiration and gratitude for the talented people who made her success possible. Nicole had told Sarah that Daniela possessed a genius for finding untried and yet supremely talented musicians to form around her and that she had given many of these their first real chance of musical success under her. Sarah could understand it. She had the feeling that Daniela was supremely gifted in tapping the resources of people around her.

That thought made Sarah wonder again why Daniela had seemed so interested in her. With a sudden start of fear Sarah realised she had made a mess of their encounter. She had given Daniela a number to reach her that, through Nicole's lamentable handling of the domestic finances, was unreachable. Daniela had promised to phone this very morning and the phone had been cut off. It became suddenly very important to Sarah to reach her new acquaintance before she might come to think that Sarah had rudely given her a line to nowhere. But how? She couldn't call Daniela and she had only the vaguest notion of where she lived. How was she supposed to find an address? She bit her lip and smiled. She didn't have to. She knew the people in the post office in Unterwasser. They would surely have had to deliver mail to Miss Daniela Devin and the address of the currently most famous inhabitant of the valley would be eminently familiar to them. She only had to hand them a letter to her and it would surely make its way to her. They could make that dinner date after all.

Excitedly she rushed from the cafe to seek out a stationery shop. She bought a tasteful little card and envelope to bear her message but still she felt dissatisfied. She ought to send some little gift; a token of apology for not being available. That promised to be a difficult one. What could you send to a girl who was rich enough to buy the whole shop if she wanted? A bunch of flowers would be nice but hardly appropriate to send by post. Sarah slapped her head. Flowers! Of course! The new idea was perfect and she dashed off in newly discovered animation to a shop she was very familiar with; the best book shop in Buchs.

If ever there was one category of shop that could lure Sarah in for the purposes of impulse shopping it was a bookshop and there happened to be rather a fine one in Buchs. Most Swiss bookshops had books in a variety of languages and most had a good collection of books in English. Sarah of course was bi-lingual and as comfortable with reading in both German and English but she had noted that Daniela, whilst perfectly able to make herself understood in German, nevertheless was much happier in English, her mother tongue. Sarah guessed that Daniela probably couldn't read German very well but in the book store in question was certainly one book that was written in English that Sarah wanted her to have. To Sarah's relief there was a copy in stock. It was a familiar book to Sarah for her own tattered copy had seen much usage over the years. It was the Collin's illustrated field guide to Alpine Flowers by Christopher Grey-Wilson and Marjorie Blamey; essential starting point and comprehensive guide to alpine flora, in Sarah's opinion. It was a beautifully illustrated guide, small enough to fit into a pocket and with a paperback cover rigorous enough to withstand extensive use in the field. It was priced at around twenty-five francs making it expensive for a paperback but perfectly reasonable for an illustrated guide and especially one so thorough in its coverage. Gleefully Sarah took her latest purchase to the checkout counter. "Can you gift wrap this for me?" she asked the girl behind the counter.

"Ja! Naturlich Fräulein."

"Oh! Moment bitte! Haben sie ein kugelschreiber veilleicht?"

"Ja. Hier. Nehmen sie Meine."

"Danke!" Sarah took the ball point pen and opened the book. It was a habit of Sarah's to mark with a cross every species of wild flower she had identified in field in her field guide. She opened the book to page 280. The fifth entry on that page was Early Purple Orchid; the flower that had so attracted Daniela the day before. Lovingly Sarah placed a little cross by the name in the text. Now Daniela would have her first entry in her alpine flower guide. She handed the book back to the shop girl, who gift wrapped it for her, and left the shop happily.

It was raining again but Sarah feeling suddenly indulgent didn't mind. In a couple of minutes she was back in the little cafe ordering a second glass of wine and borrowing a pen from the waitress. She opened the small card and took the pen thoughtfully composing words in her mind. Finally she set her pen to the card.

"Dear Daniela,

I am sorry, but only after you left me yesterday did I realise that the telephone number that I gave you was inoperable because we have our land line currently out of order. I do apologise if you've been trying to contact me in vain. I am hoping that the telephone will be working again today but in case there is still a problem I include my mobile number at the end of this note."

Sarah paused uncertainly. It sounded all a little too formal.

"I just wanted to say," she continued, *"how much I enjoyed meeting you yesterday and I hope that our date for dinner sometime soon is still on. I should be free nearly every evening for the next week or so but if you'd like to call me I'll be able to confirm and we can set a date. I hope to hear from you soon.*

With best regards,

Sarah

P.S. I hope you enjoy the little present I'm including. It's not much but just a way of thanking you for the meal yesterday and to say sorry for giving you a duff telephone number."

Sarah regarded the brief missive critically. Sarah could write excellent formal and academic prose but she was poor, she knew, in the penning of affectionate informal letters. Still, such as it was, it would have to do. Hopefully she would be able to express herself better when she was privileged to meet Daniela for dinner.

It was the thought of meeting Daniela for dinner that precipitated the next round of shopping madness. In her mind's eye, Sarah imagined herself accompanying Daniela into a fine restaurant. Daniela had exquisite taste in clothing. She would doubtless look marvellous. It was at that point that Sarah conducted a mental inventory of her own wardrobe. It came up sadly lacking. There was not an outfit in her closet that she had any faith in being suitable to accompany Daniela in public in. Her mother might have campaigned long in order to press her into more ladylike clothes but the thought of letting Daniela down in public succeeded where her mother had railed in vain. In something approaching panic, Sarah left the cafe and set about the shops of Buchs in earnest.

Even Sarah had to laugh at herself in retrospect. The sudden panic of looking ill clothed and in reflecting badly on Daniela dashed all her customary incisiveness in the matter of clothing from her head and she spent the next three hours agonising over a range of suitable attire with all the indecisiveness of any foolish young girl with money in her pocket and a special date to go to. She just could not seem to make up her mind. As a result she ended up buying not one new dress but three and a skirt and matching top to boot. In a slightly bewildered daze, she even found herself buying two new pairs of shoes and other accessories as well and, if that was not enough, she even spent the last hour or so, in a salon, having her hair restyled and her sadly neglected fingernails manicured. By the time she had staggered from the salon, feeling shell shocked, the rain had finally abated for good and Sarah was in need of yet another glass of wine.

She chose a cosy restaurant close to the bus stop and settled herself at a table, clutching her shopping bags around her, feeling foolishly indulgent and self-conscious. With a slight sense of embarrassment, she opened her bags to examine her new purchases. She was at a loss to explain the madness that had come over her, for the dresses she had bought were softly stylish and becomingly feminine items that she would normally only have been bullied into wearing for the most formal and onerous of social gatherings. In sheer disbelief she lifted a dress from its bag that had cost her nearly five hundred francs, which was more than she had spent on a single item of clothing other than high quality hiking gear for as long as she could remember. It didn't seem much for five hundred francs. It was a sleeveless, tank strapped, short summer cocktail dress in a warm gold colour with a square neckline and ruched bodice formed into an empire waist and a hemline that fell some inches short of the knee. It was a ludicrously expensive and trivial item of clothing, by her standards, and Sarah felt herself thoroughly ashamed at having been lured into buying it. She almost felt compelled to take the offensive object back to the shop and the silly high heeled sandals she had bought to accompany it as well. She was baffled by the insanity which had come over her in the shop. She must have been mad! Anyone seeing her dressed in this would be persuaded that she had completely come adrift of her marbles. The shop girl must have been on commission or something for she'd told Sarah that she looked sensational in it. The girl had been so ingenuously enthusiastic that Sarah had bought the gown against all the sober warnings of her better judgement. Perhaps she should take it back.

"Wow!" Sarah jumped at the sudden exclamation at her side. The waitress of the restaurant was stood by her table bearing a tray with her drink on it and staring at the gown in admiration. "That's gorgeous Miss. Where did you buy it?"

Sarah blushed. "Oh just some shop down the street. I'm regretting it already. I... I don't think it'll suit me."

"You're crazy Miss! You'll look fantastic in that. Can I feel the material?"

"Er.. of course. Go ahead."

The girl fondled the rich soft fabric in pleasure. "My God this must have cost you a bit. It's beautiful."

Sarah blushed even more deeply, aware that she had just blown what amounted to probably about a quarter to a fifth of this girl's monthly salary on a single dress and that didn't even take into account the cost of the shoes to go with it. She felt guilty and slightly sullied by her newfound riches. She had spent something like twelve hundred francs on clothes to a single dinner engagement! Her mother would have been proud of her.

Returning on the bus to Unterwasser, Sarah could not throw off the feeling that she had been obscenely self-indulgent and she felt almost compelled to change, at home, into her tattiest pair of old jeans and go out to the pub and drink beer. She was just in time to catch the post office in Unterwasser and at least she was able to send her package. She'd worried about the postal code unnecessarily before deciding to attach the number 9658, which was the code for Wildhaus rather than Unterwasser. It was hardly important. The postman knew of Daniela's address of course and assured Sarah that her parcel would arrive safely. Sarah walked back up the hill to Alpli burdened with her bags and feeling strange. It was the first but not the last time that Daniela would challenge Sarah's own comfortable image of herself.

Chapter Thirteen

"You went *shopping*?" Nicole was staring at Sarah is disbelief. Sarah had been surprised to find Nicole home when she returned from Buchs but not half as surprised as Nicole was upon receiving the intelligence that her frugal, penny watching housemate had just been into town and blown an obscene amount of money on feminine triviality. Sarah was blushing furiously as if she had been discovered in some guilty secret with the evidence of her sins scattered around her in shopping bags.

"I do go shopping occasionally you know Nicky." Sarah replied haughtily but her protestations sounded thin even to her.

Nicole shook her head. "Uh huh! Not you! The last time I went shopping with you in Buchs you bought a new pair of hiking boots and a bloody book on Grasshoppers. Then you spent the rest of the day whingeing at me because I couldn't make up my mind which top to buy. You *hate* shopping! You always have done."

"I do not! Shopping's one of those things you have to do now and again. I'm just not that fond of shopping just for the sake of it. I mean you must have gone around twenty bloody shops looking for that top only to return to the one you started in and bought the first top you'd seen. If you'd just taken it in the first place the whole business would have taken you about five minutes. Instead you wasted nearly three and a half hours."

"I didn't waste three and a half hours Sarah. I'm a woman for Christ's sake."

"What the devil do you mean by that?"

"I mean that men decide what they're going to buy before they ever get near to the shop then just go in and buy it. They don't want to spend any time on it because

161

it might distract from serious beer drinking time or the bloody football on telly. Women, however, are into the process. We're not that interested in the final result. It's the process we like. I didn't buy a top; I spent three and half enjoyable hours *looking* for one. To be more precise I would have enjoyed it had it not been for your continual griping."

"Are you trying to suggest that I'm deficient in oestrogen or something?" demanded Sarah indignantly.

"Well let's face it you can be a bit boyish about these sort of things."

"I resent that. I would like to point out that I am completely and unambiguously female possessed of XX chromosomes. I just do not need to assert my femininity by squandering time and money on trivial non-necessities."

"Like you did today for instance?"

"Today was different!"

"Oh yes? Just how much did you blow anyway?"

"Oh not all that much."

"Come on Sarah." wheedled Nicole amusedly. "Tell Nicole how much you spent."

"Well I don't know...."

"Don't be telling me fibs Sarah sweetheart. You've never gone into a shop in your life and not known to the last franc how much you spent."

"Well about twelve hundred I suppose." Sarah muttered shamefacedly.

"Twelve hundred! You spent twelve hundred francs?" Nicole was staring At Sarah as if she'd just announced she'd been arrested for indecent exposure on Buchs high street.

"Well I know it seems a lot but...."

"Are you trying to tell me Sarah Fuchs that you went into town to pay the bills and ended up blowing twelve hundred francs on clothes?" Nicole shook her head in wonderment. "Have you been taking drugs or something?"

"No I have not!"

"Well something's happened to you. You've even had your hair done as well."

"It's not that unusual!"

"It is for you." Nicole frowned thoughtfully. "This is bounce back time isn't it? Peter turned you down yesterday and the next thing you know you're out in town blowing all your money trying to look attractive."

"It's nothing of the sort!"

"It must be. This is so out of character for you. You're protesting rejection. There's no telling where this might end. You need to get married or at the very least get laid right sharpish."

"I did not go shopping out of a desire for sexual satisfaction Nicole."

"Rubbish! You're displaying all the symptoms honey. You're a girl in need of a damn good rogering at your earliest convenience."

"If you will allow me to elucidate Nicole dearest I will explain my motives for shopping today." Sarah was in a fine dudgeon.

"Go on then honey. Try to convince me that your shopping spree had nothing to do with your sexual frustration and spurned advances."

"That will do Nicky. If you'll just let me explain." Sarah drew a breath. "I came into some money unexpectedly today. My Dad sent me twenty thousand francs by direct debit. I'm supposed to use it to buy a new wardrobe for all the engagement parties and what have you for my forthcoming betrothal. My mother has sent dire warnings of death, damnation and exile to the furthest corners of hell if I'm not looking up to scratch for her proposed social calendar for the summer. That's why I had to buy new clothes."

Nicole collapsed onto the sofa. "*Twenty thousand*!" she squeaked. "Oh bloody hell Sarah! You mean bitch."

"Now what's the matter?"

"I'll tell you what the matter is! You've got twenty thousand to go out and blow and you didn't invite me along to help you. God! We could have gone out in Winterthur and gone on a shopping spree that would go down in legend."

"I haven't touched the twenty thousand Nicky. I'm not even sure I want to. I had enough money left from my allowance to buy some new things in any case. I'm half in a mind to send the bloody money back."

"Oh for God's sake! Just sit here for a few minutes and try to stay calm honey while I whistle up the men in the white coats to come and sit on your head and get you into the straight jacket."

"Nicky! Listen... you don't know what that money means. It's bloody emotional blackmail! My parents have got me trapped. If I take it then they've got me just where they want me. Now ok, I had to get some new clothes but I had ample money to do so without that twenty thousand. If I take that money I lose my independence. Surely you can see that. I have to prove to my mother that I don't need her charity just to have some bloody clothes."

Nicole was looking at her thoughtfully. "Well come on then let's have a butchers."

"What?"

"At what you bought you dozy bitch! Get them out and let's have a look see." Reluctantly Sarah unpackaged her purchases. Nicole's eyes grew wide as she held up the various items. She whistled softly. "Sarah these are serious threads." She lifted up the lovely golden cocktail dress that was Sarah's most expensive single purchase. "Whew Sarah!" she breathed. "I've never known you buy anything like this. Whatever came over you?"

164

Sarah felt her face glow crimson. "I... I don't know. The girl in the shop said it looked nice on me."

"Stand up. Let me look." Obediently Sarah stood to allow Nicole to hold the beautiful gown to her figure. Nicole seemed fascinated. "Incredible." She murmured. "Come on Sarah put it on. I want to see you in it."

"Oh really Nicky! Do I have to?"

"Yes honey. Just for me."

"Oh all right then!" Sarah suddenly felt shy undressing in front of Nicole regardless of the fact that her housemate had seen her undressed hundreds of times but she stripped out of her clothes and pulled the dress on obligingly. Nicole was holding the high heeled sandals Sarah had bought and looking at her strangely. Feeling oddly self-conscious Sarah slipped the sandals onto her shapely feet.

Nicole had become curiously quiet as she watched Sarah dress up and she was watching her housemate with an indecipherable expression on her face. "Give us a twirl Sarah honey." she said quietly and Sarah turned awkwardly, bemused by Nicole's sudden seriousness. Nicole seemed captivated by the vision of Sarah in the unfamiliar, softly glowing feminine attire. Sarah felt a strange tenseness in the air. Nicole stepped forward and took her hands admiring her openly. "Foxy," she said, using the pet name she had had for her friend since they had been together from school. "Have you any idea at all how beautiful you look in that dress?"

Sarah shook her head, suddenly confused by her friend's intimacy. "It... it's just a frock Nicky."

"Yes just a frock Sarah." Nicole reached down to finger the hem of the dress, rolling the fabric lovingly in her fingers. "It's gorgeous Sarah." Nicole took a deep breath. "Come on I've got the night off and tomorrow as well. Let's go down to the pub and have a drink."

"Well ok then but let me change first."

Nicole shook her head vigorously. "No Sarah. Just the way you are."

"You're loopy Nicky! I can't walk into the Alpli dressed like this."

"Yes you can. Give me a few minutes to get tarted up and we'll walk in there and blow the place wide open. We'll have a couple of drinks and then we'll walk down to Unterwasser and go dancing in the Sternen. Lock up your sons Toggenburg. Nicky and Foxy are out on the hunt!"

Sarah laughed. "You're crazy Nicky!"

Impulsively Nicole hugged her friend. "Away sweetheart. Let me do your make up and then let's hit this goddamn valley for six!"

"Nicky! I can't."

"Trust me. Tonight you can! Let's rock and roll."

Chapter Fourteen

Later that evening, in the disco in the Hotel Sternen, Sarah had found a table squeezed into a corner whilst her housemate negotiated the tricky path to the bar. Sarah was already getting a little fed up. From the moment they had walked into the little restaurant Alpli earlier, the two girls had attracted undue amounts of attention. A considerable degree of that attention could be attributed to the sight of Sarah dressed, unfamiliarly, in sparkling new clothes. Sarah looked radiantly beautiful in the gold dress and she was a revelation to anybody more used to her customary jeans and shirts. They'd walked down to Unterwasser afterwards and Sarah had rued ever allowing Nicole to talk her into going out dressed in this fashion. The steep road down to Unterwasser had been sheer purgatory in her high heeled sandals and Sarah had protested that it was better if the two of them just called the whole mad idea off. Nicole had insisted however. To Sarah's bemusement Nicole seemed to be taking a perverse pride in her newly reformed housemate. She was quite unashamedly showing her off and she was keen to display her spectacular friend in the disco.

It was quite crowded in the little rustic disco in the Hotel Sternen and the two girls had made a sensational entrance. The youthful male contingency of the Toggenburg had been swarming around the pair of them like flies around a cow-pat as Sarah had sourly observed. Sarah was unused to such openly admiring male attention. She rarely went in discos at all and if she did she was prone to sit out proceedings in some quiet corner away from the crowds. She was not comfortable in crowds at all let alone crowds that apparently seemed affixed to her presence. It was with relief therefore that having beaten off several clumsy advances from leering boys that she was able to escape into a relatively secluded corner.

Nicole was having great fun. She realised that the attention in the disco was mainly focussed on her housemate but she was not jealous of that attention. On the contrary, Nicole was revelling in it. She was truly proud of Sarah and basking in the reflected glory of her lovely friend. Jealousy and envy were not among Nicole's faults. She was genuinely warmed by the admiration that Sarah was attracting. She had often tried to cajole Sarah into dressing up and going out with her but it was rare that she ever succeeded. Most people recognised Sarah as a truly lovely girl but a rather conservative and drably dressed one for the most part. Nicole had frequently bemoaned her friend's reluctance to show herself to her best effect but now that she had finally done so Nicole was lapping it up and enjoying the experience of proving to her acquaintances just what a sensationally beautiful girl she shared her house with. Her pleasure in Sarah's appearance was manifest and Sarah was growing more self-conscious by the minute.

Nicole weaved her way back through the crowds bearing two glasses and grinning hugely. She squeezed around the table and passed Sarah a glass. "Here's looking at yer Foxy! Prost."

Sarah took the drink suspiciously. "What the hell is this?"

"Margarita Sarah; one part agave tequila; one part Cointreau and finished off with ice, lime juice and a frosting of salt and Cayenne pepper to rim the glass."

"God it sounds like cirrhosis in a glass."

"It's great! Try it." Nicole took a sip. "Hmm perfect... and all the better because we didn't have to pay for it."

"We didn't?"

"Nope! Compliments of the barman. You can add him to your fan club roster. I got a drink out of him by helping him find his eyeballs before they got trampled underfoot on the dance floor."

"Oh for Christ's sake!"

"Deal with it Sarah sweetheart. You've hit the male libido of the Toggenburg like a neutron bomb this evening. You'll probably have half the boys in the valley crooning beneath your balcony tonight. We'll have to use water cannons to disperse the crowds."

"This is pathetic!"

"Not at all. You've announced, in no uncertain terms, that Sarah is back in the valley. Come on try your drink."

Obediently Sarah took a sip. "God it's strong. I'll be rat-faced at this rate."

"Don't worry. I'll get you home before you make any serious mistakes."

"I already made one; letting you persuade me to come out dressed like this."

Nicole sighed. "I don't know what's the matter with you Sarah. You look absolutely gorgeous. Most girls would give their right arm to look like you and have every man within two hundred metres drooling over them for one evening. You though? You just look as though you trod in some dog poo on the way in. For God's sake Sarah lighten up a bit. You're beautiful. Enjoy it."

"I hate to point it out Nicky but I'm near as damn it engaged. I shouldn't be tarting up and flouncing around the village like a slut."

"You're not like a slut Sarah!" Nicole sounded indignant. "You're just dressed nicely and showing all the boys what they've missed. Anyway what's wrong with letting your hair down a bit before you tie the knot? Judie Muller got trashed on her hen party, two days before her wedding, danced in her underwear along the bar at the Hirschen, kissed every bloke she could grab hold of and still managed to look the image of virginal beauty on her wedding day. So come on. Loosen up. Alan would be pleased to hear his girl's got a bit of sass and spirit to her."

"I can't help it. I feel nearly naked in this dress."

"Don't tell the boys that! Talk about a red rag to a bull. There must be fifty guys in here at least that would be all too willing to correct the imperfect condition of your near nudity!" Nicole glanced up. "Oh oh! I see Joe Bringel and his mate Stefan looking this way and sizing up their chances. Time for some evasive manoeuvres honey. Shall we dance?"

"No way! I'm a lousy dancer at the best of times Nicky let alone in these heels."

"You're not a lousy dancer sweetheart. You've got all the right bits. Just remember to wiggle them in time to the music."

"All right then. Let me do something about the music though. This must be the third Abba track Mike's played since we came in."

"Well go and ask him for a request. I can't see him turning you down."

Sarah battled her way through the crowd to the DJ box overlooking the dance floor. The DJ smiled at her. He was a dark-haired Englishman who was a regular and popular booking at the Sternen. DJs in Switzerland tended to work one or two-month contracts in the same club and ones that became well known locally often played return bookings. The current DJ had played five or six contracts in the Sternen over the past three years. He wasn't the tallest of men but he was good looking and charming, albeit a little outrageous on occasion. Sarah knew him well and liked him. He leaned out of the disco box to kiss her politely on the cheeks. Then he stood back to admire her properly. "Sarah!" he said, "You look absolutely fabulous. Stand back and let me look at you."

Sarah laughed and took a step back. "So? Do I pass muster?" Mike was one boy that Sarah felt safe flirting with. She liked him for his genuine warmth and sense of humour and she knew that he was hopelessly devoted to his girlfriend in Appenzell.

Mike nodded. "You look good enough to eat. In fact why don't you just smear yourself in Hollandaise sauce and come up to my room once I've done trying to coax this sad crowd onto the dance floor tonight?"

"Down boy! What would Gabi say?"

Mike laughed. "Not much probably. She'd just reprocess my hide into leather accessories in her dad's factory."

"How is she anyway?"

"Fine! She's coming through at the weekend. She'd love to see you. It's been ages what with you at uni and everything."

"You seen her much lately?"

Mike shook his head. "Not enough. I've been down in Ascona for the spring and she couldn't get away too often."

Sarah raised an eyebrow. "So you'll have a lot to catch up on."

Mike grinned. "You can bet on it. We don't plan on getting out of bed for two days. Mind you I'll have to watch myself and try to remember her name. It would be embarrassing to call out Sarah whilst in the throes of passion wouldn't it?"

Sarah slapped him playfully. "Behave yourself Mike."

"I can't help it. In the presence of such radiant beauty all my sense of reason and morality goes out of the window."

"You don't fool me for a minute Mike. If Gabi was here you wouldn't look twice at another woman and you know it."

Mike heaved an exaggerated theatrical sigh. "That's the worst thing about being in love. It makes you so boringly predictable."

Sarah laughed enjoying the banter. "Look Mike do something about the music huh? Nicky and I want to dance."

"Your wish is my command dear lady. What do you want?"

It was a good question. Sarah was hopelessly uneducated about modern music. She thought for a moment. "Hey I bought three CDs today Mike."

"Oh yes?"

"Yes. From Daniela Devin."

"Good choice. A bit of local flavour too since she lives round here. You want me to play you a track from her?"

"Do you have her CDs?"

"Of course I've got her CDs Sarah. Not only is she the number one recording artist in Switzerland for the moment she also happens to hail from my home town."

"You come from York?"

"Yes. It's a long time since I was there but that's where I was born."

"Wow! I never knew that. I come from Beverly. Daniela says it's near York."

Mike raised his eyebrows "It is indeed. Daniela Devin told you that? Have you met her?"

"Yes. Yesterday. I met her up at Schwendi. Today I went out and bought her CDs."

"So do you have a favourite song?"

Sarah shook her head. "No! I haven't even listened to them yet. I haven't a clue what they sound like."

"Well do you want me to play one of her songs?"

"Well ok. That's if there's one that you can dance to that is."

Mike nodded. "Her last single is a dance number. It's about as close as she gets to a real dance hit; a bit

172

more commercial than her usual stuff but a good song anyway. Then again she rarely produces a bad song."

"I've heard people raving about her Mike. Is she good?"

"Oh yes! I've been in this business for years Sarah and I've seen artists come and go; one hit wonders that everyone's forgotten about within a few months. Daniela Devin is different though. You just know when you listen to her music that it's there to stay. She's one of those rare talents that touches everybody; old and young alike. She's special; an instant classic."

"Sounds like you like her."

"I do. You can get pretty jaded on music in this job. Some songs might sound fine the first two hundred times you hear them but they start to become irritating after that. Danny Devin's music though, I could listen to all night and not get tired of. I can't believe you've actually met the woman but never listened to her music."

Sarah smiled ruefully. "I don't listen to much music."

Mike grinned at her. "Well let's see if you can dance. I'll stick you the long version on."

"Thanks Mike. Hey let's get together for a drink sometime when Gabi comes through."

"Sure! She'd like that."

Sarah returned to Nicole feeling pleased. Nicole was looking at her suspiciously. "I hope you haven't persuaded Mike to play some awful Tyrolean folk song; all yodelling and embarrassing thigh slapping."

"No he's going to play a song by Daniela Devin."

"I thought you didn't know any of her songs."

"I don't but I bought her CDs today."

"What? All of them?"

"Yes."

Nicole regarded her friend strangely. "There's definitely something going on with you Sarah. The last time you bought a CD was last summer and it was

Beethoven's Pastoral Symphony for crying out loud. Suddenly you start buying new stylish clothes and picking up hot new sounds off the charts. Have you just emerged from a time warp or something?"

"No Nicky but I thought that if I meet Daniela again I ought to know her music a bit better. It's downright embarrassing talking to her and I've never even heard one of her songs."

"Well which song is Mike going to play?"

"Oh he said he was going to play her last single. I don't know what it's called."

"Blue Stone Lady. I already told you that."

"Oh of course. Is it good to dance to?"

"You mean you haven't listened to it?"

"Like when? I only bought the CDs today."

"God help us! Come on then this song's nearly finished. Let's get out on the floor and show this sad collection of musically retarded wobblies how it's done." Sarah allowed herself to be led out onto the small dance floor sheepishly for she was bashful about dancing in public. Her discomfort was not at all improved by Mike announcing over the microphone that the next song was for the beautiful Sarah and she turned to glare at him only to receive a wicked grin in return. As the rhythm of the song cut in she did her best however to follow Nicole who was instantly taken up in the music. Sarah was not as bad a dancer as she believed herself to be. What she certainly lacked in technicality she made up for with a degree of natural musicality and her radiant looks this night detracted attention from her occasional awkwardness. Nicole on the other hand was a superb dancer; probably the best in the Toggenburg for she had been an avid fan of dancing ever since she'd been a small girl. It was always a highlight when Nicole graced a dance floor and Sarah privately envied her friend for her prodigious talent. She had occasionally asked Nicole if she had ever thought about taking dancing up as a

174

career but Nicole had snorted derisively and told her that dancing didn't put bread and butter on the table and that the back alleys of the world of professional dancing were littered with the broken dreams of disillusioned young girls who had once thought to be Ginger Rogers.

In any case it was convenient to Sarah to let her friend do all the sharp moves for it deflected the eye away from her own less than confident steps and she was able to relax into the music and enjoy it. And enjoy it she did. To Sarah's own pleasant surprise she was instantly taken by Daniela's music. It was the first time she had actually listened to one of Daniela's songs and she would never forget the pleasure it gave her. "Blue Stone Lady" was a richly orchestrated composition laid over an infectious rhythm that was held solidly together by complex percussion and a throbbing bass line. The instrumentation of guitars and keyboards was slick and tight and the lead instruments soared to harmonious crescendo's that were exciting and spine tingling. Even Sarah's relatively untutored ear could discern that the song was a cut above the commercial dance tracks they had been afflicted with so far that evening. It was a thoroughly professional and highly technical composition that nevertheless maintained a deceptive simplicity within the structure of its rhythm and melody. Even as an instrumental track it would have been irresistible but it was raised to heights of superlatives by the vocals.

From the first moment that Sarah heard Daniela's singing voice she was captivated. Singing was one thing that Sarah knew something about and she instantly recognised a truly great voice when she heard it. She was astonished at the vocal range of her new acquaintance. She realised that a singer's technical prowess could be flattered by the technical wizardry of the recording studio but there was no hiding the awesome power and range of the lead vocals. Daniela's voice was simply mesmerising and a thrill to the ear ranging from deep contralto to soaring high notes that should have been impossible. There was a natural vibrato modulated into the voice that could send shivers down the spine of anybody still maintaining a body temperature of 37 degrees Celsius and she attacked the song with a verve that could only be described as joy. Sarah was astonished. She had had no idea that Daniela was such a virtuoso. She'd expected perhaps something sweet and tuneful but not the raw energy and masterful control she was hearing. It was a voice that teetered dangerously close to the limit for, just as you thought that Daniela had topped out on a high, she could somehow find an extra reserve and ratchet up the power and surpass it yet. It was the voice of extraordinary genius. No wonder it was taking the world by storm.

That it was taking the world by storm was evident even in this little rural disco for as soon as the song rang out over the speakers the dance floor was packed whereas it had previously held just a handful of braver souls. Sarah was grateful for the greater anonymity afforded her by the full dance floor but equally she was thrilled to see just how popular her new friend's music was. The crowd was clearly revelling in the song and the whole disco seemed to have come alive in response to it. It was as if somebody had clicked a switch and turned the whole place on. It was almost magical. Daniela had sorcery in her music.

The extended version lasted some six and a half minutes and, at the end, Nicole grabbed Sarah's hand. "It's too crowded Sarah. It's cramping my style. Let's take a time out." Sarah was grateful to be taken off the floor for she knew instinctively that any other song would be an anti-climax. They returned to their table with Sarah's face flush with excitement.

"God I never expected that!" Sarah enthused.

"She's good isn't she?" Nicole looked smug.

"She's better than good. She's bloody brilliant. Are all her songs up to that standard?"

"That's probably one of her *poorer* songs Sarah. A bit too commercial for my tastes but good to dance to."

"I'm really going to have to listen to her CDs."

"That's nothing. You want to see her in live concert."

"You've seen her? You've seen her perform?"

"Sure! I went with Ellie and Karen to see her in Zurich last December. It was amazing! She's absolutely electric live. She seems to love having a big audience in front of her. She brought the house down; three bloody encores! We thought they were never going to let her go. Best concert I've ever been to."

"Damn I'd like to have seen it!"

"Well I've got a DVD of her live at Montreaux from last summer if you want to see it. It's nearly two hours long but it's a great concert."

"Oh yes please."

Nicole grinned and slapped Sarah on the knee. "We'll make a fan out of you yet."

"I didn't know she was that good."

"Hell yes Sarah! They're comparing her with all the greatest female artists already. She's going to be massive honey." Nicole laughed gleefully. "You didn't have to buy all her CDs you know."

"Why?"

"Because I've already got them all you muppet. If you wanted to listen to them you only had to ask."

"I ... I didn't realise. I mean I didn't realise you were such a fan of hers."

"Hell yes! She's my favourite. I've even got an autographed photo of her on my bedroom wall. She signed it for me personally."

"God! Did you ask her for it?"

"No! She just gave it to me when I met her this spring. I told her I was a big fan of her music so she gave

177

me a CD and this photo which she signed. You're not the only one to fall under Miss Devin's spell you know."

"I'm not under her spell."

"Oh really? Never shut up talking about her? Go out and buy all her CDs unheard? Ask the DJ for one of her songs? You'll be putting up posters of her on your wall next."

Sarah blushed. She hadn't mentioned the poster she'd bought that day. "Well ok." she conceded reluctantly. "She seems awfully nice and she's obviously very talented."

"She's got charisma by the bucket load Sarah." Nicole sat back and eyed Sarah sardonically. "Mind you I had the feeling that you and Miss Devin would run into each other sooner or later."

"What do you mean?"

"Nothing Foxy honey." Nicole pushed her empty glass forward. "Come on sweetheart. It's your round."

Chapter Fifteen

Sarah woke, with a start, the next morning to a curious sensation. Something was tickling her left nipple. She blinked in surprise and opened her eyes. Nicole was resting half across her in bed and suckling at her breast. Sarah drew a short breath and was about to protest when she realised that her friend was fast asleep. They were in Nicole's bedroom. They'd come back late from the disco in high spirits and Nicole had suggested that they watch Daniela's DVD on her television in her room over a last nightcap and some snacks. In a giggly, tipsy mood they'd changed into night attire and climbed into bed together to watch the DVD with a bottle of port and some cheese, crackers and chocolate. The television was still switched on and there were plates, glasses and bottle strewn around the bedroom floor. They must have fallen asleep watching the DVD. To be sure they'd both drunk enough. Sarah wasn't embarrassed about sleeping together with Nicole. They'd often shared a bed when they'd been younger; whispering secrets to each other in the way young girls do. It had also not been unknown for them to cuddle each other in the dark as well for they were both affectionate and physically comfortable with each other. This was the first time however that Sarah had woken to find her housemate sucking at her breasts.

Somehow Sarah's wrap had come loose during the night and her breasts were exposed. Nicole had seemingly returned to infantilism in her sleep and sought out Sarah's breasts to suckle at and comfort herself. Her hands were resting on Sarah's breasts as she nibbled unconsciously, murmuring softly in her sleep. Sarah bit her lip and wondered how to extract herself from the predicament without embarrassment. Then she smiled suddenly and stifled a giggle. Nicole looked so childlike as she nuzzled at her breasts; her shock of dyed pink hair draped across Sarah's torso. Sarah found the situation funny and, in a strange way, quite endearing. She almost felt curiously maternal and she gently stroked Nicole's hair in fond affection feeling an oddly protective love for her volatile friend.

Nicole stirred and muttered raising her head. Hastily Sarah pulled her wrap around her and shook Nicole's shoulder gently. "Nicky! Nicky wake up."

Nicole's eyes opened blearily. "Huh what?"

"I said wake up! It's late."

"Wh.. what time is it?"

"Nearly eleven o'clock. It'll be lunch time soon."

Nicole groaned. "Oh God! My head. How much did we drink last night?"

"Enough! Come on my tipsy little madam... shift your fanny."

"Can't we just stay in bed?"

"No we can't. Come on and I'll make us some breakfast."

"I'm not sure I can manage anything Sarah."

"Of course you can." Sarah giggled. "You seemed hungry enough a while ago. Shall I fetch you a glass of milk?"

Nicole blinked in confusion. "What are you talking about? I never drink milk in the morning."

"Well it looked to me as if you had a hankering for some. I don't think you'll find any there though."

Nicole shook her head in bewilderment. "Look rewind a minute will you Sarah. I haven't the foggiest what you're blathering about."

"You were sucking on my tit."

Nicole started at Sarah in horror. "You're taking the piss!"

"No seriously. When I woke up I found you draped across me and firmly fastened to my left nipple like it was an oasis in the desert. I'm sorry I didn't have any milk for you."

180

Nicole clapped her hand to her mouth. "Oh God no! Oh Jesus! How embarrassing."

Sarah laughed and pinched Nicole affectionately. "It's all right Nicky. You were quite cute actually."

"Oh my God! I think I'm going to die of mortification. I'm sorry Sarah. I've done it before. I once tried to feed at Gerty Aldermann's breast in my sleep when we were on a school hike and staying overnight in the massenlager at Voralpsee. My mum must have deprived me when I was a baby."

Sarah grinned and hugged Nicole fondly. "It's ok. You just surprised me is all. Come on let's get a shower and then some breakfast."

"Ok but hold the milk ok."

"I'll have to actually. I forgot to get any yesterday. We'll have to drink our coffee black."

Nicole shook her head. "No I got some and there's fresh eggs and bread too."

"Great! I'll rustle up some soft-boiled eggs and toast. Do you want to use the bathroom first?"

"No you go ahead. I'll tidy up in here. God we must have fallen asleep watching the telly. The place looks like a bomb hit it."

Sarah laughed and slipped from the bed. "Ok I'll be quick." Sarah paused. "What did Gerty say anyway?"

"What?"

"Gerty. What did she say after she found you guzzling at her breast?"

Nicole blushed scarlet. "Er not a lot. I think she was quite pleased actually. She stuck to me like glue for the rest of the hike. She even picked me some flowers. I didn't know what the hell to do. I think Gerty was always a bit inclined that way if you know what I mean."

Sarah grinned wickedly. "Well, well! This is one little story I've never heard before. You and Gerty Aldermann no less!"

"Give over Sarah! It was bloody embarrassing."

Sarah laughed. "I'm just teasing Nicky. Ok I'm going to grab a shower."

After her shower, Sarah busied herself in the kitchen as Nicole used the bathroom. They had a small hi-fi system in the kitchen and Sarah took one of her Daniela Devin CDs out to play on it as she brewed the coffee and put a pan of water on the stove to boil their eggs. She was coming to love Daniela's music. The night before, she had been thrilled to watch the DVD of Daniela's live concert. They'd not watched all of it and the television in Nicole's room was small and of poor quality but she'd seen enough to understand what Nicole had said about Daniela's electrifying live performances. Daniela commanded a charismatic stage presence, belting out her songs with fire, passion and emotion; ranging from aggressive gutsy vocals all the way through to soulful melancholy. It was impossible to tear one's eyes away or not to be stirred by the thrilling music. There was true star quality to the woman. She grabbed an audience with her opening lyrics and held them spellbound to the last soaring crescendos. She was a magician on stage manipulating her audience like a virtuoso puppet handler and leaving them gasping for more. She wore her own raw emotions on her sleeve. Sarah had been astonished when a camera close up during the heart rending ballad "I Never Knew" showed Daniela's face to be wet with tears. There was soft sadness during the gentle lilting rhythms of "Soul Sister" and unfettered joy in the startling rocky "Long Time Coming". It wasn't artifice Sarah realised. This was a woman that poured her soul into her music and carried her listeners along the emotional journey and if the lyric lines were often obscure you felt, nevertheless, that there was genuine feeling behind them. It wasn't music produced for trite commercial reasons; not just catchy tunes of trivial meaning. There was the depth and perceptions of an intelligent and sensitive woman communicating her joys and heartbreaks through the medium of her richly conceived compositions.

It was hard too to put a label on Daniela's music for it seemed to be diversely influenced. There were certainly rock elements in it; a touch of blues; some west coast style light rock, a little country and western; soul; even a dash of jazz on occasion. It was very definitely Daniela's sound however for it possessed a uniqueness to it that immediately labelled it as her own. Even on short acquaintance Sarah knew that now she could hear a song and know instantly that it was one of Daniela's. The woman had come up with a sound and made it hers. Nobody else quite sounded that way.

And the music was beautiful. It is a mark of how extraordinary Daniela's music was that it so immediately touched Sarah; a person with little regard for contemporary music. It might be argued that Sarah was inclined to listen to Daniela's music favourably because she knew Daniela personally but Sarah would have stringently denied the fact. She would always insist that she would have been moved by Daniela's music even if she had never been so privileged to meet the author of it. There was something that spoke to Sarah in a fundamental way in Daniela's music, as indeed it spoke to many people. Daniela's talent was indeed something truly special and her enormous influence on contemporary music in her era is testimony to that fact. Destined to become the premier songwriter and performer of her generation Daniela was on her way to the granting of a legacy and the formation of a legend. These were early days in her development yet but the seeds of greatness were already there for anyone with the ear to hear them.

Nicole entered the kitchen drying her hair as Sarah hummed contentedly along with the irresistible little song "Chinese Whispers". "Ok so what's for breakfast?" she inquired.

183

"I already told you. Boiled eggs and toast. We've still got some cheese left though and there's some apricot jam as well."

"Butter?"

"Of course." Sarah rarely used margarine.

Nicole slumped down at the table and poured herself some coffee from the pot. "So I've got the day off. You got any plans?"

"I don't know really. I thought I might go up to the Hotel Toggenburg."

Nicole paused in the labour of drying her hair. "Oh yes? Why?"

"I thought they might have a job for me."

Nicole frowned. "What the fuck do you want a job for? You told me yesterday that your old man sent you twenty grand to see you through the summer and on top of what you already have you surely don't need to get a job."

"Maybe I want a job."

Nicole shook her head exasperatedly. "You're loopy!"

"Maybe. Anyway what are you doing today?"

"Well if you're off up to Schwendi I might come with you." She glanced out of the window. "It looks like the weather's changed for the better. If it gets warm by this afternoon maybe we can get some stuff and have a barbecue up at the Schwendisee."

Sarah eased the eggs out of the boiling water and spooned them into egg cups, passing one to Nicole. The two girls ate with pleasure; the toast hot from the toaster and damp with melted butter. "That's a good idea of yours Nicky." Sarah remarked. "Going for a barbecue I mean. We haven't had a grill in absolutely ages. I think it will be hot later on."

"Good! We'll make an afternoon of it. We can take our bikinis and get a tan."

"I haven't got one."

"What?"

"A bikini... I haven't got one."

"Oh come on Sarah! Every girl's got a bikini."

"Not me."

"I don't believe this."

"It's true. When do you ever see me going sunbathing?"

"What about when you were in Italy last summer? Surely you took a bikini."

Sarah shook her head. "No. No I never bought one. I'm not really the sort for sitting around on beaches."

"What are you like? No bikini. I seriously worry about you sometimes."

"Well I haven't got one."

"Right then! Here's the program. We'll drive up to Wildhaus and get some stuff for a grill and we'll stop in the sports shop in Lisighaus and buy you a bikini."

"Out of the question."

"Don't argue Sarah. I am not going to flaunt my body in public sat next to you dressed in your scabby old jeans and lumberjack shirt. We're getting you a suitably skimpy bikini and a sarong as a beach wrap."

"I'm not going to bare all for the benefit of any casual observer at the Schwendisee Nicky."

"You'll do as you're told Sarah. It's time you learned a few more feminine guiles. You can't keep a gorgeous body like yours under wraps indefinitely. It's a criminal waste. No wonder your sex life is so crap."

"Nicole!"

"Well it is. Come on honey. Splash out a bit of your dad's money and break a few more Toggenburg hearts."

"Absolutely not."

Nicole squirmed over to slip an arm around Sarah. "Please. Pretty please. You can't let me sunbathe alone."

"You don't have to sunbathe at all."

Nicole nuzzled at Sarah's neck. "Just for me Foxy. Please. Be a good girl."

185

"Stop it!"

"Come on! Just for poor old Nicky. Just for me."

"Oh for heaven's sake!"

"Pretty please."

"Well maybe I could...."

Nicole sat upright "Great! That's settled then."

"It's not settled at all! I was about to say..."

Before Sarah could elaborate, the peace of the kitchen was shattered by the tone of the telephone. Nicole looked pleased. "Hey the phone's back on." She stepped across and picked up the receiver. "Hello?" Then her eyes opened wide. "Oh hello Mrs Fuchs." Sarah waved her hand at Nicole and shook her head vigorously mouthing "I'm not here!" soundlessly. Nicole smiled at her evilly. "No I'm sorry Mrs Fuchs you've just missed her. She's gone out shopping. She said she needed to buy some new clothes and beachwear." Sarah glared at Nicole furiously. "What's that Mrs Fuchs? Oh yes I thought so too. No I don't know when she'll be back. You know what we girls are like when you let us loose in a shopping centre." Sarah picked up a tea towel and threatened to throw it at Nicole. "Yes of course I'll tell her Mrs Fuchs. I'm sorry to hear that Mrs Fuchs. I'm sure Sarah doesn't want to displease you. Yes I'll tell her. Of course Mrs Fuchs. Yes Mrs Fuchs!" Nicole rolled her eyeballs theatrically. "I'll be sure to tell her. Until then then Mrs Fuchs. Yes of course. Goodbye then." Finally Nicole replaced the receiver and turned to Sarah. "Quick Sarah go and turn your mobile off. Your mum's going to try and reach you on it and she's on the warpath."

Hastily Sarah reached for her mobile phone and switched it off. "What's up with her?"

"It sounds like your Dad has told her that you're kicking about spending the summer in the Ticino and she's spitting blood about it."

"Oh Great!"

"Tell her to go and eat cake. You're over twenty-one and it's your life."

"Neither of which argument will make the slightest impression on her."

"Well I'd let her settle down a bit before you broach the subject. She sounds well pissed."

"Why the hell did you tell her I was out shopping for clothes and beachwear?"

"I did you a favour Sarah. That was the only thing that mollified her. She snorted something about it being high time before mentioning that you'd probably buy something hideous without her to guide you."

"Bloody typical!"

Nicole picked up the dirty plates from the table. "Come on let's dump these in the sink and get the hell out of here before your bloody mother remembers some further grievances for me to pass along to you and I have to suffer another stream of invective."

"Where are we heading?"

"Lisighaus first; to get that bikini for you!"

"I've told you I am not going to..."

"Be a good girl Sarah or I'll phone up your mum and tell her that since you're not intending to go to the Ticino this summer you've decided that you don't need anything for the beach."

"You blackmailing bitch!"

Nicole grinned. "Come on Sarah let's go and get you into something that'll make every warm-blooded male in the Toggenburg start howling."

Chapter Sixteen

Some time later, Sarah allowed herself to be bullied into the sports and swimwear boutique in Lisighaus, grumbling mightily. Nicole was taking no prisoners today, though, and she turned a deaf ear to Sarah's protestations and very nearly pushed her physically through the door. Once inside Nicole started picking bikinis off the racks and holding them against her blushing friend's body for perusal. "Stop it Nicole!" Sarah hissed between her teeth. "There're people watching."

Nicole was oblivious. "Hmm what about this one?"

"Are you mad? There's nothing to it."

"Well you've got the body for it."

"Look if the whole point is to simply display my body why don't I just dispense with the bloody expense of buying a few ounces of purely symbolic fabric and walk around the Schwendisee stark naked?"

"Behave Sarah. It's too conservative around here. You'd never get away with it. Now if you want to go nude wait till you're in the Ticino. Nobody wears anything up the Centovalli."

"I didn't say I wanted to go nude. I was being sarcastic!"

"This one's nice too."

"Nicole Richardson you are barking mad! The bloody things got a string where the arse should be. Anyway the colour's rotten."

"Ok then how about this?" Nicole held up another small bikini in white and hot pink with string ties and at least the formality of covering the rump a little better.

"Well the colour's a bit better." Sarah conceded "But it's still too small."

"Nonsense it's perfect. Look we'll match it with this sarong and a pair of sandals and you'll look fabulous."

"Well I suppose it's at least a bit better than your other choices."

"Great! We can buy you a pair of sunglasses to match as well."

"I've got sunglasses."

"You are not wearing those horrible alpine shades of yours whilst dressed up like a glamour queen on a photo shoot Sarah."

"All right if it makes you happy. Go on then let's get the bloody thing and get the hell out of here."

"You've got to try it on first."

"WHAT?"

Nicole assumed the stance and facial expression of a person obliged to demonstrate extraordinary degrees of patience and finding it a sore trial. "Try it on Sarah... it's the usual standard operating procedure whilst purchasing an item of clothing I believe."

Sarah glared at Nicole. "I refuse! I refuse utterly to parade about virtually naked in a public shop Nicole."

"There's a changing booth at the back Sarah. This is a swimwear shop as well as other things so I'm sure you won't be the first woman to grace its interior with your partially clad body. Now stop griping and go and put the bloody thing on."

"But...."

"Get on with it Sarah."

Reluctantly, Sarah found herself coerced into compliance and blushing furiously she stripped out of her clothes in the changing booth and pulled on the skimpy little creation. It had seemed small enough on the rack but it appeared to have diminished to vanishing point when being asked to perform the modest act of covering her decently. Sarah poked her head around the curtain of the booth. "I can't wear this Nicky." she protested desperately. "The last time I was as naked as this in public a doctor slapped my arse for me."

"Come on. Let's see."

"What?"

"Step out and let's have a look at you."

"No way! Look let's just forget about..." Sarah squealed shrilly as Nicole snatched the curtain of the booth and pulled it rapidly aside. "Stop it Nicky!"

"Stop being such a bloody old woman for God's sake Sarah. Come on take a look at yourself in the mirror."

Sarah's face was flushed scarlet as Nicole manoeuvred her out of the booth and in front of the full-length mirror. A young man, on the other side of the shop perusing the snowboards, stopped even pretending to look at the last season's range of cut price bargains and was admiring her openly. Nicole regarded her in smug satisfaction. "You look fantastic Sarah."

"I feel like a complete prat! Can I take it off now?"

"Not without causing a scandal."

"I mean back in the booth you idiot!"

Nicole walked slowly around Sarah who looked as if the happen chance of a major earthquake causing the ground to open up and swallow her would have been a most welcome occurrence. "I can't understand you sometimes Sarah." said Nicole, shaking her head sadly. "Any woman would sell her soul to the devil for a body like yours and you're just embarrassed by it."

"Please can I change now Nicky?" Sarah pleaded with a whimper.

Sarah's embarrassment became further compounded as the shop assistant, an attractive young man, drifted over ostensibly to render assistance. It was a transparent pretext. He was eyeing Sarah with a brazenly predatory look. "Can I help you ladies?" He inquired with completely unconvincing innocence.

"Don't you think she looks great in that bikini?" Nicole asked him.

"Yes... er yes.... very nice." The young man was having trouble articulating.

Nicole came to decision. "She'll take it!" and ignored the furious glare from her suffering housemate.

"Of course. Er shall I wrap it for you?"

Nicole giggled. "No I'll do that." She held up the matching sarong in a pink and white floral pattern. "Come here Sarah dearest." she beckoned.

"Nicky..."

Sarah began to protest but Nicole forestalled her by wrapping the sarong around her back. "It's a long sarong Sarah so you can use it either as a long skirt or as a short full wrap." Expertly Nicole wrapped the sarong across Sarah's chest and tied the ends up around her neck. The material was a light, thin rayon and Sarah bitterly noted that it was another item altogether poorly designed for the purposes of public decency. Nicole stood back to admire her handiwork. "Gorgeous!" she declared. "Right we need a pair of sandals." She turned to the assistant. "Do you sell beach sandals?"

"Yes. Over here."

Sarah suffered the indignity of being marched across the shop to be fitted with pretty beach sandals, stylish sunglasses and even a necklace of beads that Nicole insisted upon hanging around her neck as a final accessory. By the time Nicole dragged her to the counter she was thoroughly fed up with the whole business. The final bill came to over two hundred and fifty francs and Sarah blinked in shock. "What?" she gasped. "Good God! I would have at least expected that anything I paid that much for would perform its stated function of actually covering me."

"Money well spent." declared Nicole in enormous satisfaction. "Come on give the man your card."

Sarah paid for her purchases with a groan and turned to see Nicole retrieving her clothes from the booth and folding them into a shopping bag. "What are you doing?" she demanded.

"Putting your clothes in a bag. What does it look like?"

"Oh really? And just what pray am I supposed to wear upon leaving this establishment?"

"You're dressed just fine."

"You are not seriously expecting me to walk out of the shop dressed like this!"

"Come on Sarah. We're only going up to the lake. You'd only have to get changed again when we get there and there aren't any changing booths around the Schwendisee."

"I can't walk abroad on the street like this."

"Oh stop being such a prude Sarah. You look fabulous and perfectly decent. Come on and we'll buy some munchies in Wildhaus."

In Wildhaus, Sarah discovered that there was no rest for the wicked apparently for she was subjected to the further purgatory of being bullied out of the car in order to help Nicole acquire provisions in the little supermarket there. Walking around the Migros clad in beachwear was quite the maddest thing she had ever done, thought Sarah and it was a relief when they finally climbed back into Nicole's battered old Renault for the short drive up to Schwendi.

Chapter Seventeen

The poor weather of the previous day was just a distant memory now, for the afternoon was a scorcher and Sarah began to reluctantly concede the practicality of her ensemble as the day grew hotter. Nicole laid a large picnic mat out and stripped down to a shocking pink bikini of such tiny proportions that Sarah felt quite modestly dressed by comparison. Sarah at first refused to be parted from her sarong as Nicole gathered wood from a nearby copse and set about to build a little fire in a circle of stones. It took a great deal of cajoling from her friend to finally shed the comforting cover of the sarong. Nicole took a plastic bottle of sun cream from her bag and began to smear it over herself as Sarah watched. Sarah felt a little more relaxed by now. It was really hot and they certainly weren't alone in exposing themselves to the rays of the sun. The hot weather had lured a number of people to the cool banks of the little lake in their swimwear and there were even a couple of girls sunbathing in a pasture close at hand that appeared to have economised in their own swimwear purchases by only buying the bottom halves of their bikinis.

In any event, it was impossible to remain annoyed with Nicole for long. Nicole was so plainly enjoying herself and her happiness was infectious. Sarah felt the odd feeling that she had experienced the night before in the disco; the feeling that Nicole was enjoying showing off her beautiful friend in public. She realised that the whole charade about buying a bikini had been devised with this aim in mind and Nicole's satisfaction of stripping her best friend down for public approval was evident. Sarah was bemused by Nicole's satisfied delight in her. It wasn't something that she could readily understand for she could never admit her own beauty but she nevertheless felt strangely moved by Nicole's obvious pride in her.

Nicole was humming to herself as she rubbed sun cream into her legs and Sarah found herself examining her friend closely. It was often easy to forget, given Nicole's penchant for shocking hairstyles and outrageous clothes, just how pretty a girl she was. She had a small trim body with shapely legs and small but pert breasts. Her feet were lovely, Sarah noted although the scarlet nail varnish on her toenails distracted from their shapeliness. Nicole had a tattoo of an angel on her left shoulder blade that had once been a serious bone of contention between them. Sarah had been furious with her when she had had it applied in a shop in Winterthur and they'd been barely on talking terms for two days. It wasn't just the tattoo itself that had caused the friction, although that was bad enough. What had really caused the rift was the fact that in the wreath about the angel's feet Nicole had had the name "Sarah" inscribed. She had just wanted to have the name of her best friend tattooed on her Nicole had protested miserably as Sarah had berated her for her foolishness. Sarah had told her she was an idiot and that even friendship was no reason to so mutilate your body for life. They rarely mentioned the incident or offending brand on Nicole's skin anymore. Sarah had forgiven her friend and Nicole had never had another tattoo inflicted on her body. If Sarah ever did mention the tattoo it was with distaste and exasperation but deep down, in a place she would never admit to anyone, there was a little part of her that was secretly touched by the fact that her best friend had her name permanently etched on her flesh.

Sarah borrowed the sun cream and applied it to herself. Her years in the mountains had long since taught her the folly of exposing bare skin to the intense ultra-violet rays of the sun in the thin air of high altitudes. Alpine strength sun creams were the strongest of all.

They had to be for it was easy to burn very quickly in the mountains. "Shall I do your back?" Nicole asked.

"Yes please." It was a pleasure that Sarah readily succumbed to. Nicole was quite a good masseuse and she had often rubbed Sarah's shoulders for her. Sarah loved having her back massaged. For a few minutes she basked in the sun as Nicole ran firm hands over her back. There were bees buzzing among the flowers and the sounds of laughter and splashing from the lake where several people were swimming and cavorting in the water. Sarah began to feel sleepy.

Nicole slapped her sharply on the rump. "Come on let's eat. I'm hungry now."

Food eaten out of doors in the wild and cooked over a little fire always tastes better than the same food elsewhere. They cut lengths of green twigs and skewered heavenly seasoned sausages on them to roast over the embers of the fire. Nicole cut up some pieces of steak and skewered them with pieces of onions, green peppers and mushrooms on long twigs to grill in the fire whilst Sarah wrapped potatoes in silver foil to bake in the hot embers to be eaten with cheese and butter melted in them. There was a tub of coleslaw they shared between them and cherry tomatoes, pickled onions, olives and good crusty bread. They dipped their bread into a bowl of tzatziki; Greek style yoghurt with chopped cucumbers, olive oil, pepper and garlic and washed it down with a crisp white wine. It was a feast.

Finally Sarah shook out her hair and leaned back on her elbows to stretch replete and contented. "That was just heaven." she sighed.

Nicole watched her friend in pleasure. Sarah had never seemed more beautiful. Her hair fell in a great wave over her bare shoulders and gleamed in the sun and her fine muscled body shone slightly with a sheen of perspiration. She looked happy and relaxed as she closed her eyes and luxuriated in the warm rays of the sun. With a glint Nicole reached into her bag. Sarah heard the click and soft whirr and opened her eyes in surprise. Nicole was holding her digital camera; an expensive model she'd received as a Christmas present the year before. "What the hell are you doing?" Sarah demanded.

"Just taking a photo of you."

"You might have asked!"

"Oh come on. It's only a photo."

"I think it would be diplomatic of you to *ask* before you take a picture of me with next to no clothes on Nicole." Sarah stated with no lack of firmness.

"It's only a photo Sarah. You looked so nice there I just took a photo."

"Well really Nicky! You're too bad."

"Away Sarah. Let's have another one."

"Nicky! I'm barely dressed."

"Oh for heaven's sake Sarah. Are you the only girl in the world that hasn't had her photo taken in her bikini on holiday or something? Bloody hell sweetheart! Sometimes I feel like I've just stepped back into the nineteenth century talking to you."

Sarah had the good grace to look abashed. "I'm just not used to it Nicky." she murmured.

"Blimey honey." Nicole was looking at the image of the first shot on her digital display screen. "You look great. I could probably flog this to a modelling agency."

"Don't you dare!"

"Come on honey... let's have another one."

"All right but just one mind."

"Well look at the camera and smile this time ok!"

Nicole seemed so childishly pleased that Sarah couldn't help but smile as she posed for a second photograph. Nicole's breath caught in her throat as she peered into her camera. Sarah looked stunningly radiant. With deep satisfaction Nicole put her camera back in her bag. She passed a hand over her brow. "Whew it's hot. I'm going to go have a dip in the lake."

Sarah was instantly concerned. "Be careful Nicky. It's dangerous."

"Sarah! I've been swimming in that lake since I was six years old. Stop fussing."

Sarah realised that she had little to worry about as she watched her friend slide into the still water of the little lake. Nicole was a superb swimmer; far better than Sarah, and she covered the distance to the moored platform in the centre of the lake in an effortless glide. The lake was a picture in the gentle afternoon light. The water was barely ruffled by any breeze and pair of mallards was dabbling about in the marginal lilies. Nicole was a splash of pink against the verdant backdrop of the green pastures and lilies as she sat on the platform and dabbled her legs in the cool water. Sarah regarded her with an affection amusedly mixed with a slight sense of exasperation. Her singular friend had a habit of leading her into the sort of situation she had had to endure today but that was just Nicole's way and Sarah loved her for it. She shook her head fondly as she thought of how she had somehow been paraded through half the upper Toggenburg in a bikini and sarong. Nicole would relish such a mischievous misadventure. But there was something more Sarah felt. Ever since her return to the Toggenburg Sarah had sensed that Nicole been utterly delighted by her return; had never seemed happier in her company. She must have missed her, Sarah thought. Nicole needed her in a fundamental way; felt incomplete without her lifelong friend. What would she do when Sarah married and moved away? It was a sad thought on a beautiful day.

Eventually Nicole slid back into the water and swam back to the bank; easing herself out in a place where the banks were boggy and covered with lush marshy vegetation. It was a mistake. The boggy areas around the lake were infested with leeches and as Nicole padded her way across the swaying, treacherous swampy ground she uttered a venomous oath of disgust. A large black leech was clinging to the lower part of her calf. "Don't pull it off!" Sarah called "Come here. I'll deal with it."

Nicole hurried across her face distorted with distaste and approaching on panic. "It's horrible! Get it off me Sarah!"

"Come to the fire. No don't pull at it. If you pull it off it just leaves its head buried in your skin and it can go bad. Here sit down."

Nicole looked almost in tears although in truth the leech wasn't painful. "God it's foul Sarah! Do something!"

"Oh stop being a drama queen Nicky. It's only a leech." Sarah pulled a partially burned sliver of wood from the fire and blew on the glowing end to make it burn brighter.

"What are you going to do?" asked Nicole fearfully.

"Just hold still. I'm not going to hurt you." Gently Sarah took firm hold of Nicole's leg and brought the glowing ember down onto the leech. It squirmed under the heat and pulled itself clear falling from Nicole's leg and leaving a little drop of blood. "That wasn't so bad was it?" asked Sarah patting Nicole's leg. "Pass me my rucksack. I've got my hiking first aid kit in it." Quickly Sarah applied a little antiseptic lotion to the wound and dressed it with an adhesive plaster. "There now. You'll live."

Nicole was looking at her strangely. "Sometimes I can't get my head around you Sarah."

"What do you mean?"

"I mean if you're asked to do something as simple and as normal as appear in public in anything other than a pair of tatty old jeans and a shirt you're a pusillanimous whimpering coward but face you with a crisis that would have most girls running around in circles screaming their heads off and you're not fazed in the slightest. How did you do that so calmly? I couldn't bear to look at the horrible thing."

"It's not the first time I've had to deal with a leech Nicky. It's no big deal."

"You're seriously weird Foxy."

Sarah laughed. "That's rich coming from you!" Sarah ran a hand over her shoulder. "This sun's getting too hot Nicky. I've not shown this much flesh to the afternoon sun all year. I'm getting red. I'm going to put my sarong back on."

Nicole picked up the wine bottle. "Yes and we're out of wine too. Let's gather up our stuff, put the fire out and walk round the lake and have a drink at the restaurant in the shade of a parasol."

Sarah looked uncertain. "Can we go to the restaurant dressed like this?"

"Everybody else does Sarah. Half of their revenue in the summer is from people sunbathing down by the lake."

"Well I suppose so then."

They found a table in the garden of the restaurant. It was the very same that Sarah had shared with Daniela just the day before yesterday and it was a relief to shelter from the fierce sun in the shade of the big parasol at the table. Monika, the German waitress, brought them a carafe of chilled white wine and a bottle of sparkling mineral water to water it down with. Monika was bursting to talk to Sarah. "I didn't know you knew Daniela Devin Sarah!" she blurted out. Monika's Swabian German accent sounded strange in contrast to the Swiss German that prevailed locally.

Monika had difficulty understanding Swiss German so Sarah responded in High German out of politeness. "I don't know her really Monika. I only met her the day we came into the restaurant."

Monika looked disappointed. Doubtless she was fishing for gossip. "Oh! I see. Well thanks for bringing her in. She left nearly seventy francs as a tip."

"I know. Actually I didn't bring her in. It was her idea."

"Well she can come in anytime she feels like if she's going to leave tips like that."

"Has she never been in before?"

"Once or twice but never when I've been on duty. I've never been so close to her before. If you see her again will you thank her for the CD she signed for me?"

"Of course! Did you like it?"

"Yes! It's Geil! I love her music. I had to share the tip with Jacky but the CD's *mine.*"

"I'll tell her that if I see her."

"Thank you." Monika skipped away happily.

Sarah smiled in wonderment. "Is the whole valley loopy over Daniela Devin?"

Nicole nodded. "I'd say the whole of Switzerland is Sarah; and the rest of Europe to boot. The papers are calling her a phenomenon."

"It's crazy. Mind you I can understand it, now that I've heard her music. She's fantastic."

Nicole took a sip of wine. "Yes she is."

Sarah regarded her friend worriedly. "Steady with the wine Nicky. You still have to drive us back."

"I'll be alright honey. I've driven the road so many times I think the car could find its own way back even if I fell asleep at the wheel. Are we going over to the Hotel Toggenburg then?"

Sarah sighed. "I don't know. I seem to have lost the whole purpose of the day letting you talk me into strutting around like this. I can hardly go looking for a job dressed in a bikini and sarong can I?"

"I'm sorry Foxy."

"Oh don't be. I've still got time to look for work. It was just nice having a day out with you. I can always go up to the Toggenburg when you're at work."

"They think the sun shines out of your arse in the Hotel Toggenburg Sarah. They wouldn't care if you walked in dressed in your underwear. They'd still take you on. Frau Fritzl says that you're the best waitress she's ever had."

"Well I'm not walking over there dressed like this. It wouldn't be polite."

"Well I suppose you've got a point. Hey have you still got your phone switched off?"

"Yes! I suppose there are about fifty vitriolic messages from my mother on it by now."

"You ought to look at it Sarah. You can't hide from your mother indefinitely."

Sarah heaved a sigh. "No I suppose not. I'll take a look."

There weren't fifty messages from Sarah's mother on the phone but there were half a dozen of increasing frustration including two voice mail calls on the answer machine. "Why is your phone switched off Sarah?" her mother had demanded imperiously on the last one. "I've been trying to get hold of you all day. For heaven's sake call me back! We need to talk seriously." Sarah groaned at the message. There was an uncomfortable interview looming. In addition to her mother's calls Sarah saw that she had a message from Alan. It was succinct and devoid of emotional content. "WILL CALL U TONITE" Sarah bit her lip. That was another upcoming interview she was beginning to dread. For a moment she felt forlorn. Alan was usually a busy man she realised but surely tapping out a simple "LUV U" on his phone wouldn't have taxed the time demands of corporate finance. There was another message on her answer phone and Sarah accessed it expecting another burst of impatient elbow jiggling from her mother. Instead a warm melodic voice

201

greeted her on the answer machine. "Hi Sarah! Danny here. I'm just calling to say thank you for your note and the present you sent me. It was so sweet of you! I shall treasure it. I looked up Early Purple Orchid and found the kiss you'd marked it with. Thank you for that. I was touched. I'll try and call you later and perhaps we can arrange that dinner sometime. Until then a big kiss and take care of yourself. Bye." Sarah pulled a wry face. Daniela had seemingly misinterpreted the little cross she had placed by the entry for Early Purple Orchid in the field guide she'd sent her. She could hardly tell Daniela that it had been just a cross and not a kiss though could she?

"Well?" Nicole was asking.

"Yep. Half a dozen messages from my mother and one from Alan. He says he'll call tonight. Oh yes and a voice message from Daniela."

"Oh wow! What did she say?"

"Just thank you for the present I sent her. She says she'll call later and sends me a big kiss."

Nicole raised her eyebrows. "Oh really? Hmm! You might have to be careful there."

Sarah glanced at Nicole sharply. "Whatever for?"

"Remember that story about a bust up in her band?"

"Yes didn't one of her backing vocalists run off with her boyfriend or something?"

"She ran off with the lead guitarist Sarah but he wasn't Daniela's boyfriend."

"So?"

"No. It was the other way around so the story goes."

"What do you mean?"

"I mean the backing vocalist was Daniela's *girlfriend*!"

202

Chapter Eighteen

Sarah was still shocked by Nicole's revelation as the two girls left the restaurant and made their way back to the car. "I can't believe that Daniela is a lesbian." Sarah stated with a shake of her head. "I would just never have seen it."

"Why not?" asked Nicole in amusement.

"Well she just doesn't seem like one."

"Lesbians don't come with labels attached, Sarah, and your normal clichéd image of some butch dyke doesn't fit most lesbians either. Remember Maria Walliser?"

"She wasn't a lesbian."

"Sarah darling, she married her girlfriend under the new Federal law as a registered partner in April. They've been living together for nearly three years."

"You're joking! She can't be a lesbian."

"Why? Just because she's all girly and feminine?"

"Well yes. I suppose so. I mean she was popular with the boys."

"Doesn't mean a thing Sarah. I knew a girl in Buchs that was notorious for jumping into bed with anything wearing trousers and she eventually settled down with a woman in Graubunden. They've even got a kid. God knows what the parentage is."

"But Daniela told me that she was married once."

"So what? Wolfgang Kopli's wife ran off with an air stewardess and they'd been married for nearly ten years."

"But Daniela? No I can't believe it."

"Well I don't know all the facts Sarah but she has a reputation for liking girls. I don't think that's the whole story because she's been linked romantically with a few men as well according to the tabloid press."

"You're telling me that she's bi-sexual?"

Nicole frowned as they approached the car. "I'm not sure I like labels like that Sarah. We always put people into categories don't we? They're either homosexual, heterosexual or bisexual. I've got the feeling that it's not quite as easy as that. There's an awful lot of leeway in those definitions isn't there?"

Sarah paused at the car and leaned on the roof thoughtfully. "How do you mean Nicky?"

"I mean you shouldn't be too quick to label someone Sarah. Look what does bi-sexual mean? Does it mean that you are attracted equally to men and women? Or does it mean that you mostly like men but have been known to sleep with a girl too. Things are never quite that black and white. Brigitte Coppette slept with a hairdresser from Wil and he was one of the campest gay guys you've ever met; all limp wrists and you could have covered him in mashed potatoes and called him a cottage pie. Now does that make him gay or bi-sexual? If you take a line between being exclusively attracted to men through to being exclusively attracted to women whereabouts do you point to on the line and call that bi-sexual. I think most people have experienced some sort of ambiguity in their sexuality at some stage in their lives. I had a crush on Miss Hirtzel, our music teacher when I was fourteen."

Sarah laughed. "Everybody had a crush on Miss Hirtzel Nicky. She was lovely. That was just schoolgirl vapours. That doesn't make you bi-sexual."

"So what does?"

Sarah frowned. "I don't know. I suppose it's if you sleep with women as well as men."

"Lots of people that call themselves straight have slept with their own sex Sarah."

Sarah pondered that for a moment. "Have you Nicky? I mean have you ever slept with another girl?"

"None of your bloody business!"

Sarah pulled as rueful face. "I nearly did."

"WHAT?" It was Nicole's turn to look shocked.

"Oh it was nothing really. It was while I was at uni. We went with a bunch of us down to Interlaken to a party that some friends were throwing. Well we'd all drunk too much so we ended up having to stay the night and I ended up sharing a bed with a girl from uni. Anyway, in the middle of the night, I woke up and found her hands on me and trying to kiss me."

Nicole laughed. "Oh brilliant! What happened?"

Sarah blushed. "Well I didn't know what to do so I pretended to be asleep. She didn't stop though and...."

"Yes? Go on..."

"Well she slid her hand up under my T-shirt and started stroking me."

"Oh God! This I would have loved to have seen."

"Stop laughing Nicky. It was embarrassing. I didn't know what to do."

"Did you stop her?"

"Well yes... eventually."

"*Eventually*?"

Sarah's face was crimson. "Yes. I... I... well it wasn't unpleasant."

Nicole slapped her hand on the car roof and burst into renewed laughter. "Oh God! Don't tell me you were *enjoying* it."

Sarah pulled a face and nodded miserably. "I... I started to get aroused. That's when I had to stop her."

"Otherwise your squeaky-clean reputation would have taken a serious hit?"

"Please stop laughing Nicky. It was awful! The girl was devastated about it. She told me that she'd been in love with me for two years. I felt awful. She was crying and everything, and I felt rotten. I liked her too. She'd always been nice to me and I'd had no idea that she had feelings for me."

Nicole gave a little snort. "Well for God's sake don't let that story become common knowledge.

There've been enough question marks about you in the past as it is."

Sarah's eyes flew open in shock. "What the hell do you mean?"

"Come on Sarah. You can't be that naive. I mean at school you never dated boys and let's face it there was always something of a tomboy about you."

"That's a monstrous thing to say!"

"I'm not saying it Sarah. Plenty of people did though. There was quite a bit of talk about you before you started getting serious with Alan."

Sarah tossed her head and placed a hand on her hip in exasperation. "Oh just great! So everybody at school thought I was a lesbian then?"

"No of course not. There was some speculation that's all."

"Fantastic! And now of course I've been seen walking hand in hand with a well-known lesbian into the Schwendi restaurant. Just brilliant!"

Nicole looked at Sarah in surprise. "You were holding hands with Daniela?"

"Yes she took my hand. How was I to know that she's lesbian?"

Nicole grinned wickedly. "You must have made a lovely couple."

"Shut up Nicky! It's not funny. God it must have looked awful."

Nicole looked piercingly at Sarah. "So if you'd known would you let her take your hand?"

"No! Well probably not. Oh hell... I don't know...." Sarah trailed off in confusion.

Nicole was looking at Sarah quizzically. "I'd say she was a hard person to say no to. Wouldn't you?"

"What do you mean?"

"Just that she's a pretty intense person from what I've seen of her. If she took *my* hand I can't see me telling her to keep her hands to herself. I'd probably just let her."

Sarah looked at Nicole intently. "Anyway I've told you some secrets. What about you?"

"What about me?"

"Well have you ever... you know... fallen for a girl? I mean apart from Miss Hirtzel that is."

"Just one Sarah."

"Oh really? Who?"

"Like I said.... none of your damn business. Come on. Get in the car."

Chapter Nineteen

Nicole was curiously quiet as they drove home, as if the subject was not one she wished to discuss further and Sarah's intrigue grew. Nevertheless she decided to drop the whole embarrassing subject. The more she thought about her encounter with Daniela, the more she became confused by it. She could see now that a good deal of Daniela's words and deeds pointed to an attraction for her. She'd openly admired Sarah and complimented her. God she'd hardly been able to take her eyes off her, Sarah realised. Sarah cringed inwardly as she pictured the scene in her mind. The conversation had bordered dangerously on intimacy. If anybody had been watching, then it would have seemed as if they were very close. Monika had even assumed that they were close.

It wasn't just that Daniela had demonstrated an attraction for Sarah either. In a part of her where Sarah was apt to be honest with herself, she had to concede that the attraction had been mutual. She had been entranced by her glamorous new friend. She now realised just how dangerous that enchantment could be. It hadn't escaped her notice either that the previous day she had not only bought all of Daniela's CDs but also a large poster of her as well. She'd better keep *that* out of Nicole's sight she thought grimly. She'd never hear the last of it if Nicole found her to be in possession of a large naked portrait of her new friend.

At home Sarah showered and hung up the little bikini and sarong in her wardrobe. She paused to stroke the material of the sarong sensually. Since it was time to be honest with herself she acknowledged privately that she had actually enjoyed being so scantily dressed today, in spite of all her protests. Alan had better get home soon she decided. She was a walking time bomb of bubbling frustrations. The hot summer days were leading her perilously close to indiscretion.

She took a deep breath and pulled on a pair of jeans and a T-shirt before going downstairs. She found Nicole sat in the kitchen with a cup of coffee listening to Daniela's CD that Sarah had left in the little hi-fi they had in the kitchen. Sarah hadn't taken it out since breakfast. Nicole looked thoughtful. The song "Blue Stone Lady", Daniela's single release from the album, was playing. "It's a song about a girl Sarah." She observed. "I've never really listened to the lyrics before but if you do it's a song about a girl breaking her heart."

Sarah paused to listen.

"Blue Stone Lady, eyes so blue,
I never asked, I never lied,
But yet again I promise you,
Blue Stone Lady I have cried,
In the whispers of my mind,
I have cried and cried for you."

Sarah pondered. "It could mean anything Nicky."

Nicole shook her head. "It's a lament Sarah; a lament of impossible love. Listen to the whole song and you'll...." Nicole was interrupted by the telephone.

Sarah winced "If that's for me Nicky it could be one of three people; none of which I'm particularly looking forward to a conversation with."

Nicole nodded. "I'll get it." She picked up the phone. "Hello? Oh Hi there! Just one moment." She covered the mouthpiece of the phone quickly. "Sarah! It's Peter!"

Sarah slumped down in a chair resignedly. "Sorry. Make that *four* people."

"You've got to talk to him."

Sarah nodded with a heartfelt groan and took the phone. "Hello Peter. This is a surprise. I thought you were still up at Gamsalp."

"I am. I've walked around to the restaurant to have a beer and phone you. I've been worried about you."

"Whatever for?"

"Well you seemed well... a bit upset with me the other day."

"Oh take no notice of me Peter. I was just in a funny mood."

"Sarah I always take notice of you, especially when you seem upset."

Sarah cringed inwardly but battled on bravely. "Really Peter it was nothing. I was just being silly. I haven't been up in the mountains for months now so maybe the high-altitude air was getting to me."

"You've got mountain air in your blood Sarah. That wouldn't cause it."

"Oh Peter just forget about it ok. I'm sorry if I was in a funny mood. I'm just going through a funny patch what with my engagement looming and all."

"I kind of gathered that Sarah. I wanted to talk to you about it."

"How do you mean?"

There was a pause on the line and when Peter resumed talking he sounded embarrassed. "Well I just wanted to talk to you. There're things we have to discuss... discuss about you and me and your marriage and everything."

Sarah frowned. "I'm not sure I'm following you Peter."

"Oh hell I'm saying this all wrong. Look Sarah I've been thinking about you ever since I met you the other day and about the things you said. I can't get it out of my mind and I need to talk to you. There're things I have to say... private things about me and you and how I feel about you. I've wanted to talk to you for a long time now but the other day, when you came up here, it made me realise that I have to see you urgently and to... well clear the air about us as it were."

"Peter you can always talk to me."

"Not about some things Sarah. I.... I've been frightened of losing you Sarah. I'm still frightened of losing you. You've been a part of my life ever since I was a kid. I can't bear the thought of losing you."

Sarah bit her lip. "Peter.... I've never heard you talk like this before."

"You're not the only one going through a rough patch Sarah. I took this job up here for a couple of weeks just to get away from things and sort my head out. You get an awful lot of time to think things through when you're stuck up in an alp with no other company than a load of dumb cows."

"You were thinking about me?"

"About a lot of things Sarah; about my life, about where it's going and about... well lots of things I suppose. When you came up the other day maybe I realised I couldn't work things out on my own. I can't hide up here forever. I want to talk to you and well there's you getting married at the end of summer and everything and it might be too late then."

Sarah took a deep breath. "Peter, the only people saying that I'm getting married at the end of summer are my parents. I haven't said so yet. In fact I haven't even been asked. I think the bride's consent is generally regarded as an obligatory requirement for a wedding in our culture, wouldn't you agree?"

There was an even longer pause on the other end and Sarah could almost hear Peter wrestling with his words. "I... I know Sarah. You sounded the other day as if you're having second thoughts Sarah. That's what I wanted to talk to you about. I wanted to talk to you before you made any decision on your marriage."

"Peter! Are you telling me that you.... well you...." Sarah paused unsure how to continue.

"I'm telling you only Sarah that I want to talk to you before you make a final decision on your marriage...

211

before you make a mistake or something. I'm sorry. I'm making a hash of this. I'm not very good at this sort of thing."

"I understand Pete. Do you want me to come up the alp again?"

"No Sarah. I'll be finished up here next week. Can we meet up then?"

"Sure. One of the pubs in the valley?"

"No Sarah. I... I'd prefer not to. I'd like to talk privately away from prying eyes. I have to be in Winterthur next week. Can we meet there?"

"Winterthur! What the devil are you doing in Winterthur? You never go to town."

"I just have things to do there. I'm staying for a couple of days and it's a nice neutral place to meet up. Would that be alright?"

"Well if you want of course it's alright. I'm just shocked at the thought of you staying in Winterthur. Do you know anywhere there?"

"There's an English pub on the main shopping street. I thought we could meet there."

"Yes I know it. When do you want to meet?"

"Would Wednesday be all right?"

"Fine by me."

"About three o'clock in the afternoon?"

"It's a date."

"Thank you Sarah. I'll ring off now. I just want to say...."

"Yes?"

"Just that I love you. Until Wednesday then." The line went dead leaving Sarah holding the receiver foolishly.

Nicole was hopping about excitedly in the background. "Well?" she demanded.

"Oh hell Nicky! Now what am I going to do?"

"Skip the enigmatic lamentations Sarah. What did he say?"

"He says he loves me and that he doesn't want me to make any final decision on my marriage until he's had chance to talk to me about it!"

Nicole snorted and shook her head. "Men! They're like sodding buses! You wait half the day for one and then half a dozen turn up at once."

"What the hell am I going to do Nicky?"

"When does he want to talk to you?"

"Next Wednesday."

"Well then you'd better talk to him."

"And what the hell is he going to say?"

"Well tell me exactly what he said." Briefly Sarah gave a synopsis of the conversation and Nicole nodded in understanding. "Well it's not exactly rocket science Sarah. Obviously he's peed off about you marrying Alan and presumably wishes to present a counter proposal."

"I've been Alan's girlfriend for three years now Nicky. Why has Peter suddenly decided he's not happy about it?"

"Because now he's looking at a set wedding Sarah. Maybe before he thought he might still be in with a chance but now it's looking like a fixed date. It's now or never for him."

"That's crap Nicky! There's been an understanding that I'd marry Alan for at least the last two years."

"An understanding isn't a commitment. It focuses the mind knowing you're going to be executed in the morning."

"When you've finished misquoting Samuel Johnson at me, it still doesn't hold water. Whether or not there has been a lack of a fixed date for the wedding there has been nevertheless a firm commitment to this wedding Nicky. Peter has known for ages that I'm marrying Alan. He even approved of the match for God's sake. He's told me that Alan will make a fine husband for me and he's never once expressed any concerns about it until now. Why the sudden change?"

213

"Because of you Sarah. Come on honey. You can't be that thick. Think it through. Ok while you were committed to Alan Peter would never express any disapproval. Of course he would wish you well and tell you that Alan was a great choice. He would never try to steal you from Alan. He's not that kind of bloke. He's a sweetheart and if he was distraught because you were marrying another man he would just bite the bullet and resign himself to the fact. Maybe he'd be heartbroken but he'd never show it. He'd just get on with it. That's just the way he is. Now though it's different isn't it?"

"Why?"

"Oh God Sarah! You can be a brainless bitch sometimes. What happened in the alp the other day?"

"Well not much."

"Bullshit! You expressed doubts about your marriage to him. For the first time you actually told him straight up that you weren't exactly one hundred percent behind your forthcoming marital bliss. Worse yet you even told him that you'd previously thought of marrying him. God Sarah! Talk about laying it on a plate for him. You opened the door for him and let a ray of hope shine through. This is what all this is about."

"Well that's not the impression he gave me when I talked to him Nicky."

"So you caught him by surprise. He wouldn't have known how to react. Come on... we're talking about Peter here, not one of the world's great mercurially impetuous decision makers. It probably takes Pete about ten minutes just to decide which pair of socks to pull on in the morning. He'd hesitate about jumping in even after the angels told him the water was lovely. How much do you want to bet that he's gone away after the other day and been agonising over it ever since."

"Well yes he said as much."

"Of course he has. He'll have gone away and thought about it; then he'll have thought some more;

then a bit more and when he was finished he'll have gone and thought some more. Two days of soul searching contemplation before reaching a decision is pretty dynamic action by Pete's standards. He must really be under the gun. I'd say that Alan has an official competitor in the market for your hand."

Sarah groaned and leaned heavily on her elbows on the kitchen table and burying her face in her hands. "Oh Blast it! What am I going to do?"

"Well exactly what Peter said. Do nothing. Do nothing until you've spoken to him. Now my guess is that on Wednesday you're going to get a long monologue concerning his undying love for you, an agonised attack of conscience and guilt and, just possibly after a few hours of hand-wringing baring of the soul, a heart rending, feeble and humble plea that you might, just might, reconsider your marriage to Alan and contemplate the extraordinary and presumptuous proposal that you condescend to consider the suit of this unworthy miserable and abject creature to be joined in holy matrimony as your lawful wedded husband. It'll probably be hard going and require a certain amount of prompting but that I would think would be a likely scenario."

Sarah lowered her hands and glared at Nicole. "And then what the hell am I supposed to do?"

"Why you do what any warm-blooded female does Sarah. You stall. Play for time. Thank him sincerely for the honour of his proposal and tell him that you'd like some time to think things over. Then you go away and start thinking seriously about the sort of person you really want to spend the rest of your life married to, which is what you should have been doing in the first place and not letting yourself be Shanghaied into a marriage by your family's ambitions. You've been displaying even less powers of decision making than Peter has Sarah. You've let your family make your

215

decisions for you. Well it's time to grow up now Sarah. You're nearly twenty-two and it's decision time. Do you marry Peter, Alan or none of the above. Whatever you do it's time for *you* to decide. Nobody else. You!"

"Nicky it's not that easy."

"Then simplify it."

Sarah sighed heavily and ran a hand through her hair. Before she could reply the telephone rang again. Nicole looked at her seriously. "Nine gets you ten that's going to be your mum Sarah. Have you got the guts to talk to her? And if you have, what are you going to say to her?"

Sarah took a deep breath. "Give me the phone."

It *was* Sarah's mother and she sounded distinctly peeved. "Where on earth have you been all day Sarah?" she wanted to know. "I've been phoning you and sending messages all day and devil the sign of you. Why on earth has your mobile been switched off? How is anybody supposed to get hold of you? Are you deliberately trying to avoid me?"

Sarah fought down the prickling of rebellion that surfaced every time she was obliged to talk with her temperamental and domineering mother. "How are you mother?"

"What? Oh I'm fine. Now listen Sarah..."

"I'm fine too mother. Thank you for asking."

"I'm very cross with you Sarah."

"Oh so you're *not* fine?"

"What the blazes are you talking about Sarah?"

"Well you just said you were cross. I'm sorry to hear that."

"I am *understandably* cross Sarah. I've spoken to your father and he tells me that you are still in the Toggenburg."

"Yes mother. That's right. It's where I *live*."

"Sarah it is where you have *been* living. I think now though, with your changed circumstances, you ought to be able to put the Toggenburg behind you. I expected you down here in the Ticino for the summer Sarah. There's a room ready for you here and there's absolutely no reason for you to be idling away your time in the Toggenburg while we have things to arrange. I can't think why you didn't come straight to the Ticino once you'd finished university."

"I am not "idling" my time mother! As to my coming to Ticino why the devil should I? I live here. All my belongings are here. Why on earth would I have gone to Ascona when the academic year finished? This is where I live."

"Well then I suggest you wake up and realise that you are about to have a change of address Sarah dearest. You've had enough time now to wind up your affairs in the Toggenburg and get yourself here. If you've got too much stuff then put it into storage and just bring what you need for the summer. You'll be getting rid of most of your stuff anyway once you're married I presume. Now if you apply yourself then it shouldn't take you more than a couple of days to put your affairs in order. I shall expect you here by next week at the latest."

Sarah felt her hackles rising; a common reaction to her mother's imperious commanding tone. "Why may I ask is my presence in the Ticino required so urgently then pray?"

Sarah's mother clicked her tongue exasperatedly. "In case it had escaped your attention Sarah we have a wedding to organise."

"Oh really? Whose wedding is that then?"

"Are you being deliberately obtuse Sarah? Yours of course!"

"I wasn't aware that I was getting married mother."

"You are either being particularly stupid or you are deliberately trying to annoy me Sarah. You are perfectly aware that you and Alan are to be married at the end of summer. Alan's family are completely in agreement and

217

they tell me that Alan is perfectly amenable to the provisional date we are setting. Now we've got less than three months to get this thing organised and we can hardly do that while the bride is sat on her backside several hundred kilometres away."

"I am not being stupid mother and as to annoying you it would hardly seem necessary it appears. I repeat I am not aware that I am getting married."

"Don't you dare be having second thoughts Sarah."

"I wasn't aware mother that my *first* thoughts had yet been considered."

"What on earth are you talking about girl."

"Do you know what I'm looking at mother?"

"Of course I don't know what you're looking at Sarah. How could I?"

"My left hand."

"Your left hand? What are you babbling about?"

"Just that mother; my left hand. It seems curiously devoid of ornamentation; particularly any ornamentation in the form of amorphosised crystallised carbon set in precious metal. I would conclude from this lack of such ornamentation, that I am not officially engaged. I believe it is a customary condition, upon taking a future bride, that her consent is first obtained and that she be asked to wear the afore-mentioned decorative item as a token of that consent. Since none of those conditions has been met mother I can only conclude that I am, as yet, a single woman with no immediate future prospects of marriage."

"Don't talk nonsense Sarah! Of course Alan wants to marry you."

"Well then he can damn well do me the courtesy of asking me first."

"How can he do that while he's in America Sarah?"

"He seems perfectly capable of consenting to a marriage with his family and mine mother. Perhaps somebody ought to point out to him that he hasn't as yet sought out the most important consent required; to wit, that of the person projected to be his future wife."

"You're being peculiarly obstinate Sarah."

"What, simply because I'd like to be asked before being dragged down an aisle into matrimony mother?"

"Sarah your marriage to Alan has been the subject of an understanding for the last two years."

"An understanding is not a commitment mother. If Alan wants me then he's damn well going to have to ask me."

"I'll get him to phone you and maybe he can knock a bit of sense into your head."

"You damn well will not! If Alan wants to marry me then he will have to present himself in person and have the common courtesy to personally ask for my hand in marriage. I'm an old-fashioned girl mother. I'll require bended knee, solemn oaths of undying love and the offer of the biggest rock his not inconsiderable income can afford and then, and only then, will I seriously consider his suit. Until such an occasion, I will continue to consider myself as officially unengaged and I refuse to indulge in the logistic planning of a wedding to which I have not yet been invited as the primary guest of honour!"

"Alan won't be back for weeks yet Sarah."

"Then consider the wedding preparations suspended mother. Alan knows where to find me. I'll be here; in the Toggenburg."

"Now listen here Sarah..."

"No mother! You listen! Alan has never once asked me to marry him although he's not above a little cosy deal making with my family to obtain their daughter. Well I'm sorry but I'm not some financial contract he can broker a deal over through third parties. I am the person expected to spend the rest of my life married to him and the least he can do is ask me if I consent to that arrangement."

"You're being disrespectful Sarah. What will his family say?"

"Disrespectful? I'm the one whose considerations are being disrespected mother! I'm sure Alan's family will understand that the fundamental starting point for any marriage negotiations is the consent of the bride to be. If they do not respect my right to choose to whom I am to be married then they can take their wedding plans and shove them where the sun doesn't shine!"

"Where do you get this boneheaded obstinacy of yours from Sarah?"

"I can't imagine mother."

"Well you can get rid of it. You know damn well that you and Alan are unofficially engaged. I'm certain that Alan will make that engagement official as soon as he returns from America. All we're doing is anticipating that in advance and going ahead with the planning for the marriage and for that I need you down here. Now I'll not hear another word Sarah. I want you down here next week at the latest. We can discuss making your engagement official at our leisure once you're here. I was planning to hold a party to announce the wedding date when Alan returns in any case. You can announce your official engagement at that. That might be some weeks away though and we can't afford to lose any time waiting for that."

"You haven't listened to a damn word I've said have you mother?"

"I've heard all I need to hear Sarah."

"Well let me reiterate it in any case. I am *not* coming to the Ticino next week. I am not even going to consider a marriage until I have been officially consulted on the matter by my prospective spouse. You can do all the planning you want mother but without me. If Alan returns from America with the intention of asking me to be his wife then fine; we'll take it from there. Until then I'm going nowhere."

"For heaven's sake grow up Sarah!"

"I already have done mother. I'm not a little girl you can order about at your whim anymore. I'm a grown woman and I know my own mind. This is *my* marriage mother not just a date on your social calendar. I'm the person that has to live with the consequences of this marriage for the rest of my life. It's not immaturity to consider those consequences seriously. I shall hear Alan's proposal carefully and base my decision upon the terms of that proposal. Until I make that decision there is no engagement, no marriage, no reason for you to make any plans and certainly no compelling reason for me to leave my home and spend the rest of the summer in the Ticino."

"I'll talk to your father. Hopefully he can make you see sense."

"That's my last word on the subject mother. Now if you'll excuse me I have pressing engagements."

"Now listen here Sarah...."

"Goodbye mother." Sarah hung up the phone firmly.

Nicole was sitting across the table blowing a soundless whistle. "Damn Sarah! That was telling her."

Sarah slumped in her chair. "God I can't believe I talked to my mother like that. She'll be furious."

Nicole pulled a face. "Well let her be. You're right. It *is* your marriage. She'll just have to accept that."

Sarah grimaced. "Fat chance. She's not a woman comfortable with not getting her own way. I haven't settled anything. Those were just the opening shots of the battle. I'll give you better than even money that she'll be back on the phone within minutes for round two." Almost on cue the telephone rang again. Sarah sighed heavily. "I don't know why I paid the phone bill just to have this stress." Wearily she picked up the phone. "I've told you mother." she stated firmly. "This conversation is at an end."

"I beg your pardon." The soft voice on the end of the line was most definitely not Sarah's mother.

Sarah sat bolt upright. "Daniela! Oh I'm so sorry! I... er I thought it was my mother."

There was an amused chuckle. "So I gathered. Look is this an inconvenient moment?"

"No... no not at all. Of course not."

"Are you sure? I mean you sound as if you're in the middle of something."

"Oh it's nothing Daniela; just a torrid conversation with my mother."

"Oh I'm sorry to hear that Sarah. Mother's will be mothers though and don't always see eye to eye with their daughters."

"Oh I get along with my mother just fine Daniela as long as I agree with everything she says and do everything she tells me to!"

Daniela laughed gently. "I get the picture. Look what are you doing tomorrow night?"

"Er I didn't have anything planned as yet." Sarah told her guardedly.

"Well how about that dinner then? I don't have to work as I thought this week and so I thought perhaps you'd grant me that dinner date you promised me."

Sarah thought furiously. "Er where were you thinking of going Daniela?"

"I haven't a clue Sarah. I was going to leave the choice of restaurant up to you since you know the area better than me."

"Well there's the Gade."

"Oh yes? Where's that?"

"You might have seen it. It's a lovely old rustic restaurant in a converted cowshed on the way down from Schwendi to Unterwasser."

"Oh yes! I know it. Just on the right just past Schwendi?"

"That's the place."

"Yes I've stopped there for a drink out in the garden before. It looks lovely."

"The food's good too."

"Well then it'll be just perfect. Shall we make it a date?"

"Yes... yes I'd like that."

"Fantastic! I'm looking forward to it. Do you want me to pick you up? I mean it's quite a long way for you to go over to Schwendi."

"Oh no Daniela. I'm sure I can find my own way there."

"Well shall we say seven o'clock then?"

"Yes... yes that'll be fine."

"Great! I'm so looking forward to seeing you again. Did you get the message I left on your phone?"

"Yes I did. Thank you."

"I should thank you Sarah. I was very touched by the present you sent me. It was very..." There was a momentary hesitation. "It was very sweet and thoughtful of you."

"Oh it was nothing Daniela."

"It was more than nothing Sarah. It meant a great deal to me."

Sarah was thankful that Daniela could not see her blush. "Well I'm pleased that you liked it."

"I did indeed Sarah. You couldn't have sent me anything nicer. It was just what you would have thought of. You're a very special person Sarah."

"Oh good Lord no! Nothing special about me."

"Oh but there is! Are you at home alone?"

Sarah swallowed. "Er no. My housemate Nicole's here with me."

"Oh well say hello to her from me. I like Nicole."

"Yes... yes I will."

"Good. Well in that case I'll see you tomorrow at the Gade."

"Yes I'll see you then."

"I can't wait. Bye bye Sarah!"

"Goodbye Daniela."

Chewing her lip thoughtfully Sarah replaced the handset. "Oh hell!" she muttered.

Nicole raised an eyebrow in amusement. "Trouble with the girlfriend Sarah?"

"It's not funny Nicky. She's invited me out to dinner tomorrow evening."

"Well we'd better find you something nice to wear. I mean you'll want to make a good impression on a first date won't you?"

"Are you asking for a slap Nicole?"

Nicole giggled mischievously. "Well it would be one way to postpone your upcoming nuptials wouldn't it? I mean your arranged marriage is going to go tits up right sharpish when the prospective parties discover that you're seeing another woman."

"I am not finding this amusing Nicole. What the hell am I going to do? Daniela sounded pretty keen to see me again. She even asked if I was alone. God knows what she'd have said if I had been."

"You could have said no Sarah; prior engagements and all that."

"You've said it yourself Nicky. She's not an easy person to say no to."

"Well just chill it a bit when you see her. Tell her you're engaged to a fellah. That should send a strong enough message."

"Right! And this just after determinedly telling my mother that I'm *not* engaged."

"Daniela doesn't need to know that."

Sarah ran a hand through her hair in agitation. "God what a bloody day this is turning out to be. I only need Alan to phone up to muddy the waters even more."

Nicole nodded. "Yep and from what I gathered from hearing your side of the telephone conversation you had with your mum that's going to be awkward."

"How do you mean?"

"Well am I right in saying that you told your mum that your sole concern over the marriage is simply that you haven't been asked yet?"

"Well I *haven't* been asked and I'm damned if I going to get married without the simple bloody courtesy of being asked for my consent. I mean ...."

"So what happens when he *does* ask?"

"Sorry?"

Come on Sarah. You've told your mum that you are not going to the Ticino to plan your marriage simply because you haven't been asked yet. Ok that's fair enough. As a way of stalling it's pretty sound for the moment. The only trouble is that it's easy to finesse. The first thing your mother is going to do is call up Alan and kick his backside. That means that, as soon as Alan arrives back in Switzerland, he's going to slap a bloody great diamond ring under your nose and say, "Right You've now been officially asked so can we stop pratting about and start getting this thing organised?" and you've no idea what you're going to say to that. You've painted yourself into a corner Sarah. By indicating that your objection to the marriage is simply that you haven't been asked, you have, in effect, indicated your automatic acquiescence once that objection is removed. You need a backup plan Sarah. You've got more issues with this marriage other than the fact that nobody's had the decency to ask if you agree to it. You don't want to put yourself in a position where anybody can say that you've said you'll agree if only you're asked. You still have to retain the right to refuse the proposal. Right now if Alan does ask you to marry him you're trapped because you haven't given yourself a fall back negotiating platform."

"I did say that I would make a decision once I was asked."

"Well that's something I suppose. Most importantly though don't let yourself be manoeuvred into a position whereby you have to say immediately yes or no once confronted with the proposal."

"That'll just seem like I'm stalling."

"Well you *are* bloody well stalling! Good God Sarah! Every woman has the right to go away and think about it before granting consent to marry."

"I've had several years to think about it Nicole."

"And still haven't made up your mind?"

"Well it's different now isn't it? I mean it's never been this immediate before."

"No it hasn't. Does it occur to you as significant that the more imminent this marriage becomes the more doubtful you are about it?"

"I should imagine every woman has eleventh hour misgivings on the eve of their marriage Nicky."

"Which is exactly what your mother will dismiss them as!"

Sarah buried her head in her hands in despair. "Oh God I don't know!"

"Then there's Peter." Nicole pointed out.

"I know! I know!"

Nicole grinned. "What with Alan and Peter and now Daniela Devin competing for your affections Sarah you're turning out to be one popular girl for the moment; the most eligible unmarried woman in the Toggenburg. We'll have to start up a rota of visiting hours for all your suitors."

"Give me a break Nicky."

"And what are you going to say when Daniela tells you that she's in love with you?"

"Don't be ridiculous Nicky. I've only met the woman once. She's not in love with me."

Nicole regarded Sarah strangely. "Why not Sarah? Everybody else is."

Chapter Twenty

Late in the afternoon the following day, Sarah found herself on the road to Schwendi just outside the Gade restaurant. Nicole had a split shift that day and had dropped her in the car before driving to Wildhaus for the second stage of her day's labours. Sarah still had some hours to kill before her rendezvous with Daniela but she intended to put them to good use. She looked beautiful. There was no earthly point in returning home before meeting Daniela, so she had dressed for the evening before leaving the house. It had been an ordeal because Nicole had fussed over her appearance with a dedication that might have led one to believe that Sarah was about to be presented to the crowned heads of Europe and not just dressed for a dinner date at an undoubtedly rustic restaurant. Nicole was certainly a better judge of Sarah's appearance than she was of her own for she had done a fine job on Sarah's hair and make-up and even insisted on shaving Sarah's legs, despite the fact that Sarah had very little in the way of bodily hair and her legs were as smooth as a baby's. Nicole had treated all Sarah's objections with contempt, however, for, rummaging through Sarah's purchases from Buchs, she had found the lovely little sexy summer dress that Sarah had been hiding from the light of day like a guilty secret in her wardrobe.

It was strictly speaking a day dress and, in fact, it could have been classified as a beach dress for the material was light and thin enough to make one cautious about being silhouetted against strong light. It had a tied dyed pattern in white and jade green with a ruched empire waist, a plunging neckline and a halter top that tied at the neck, leaving the arms and shoulders bare, and a built in shelf bra to compensate for the fact that the backless and shoulder-less creation was not designed to be worn with any accompanying underwear, other than perhaps the most in-obtrusive of thongs or tiny knickers. It was short too; cut well up on the thigh and exposing a generous length of those long, elegant and smooth legs that Nicole had so agonised over.

Sarah herself did not know exactly what madness had come over her in purchasing the dress although she loved the soft material of it on her skin. Nicole's eyes had lit up when she had unearthed the creation from the inner-most darkest corner of Sarah's wardrobe and held it up to the light of day. Sarah had protested feebly that the dress was inappropriate for an evening dinner date and that it had been a mistake to buy it in the first place. It had cost her over two hundred and fifty francs and, although it had been out-priced by the gold cocktail dress she had worn to the disco on the night of her shopping trip to Buchs, it was undoubtedly a stunningly daring little number and quite outside Sarah's comfort zone. Nicole had taken one look at it and fallen in love with it. From that moment on, all Sarah's resistance had been futile and the chances of her wearing anything else to dinner that night had essentially diminished to vanishing point. Nicole had even dipped into her own jewellery and accessory collection to adorn her housemate and Sarah had found herself bedecked in Nicole's jade earrings and a matching jade bracelet and a sash in the same colour about her waist. A pair of white high heeled sandals had completed the ensemble and it was a lovely looking Sarah, if a cringingly self-conscious one, that hesitated on the roadside by the little path that led down to the Gade restaurant.

Sarah sighed and, clutching her handbag and the pale green shawl she had brought to cover her shoulders in the cool of the evening later on, she stepped off the road and onto the path. The path, such as it was, was merely a series of flagstones descending the slope across the little meadow that separated the restaurant from the main road perhaps a hundred metres long. It was not the most comfortable of routes to negotiate in high heels, especially for a person like Sarah who was unused to the more impractical of feminine footwear and far happier in comfortable boots or trainers. Nevertheless, stepping gingerly over the flags, she successfully surmounted the obstacles to the sun terrace in front of the restaurant. The afternoon sun was hot and she gratefully slipped onto a table beneath the shade of a large parasol. The restaurant was quiet for the moment and she had the terrace to herself. Doubtless some locals would be inside quaffing beer at the Stammtisch but she was alone on the terrace with nought but the bubbling sound of the brook in the little cleft behind the restaurant to disturb the afternoon tranquillity.

Sarah welcomed this little period of calm in the tumultuous events of the past days for she had much on her mind to reflect upon. The painful telephone interview with her mother had disturbed her greatly and she knew she had to steel herself if she were to emerge from that conflict unscathed. Then there was her father who was being unreasonably gentle and understanding with her; a far greater pressure on her she realised than her mother's obstinate hectoring. Just to add to the pressure Alan had telephoned last night as well. Alan seemed to be blissfully unaware of international time zones for he had phoned her in the late evening in America and had seemed a little put out by Sarah's undisguised annoyance at being woken at three o'clock in the morning to hear him enthusing about his career prospects.

It had not been a satisfactory phone call, Sarah had to confess. She had been irritable and barely interested in Alan's account of his successful work in America. It was unfair, she was honest enough to concede. Alan was really phoning to make her aware of just how bright his future prospects were and reassure her that that her potential fiancée had fine opportunities before him and would be able to keep his wife in a fashion which he considered she deserved. A promise of financial security and wealth was about as close to an expression of affection as Alan's inhibited emotional character was able to enunciate, Sarah realised and perhaps she should have been more sympathetic to it. Nevertheless she wished that just once he might be able to say, "I love you and I miss you terribly!"; a short sentence that would have elicited a far more positive reaction from her than the detailed accounts of his dealings with some firm apparently manufacturing air-conditioning units. Sarah had no head for the finer nuances of corporate finance and, at three in the morning, Alan might as well have been talking about the wave properties of sub-atomic particles for all that she could make head or tail of it. In the end she had cut him off quite abruptly, saying that she needed her sleep and had exacted no further meaningful content from the conversation other than that he hoped to see her soon. Her last thoughts before returning to slumber were that she dearly hoped he would have something more interesting to talk about when next they did meet.

Then of course was the looming confrontation with Peter to worry about. Sarah's heart fluttered in her breast every time she thought about that upcoming meeting. It presented an insolvable paradox for her. If Nicole was right then Peter was about to stake his own claims for Sarah's affections and that opened up a Pandora's box of complications. On the one hand there was a part of her that truly desired to hear Peter's declaration of love for her. It was something that deep down she had expected to hear for many years but it had not been forthcoming. Now it seemed as if it might and that would really throw the cat among the pigeons. What if he asked her to leave Alan and marry him? What the devil would she say? If she said yes then she would be defying the wishes of her family in even more dramatic a fashion than her sister had. It would be carnage! Total alienation didn't even come into it! Alan's family was nearly joined at the waist to Sarah's. To turn Alan down for what, to be honest, was a humble cowherd would bring the wrath of her family down on her head like all the demons of hell. Her sister had, it is true, defied her family in marriage but she had, at least, had the sense to marry someone with some future prospects, albeit ones that were not immediately evident. Eventually they had achieved financial security and her sister had been able to thumb her nose at her family's misgivings. That was not a particularly obvious option in Peter's case. Peter was a dear man, gentle to the core and she loved him greatly, but he was about as ambitious as one of the cows he was currently spending his time attending to. Sarah wished fervently that he could show a little more personal aspiration. Her carefully husbanded finances would seem awfully thin in a prospective marriage to a person of such unworldly sense of enterprise.

Should she marry for love then? Was her love for Peter sufficient to ride the inevitable shoals of financial crisis that would be part and parcel of their life together? Alan after all, despite his faults, was a good man and certainly destined to be a rich one. Would she, could she abandon that safety net for a man who, however sweet he might be, she would spend her life with worrying over how they would pay the bills and with her family unforgiving in their rejection of their chosen suitor for her? If Peter declared his hand she would have some terrible decisions to make.

Last but not least among Sarah's ruminations was Daniela Devin. There at least was one forthcoming encounter she was looking forward to. Oddly, it had not hugely disturbed her to learn that Daniela was possibly lesbian. Sarah felt that Daniela was not a woman that would exploit her celebrity status to seduce a confused young woman. There was a genuine warmth to her that transcended sexual roles. She might be lesbian but Sarah did not feel threatened by that. Sarah felt sure that Daniela would respect her and be fully aware that she was in a relationship with a man. She would be able to tell Daniela that she was not inclined towards her own sex and Daniela would fully understand and respect that without it souring their friendship. Nicole's teasing and stories of rumours concerning Sarah's sexual ambiguity notwithstanding, Sarah was not a lesbian was she? She had never had sex with another girl. She had always been completely heterosexual in all her relationships hadn't she? Of course she'd experienced the girlish crushes that every young teenager went through during their formative years and some of those had involved other girls but that was completely normal, wasn't it? She had never, in spite of her somewhat rebellious rejection of the trappings of femininity, ever given anybody any reason to doubt the orientation of her sexual preferences had she?

Until now. Yes there was the rub wasn't it? Sarah took a deep breath on the quiet of the Gade terrace. The waitresses hadn't seen her apparently for she was still waiting to be served. She didn't mind. Her head was suddenly in turmoil. Sarah, as it has been already noted, was a girl capable of being honest with herself and that honesty was troubling her now. Why, she asked herself, was she more excited about the prospect of meeting a beautiful and charismatic woman than in meeting either of the two men to whom she might find herself married? It wasn't just Daniela's celebrity status she knew. She was genuinely thrilled at the thought of spending an evening with the woman that had touched her deep in some part of her that she had never seen before. She knew that she looked beautiful today. Even without Nicole's interest in the affair, she would have dressed to her best for this meeting. Sarah smoothed the soft material of her dress. It was telling that dress she realised. She had never gone to such trouble to dress attractively for a man before. She actually *wanted* Daniela to find her attractive. Nicole's teasing had been very close to the mark. This was not simply a matter of dining out with a friend. It was a date! She had got dressed up for a date.

Sarah shook her head in confusion. How did you dress for a date with another woman? Daniela was the most feminine of women. Were you supposed to dress in a more masculine style to attract her or was that just a cliché that a feminine woman was attracted to a masculine woman? In any event Sarah was dressed in a more feminine style than she could recall ever having done before. She was dressed positively flirtatiously. Why had she felt the need to show her femininity to this woman when she had rarely if ever done so to the men in her life?

Sarah bit her lip and, in an uncharacteristically sensual motion, she stroked a fingernail across her bare cleavage. "Am I attracted to her?" she asked herself brutally. The answer came from a deep and secret well within. "Yes I am! She is soft and sweet and oh so ever beautiful and I want to stroke her, caress her, taste her lips on mine and....." Sarah shook the disturbing thoughts from her mind. In shock she realised that she had been caressing her breast as she thought of Daniela. "Stop being so stupid!" she told herself. "You're letting yourself be beglamoured by a famous beautiful woman. Even if she was a lesbian whatever makes you think she would look twice at you? She must have thousands of silly young girls she could bed. She's a rock and roll star! She's probably got groupies crawling out of the woodwork."

Sarah set her lip and watched a little White Wagtail that was flitting around on the fringes of the restaurant terrace. It was a handsome little bird in blacks, whites and greys; its impossibly long tail constantly twitching as it scampered restlessly about seeking crumbs that previous occupants of the terrace had left. Sarah regarded it fondly willing tranquillity on herself. Daniela had told her she was special. Did she mean that? Or was she, Sarah, just a little bird wagging its tail around an illustrious star seeking crumbs?

"Entschuldigung Fräulein! Ich habe sie nicht gesehen!"

Sarah span in her seat in surprise. The young waitress was hovering behind her. Sarah recognised her. "Hoi Maggie! Wie gehts?"

"Oh it's you Sarah. Good thank you. Can I get you something?"

"Just a coffee thank you Maggie. I'm going up to the Hotel Toggenburg after a job shortly and it won't do to be smelling of alcohol."

"Ok. Straight away."

"Oh and another thing Maggie. Is the restaurant booked up for tonight?"

"Not as far as I know Sarah. Were you wanting to book a table?"

"Yes please. Are you still doing a Tartar Hut?"

"Yes. Is that what you wanted?"

"Yes I'd like to pre-order that."

"No problem. How many people?"

"Just two."

"Is Nicky joining you?"

"No she has to work tonight."

"Oh er... somebody special then?"

"Just a friend Maggie."

"Ok I'll put you on the best table upstairs. What time shall I book you for?"

"About half past seven. Is that ok?"

"Yes of course."

"Oh yes and Maggie.... I don't want my guest to pay for the meal so can I prepay everything?"

"Sure Sarah. Just give me your card and I'll set up a tab for you."

"Great! I'll want a Tartar Hut for two and could you bring me the wine list so I can pre-order?"

"Will do Sarah. Do you want me to put aperitifs, coffee and digestifs on your bill too?"

"Yes please."

"Ok I'll just open a tab on your card and you can sign for everything at the end."

"Thanks Maggie."

"Ok I'll go and get your coffee."

From the wine menu, Sarah chose a fine red wine; a Premier Crus Pinot Noir from the Clos Saint-Denis in the Burgundy of France. It was indulgent, she knew, and it was the most expensive red wine on the menu but it seemed a shame to spoil the ship for want of a ha'porth of tar. The whole meal was liable to cost her a considerable amount but Sarah's normal frugality was tempered by a desire to demonstrate that she came not to the meeting as some star-struck young supplicant in thrall to Daniela's fortune. She had her own money. She would not have it said of her that she was a parasite upon her new friend's riches. Daniela might protest that she should pick up the bill for the evening's fare but Sarah was prepared to be stubborn and insistent. She would meet Daniela as equal or not at all.

Satisfied with her choices for the evening, Sarah finished her coffee and took once more to the road. It was not a long walk up to the Hotel Toggenburg but it had rarely taken Sarah longer to negotiate. She reflected ruefully that she seemed destined to meet Daniela whilst suffering from podiatric problems for the unfamiliar high heels were a purgatory as she winced on her way up the hill in less than elegant fashion. There was a short cut across the meadows from the Gade but her choice of footwear precluded her taking that option. She considered removing her sandals and walking the distance barefoot but she could imagine Nicole falling down in a dead faint at the thought. Nicole had spent some time on her pedicure; trimming and painting her toenails and she would have been more than dissatisfied by Sarah undoing all her careful ministrations by subjecting her feet to the less than tender mercies of a dirty tarmac road. Sarah paused to lean on a fence post to rub her feet with a sour face. She was learning that femininity came at a price.

Chapter Twenty-One

The big hotel, on the top bend, at Schwendi was quiet as Sarah stumbled in through the foyer. The reception desk was empty and so, wriggling her toes to ease their discomfort, she walked through into the restaurant. It was deserted. Sarah supposed that whatever guests the hotel had were out for the day. Feeling a little foolish, she took a table in the big window overlooking the grand view of the valley beneath. Taking her seat, Sarah noted she was not entirely alone in the hotel for an elderly couple occupied a table on the sun terrace beyond her window. They formed a touching tableau Sarah observed in pleasure for, despite their advanced age, they were holding hands affectionately. With a flutter in her heart Sarah wondered at the kind of love that survived even into the twilight of one's life. The old lady's hair was grey and thinning and her face was deeply wrinkled but, to her old husband clutching her hand, she had seemingly never lost the beauty that had carried his heart in his youth. Sarah found the old man's evident pleasure in his wife curiously moving.

The elderly couple were evidently awaiting their order it seemed for, at that moment, a young waitress hurried out from the kitchen doors bearing two plates full of food; lean sliced veal in mushroom and cream sauce with rosti Sarah saw; a speciality of eastern Switzerland called veal Zurichoise. The waitress noted Sarah with a shock and nodded an acknowledgement to her before taking the steaming plates out to the terrace. She was a small dark-haired girl Sarah had never seen before. After delivering the food to the elderly couple, she was at Sarah's table briskly, taking an order pad from her apron.

"Greuzi Fräulein. Was kann ich sie bringen?"

"Oh just a coffee please. Tell me is Frau Fritzl in the house?"

"Yes Miss. At least she was a minute ago. You wish to speak to her?" The girl had a Latin sort of accent that Sarah suspected was Portuguese.

"Yes please. That is if she's not too busy."

"Do you have appointment Fräulein?"

"No I'm afraid not but I know Frau Fritzl well."

"What name shall I give Fräulein?"

"Sarah, Sarah Fuchs."

"Thank you Fraulein Fuchs. I go see her after I bring your coffee."

Frau Fritzl was never too busy to see Sarah for she adored her and the intelligence that Sarah was in the restaurant. desirous of speech with her, brought the matron of the Hotel Toggenburg quickly in typically flamboyant fashion. "SARAH!" she boomed rushing into the restaurant with her arms held wide. "Liebchen! Great God! How wonderful."

Sarah rose politely to her feet but her eyes danced with amusement and affection for her old boss. Frau Fritzl was a tall willowy brunette, in her middle years, of passionate temperament and dramatic theatricality. Sarah held out her hand but Frau Fritzl ignored it in her haste to rush to Sarah and clasp her to her bosom. She nearly danced Sarah around the restaurant in her glee at seeing her favourite once more. "My darling!" she enthused, "My lovely Sarah! Where have you been? They told me you were back in the valley. Why haven't you been to see us before now? It's too bad of you. What have you been doing?" Sarah found no chance to answer the barrage whilst being crushed to Frau Fritzl's chest in what appeared to be a particularly incapacitating wrestling hold and having her face smothered with kisses. "Magdalena!" Frau Fritzl barked. "Champagne! Fetch us a bottle of the Dom Perignon on ice as quick as

238

you can now. Our Sarah is home again and we'll drink only the best."

Sarah gasped for breath. "Whoa! Slow down Frau Fritzl. I've got a date for dinner later and I can't get tipsy."

"Nonsense! It's nearly a year since I saw you. You'll have a drink with me."

Sarah realised that resistance was pointless. "Very well then but just one glass."

"Magdalena fetch us some olives and cheese crackers too." Frau Fritzl ordered, seemingly oblivious to Sarah's protests. Then she held Sarah at arm's length the better to look at her. "My God you look beautiful Sarah!" she enthused, "I've never seen you look so lovely. You've grown up a lot darling. University life must agree with you. What a beautiful dress."

Sarah blushed but with pleasure. "Oh I'm just dressed up to go out to dinner this evening Frau Fritzl."

Frau Fritzl grinned and pinched Sarah's cheek playfully. "With somebody special perhaps?"

"Oh just with a friend." Sarah assured her hastily.

"But of course. I'm stupid. You'll be getting married soon won't you? How is that boyfriend of yours?"

"Alan's fine but he's in America for the moment. He won't be back for weeks yet."

Frau Fritzl snorted in disgust. "The man's a fool! Fancy jetting off to foreign parts and leaving a girl like you to your own devices. If he's not careful somebody else will be snapping you up whilst he's away, playing the fool, so far from home." Frau Fritzl snatched Sarah's left hand and perused it distastefully. "He hasn't even got the sense to have put a ring on your finger. I'm telling you he'll be losing you if he doesn't look out. Men have got no sense at all. They think that they can just go gallivanting off and expect women to stay at home waiting for them. If Alan had half the gumption God granted a sparrow he'd have had you in a church long ago."

Sarah squirmed uncomfortably at Frau Fritzl's evident outrage. "Er our parents are making the arrangements for our marriage in Alan's absence Frau Fritzl. My mother is talking about us marrying at the end of summer."

"Hmmph well they'd better hurry up. A jewel like you won't be left hanging around forever. Ah here's Magdalena with the champagne. Come let's sit for a while and you can tell me all your news."

For the next half an hour Frau Fritzl grilled Sarah assiduously for news and for information on her upcoming marriage. From another person Sarah might have found the barrage of questions intrusive but Frau Fritzl was such a big-hearted lady and she so clearly adored Sarah that it was hard to be offended by it. Sarah fielded the stream of inquiry with as much diplomacy as she could muster but, beneath her exterior bonhomie and theatricality, Frau Fritzl was a shrewd woman and she began to perceive that not all was well. She was shocked to learn for instance that Alan had not yet made the engagement with Sarah official by formally asking for her hand. "Whatever is the man thinking of?" she demanded indignantly. "How the blazes does he expect to marry you at the end of summer when he hasn't even got around to asking you properly yet? Has he got bird shit for brains?"

In spite of the fact that Frau Fritzl had articulated the very objection that Sarah herself had presented to her mother Sarah found herself defending Alan. "Oh there's been an understanding for quite some time Frau Fritzl. We... er... we just decided not to become officially engaged until after I finished university. It would have distracted me from my studies if I had a marriage looming up. The trouble was that Alan had to be away on business for most of the summer so we couldn't make it official. I'm sure that once he returns he'll ask me properly. Certainly my parents and his parents expect him to do so. My mother's already been picking out wedding dresses for me."

Frau Fritzl wagged a finger under Sarah's nose. "Don't you be letting your mother hi-jack your wedding Sarah. I know what Alisha's like. If she has *her* way, she'll turn it into her own damn fashion statement. You just tell her that it's your damn wedding and you'll choose your own wedding dress, thank you very much. Take her advice by all means but, in the end, it's you that's getting married, not her."

Sarah grimaced ruefully. "That's easier said than done Frau Fritzl. She's already planning the whole thing together with a series of parties and social events leading up to the wedding. In fact she wants me down in the Ticino straight away so she can start to put everything together in earnest."

"Where are you supposed to be getting married?"

Sarah shook her head. "I've no idea really. I suppose my mother wants me to marry near Ascona."

"You can't get married in the Ticino Sarah. They're all bloody Catholics down there."

"Alan's family are Catholics Frau Fritzl."

"Good God! You mean you'd have to convert?"

"I... I don't know. I haven't really thought about it to be honest. I'm not very religious I'm afraid. I suppose we could get married in a civil ceremony."

Frau Fritzl shook her head. "Your mother would never go for that Sarah. If she's after planning a big wedding then it'll be a church wedding with all the trappings even if it means turning you into a papist."

"Well surely there are protestant churches in the Ticino as well."

"A few perhaps, which would mean Alan having to renounce his Catholic faith."

Sarah grimaced in confusion. "I don't think Alan is much concerned by religion Frau Fritzl. I can't ever recall him attending church except for weddings and funerals and what have you."

"And his family?"

"I think they worship the power of the almighty dollar to be honest Frau Fritzl."

"Well you'd better sort it out Sarah. I know a lot of people only pay lip service to religion in this day and age but it's important nonetheless. Do you convert to Catholicism to pander to Alan's faith or does he renounce Catholicism to embrace yours? I mean which religion do you want your children baptised into? You ought to think about it."

Sarah frowned thoughtfully. She'd never even thought about the religious complications of marrying a catholic. Sarah had a very secular view of the world. She was not atheist as such for the teachings of the Christian faith had rooted in her as a child and she had some sort of vague notion of a Christian God. Certainly, however, she was not a practising Christian and she tended to think of churches as purely ceremonial institutions because you had to hold weddings, funerals and christenings somewhere. They were just simply symbolic punctuation marks on one's journey through life and they held little spiritual meaning for her. Nevertheless it was another disturbing thought. Her mother was Anglican and her father Lutheran and Sarah had been brought up in a solidly protestant background. Inherent in that was a vague mistrust of the trappings of the Catholic faith and that was especially true in the Toggenburg.

Modern Switzerland was generally speaking a model society of religious tolerance but it had not always been the case. Indeed the Toggenburg was one of the fault lines of history when it came to religious strife within Switzerland. The great protestant leader of the

Reformation, Huldrych Zwingli had been born near Wildhaus in 1484 and died in battle with the Catholic Cantons some 47 years later. In 1712 there had even been a religious war that grew out of the Toggenburg protestant's dispute with Catholic St Gallen that was known as the Toggenburg war and led, following Catholic defeat at the battle of Villmergen, to the end of Catholic hegemony in the Swiss Confederation. The old ghosts of religious rivalry ran deep in the Toggenburg, where Zwingli's old wooden house still stood and was revered as a museum in Lisighaus.

Sarah almost felt that the renunciation of her protestant upbringing would be akin to a surrender of her Toggenburg identity. Her mother had no such allegiance to the valley and would never understand Sarah's deep-rooted feeling of belonging within it. Toggenburgers were protestant. There was a beautiful high pass out of the Toggenburg which at its height separated the Toggenburg from the Canton of Appenzell. It was called, in the Toggenburg, the Zwingli Pass but it had quite a separate name in the catholic Canton of Appenzell whose inhabitants would never acknowledge the great protestant reformist. If you scratched the surface of tolerance in the Toggenburg you'd find the old mistrust never far beneath.

Sarah shook her head with a sigh. It was just one more complication to add to her growing misgivings over her marriage. "Anyway," she said taking a cautious sip of her champagne. "I didn't just come here today on a social call Frau Fritzl."

Frau Fritzl raised her eyebrows. "Oh Really?"

"No I was wondering if you had well any work going for the summer. I know it's a bit late in the season to be looking for a summer job but I just wondered if you had any positions available."

Frau Fritzl narrowed her eyebrows and looked at Sarah carefully. "You want your old job back?"

Sarah nodded. "Well yes but, if not, anything else that's available."

Frau Fritzl bit her lip and tapped out a cigarette from the packet on the table. "I see." She took a long time to light her cigarette, marshalling her thoughts. "Well Sarah," she continued at last, "I'll be honest with you. I've more or less filled all the positions for the summer. Now if you'd asked me a month ago I'd have bitten your hand off. I wish you *had* asked me. I'd have kept a place open for you without doubt. You're the best worker and the most reliable I've ever had. Certainly you could have taught the girls I have got a thing or two. Magdalena there is a dear girl but she's apt to be a bit lazy and she has the devil of a job getting out of bed in a morning. I'd have loved to have you for the summer Sarah but I haven't any grounds to dismiss the girls I've got now so I couldn't in all honesty offer you a full-time job. Now that doesn't mean that there's no work going at all. In fact we've got a busy summer ahead of us and we've got some big parties booked, as well as a few big functions and I'll need to take on temporary help to take up the slack from time to time. Now if you were looking for some temporary work we could do business Sarah but, I'm afraid, unless we lose somebody along the way, that it will only be that temporary work when I'd maybe have to call you in for a couple of days a week as and when necessary."

Sarah nodded in understanding. "Well I still might be interested Frau Fritzl. I'm really looking for something to supplement my finances through the summer. Even if it was only a couple of days a week I'd be interested."

"I don't know that it *would* be a couple of days Sarah. There might be times when I'd need you all week and then others when I didn't need you at all. It would have to be very flexible according to what we had on that week. Now I'd love to have you but I'd quite understand if somebody else offered you something a little more reliable as regards working hours."

Sarah leaned back in her chair thoughtfully. "Well actually this might work out rather well Frau Fritzl. If I have marriage plans coming up then I'll need to stay flexible as well. It's probably to my advantage to not have permanent commitments. If I were to let you know when I'm available you'd be able to call me up in the event of your requiring somebody at short notice to cover some eventuality and we'd both gain."

Frau Fritzl took a long drag of her cigarette and regarded Sarah in puzzlement. "Why Sarah?"

"Well you'd have somebody available at short notice without having to pay them a regular salary and..."

"No, no Sarah. I don't mean what's the advantage to me. What I want to know is why you need a job."

"Well Frau Fritzl I do have some money for the summer but I'd still welcome some extra income. If I'm getting married at the end of summer I don't want to exhaust my savings do I?"

Frau Fritzl shook her head slowly. "You're not happy about this marriage are you Sarah?"

"Whatever do you mean?"

"Sarah I don't know exactly whatever it is that Alan does for a living but I do know that he earns a large salary doing it. He earns a large enough salary to afford an expensive car, to fly down to Portugal to play bloody golf and to deck himself out in expensive designer clothes. I am certain beyond doubt that he earns enough money to relieve you of personal financial worries whilst you wind up your affairs in the Toggenburg and concentrate on planning your marriage. Even if *he* doesn't support you for the summer your family will Sarah. Now I know from experience that putting a marriage together is a lot of work Sarah and taking on a job you don't really need doesn't seem to be particularly conducive to that end. So why do you want a job?"

Sarah sighed and put down her glass. "I don't know Frau Fritzl. Pride, I suppose. I don't want to be a kept woman. I want to show that I'm more than capable of looking after myself; that I can make my own money. I don't want to be bartered off into marriage as a prize cow. I want to prove I'm independent. I don't just want to be a kept housewife."

"It's a full-time job being a housewife Sarah."

"Perhaps but I haven't spent three years at university to gain a degree just to clean house and cook meals for the rest of my days."

"You don't need to have a university degree to wait on my tables either."

"No but at least it will be something I'm doing on my own. It might not be the career I wanted but it's something."

"What career did you want?"

Sarah shook her head sadly. "Well I suppose I had dreams once.... you know taking a Master's degree maybe even a Doctorate but...."

"But you're getting married instead?"

"Oh hell! I don't know. Do you have to give up all your dreams just to get married? Men don't seem to."

"You're right they don't. On the contrary a good marriage can be a sound career move for them. It can be tough being a woman Sarah."

Sarah nodded in wry agreement. "Tell me about it. Sometimes I wonder if Emily Davidson died in vain."

Frau Fritzl snorted in amusement. "In this country she probably did Sarah. Don't forget that Switzerland was the last country in Europe or any western democracy come to that to grant women universal suffrage. We didn't get suffrage until 1971 in Federal elections and even then some Cantons held out against female suffrage in Cantonal elections until well into the eighties.

Appenzell Inneroden didn't finally give women the right to vote until 1990 for God's sake! You're living in the dark ages when it comes to women's rights in this country Sarah."

Sarah frowned. "Are we still second-class citizens then?"

"Well not according to the Article 8 of the revised Federal Constitution, which was altered following a referendum in 1981 Sarah, but it seems that nobody's mentioned the fact to our men folk sometimes." Frau Fritzl paused to extinguish her cigarette. "I think I can work out what all this is about Sarah. I think you're uncertain about this marriage and you need time to think about it. Am I right?"

"I guess you're not far wrong Frau Fritzl."

"Well Sarah I married for all the wrong reasons and it took fifteen years of hell for me to finally get shut of my husband. I'd hate you to make the same mistake I did. Ok then, as far as I can, I'll help you. I think what we've talked about is a fine idea. I'll certainly need extra help from time to time over the summer and what's more I know nearly every other hotelier and restaurant owner in this valley and they'll certainly need extra help on occasion as well. If you like we can set up a situation where you'd be available to expedite in any locale, requiring your services at short notice, throughout the summer. Between all the hotels and other places we can certainly keep you busy until autumn and you'd still be free of any long-term commitment should your wedding plans require it. Would that give you the independence you require?"

"It sounds great Frau Fritzl."

"Well it could work out rather well. There's always a need for people that can pop in to help out when there's a sudden rush on or when somebody falls ill or whatever. You'll probably find yourself with more work than you need but you'll be able to pick and choose where and when you want to work. Would that suit you?"

"Yes! Yes it would."

"Ok then give me a couple of days to make a few phone calls and we can set you up. Now then stop looking so glum and have some more champagne."

"Oh I really mustn't Frau Fritzl. I've got a date for dinner and I don't want to turn up half canned."

"Just who are you meeting for dinner?"

Sarah blushed and hated herself for the overt demonstration. "Well actually it's a girl I met recently that's come to live in the Toggenburg. I don't think she knows many people locally and I said I'd take her out to dinner to get to know her. She's very nice and quite famous apparently."

Frau Fritzl laughed shortly. "She wouldn't happen to be called Daniela Devin would she Sarah?"

"Why yes! Do you know her?"

"Oh Sarah everybody in the valley knows of Miss Devin. I've met her several times myself. She often pops in here for a drink or a bite to eat. She's a lovely girl and very talented."

"Yes she seems so."

"Oh she is. She's one of those people you just can't help liking and fame doesn't seem to have gone to her head. She's always very polite and friendly. My girls love it when she pops in because she's always generous with her tips."

"Yes I've seen that." Sarah told Frau Fritzl with a laugh.

Frau Fritzl picked up her cigarettes with an amused smile and tapped out another one to light. Sarah worried that she was smoking too much. "You know it's funny Sarah."

"What is Frau Fritzl?"

"Oh call it a hunch; an intuition if you like, but I had the feeling that you and Daniela would meet up at some point."

Sarah frowned. "You're not the first person to say that Frau Fritzl. But why; I mean what makes you say that?"

"I don't know myself Sarah. I guess it's just because you and Daniela seem to be cut from the same cloth; kindred sisters if you like."

Sarah laughed. "I'm hardly a rock and roll star Frau Fritzl."

"No your talents lie in other directions Sarah. Nevertheless there's something akin between the two of you. You're both brilliant, beautiful and have that special quality about you that makes people love you. You'd make natural friends. You'd gel together instantly and make a force to be reckoned with."

Sarah looked at Frau Fritzl intently wondering if there was some hidden meaning behind her words. "Nicole tells me that Daniela might be a lesbian Frau Fritzl. Is that true?"

"I have no idea Sarah. It's not generally my policy to ask my customers personal questions."

"I'm sorry! Of course not."

"Are you worried about it Sarah?"

"Well I don't know. A little bit I suppose."

"Are you lesbian Sarah?"

Sarah's eyes shot open in shock. "Good God! Whatever makes you ask that?"

"Oh don't get so het up Sarah. It was just a question. I just noted that when you said you were seeing Miss Devin you blushed to the root of your hairs. I've known you for a long time Sarah and I've never seen you dress up so nicely to go out to dinner with somebody before. Then you tell me that you're having doubts about your marriage and now you're going out to see a woman who may or may not be inclined towards members of her own sex and you put your sexiest frock on for the occasion. Well I can't help it if I ask questions now can I?"

"Frau Fritzl! I can't believe you're thinking this. I have a boyfriend for heaven's sake."

"So? I had a husband for fifteen long years before I got rid of the bastard."

"But you're not lesbian."

"Well don't tell my girlfriend that."

"*WHAT?*"

"I said don't tell Angelica that."

"Angelica? The lady that helps out in the hotel?"

"Yes! My girlfriend, my beloved, my, how do you call it nowadays, my significant other half."

"*Impossible!*"

"All too possible Sarah. I'm surprised you don't know. I don't hide the fact. Angelica has been my partner for five years now and I'm proud of it. She's given me more love and joy than ever I got out of fifteen years with the scumbag I married."

"I don't believe this. I never knew."

"Does it make you feel any the less respect for me Sarah?"

"No. No of course not. It's your own private affair Frau Fritzl."

"Yet you seemed shocked when I asked you if *you* were lesbian; quite outraged in fact; as if you thought it was a mortal insult."

"I... I didn't mean to... well to cast aspersions Frau Fritzl."

"Perhaps you were so shocked because there was some truth in it Sarah. Tell me something. Are you attracted to Daniela Devin?"

"I can't possibly answer that question Frau Fritzl!"

"Elke!"

"What?"

"Elke Sarah. It's my name! Stop calling me Frau Fritzl for heaven's sake. It makes me sound like somebody who runs a chip stall."

"I'm sorry but you've always been Frau Fritzl to me."

"Well not anymore. If I'm going to tell you private details about myself you can damn well call me by my Christian name. Now you don't have to answer my question Sarah because I can read the answer on your face. I just want to tell you to be careful Sarah. I don't have a daughter of my own but I've always thought of you as a surrogate daughter Sarah and I'm worried about you."

"I'd be proud to be your daughter.... Elke."

"You should be proud of the mother you've got as well Sarah. Oh I know Alisha's a difficult woman at times and I've not always seen eye to eye with her but she's a fine woman for all that. She was a great beauty in her day Sarah. You get your looks from her. But people get older and start to lose their looks. It's harder on some people than others Sarah and I think it's hard on your mother. I think she looks at her life and sees all the things that might have been; the things she missed and maybe she's a little too demanding on her children as a result. You should understand that Sarah."

"You're changing the subject. You said you were worried about me. Why?"

Frau Fritzl sighed. "Because I think you might be heading for a crisis Sarah. Don't ask me why I think that because it's only a hunch. I don't think you're ready for marriage yet. I think you still have some issues to be sorted out."

"Issues?"

"Yes. Issues such as Daniela Devin or, if not her, then somebody like her."

Chapter Twenty-Two

It was nearly twenty past six before Sarah finally left the Hotel Toggenburg. The champagne she had been unable to refuse was going to her head but she was not yet tipsy. Her mind, instead, was fixed on the strange conversation she had shared with Frau Fritzl and the complex ramifications of it. In a sense, the visit had been a success. Sarah had obtained just what she wanted in regard to a job. It was an excellent solution, as far as she was concerned. There'd certainly be enough temporary work around the valley to keep her in pocket and, with Frau Fritzl to recommend her, then there'd be people jumping into her lap to employ her. Frau Fritzl was deeply respected in the valley and her opinion valued. With luck then, Sarah would have all the employment she desired.

Nevertheless Sarah was discomfited. It had shocked her when Frau Fritzl had confessed to being in a relationship with another woman. Sarah wondered if Nicole knew about it. Certainly she had never mentioned it. Sarah had been even more shocked when Frau Fritzl had obliquely suggested that Sarah also had feelings for women. It wasn't something Sarah had actually ever really examined about herself until now. She'd always considered herself unambiguously heterosexual. She found men attractive. There was no doubt about that. There were some men that she truly thought sexy. Alan was an attractive man. Anybody could have told you that. He was tall with handsome classical features and fine physique. Most girls thought him a dream of a man. Peter in his own way was also a very good-looking man with his fine muscled body and his dreamy romantic eyes. Sarah knew that, had he ever shown a physical interest in her, then she would have been a pushover to drag into bed.

So why now were there question marks over her sexuality? First Nicole and now Frau Fritzl had, in a round-about sort of way, suggested that Sarah's own sexual orientation was not as clear cut as she had fondly believed and the main reason for this was the introduction into her life of a beautiful woman, over whose own sexual preferences there was raised some considerable question mark. Sarah told herself that it was ridiculous that people might consider her lesbian just because she was meeting a girl who might possibly be so. After all she had known lesbians before.

At university, there had been several girls who had made no attempt to conceal their sexual orientation in that regard. One of them had even been a friend of hers and apt to join her circle of friends in the university bar. There'd never been the slightest hint that Sarah would ever have been attracted to her. The girl had been into dressing in a Goth style; all garish face paint, black and blood red outrageous clothing adorned with pewter skulls, silver gargoyles and other Gothic imagery. She'd worn a blood red highlight in her jet-black hair, worn black fishnet tights with holes in them, under startlingly short skirts, and had shown a penchant for bondage paraphernalia and skin piercings. Sarah had liked her. She'd been a lot of fun, although apt to drink too much on occasion. In their last year at university, the girl had gone steady with a girl studying sport sciences and it hadn't worried Sarah in the slightest. She'd always considered herself as tolerant of people's sexual orientation. So why was she so disturbed to find that other people were starting to question her own?

The truth was that, for the first time, Sarah was posing that very question herself. Frau Fritzl had seen it and, in another sort of way, so had Nicole. Sarah *was* attracted to Daniela. She was excited about meeting her. In fact Sarah had not felt so excited about a date in years. It had that quivering feeling of anticipation you felt

253

when a really gorgeous man invited you out for a date; a feeling that the night ahead held promise of enchantment and excitement. Sarah's limited sexual experience gave her few comparative scenarios to judge her mood by but she knew that she was captivated by Daniela. Every time she thought of her new friend her eyes grew misty, her face softened and she found herself stroking the material of her dress sensually.

Still with her mind in turmoil, Sarah descended the road toward the Gade restaurant. She was early. The meeting was for seven o'clock but Sarah saw no reason not to arrive early and make sure that everything was in order with her booking. As soon as Sarah stepped onto the path leading from the road to the Gade, she saw Daniela. She was sitting on the terrace at the back, glorious in a pleated blue and white empire waisted halter cocktail dress. There were sapphires set on a white gold chain about her neck, matching her earrings and her wavy golden hair had a blue flower set among its luxurious tresses. There were expensive white, rhinestone encrusted, open toed, high heeled sandals on her delicate feet and a bracelet of lapis lazuli about her slim right wrist. Sarah caught her breath. Daniela looked beautiful; heartbreakingly beautiful.

Daniela didn't see Sarah for she was engaged in conversation with some people at the next table. In a trance like daze, Sarah descended the path toward the terrace her eyes never leaving Daniela; willing her friend to look around and see her. Daniela did see her for her eyes were flickering constantly in the direction of the road. Sarah saw to the moment when Daniela recognised her presence. Daniela jumped to her feet; her face suddenly radiant with unconcealed delight. She seemed to glow with sudden joy and Sarah felt her heart jump in her breast. Daniela's partners in conversation found themselves neglected as Sarah stepped over the last flagstones of the path and Daniela rushed to meet her.

Sarah had been worried about this moment; about how she would greet Daniela. She'd worried about the right mixture of warm formal greeting and friendliness. In the event the situation was taken out of her hands for Daniela was overtly affectionate and she grasped Sarah in her arms and pressed her lips to her cheek. Sarah felt curious sensations overwhelm her as Daniela pressed her body close and hugged her without, it seemed, any desire to let her go. "Oh Sarah! You came."

"Of course I came. I did say I was coming."

Daniela laughed. "Forgive me Sarah. I was worried you wouldn't come. Silly of me."

"You're early." Sarah told her with a smile.

"So are you."

Sarah glanced at her watch guiltily. It read half past six. "Yes er... I suppose I am."

"We must both have been looking forward to seeing each other." Daniela took a step back and held Sarah at arm's length by the elbows. "Let me look at you. God you look fabulous; sensational! You're wearing green. That's brilliant!"

Sarah grinned. She found Daniela's uninhibited pleasure and enthusiasm infectious. "Why should it be brilliant that I'm wearing green?" she asked in amusement.

Daniela laughed and grasped Sarah once more to kiss her on the cheek. "Ah now that's a surprise but I'll tell you later. Just let's say that it's perfect." Daniela grasped Sarah's hand and pulled her to her table. "Come on, let's sit down and have an aperitif before we eat. Beguiled by her friend's obvious pleasure, Sarah allowed herself to be steered to the table. Daniela would not allow her to sit opposite her but instead pulled her down onto the bench to sit next to her and refused to relinquish her hand. Daniela's lovely blue eyes were dancing with pleasure and Sarah realised that she was not the only one that had been anticipating this meeting with excitement.

"Oh God Sarah I have been so looking forward to this evening." Daniela told her whilst squeezing her hand.

"I've been looking forward to it too Danny." Sarah choked, cursing herself that her voice didn't seem to be working properly.

Sarah glanced around her nervously. The restaurant terrace had filled up since her visit in the afternoon and a number of people were regarding Daniela's effusive greeting of her with interest and amusement. Some people were overtly staring. It didn't seem to worry Daniela however. "We have so much to talk about." she told Sarah enthusiastically. "Let's get you a drink first though. What will you have?"

Sarah laughed. "I'd better go easy Danny. I've just soaked up half a bottle of champagne complements of Frau Fritzl at the Hotel Toggenburg."

Daniela cocked her head on one side in interest; a gesture that was characteristic of her. "Oh really? I know Frau Fritzl. I like her."

"She's very fond of you too Daniela. Before I left, she said to say hello to you."

Daniela smiled hugely. "That was sweet of her. What were you doing drinking champagne with her?"

"Oh it's just a long time since she's seen me and she's a bit of a flamboyant sort of person; insisted on sharing a bottle of bubbly to mark my return to the valley. I had to tell her to slow down or I'd have ended up rat-faced. I didn't want to show you up in public."

Daniela's grin became even wider and she impulsively raised Sarah's hand to her lips to kiss her fingers. "Don't worry darling. I'll make sure you get home before you disgrace yourself."

Sarah's heart fluttered at the intimate gesture that seemed to come so naturally to her uninhibited friend. "Oh er... don't worry I er... managed to make her drink most of it."

Daniela tossed her hair and laughed. "When I'm in those situations I usually try to place myself strategically by a large potted plant. I must have killed dozens of perfectly innocent pot-plants with alcohol poisoning down the years."

Sarah laughed enjoying Daniela's company immensely. "Well I think I put a bit of a backward stagger in her rubber plant but for God's sake don't tell her that."

"Were you visiting her socially then?"

"No actually I was after a job."

"A job?"

"Yes I used to work for her and I went up to see if I could have my old job back."

"Well she'd better have enough money to pay you well."

Sarah frowned. "I'm sure she'll pay me properly Daniela. What makes you think otherwise?"

"Well because I'll offer you a job; my personal dinner companion and mountain guide and I'll out-match anything Frau Fritzl cares to put on the table."

Sarah couldn't help but laugh. "Stop it Danny! You're embarrassing me."

"Well God forbid I should do that. Where is that waitress? You must be thirsty. Maybe we'd better ask her to bring us some menus too."

Sarah grimaced in embarrassment. "Oh Danny I hope you won't be angry with me but I've already ordered our dinner."

Daniela inclined her head and regarded Sarah quizzically. "You've already ordered? How did you manage that trick? I'd swear I haven't taken my eyes off you since the moment you arrived. Did I faint or something and you managed to get the order in while I was unconscious?"

Sarah laughed. "No Danny. I came here earlier on my way up to the Hotel Toggenburg and pre-ordered our dinner."

Daniela smiled. "May I be allowed to ask what we're having then?"

"I've ordered a Tartar Hut for both of us. It's a speciality of the house."

Daniela frowned. "You mean steak tartare?"

Sarah shook her head. "No Danny although the name has a similar origin. Steak tartare is a dish of raw minced beef seasoned with spices, onions and capers that is supposedly named after the Tartar nomadic tribes of Central Asia according to legend. Actually it's a myth. Steak tartare is actually named after tartar sauce which was served on the side when the dish was first introduced in French restaurants at the beginning of the twentieth century when it was more usually known as Steak a L'Americaine or Filet Americaine. The story that the dish got its name from the raw beef that Tartar horsemen kept under their saddles to tenderise during the day's riding is almost certainly fabrication."

Daniela's grin became huge. "Every time I ask you a question I get an in-depth resume and analysis. Where do you get all this stuff from?"

"Oh I'm sorry. Was I boring you?"

"Not at all. I find your depths of knowledge fascinating. It's like having Google on draft."

Sarah smiled sheepishly. "I'm sorry Danny! I just have the sort of head that soaks up trivial information. I'm always boring people with useless facts. Just slap me if I start to ramble."

"I wouldn't dream of it. I could listen to you all night. So tell me then, what is Tartar Hut?"

"Well it's a bit of a Swiss speciality and it's called Tartar hut after a Tartar's hat which is the meaning of the word hut in English."

Daniela grimaced comically. "Is this the beef they kept under their hats then? It would appear that they either consumed meat that had been festering under their hats all day or alternatively been residing under their backsides. Now I may be wrong but I'm guessing that a nomadic tribe of horsemen weren't overly big on personal hygiene so if I'm ever unfortunate enough to be invited to dinner with a Tartar family, I think I'll decline!"

Sarah laughed, enjoying her friend's company immensely. "Oh no it's nothing like that. The Tartars were known for wearing conical hats with a wide upturned brim. The meal gets its name from the shape of their hats."

Daniela lifted up her hands in surrender. "Ok I'm baffled. I guess I'll just have to wait and see."

Sarah nodded with a grin. "Yes. I'm sure all will become clear in due course."

"Are we drinking wine with the meal? I've left the car at home so I wouldn't have to worry about driving home if I get tiddly."

"Oh I wondered why your car wasn't on the car park. Have you walked over here then?"

"Yes. It's not that far from Oberdorf."

Sarah pointed to Daniela's feet. "It is in those heels!"

"I took my shoes off and cut through the meadows where I could. I love feeling the grass under my feet." Daniela nodded at Sarah's feet. "You've got high heels on as well and you've a lot further to come than me."

"Oh Nicole gave me a lift and she says she'll pick me up after work as well, which is a good job because I can't walk any distance in these wretched shoes. It was torment enough just getting up the road to Schwendi."

Daniela smiled slowly. "Well you look lovely in them Sarah. You have beautiful feet."

Sarah frowned in puzzlement. "I never really think about my feet very much other than as a purely functional set of appendices. I mean it never occurs to me to think of them in decorative terms."

"Well you should because you have lovely shapely feet. Anyway you seem to have taken some trouble over them. I see you've painted your toenails."

"Oh hell that wasn't me! Nicole insisted on giving me a pedicure job before I left the house. She did my hair and make-up as well and she made me wear this dress. I'm hopeless with things like that. Nicole's always badgering me to dress up a little."

"Well her efforts are well rewarded. You look stunning."

Sarah swallowed hastily. "Anyway I never answered your question. Yes we are drinking wine. I've already ordered a bottle."

Daniela lifted her eyebrows in amusement. "You seem to have organised things very thoroughly Sarah."

Sarah blushed. "I... I didn't wish to be presumptuous Daniela."

"I'm not offended Sarah. On the contrary; I'm touched. I'm touched that you went to so much trouble."

Sarah raised her eyes to look at Daniela sheepishly. "I... I'm sorry Danny... I didn't want to well... be too forward. I'm afraid I have a confession to make."

"Oh really?"

"Yes I... well I didn't just pre-order the dinner... I... well I've prepaid it as well. I wanted this evening to be my treat for you. I didn't want you to pay a thing."

"Sarah!"

"It's no good protesting Danny. I know you've got far more money than I have but I'll not hear of you paying for anything. This is my treat."

Daniela grasped Sarah's hand impulsively and gazed into Sarah's face; the impossibly blue orbs searching Sarah's features intensely. When she spoke her voice was husky with emotion. "Sarah have you any idea how long it is since somebody actually took me out and bought me dinner? Thank you. I... I feel truly privileged. You've no idea how much this means to me." To Sarah's shock Daniela turned her head aside quickly and reached into her handbag for a tissue to dab away a tear at her eye. "Thank you Sarah." she repeated. "This is very special to me."

Sarah sat transfixed, unable to speak as she watched Daniela struggle with her emotions. "Please," she said feebly. "It's nothing really." Sarah's words sounded trite and meaningless to her and she realised that somehow the underlying tensions in this meeting had notched up a little.

Daniela took a grip on herself and raised her face to Sarah once more. Sarah's heart fluttered at the beautiful face, softly illuminated with a gentle but sweetly sad smile. "No Sarah it's everything. Forgive my foolishness. I find you touch me in ways that I thought were lost to me. You truly are somebody special." For long seconds they stared at each other and, for one mad moment, Sarah felt the urge to lean over and kiss those captivating lips. She knew it was madness. She knew that once she took that step she would be irrevocably lost. At this inopportune time Maggie, the waitress, finally arrived and the moment was lost.

They ordered Campari Oranges for an aperitif and the chilled cocktails were both sweet and tart with bitterness; sharpening their appetites as they sipped them slowly, pausing often to look at each other, both clearly fascinated by what they saw. They talked quietly to each other and, if their conversation was seemingly without serious content, then their hands touching on the table told a tale that went deeper than the triviality of their words. In the evening sunshine on the terrace Sarah found herself swimming in unfamiliar waters.

She had never known an intensity in another person's presence to match that she experienced with Daniela. She found herself even glancing at Daniela's bosom fascinated by the soft curves of her breasts and the inviting valley of her cleavage. She was entranced by the great waves of silky blond hair that cascaded over Daniela's shoulders, in such luxurious abandonment, and the urge to stroke it was like an unfulfilled ache in her belly.

Daniela had a characteristic gesture in which she would frequently lift a hand to stroke a finger down the side of her long neck. To Sarah's fevered mind the gesture was almost an invitation; a seductive enticement to stroke that neck for her and to tease it with soft kisses. In her imagination she could see Daniela close her eyes at the touch of the caress and part her lips, glistening with moisture and her face flushed pink as the blood rushed to the surface. Sarah found her breathing grow deeper at the thought and she knew her own face blushed revealingly. What was more disturbing yet than these thoughts was the knowledge that Daniela was equally entranced by her. Daniela couldn't seem to tear her eyes away from Sarah. She stared at her openly and hopelessly fixated in wonderment as if she was scarcely able to believe the evidence of her own eyes. At one point, a small insect of the evening flew into Sarah's hair and Daniela leaned across to brush it away for her but her fingers lingered a second to feel the softness of Sarah's dark brown hair and Sarah's longing leaped in her loins in a sudden quickening flare.

At last Maggie came to announce that their table was ready and that their dinner would be served shortly. The two girls rose and Daniela slipped an arm around Sarah's waist to guide her into dinner. No longer understanding what she was doing Sarah reciprocated and slid a hand around Daniela's slender waist feeling the warmth of her body beneath the thin fabric of her dress. She knew how the gesture would be interpreted and she was conscious of the stares from the other inhabitants of the restaurant terrace but, in her infatuation, she cared not. With their arms about each other they went upstairs for dinner.

The upstairs room of the Gade was beautiful. The Gade itself was an old converted wooden barn and the dining room was a rustic high roofed old construction of rough timber beams with antiquated old farming implements hanging on the bare wooden walls. There were flowers in boxes everywhere and the tables were covered in pink and white, chequered tablecloths and softly lit by candles. There were spotless, white linen napkins folded into fans at each setting and the table was adorned with a little floral display in the centre. Daniela took her seat in pleasure. "This is lovely." She exclaimed looking around in delight. "I never knew the upstairs of this place was so nice."

"It's one of my favourites." Sarah told her shyly. "I love this old place."

Daniela grinned and took Sarah's hand. "You keep coming up with these surprises tonight Sarah. I can't help but wonder what you're going to surprise me with next."

Sarah cleared her throat. "Er here comes Maggie with the wine." She warned.

Daniela relinquished Sarah's hand reluctantly and Maggie poured a tiny amount of the rich red wine into Sarah's glass for her to taste. Sarah knew Maggie well but the girl's face was unreadable, as she stood politely holding the bottle, as Sarah raised her glass to her lips. Sarah could well imagine the gossip that would be born this night. "It's fine Maggie." Sarah croaked and bit her lip. Maggie poured the wine and departed, leaving the bottle on the table.

Daniela took a sip and tilted the bottle to read the label. "Sarah," she said, "I don't know much about

Tartars but I do know a good wine. This is a top class Premier Crus Pinot Noir. You have fine tastes darling."

"I... I'm glad you like it."

"Oh I do." Daniela raised her glass. "A toast then."

"To what?"

"To the most beautiful girl in the Toggenburg."

Sarah grinned mischievously. "You can't propose a toast to yourself."

"Who said I was talking about me?"

"I did! There's only one contender for that title."

Daniela laughed; the liquid tone of her laugh infectious. "I disagree."

Sarah's eyes danced as she raised her glass. "Well then let's toast the most beautiful girl in the Toggenburg whoever she might be."

Daniela shook her head. "No. Better. Here's to the *two* most beautiful girls in the Toggenburg. To us."

Sarah took a breath and held Daniela's eye. "To us!" The wine goblets were huge, like small goldfish bowls and they chimed prettily as the girls tapped their glasses together.

There was a flurry from the dumb waiter and Daniela turned to regard the source of the activity. "Oh my God! What on earth is this?" Maggie and a colleague were carrying a large board between them upon which rested a large iron cone. They were carrying it carefully for the cone was obviously very hot. Gingerly they eased the apparatus onto the table and Maggie lit an oil burner beneath the hollow cone. Around the cone was a wide brim and Maggie's colleague ladled grated vegetables into the rim before filling it with hot, clear bouillon from a jug. The clear soup bubbled in the hot metal. Daniela was watching these preparations in fascination tinged with trepidation. "What the blazes is this?" she wanted to know.

"A Tartar Hut." Sarah explained. "See it's shaped like a Tartar's hat. Don't touch the metal. It's red hot."

"What the hell are we supposed to do with it?"

"You'll see."

And she did, for, next, Maggie brought out a great silver platter full of slices of uncooked meat; lean beef, veal, slivers of ostrich meat and streaky bacon. Maggie's colleague loaded up the table with bowls of salad, half a dozen different sauces in bowls, pickles and a large bowl of thin French fries. Daniela shook her head in amazement. "You can't possibly expect me to eat all this. I'll be a ruined woman."

"I'll take you hiking in the mountains. You'll soon work it all off."

"Well what do we do?"

"We use these long forks to pick up the meat and lay it on the side of the cone to grill on the hot metal. See there are spikes sticking out to hold it in place. Once it's cooked we dip it in one of the sauces and eat it. All fairly straightforward!"

"What's with the soup in the rim?"

"Oh that's for afters. As the meat cooks, all the juices trickle down the side of the cone into the soup and flavour it. When it's to our liking we drop a shot of sherry into it and drink it with a spoon." Sarah paused in her explanation to pick up a piece of bacon with her fork. "Grill the bacon first Danny because that leaves a layer of hot fat on the metal to cook the other meats in."

"This isn't a meal, it's a bloody coronary looking for somewhere to happen."

"Try it. You'll enjoy it."

Daniela did enjoy it. The meal was both fun and deeply satisfying. They would both admit that they ate too much but they took their time plucking the sizzling morsels from the hot metal to eat them with pleasure dipped in barbecue sauce, or tartar sauce, another sauce spiced with hot chillies or garlic laced mayonnaise; laughing as one of them accidentally dropped one of the pieces of meat into the rim of soup and having to recover it with a fork. They paused often to sip at their wine, nibble at some pickles or eat a couple of fries. Sarah encouraged Daniela to try one sauce by dipping a French fry into it and holding it for Daniela to pluck from her fingers with her mouth. Sarah was messy for some of the sauce dribbled onto her finger. She gasped quietly as Daniela held her hand and licked it from her finger, her eyes never leaving hers. They sampled the soup often, declaring pompously that it needed just a little more to make it perfect and giggling helplessly at the silliness of it. They were becoming tipsy too for the first bottle of wine soon became a sad and empty container to be replaced by its virgin companion. Maggie's face as she poured the second bottle was a mixture of amusement and restrained astonishment to see Sarah so uncharacteristically flirtatious and with another woman at that.

Sarah was past caring. She had never had so much fun at a dinner engagement. Everything she did with Daniela seemed so full of pleasure and laughter. It wasn't all silliness and gaiety for there were moments when they talked seriously. Sarah listened soberly as Daniela told her something of her life as a pop star and the pressures and heartbreaks that could entail. Sarah didn't press her for personal details but she could discern some of the cost and toil that Daniela's career involved. She detected a strand of loneliness behind a person who was forever in the public eye and who must need conceal her private world from the unforgiving spotlight of fame. She realised early that Daniela's pleasure in this evening was simply the gratification of relative obscurity; of a normality often lacking in her public career. She began to understand how deeply Daniela would be moved just by the gesture of a friend taking her for simple meal and how greedily she would embrace such a private moment when she was not obliged to be anything but herself. Such moments would be precious indeed to her; to be

266

savoured and jealously guarded. Such moments might be taken for granted to a person not afflicted with the trappings of fame but so terribly important to those for whom such interludes were sweet relaxations of their public lives.

In her turn, Sarah found herself talking openly and honestly about herself in far more private a fashion than she would have normally credited, given that she had known Daniela for such a short time. Once again, Sarah noted that Daniela was a good listener, rarely interrupting her except for clarification. To her own surprise, Sarah talked about her forthcoming marriage and described her misgivings with startling candour. Daniela just nodded in understanding and refused to be judgemental. Only once did Daniela venture a remark that could be interpreted as a criticism of Sarah's proposed marriage. Sarah had described her conversation with Frau Fritzl and how that lady had stated that instead of a career she was getting married instead. Daniela nodded in agreement. "I think she's right Sarah. You're way too qualified to be a housewife."

Mostly, however, they just talked of neutral matters. Sarah discovered that Daniela had a repertoire of outrageously funny anecdotes about people in the show business world and she lampooned the rich and famous mercifully although not in any way arrogantly for she was quite as ready to tell a funny story about herself. Daniela, in turn, seemed fascinated by Sarah's love of the high mountains and she grilled her incessantly on them, as if they were some mystery she longed to unravel. It seemed Daniela had been reading the field guide to alpine flowers that Sarah had given her assiduously for she frequently asked questions about it; seeking understanding of the alpine environment and its rich and specialised flora. Sarah was delighted to find such an interested and enquiring student. There was never any sense in the conversation that the famous and talented Daniela was the most interesting of the two of them. She often seemed to dismiss her own, admittedly fascinating, life to dwell on what Sarah might have considered her mundane one. Sarah had been concerned that she might not be able to meet Daniela as an equal. Daniela, it appeared, had no such qualms. It wasn't artifice either, Sarah began to understand. Daniela really accepted her as fully equal and considered her own fame as a purely accidental condition of existence and not something to boast about. Many a pop star of such renown might have been egotistical and demanding of attention. Such a condition seemed alien to Daniela.

At last they pushed their plates aside with the groans and deep breaths of two young women who have eaten far more than they considered good for them. Sarah estimated that they'd managed to consume about three quarters of the fare laid before them which was a formidable achievement for two women that looked as if neither of them had previously consumed an excess calorie in their life before. "Oh my God! I'm stuffed!" Daniela protested theatrically. "Do they have porters here? I need a couple of strong men with a sedan chair to carry me home."

Maggie came to clear the dishes. "Will you be having dessert?" she inquired innocently and Sarah dissolved in giggles as Daniela looked at her as if she'd just uttered an obscenity. But if there wasn't dessert, at least there was coffee, rich and strong and Sarah insisted, in spite of her better judgement, on two balloon sized glasses with a shot of the restaurant's fine XO cognac in them. To complete the devastation Maggie brought them a little tray of liqueur chocolates to accompany the coffee and brandy and tempt their sated palettes.

Sarah smiled at her friend agonising over the small choice of chocolates. "Let's go and sit outside awhile Danny and drink our coffee." She suggested. "It's a lovely warm evening and I love the view from up here by night." In deep contentment, they drifted back out onto the restaurant terrace to find themselves alone in the night.

Chapter Twenty-Three

It was a warm muggy evening and there were the hints of lightning flashes across the valley over the bulk of the Santis. It was dark by now and the lights of the villages and farmhouses were little points of warmth in the valley below. They sat below one of the lamps on the restaurant terrace and watched the evening moths dancing in the glow. A little pipistrelle bat fluttered across the terrace hunting and Daniela exclaimed aloud in pleasure to see it. They sat close together alone on the terrace, their legs touching and held hands as they listened to the chirping of the crickets in the meadows and the chorus of frogs from the boggy fields below them. Sarah sipped her coffee, sampled the warming glow of her cognac and felt as close to heaven as she ever had.

Daniela sighed blissfully. "Sarah I've had a wonderful evening."

"Me too Danny."

Daniela brushed her hair aside and leaned back with her eyes closed to breathe in the scent of the evening; aromatic with the meadow flowers. "We really must do this often Sarah."

"I agree."

In a sudden movement Daniela reached out to lay a hand on Sarah's cheek. Sarah jumped at the sudden contact but she lifted her hand to cover Daniela's with her own and hold it to her face. Daniela hesitated and took a breath. "Sarah I hope you won't be annoyed with me but I've brought you something; a little present."

"A present? For me?"

"Yes it's just a little thing Sarah; just something to say thank you for your kindness and for sending me that gift of yours. Please don't be offended."

"I... I don't know what to say Danny."

"Well here." Daniela rummaged in her handbag and produced a tiny box. "It's just something small Sarah; nothing really."

Sarah took the little box and opened it in puzzlement. It contained a thin, white gold chain necklace from which hung a little heart shaped pendant in white gold at the centre of which reposed a single green stone. Sarah gasped. "Oh Danny it's lovely!"

"I'm pleased you like it."

"Danny please don't tell me that this is real gold."

"Of course it's real gold. You don't think I'd risk subjecting your beautiful neck to the possibility of non-precious metal allergic reaction do you?"

"But please tell me that that's not an emerald."

"I think of green when I think of you Sarah; the green of your valley and your lovely meadows. It suits your hair. Did you know that your hair has a chestnut sheen in the sunshine? That's why I was so pleased when I saw that you were wearing green tonight. It suits you perfectly."

Is it or isn't it an emerald?" Sarah insisted.

"Yes it is Sarah. Emerald is the stone of life and love and the love of nature. Your birthday is in May you told me, so it is also your birthstone and it symbolises the freshness of spring and the joy of life. I can't think of a better thing to hang about your neck."

"Danny I can't possibly accept this."

"Why not?"

"Because... because it's too much Danny. It's far too precious for me. I hardly know you."

"I'm sorry if I've offended you."

"You haven't. It's just... well it's just too much."

Daniela placed a finger on Sarah's lips. "Sarah listen to me. I don't have many friends; not true friends. Oh I have hundreds of people that call me their friend but, in my business, really genuine true friends are hard to find. Sycophants are two a penny. I want to be your

271

friend Sarah. From the moment I first saw you I've thought of little else. You must know how I feel about you." Daniela pointed to the necklace in Sarah's hand. "That little insignificant piece of beryllium aluminium silicate coloured with traces of chromium and vanadium is nothing Sarah. It cannot compare in beauty or preciousness to a single strand of your hair. It's just a token Sarah. It's a token of my... my esteem for you. It can never glitter as brightly as a single twinkle of your eyes nor shine so wondrously as your smile. It's just a token. Its value could never match the value I'd place on the thought that you wore it about your neck and thought of me. If it offends you then let us take it to that little brook over there and cast it into the water and let it lie until some little nymph of the stream finds it and sits upon a rock, to hang it about her neck there to wonder from where it came and what sadness caused it to be cast away."

Sarah stared at Daniela in something approaching desperation. Nobody had ever talked to her like this before. In a flash she saw the romance; the sheer unadulterated magic of this woman's inner poetry and understood from which deep well this woman's lovely music came. "I... I don't know what to say." She repeated foolishly.

"Then say nothing my lovely. Just take my gift for your own and know that I'd lay every emerald that ever came from the mines of Coscuez at your feet in exchange for a single smile."

Sarah nodded dumbly and lifted the necklace from its box. Her fingers fumbled clumsily with the clasp on the chain. "How does this open?" she asked biting her lip.

"Here let me help you." In a fluid motion Daniela rose to stand behind Sarah and took the necklace from her trembling fingers. "Hold your hair up out of the way." Obediently Sarah lifted her long hair. The gold of the chain was cool about her throat as Daniela fastened the necklace behind her neck. Sarah reached up to touch the emerald with her fingertips, hardly daring to breathe. Once the necklace was fastened Daniela bent and kissed Sarah softly on the side of her neck. Sarah shivered at the contact and raised her free hand to Daniela's head. The hair was as soft and lush as she had imagined. Daniela whispered in her ear. "A necklace is always a gift of love Sarah. Thank you for accepting it."

"I... I don't know if I'm ready for this Danny."

Daniela straightened up and stroked Sarah's hair fondly. "I don't know if I'm ready either Sarah." she sighed wistfully. "I'm not a person known for caution and prudence. I just go with my heart and it usually gets me into trouble." She laughed suddenly and resumed her seat. "Come let's stop being so serious. Let's just enjoy the night air. Do you think we can risk another of those brandies without making an exhibition of ourselves?"

Sarah laughed, disarmed by Daniela's mercurial return to gaiety. "Oh I think so. But it's my treat remember so I'll go in and order them."

"Your wish is my command my lady!"

Sarah stepped back in the restaurant feeling conspicuous with Daniela's gift about her neck. She found Maggie in the downstairs bar polishing glasses. "Maggie can we have two more cognacs please?"

"Of course. Hey I didn't know it was Daniela Devin you were dining with tonight. I didn't know you knew her."

"Well I don't. Well not very well anyway. I mean I only met her recently...." Sarah tailed off aware that she was starting to babble and making herself look foolish.

Maggie grinned. "Well you seem to be getting on like a house on fire considering you've only just met her."

"She's just a friend." Sarah protested feebly and could have kicked herself for her imbecility.

Maggie's eyes glinted. "Nice necklace." Maggie missed nothing it seemed.

Guiltily Sarah grasped the necklace and swallowed. "Oh er do you like it?"

Maggie laughed. "I'll get you those cognacs." she said.

Sarah leaned against the bar and cursed herself. She might just as well have given Maggie a written memo. A musical chime from her handbag alerted Sarah to a call on her telephone. With a shock she realised that it must be Nicole. Nicole had promised to phone as soon as she'd finished work. Sarah hadn't realised that it was so late. She groped in her bag and retrieved the phone. "Hi Foxy!" boomed Nicole. "I'll be finished soon. You still want me to come pick you up?" Sarah took several deep breaths and glanced at the door leading out to the terrace. "Hello? You still there?" asked Nicole.

"Yes... yes of course I'm here."

"So do you want picking up or not?"

"Well of course I want picking up. You don't think I'm going to walk all the way down to the valley and back up to Alpli in these damn heels do you?"

"Ok, ok! Keep your hair on. Just asking. You hesitated so long I thought you might have other plans."

"Just come and pick me up Nicky."

"All right. I'll be about half an hour. You still at the Gade?"

"Yes."

"Ok I'll come and get you." Nicole giggled. "How was your date?"

"Give me a break Nicky. I'm having a bit of a torrid time."

"Oh not so good huh?"

"No it was lovely. I just..... look just come and pick me up. I'll tell you about it later."

"Ok see you soon."

274

With a sigh, Sarah hung up. Her heart was beating loudly in her chest. She ventured no more conversation with Maggie but took the drinks with a polite thank you and carried them out to the terrace. She tried to look off-hand as she handed Daniela her drink and spoke. "Oh er Nicky, that is Nicole my housemate, phoned. She's coming to pick me up in half an hour or so. Do you need a lift home?"

Daniela's face was in shadow and her expression unreadable. "That's kind of you Sarah but I think I'd rather walk. The night air's lovely and I'd like to walk home in the dark."

Sarah pictured Daniela walking alone in the darkness her golden hair shining faintly in the faint illumination and her bare feet padding on the soft grass. "I can understand that Danny. I like to walk by night too."

"You could walk back with me Sarah."

Sarah shivered. There it was. The invitation; bold and brutal in its honesty. You don't have to go home to your lonely bed. You can walk back with me through the sweetness of the night and clasp my hand in the stillness of the night air. Will we even make it back to the house in Oberdorf before we clasp each other in our arms and seek each other's lips? You can phone Nicole and tell her not to bother coming for you. You can walk back to my house, to my arms and to my bed. You only have to cast caution aside and tonight we'll rest naked in embrace and the devil take tomorrow. Daniela was watching her saying nothing. "I... I can't Danny. Sarah stammered at last. "I just can't."

Daniela lowered her head. "I know Sarah. Forgive me. It was wrong of me to ask."

"Please Danny. You don't understand."

"Oh I do Sarah. Better than you might think." Slowly Daniela rose to her feet. "I'd better go Sarah before your friend gets here."

Sarah jumped to her feet. "Oh you can't go yet Danny. Stay and have a drink with Nicky and me. She'll be devastated not to meet you."

Daniela shook her head. "No Sarah. It's better not. I'm just being selfish. I want to remember tonight as just the two of us. I don't want to share the memory with somebody else."

"Don't be silly Danny. It's just Nicky."

"Please Sarah. I'd rather go now. That way the last sight I'll have of tonight was you and you alone. It'll be something to take to my dreams."

"Oh Danny be careful walking home. It's dark on the road over to Oberdorf."

"I'll be careful, I promise. Will you phone me tomorrow?"

"Yes. Yes of course."

"I'm afraid I won't be here much this next week. I have some stuff to do in the studio so I'll be away. Are we still on for that mountain hike?"

"Of course. I look forward to it."

"I'm looking forward to it too."

Daniela took Sarah's hands and held them in a soft grip. "Thank you for tonight Sarah. It was wonderful."

"Thank *you* Danny. I enjoyed it too."

"May I ask a great favour of you Sarah?"

"But of course."

"Will you kiss me?"

"Kiss you?"

"Just a little kiss Sarah; a little kiss to tell me I'm forgiven for imposing on you with my feelings for you."

"Oh Danny there's nothing to forgive."

Daniela moved closer. "Ever such a little kiss Sarah."

"I... I suppose... oh of course."

Daniela folded her in an embrace and turned her face up; her eyes searing Sarah with their sadness. "Just a little kiss Sarah. I fear what I might do if it's more than a little kiss."

Sarah had never kissed a woman on the lips before. Daniela's mouth was sweet and her lips so soft. The kiss lingered and Sarah felt Daniela's body stir against her and her own body responded. Daniela's hand strayed to Sarah's hair and caressed it and Sarah's hand brushed Daniela's naked back eliciting a soft exhalation of air from her and a quickening of her lips. They were disturbed by a chorus of laughter from the restaurant within and Daniela broke the kiss laying her head on Sarah's shoulder breathing heavily. "Thank you." She breathed hoarsely. She was shivering.

"You're cold Danny." Sarah admonished her in concern. "You haven't anything warm to wear to walk home in."

"I'll be fine Sarah."

"No you won't. It's a good twenty-minute walk back to Oberdorf. You'll catch your death." In sudden decision Sarah took her shawl and wrapped it about Daniela's shoulders. "Look take my wrap. I don't need it if I'm going home in the car."

Daniela took a corner of the shawl and held it to her face. "Thank you Sarah."

Sarah took her face in her hands and kissed her once more; a sisterly kiss but nonetheless sweet. "Take care Danny."

"I will do. Let me go now."

Sarah relinquished her grip and felt suddenly so terribly alone without the warmth of Daniela's body against her. "I... I'll call you." she croaked breathlessly.

"I'll count every minute until you do. I'm sorry Sarah."

"For what?"

"For falling in love with you. I know it wasn't fair of me. Goodnight Sarah." And then she was gone, walking back up the path to the road, her pale dress luminous in the glow from terrace lamps like a spectre disappearing into the night. Sarah watched her go feeling that she ought to say something, but no words would come. When the night had finally swallowed her Sarah collapsed into her seat on the terrace. It was getting chilly outside now but Sarah felt no urge to stray indoors into the warmth. She sat alone with her bewildering thoughts and felt tears of desolation on her cheek. Her senses screamed at her to fling aside her shoes and fly up the road after Daniela but her in built propriety held her back; encased her in a hopeless loneliness she had never known before. And so, presently, Nicole found her.

Chapter Twenty-Four

Are you all right Sarah?" Sarah jumped. She'd had her face buried in her hands and she'd been so far away with her thoughts she'd not even seen Nicole's car pull up at the road above or her approach to the restaurant. Nicole was standing staring at her, her face in a concerned frown. "What the hell are you doing sat out here on your own? It's bloody freezing! Where's your wrap?"

"Oh Nicky! You startled me."

"What's up Sarah? Where's Daniela?"

"She's gone home Nicky. She's walking home so I gave her my wrap to keep warm."

"While you just sit out here freezing your butt off. I know you're a bit loopy Sarah but this takes the biscuit. Why's she gone home? You haven't had a row or something?"

"Don't be silly. Of course not."

"So why are your eyes red? You've been crying haven't you?"

"I have not! I just got some pollen in my eyes that's all. I always get a bit of hay fever at this time of year."

"So no tiff with the girlfriend then?"

"Don't be ridiculous Nicole. And stop calling her my girlfriend. She's just a lovely girl who doesn't know many people in the Toggenburg and we've had a lovely evening."

"Hmmph! Well for God's sake come inside and get warm. You'll catch bloody pneumonia out here and I could do with a beer. I've had a rotten night at work."

"Ok but I could do to use the loo first."

"Right then I'll get the beers."

"Don't bother on my account Nicky. I've soaked up enough alcohol for one day and I haven't even finished my brandy yet."

Nicole reached down and picked up Sarah's glass to sniff it. "Hmm expensive brandy as well. This is what comes of going out on a date with a millionairess."

"Just for your information, I paid for everything."

"Now I know you've come adrift of your marbles. Why the hell did you pay for everything? Daniela Devin could probably have bought the whole restaurant."

"Call it pauper's pride."

"Call it a severe infestation of bats in the upper stories. Come on. For God's sake let's go in."

When Sarah returned from the lavatory, she found Nicole sat in a small window alcove in the downstairs bar, nursing a beer and looking thoughtful and worried. As soon as Sarah eased herself into the alcove Nicole confronted her. "Sarah what the hell's going on?"

"What on earth do you mean?"

"Don't play the innocent with me Sarah Fuchs. You know damn well what I mean. I've just been talking to Maggie while you were in the loo."

"Oh!"

"Yes! Oh! She tells me that you and Daniela Devin have been cooing over each other like a pair of demented love birds all night; all touchy feely and long lingering looks. They nearly had somebody come out of the kitchen to throw a bucket of water over you before you scandalised the rest of the clientele."

"I've never heard anything so ridiculous. Maggie's exaggerating."

"Oh yes? And what's *that*?" Nicole stabbed an accusing finger at Sarah's throat.

Sarah started and covered up her emerald necklace guiltily. "It's nothing. Just a little present from Daniela; just a cheap trinket to say thank you for that book I bought her."

"Let me see it."

"Really Nicole! You're being ridiculous."

"I said let me see it."

"Nicky please..."

"Come along Sarah. Don't be shy. I'm quite an expert on cheap trinkets."

Reluctantly Sarah let Nicole examine the necklace. Nicole's face grew stern. "Oh cheap trinket huh? Twenty-two carat gold and a bloody emerald that has to be at least one and a quarter carats if not more. She didn't pick this up on the cut price costume jewellery shelf at Globus Sarah. It looks like a top quality gem to me; dark green with just a hint of blue and well cut by the look of things; good colour and good transparency. There's a tad of an inclusion on the back but that's normal with emeralds. Quite a return on a twenty-five-franc book isn't it? If your new girlfriend paid a rappen less than five grand for that then I'll join a bleeding nunnery."

"Don't be silly Nicky. She wouldn't give me anything as valuable as that. I hardly know her."

"Sarah dear, Daniela Devin is loaded. She's got millions! She could have paid for that little trinket out of the bloody milk money. Hardly have cost her a thing comparatively speaking; especially if it helps her get inside your bottom drawers. She'll have recovered the loss in interest in the time it took you to hang it around your neck." Nicole paused. "You did hang it around your neck didn't you Sarah? I mean don't tell me that she did it for you."

"Well yes she did as it happens. I couldn't work the clasp."

"Oh my God! You brainless bitch!"

"Nicole!"

"Well you are sometimes. Honestly Sarah have you no sense?"

"What do you mean?"

"I mean Sarah that when somebody hangs a necklace that's a gift around your neck they are giving you very clear, unambiguous statements of intents and by letting them do it you are cooperating towards those intents; and by intents I don't mean a day's camping unless you like sex under canvas and possess a double sleeping bag."

Now you're being as bad as Maggie."

"Sarah honey. Listen to me. Have you thought all this through?"

"What are you talking about?"

"Look I know that you're going through some rough patches with the men in your life who aren't exactly lining up to drag you into the haystack. I know frustration can be a rotten thing and maybe you're turned on by the thought of a little adventure on the other side of the street but this is downright reckless. You've got to chill this thing with Daniela before it gets out of hand."

"You're talking absolute rubbish Nicky."

"I'm not talking rubbish Sarah and you know it. Think about your reputation."

"Well, according to you, it's already pretty shaky."

"Not half as shaky as it's going to be once Maggie's finished doing a number on it. Maggie's a dear girl but she's the worst gossip in the valley. By tomorrow evening the whole Toggenburg will know you were kissing and cuddling with Daniela Devin."

"I was *not* kissing and cuddling."

"Couldn't keep your hands off each other, the pair of you, according to Maggie, and you can bet that that story will improve with every telling."

Sarah folded her arms crossly. "I don't care what they think. I know what really happened."

"Oh yes? And what happens when this little episode comes to the attention of your parents and Alan?"

"How could it? They live in the Ticino."

"Where I presume they have newspapers."

"Newspapers? What are you talking about?"

282

"Newspapers, Sarah dear. They're the things made of paper you buy in kiosks and the like. What are you going to do when the story hits the papers?"

"Why on earth would it get in the papers? You're just being silly."

Nicole sighed and rubbed her eyes. "You know Sarah for a brainy girl you can be a right dumb cow sometimes. Daniela Devin is a national celebrity. Everything she does is scrutinised by the tabloid papers. Last year we had paparazzi crawling all over the place when she moved into the valley. Now it cooled down a bit when she settled in and lived quietly but if word gets out that she's out and about with a new girlfriend then you can bet your bottom dollar that you'll have reporters and photographers squirming out of the woodwork. I wouldn't trust Maggie's discretion as far as I could pick it up and throw it. Now think what your dear mother is going to say when she sees a bit fat photo of you on the front page of the Blick and a headline announcing you as the new love in pop star Daniela Devin's life. The explosion is going to make Bikini atoll look like a firecracker. And what is your prospective fiancée going to say; or his family. There's going to be a distinct tonal lack in the timbre of the old wedding bells isn't there? For God's sake Sarah! If you fancied a little experiment with your own sex for a change couldn't you have picked someone a little less high profile to do it with?"

"This is too bad of you Nicky. For heaven's sake you were the one that made me get all dressed up prettily to meet Daniela. You damn well went out of your way to encourage me!"

"I know Sarah but I didn't think it was going to get this steamy. I thought you had more sense. God knows why."

"Nothing has happened between Daniela and I Nicky. I'd like to point out that I am in fact sat here

283

talking with you and not back at Daniela's villa rolling about in bed."

"Did she invite you?"

"None of your damn business!"

"She did huh? Well at least you retained the presence of mind to turn her down. Your reputation is still going to take a knock though."

"Nicole the whole Toggenburg knows that I'm engaged in all but name to be married. Nobody thinks I'm a lesbian in spite of what might be considered damning evidence to the contrary."

"What evidence?"

"Well the fact that I've shared a house with another girl for the last few years for example."

"Oh great! Now you're dragging my reputation into it."

"Well it's likely to reflect on you isn't it? I mean people see us as inseparable and it's you I'm going home with, not Daniela Devin."

"You can't think that people are going to talk about us in that way can you?"

"Why not? After all we were both seen barely dressed together in public the day before yesterday; first in a sports shop, then the Migros and then at the Schwendisee and the adjoining restaurant. If people wanted to gossip there'd be plenty of scope there wouldn't there?"

"Oh hell! What are you trying to say?"

"Just this Nicole. People will gossip whatever you do. You're being overly paranoid. We both know that there is nothing scandalous in our friendship and I've done nothing to be ashamed about with Daniela. Yes she let me know that she was attracted to me and yes she's an affectionate girl, that can be a little overpowering and very tactile, but nothing happened. I told her that I couldn't go home with her and she understood. I'd like to think that we'll remain friends because she's a dear but she's not my lover Nicky. Ok maybe I shouldn't have accepted this necklace from her but she was very sweet about it and looked heartbroken when I refused it at first so I didn't have the heart to insist. Perhaps I ought to send it back with a contrite apology. I'll have to think about it. The long and the short of the matter, however, is that I'm not Daniela's lover and the bloody gossips can speculate to their heart's content. And if the bloody newspapers suggest otherwise I'll sue their arses from here to Fleet Street and back. The future of my marriage does not depend on a perfectly innocent evening out with a lovely lady, famous or otherwise."

Nicole held up her hands. "Ok, ok Sarah. Calm down. I'm just worried is all."

"Why Nicky? I mean why are you suddenly down on me seeing Daniela? You weren't like this when we talked about her earlier. Is it just because your own reputation might suffer through association with me?"

"I just worry about you Sarah. I couldn't give a flying fuck about my reputation."

"There's more to this Nicky. What is eating you?"

"I've told you Sarah. I worry about you. You haven't always had a good track record when it comes to affairs of the heart."

"Your own past form is hardly a sound basis to be giving *me* advice from Nicky."

"Ok I'll shut up. It's your business after all."

"Yes. Yes it is."

Nicole pursed her lips and stared at her beer glass thoughtfully. "Just one thing though Sarah."

"Yes?"

"Did you... I mean were you... well you know... tempted... I mean when Daniela asked you home."

"And why the devil is that your business?"

"It isn't. I'm just curious. You don't have to answer."

"Nicole when I was a little girl I found some money somebody had left around at home. I was tempted to take it but I didn't. Remember what they taught us in RE lessons. The devil puts temptations in front of us all the time. The temptation isn't the deed however. It's what you do about the temptation. Just for the record yes I was tempted. But nothing happened and I'm sat here instead listening to you being an old woman about it. Does that satisfy you?"

Nicole nodded. "Yes Sarah but Sarah...."

"Now what?"

"Just be careful ok. Just cool it with Daniela all right."

Sarah sighed and looked out of the window at the lights glinting in the valley below. "I think it already got chilly Nicky."

Chapter Twenty-Five

There was a chill wind in the Sarah and Nicole household for the next couple of days as well. The altercation the two girls had had in the Gade drove a certain rift between them and whilst admittedly not serious enough to preclude their speaking to each other it was, nevertheless, not without a degree of tension. Sarah kept her promise and phoned Daniela the following day but she made sure that Nicole was out of earshot when she did so. Daniela sounded enormously pleased to hear from her but her joy was tinged with a subtle air of sadness too, which Sarah found perplexing. Daniela was due to go to Zurich to the recording studio the following day and she sounded desolate that her absence for several days would not permit her to see Sarah. Sarah bit her lip and tried to keep the conversation light but there was no denying the undertones to it. The conversation ended unsatisfactorily with Daniela extracting a promise from Sarah to phone and a further promise to meet again as soon as Daniela's commitments would allow. Sarah discreetly kept this information from Nicole, not wishing to add to the already strained atmosphere in the house. Nicole seemed sullen and irritable and it was notable that Daniela's music was pointedly absent from the fare on the house stereo systems.

On Sunday, as if Sarah didn't have enough troubles, she had to face another major assault from her mother who simply was refusing to accept that Sarah intended to remain in the Toggenburg until such time as she received a firm statement of intent from Alan. The telephone conversation had descended into an unseemly row and Sarah found herself exhausted and dispirited. There was no word from Frau Fritzl regarding possible work either and by Monday morning Sarah was thoroughly fed up. She felt confused and in a turmoil with little help from

Nicole who greeted her every lament against the slings and arrows of outrageous fortune with non-committal grunts.

Monday brought a new domestic crisis for a delivery man turned up on the doorstep with the biggest bunch of flowers Sarah had ever seen. Unfortunately, as chance would have it, Nicole had answered the door and taken delivery and she tossed the floral offering onto the kitchen table sourly. "For you!" she snorted, "The girlfriend's obviously pining for you."

Sarah bit back the rude word that immediately came to mind and picked up the bouquet to examine the card. It was indeed from Daniela. The card read,

"Dear Sarah,

I'm sorry if I left in a bit of a strange mood the other night. Forgive me. I'm just a little emotional for the moment. I just wanted to say how much I enjoyed the other evening and how much I look forward to seeing you again. I'm away for a few days but I hope that when I return we can meet. I'm thinking about you always.

With all my love

Daniela.

It was not a message designed to alleviate the domestic tension and, when Nicole took herself off to work, Sarah gave vent to an uncharacteristic display of petulance by kicking the odd cushion about and using the sort of words that she would rarely, if ever, use in public. Finally, unable to endure another day of recriminations, she donned her hiking gear and took off for the mountains leaving a note for Nicole to say that she would be back on Tuesday. It was a pure escape, she knew, but she needed time with her thoughts.

There was still some snow clinging to the mountains this early in the summer but Sarah's hike was not an overly ambitious one. She took the route up the long valley from Gamplut to climb high onto the flanks of the Altman and to the little and very basic mountain hut on the Zwingli Pass. The high mountains were a balm to her turbulent mood and she paused often on the rocky flanks of the mountain, finding some solace in the little Alpine snowbells poking their pale purple heads from the damp patches of ground where the snow had so recently melted.

It was Sarah's first real climb of the season for the SAC hostel at Zwingli pass was over 2000 metres up and her legs felt the strain on the long haul up. The hostel was a rough stone building on an outcrop of rock among the boulder fields descending from the Altmannsattel and it looked bleak and lonely set in desolate isolation amid the grandeur of the peaks around it. It did not look at all hospitable but the hostel was manned and the warden greeted Sarah warmly for she was the only visitor to the hostel that evening. There was even food although, after her gastronomic heroics of the weekend, Sarah would have been perfectly content with the food she had packed in her rucksack. The food was as basic as you could get but the thick barley and mutton soup and crusty bread was just wonderful to an appetite sharpened by an afternoon's hard climbing. Drink came in the form of fruit juice or bottles of Appenzell beer and the hostel's communal room and dining quarter was at least warmed by the stove in the corner. The warden would have lingered in conversation with Sarah for it was a solitary existence on the mountain when you had no guests and an evening of congenial conversation with a beautiful girl, hiking on her own, would have been most attractive. Sarah, however, was curiously uncommunicative and the warden, being a sensitive man, sensed her desire to be alone and discreetly busied himself with chores elsewhere about the hostel. Sarah finished her evening meal and took a bottle of beer outside, where she walked a hundred metres away from the hostel to perch on a rock and gaze down at the vista below her.

Evening was setting over the mountain and there was barely a breath of breeze. The calls of the Alpine Choughs echoed mournfully against the cliffs of the mountain behind her and there were the croaking calls of Ptarmigan from the boulder fields. A single Water Pipit flew over with a sharp *"phist"*; the plaintive little cry somehow emphasising the loneliness on the mountain flank. Normally Sarah would have loved this quiet solitude in the still of the evening in the mountains but, today, it felt like a sorrowful harmony to the lonely void in her own heart. For the first time in her life, Sarah felt truly lonely.

Such a feeling had rarely, if ever, occurred to Sarah before. She was, after all, well-loved and popular. She had a caring and supportive family and many good friends throughout the Toggenburg who worshipped her. She had friends from university all over Switzerland who would have joyfully taken her into their homes at the merest courtesy of a phone call to announce her arrival. She had a boyfriend who was the envy of many of her friends; tall, handsome and wealthy and who was counting the days until he could vow himself until death as her husband. She had a dear male friend in Peter with whom she could share her love of the wild mountains of her homeland. She had in Nicole an endlessly diverting companion in life to whom she was devoted. Sarah never made enemies. She could not, in all honesty, name a single person who truthfully disliked her. Many a beautiful girl at school might have attracted envy and jealousy among her peers but Sarah's quite obvious lack of vanity and her singular goodness had disarmed even the bitchiest of perceived rivals. She was just impossible to hate.

So why, therefore, should a girl, with such a reservoir of love and good feeling toward her, suddenly find herself feeling so desperately isolated and lonely. Sarah didn't understand it herself. She only knew that, from the moment that Daniela had walked away into the night at the Gade, there had been an aching cavernous hole in her heart; a void that should have been filled by the warm certainty of another person's presence. It had taken Daniela, Sarah realised, to show her just how insufficient the other relationships in her life were.

Nicole might dismiss Daniela's advances as predatory lesbian intent but Sarah knew it wasn't that simple. She had never had anybody look at her in that way; never had anybody so sweetly and gently express their adoration of her in that way. It was more than just desire. Daniela loved her. Incredible though it was, this woman, this extraordinary woman, had fallen hopelessly in love with her. Sarah guessed that Daniela was a woman of immediate and all-consuming passion. She would not lie about the imperatives of love. Her words were not just sweet nothings to lure a person into sexual intimacy. She was a person who would love completely; without ambiguity; pure and honest. It would not be a casual fling with Daniela; not, how had Nicole phrased it, an adventure. It would be all consuming; a blazing fire and a terrible leap into the unknown.

It could have happened too, Sarah was honest enough to admit. Nicole had saved her. Had Nicole phoned just a little later on Saturday evening; had Daniela lain her gentle invitation upon the table before Sarah had had a chance to tell Nicole to pick her up then she could have been lost. She could so easily have acquiesced and flung herself into Daniela's arms; surrendered to the insanity of the feelings overpowering her and marched down the road to catastrophe.

Sarah shivered as she thought of the consequences of that tiny balance of chance. She would have been alienated from her family, have destroyed her marriage prospects, laid waste to her reputation and perhaps even have lost the respect of her dearest friend. It had been so close. She had been bewitched by the charisma of a powerful woman; so bewitched she had been magnetically attracted to her in contravention of everything she had been before. It was as if some terrible enchantment had been cast over her, to cast her life aside for the warmth of a woman she hardly knew, in deference to feelings she could not comprehend and with consequences so terrible she could hardly bare to think about them.

It had been the right decision to reject Daniela. It was the only decision possible. She had stepped to the brink and, against all the illogical impulses of her emotions, had taken a step back and thus redeemed herself with salvation. She had stared into the face of insanity and somehow recovered. She remained the Sarah that everyone knew and the strange creature, she might have become, cast out into the wilderness of impossible dreams. But it had cost her. It had cost her dearly. The chasm in her heart told her that.

Sarah shook her head and gazed hopelessly at the bare mountainside below her. Why she asked; why should she feel so desperate and miserable? It had always been the right thing to do so why did it feel so terribly wrong? Sarah stared at her beer bottle. It was nearly empty. There were more in the cool storage hut beside the hostel. The warden had told her to help herself and just leave the money in the jar by the stove in the dining room. She stared at the beer bottle in her hand as if it held some key to enlightenment. "Why" she asked herself again, "am I beguiled by another woman? I'm not a lesbian! I'm a normal woman." She started guiltily realising that she had voiced her thoughts aloud and she glanced around, fearing that the warden might be in earshot. But she was thankfully alone. She turned back to her perusal of her beer glass and murmured more quietly. "I am a woman." A woman! The thought seemed to stick in her brain like a persistent itch.

Yes she was a woman. But look at her now. Take a look at her grubby jeans and her scuffed hiking boots; her hair tied back in a tail and her rough cotton shirt and thick woolly pullover. Look at her now drinking beer straight from the bottle and wiping her mouth over the back of her sleeve. Not exactly the image of femininity was it she conceded ruefully. And this was normal garb for her; so normal it was almost characteristic of her. Her mother despaired of her lack of female refinement. Even Nicole berated her for it. When she did dress in feminine attire, then everybody remarked upon it for it was so unusual. Peter had joked about her legs as if he had never seen them before. Even when out with Alan she was most likely to don a pair of jeans. He had once irritably asked her why she didn't put some nice clothes on for a change and she had been annoyed with him for her jeans had been new and she'd worn a blouse she'd imagined was smart. Sarah frowned. She didn't dress like a woman and she didn't much act like one either, if she was honest.

"But I *am* a woman!" she repeated to herself, "I have no inclination or desire to be masculine. I don't feel boyish or butch. I am perfectly content to be a woman. I have no gender issues; no inner envy of maleness. On the contrary I'd hate to be a man. I am a woman pure and simple and perfectly at ease with my gender." Nevertheless it was inescapable that she neither advertised nor openly indulged in her femininity. She was the way she was, an attractive girl who felt no particular need to emphasise that attractiveness. Until now, that is.

Sarah bit her lip. Yes! Until now. Sarah had to admit that she had gone slightly mad over the past few days and the blame for that insanity could be placed firmly at the door of Daniela Devin. It had started with their first meeting up at Schwendi. The very next day she had completely lost it and spent a small fortune on feminine clothes. It was true that it was mostly her father's money she had spent. He had told her to go out and buy herself something nice; some new clothes. Sarah winced at the thought. Even her father, it seemed, bemoaned his favourite daughter's failure to dress a little more girlishly. But it wasn't her father that was the driving force behind her momentary shopping madness Sarah knew. It was Daniela and the thought that the next time she should meet her that she should look her best; look in fact like a woman. She'd even gone out to a disco with Nicole dressed (and Sarah cringed at the recollection) sexily; even danced (danced for heaven's sake!) to a Daniela Devin track. The next day she had been so softened up by her new-found opening she had even allowed Nicole to bully her into buying a bikini; an item of wear she had not possessed since she was a young girl. Then, to cap it all, she had spent two hours doing her hair, her face, her hands, her feet for God's sake and bedecked herself in softly alluring feminine clothes and adorned herself with jewellery just to go to dinner with Daniela. It was lunacy! She had never gone to so much trouble to dress up for dinner in her life. She had wanted to look pretty. She had wanted to look attractive. She had wanted, God forbid, to look *womanly*!

Yes womanly. She'd wanted to look like a woman. And she had succeeded. The crazy thing was that she had enjoyed being a woman for Daniela. Sarah frowned and tried to grasp the meaning of the disturbing thoughts. Why did she not feel the same wish to demonstrate her femininity to Alan? But then Alan would never admire her so warmly and frankly. Not even Peter could do that. Alan would never have told her so often how beautiful she was. He would never have toasted her as the most beautiful girl in the valley. He would not have thought to find her birthstone and honour her life with an emerald on a gold chain or hang it with love about her neck and bless it with a kiss. He would not have told her that a single strand of her hair was more precious and beautiful than all the emeralds in Colombia. He would not have thought to send her flowers to thank her for a wonderful evening and to let her know he thought of her. Only Daniela had done that. In all her life, only Daniela had uncovered that female side to her. Only for Daniela had she truly wanted to be a woman and only Daniela had so validated her for being so. Only Daniela had treated her like a woman. It had taken another woman to make her feel it; to make her feel like a woman.

In agitation Sarah jumped to her feet and stalked back to the hostel for more beer. At the hostel she slapped her hand against the rough stone of the side of the building by the door and leaned against it breathing heavily. She closed her eyes in anguish. Of course she was not treated like a woman. She didn't behave like one. She could hardly blame the men in her life for not acknowledging her femininity when she went to such lengths to obscure it. She opened her eyes slowly. Well maybe she could change it. With a heartfelt sigh she stepped inside.

Bernhard, the middle-aged warden, was sitting at his ease in the common room, with his boots off, drinking a bottle of beer and filling the room with acrid smoke from a foul smelling Villiger cigarillo. He raised his head to greet her cheerily. "Hoi Sarah. Getting cold outside is it?"

"No it's fine Bernhard. I just came in to grab another bottle of beer."

"Well there's plenty in the cool cabinet. It might be a bit cold in the dormitory tonight but I've put plenty of blankets out."

"Thanks Bernhard."

"What time are you leaving in the morning Sarah?"

"I don't know Bernhard. I'm only going to hike back down to Gamplut and then over to Alpli. I've got all day to get back so I'm not in a hurry to be away in the morning. Why?"

"Well it's just that I have to be out early to fix some cabling on the track over Altmannsattel so, if you aren't going to be up early, I wondered if you'd mind seeing to your own breakfast. There's coffee in the jar in the pantry with sugar and jam. There's fresh bread in the bin and milk and butter in the cold room. There's some cheese as well if you want it."

"Yes that's fine Bernhard. I'll manage. How are we for water?" In the high limestone mountains of the region, water was commonly scarce on the surface at high altitude and needed to be carefully husbanded.

"No problem. We've had hardly any guests up here yet and we've loads. I'll light the stove before I go out in the morning and you can stick a pan of water on it if you want hot water to wash in."

"That'll be great Bernhard." Sarah took another bottle of beer from the cabinet and flicked the plastic top off. "I think I'll sit outside a little while longer." She paused in consideration. "Bernhard?" she began hesitantly.

"Yes?"

Sarah agonised. "Well... you've known me for years."

"Ever since you were about eight years old Sarah. That's few years now."

"Well do you think that I'm....." Sarah hesitated in embarrassment.

"You're what Sarah?"

"Well sort of well... I don't know... sort of tomboyish... you know... not really girly?"

Bernhard looked at her in surprise. "Whatever brought that up?"

"I don't know. I just wondered if... well if I was well just a bit too well butch I suppose. People keep telling me that I ought to behave more like a lady."

Bernhard chuckled and applied a match to the obnoxious brown rough stick of tobacco in his mouth. "Well you always were a bit of a tomboy Sarah. I remember hiking over the Lysengrat with you and your Dad, the year after I lost my first wife. You must have been nine or ten years old at the time. I can still see you now with your hair in a pony tail skipping across that arête like it was a ride in the park. You were fearless. No girly vapours from our little Sarah. You'd swarm up the mountainside like a little steinbock and put all the lads to shame. We used to call you our little murmeltier."

Sarah winced at the comparison between herself and the Alpine Marmots; the fat ground squirrels that inhabited the high mountains but she grinned in spite of herself. "You're not really helping me here Bernhard."

Bernhard smiled at her fondly and blew a cloud of blue smoke from his wretched old stogie. "It was a good name for you Sarah. You belong on these mountains; always have done."

"I'm trying to fish for assurances that I'm a proper lady Bernhard not an overweight rodent that digs holes in the scree slopes."

"What's bothering you Sarah? Why this sudden concern about being a lady?"

"Because I'm supposed to be getting married at the end of summer Bernhard and people are telling me that it's time that I grew up and became a lady. I've spent most of my life walking about on these mountains in a pair of old jeans and my hiking boots. I don't know *how* to be a lady."

Bernhard nodded sagely. "Ah so that's what's bothering you. Well Sarah I wouldn't worry if I was you. You've grown up just fine. I couldn't help noticing what a fine looking young woman you've turned out to be when you walked in this evening. Don't let anybody tell you otherwise. If you're worried about being a lady... well don't. That'll come in time. It's hard to grow up Sarah but when you're away, married in a fine house, you'll soon learn the graces of a lady. Then there'll be children on the way and you'll find that you're woman enough for that too. Just remember one thing."

"What's that Bernhard?"

"You'll always be Sarah. You were born for these mountains and you've lived most of the length of your days among them. Don't ever forget your roots. The mountains are a jealous mistress Sarah. They'll give you no peace if you turn your back on them for the genteel surroundings of a lady's drawing room. There'll always be a part of you that wants to cast aside her fine clothes and put her old boots down on the good solid stone of the mountainside. Don't ever forget who you are."

Sarah nodded sadly. "You're right Bernhard. I can never leave this behind."

Bernhard shook his head with a chuckle. "Come girl! Enough seriousness. Keep an old man company for an hour or two." He reached into a drawer in a rough little cabinet beside him and withdrew a pack of Swiss playing cards. There were thirty-six cards in the pack arranged in four suits of bells, shields, acorns and flowers. "We've time for a few hands of Jass before we turn in for the night."

Sarah smiled. "I'd like that Bernhard."

"Well pull that table up and a chair and let's deal. We'll make it ten points a rappen. Do you want to keep score?"

"Ok."

"Fine. I'll shuffle the cards. Be a good girl and get us a couple more beers."

Sarah played badly for her mind was distracted and she was several francs poorer when Bernhard finally put away the cards, stretched his legs and announced that it was time for him to retire. Sarah sat up for a little while longer before the stove, nursing a beer. There was a rumble of thunder from further up the pass and Sarah guessed there was a thunderstorm brewing over the high peaks. It didn't worry her. Thunderstorms were common occurrences in the mountains especially in the late afternoon which was why you always tried to reach your destination early at high altitude. Sarah was used to thunderstorms and, assuming she was safely indoors, she quite enjoyed them. There was something exhilarating about a wild storm on the mountains.

Sarah thought of the coming week. There were challenges ahead for her, not least of which would be her upcoming meeting with Peter in Winterthur. The more Sarah thought about that meeting, the more puzzled she became. For Peter to suggest a rendezvous in town was hopelessly uncharacteristic of him. She found herself intrigued. At the same time, she knew she had to come up with a strategy to deal with the confrontation and that was no easy matter. If, as she half expected and Nicole certainly seemed to believe, Peter was about to declare his hand then the meeting was tantamount to betrayal; cheating on Alan. This, Sarah postulated, was the most likely reason why Peter had asked to meet her in a neutral place away from the sight of their acquaintances. Winterthur didn't strike Sarah as the sort of place *she* would have chosen for a secret lover's tryst but it was apparently the best that Peter could come up with. It all seemed a bit shady. What if Peter intended to take a hotel room? What if he suggested they share it? What on earth would she do in that instance? Here she was just months away from her marriage agreeing to meet another man, away from prying eyes, in whom she had expressed an interest in and who was tentatively returning the compliment. If the tale ever got back to Alan it was going to look very bad indeed.

How was she going to conduct herself? She knew that she needed to know what Peter's feelings for her were. In the last days, Peter had re-emerged from the pack as the other man in her life; the alternative to marriage with Alan and she could not dismiss that alternative out of hand. Nicole was right in that she had to make some decision about it. First of all she had to hear Peter's suit. Once all the cards were on the table she would beg time to make a judged response. After long years of never declaring himself to her, Peter was hardly in a position to demand an immediate answer. She would hear him out sympathetically but she would defer her decision. She needed time.

She would not sleep with him Sarah decided. For one thing, that would be tantamount to declaring her own hand and, on the other, it would be unethical whilst still attached to Alan. If Peter had some idea of a romantic adventure in Winterthur, then she would tell him gently, but firmly that she would not be unfaithful to Alan. It would be grossly unfair. If she decided against marriage to Alan then it was her duty to formally end the relationship. It was a daunting prospect but she would have to do it. She would not lose the moral high ground by sleeping with Peter whilst still in a relationship with Alan. Only once the relationship was ended, would she enter into intimacy with Peter and all that depended upon the nature of Peter's suit. If she was to break with Alan, with all the upheaval that was likely to cause, then he had better have a very good argument for her doing so.

How much did she want Peter to make a good case she asked herself. The answer to that was that she didn't know. In a real sense Peter was her first love; the first man who had ever dominated her dreams and excited her fantasy. It had always been an unrequited love but she had never lost her attraction to him. Peter had been a dominant figure in her life to such an extent that it had been taken for granted among her peers, if not among

300

her family, that one day they would combine. It had never happened and Sarah frequently rued the fact that it had not. Presumably Peter was now also waking up to the reality of the missed opportunity. Well she would give him every chance. She had already decided to award Peter the fruits of her newly awakening femininity. If the curious madness that had come over her with Daniela had at least one positive aspect, it was that it had alerted her to her failings in this regard. It would be a new Sarah that Peter would meet in Winterthur on Wednesday. He would see that his childhood friend was a woman and if he hoped to win her hand then he'd better damn well start treating her like one.

On that note of determination, Sarah rose and cleared away the remnants of beer bottles and emptied out Bernhard's acrid ashtray before retiring to bed. The dormitory of the hostel was typical of the sleeping arrangements in alpine huts. There were three broad wooden shelves in three layers each of which could have accommodated some ten people sleeping on them. There were thin foam filled plastic mattresses laid on the wooden boards and pillows and coarse woollen blankets folded at the foot of each mattress. Sarah carried a lamp for there was no electric light in the dormitory and, after discarding her boots, climbed the ladder to the top shelf. She was quite alone in the dormitory which precluded the usual hazard of stepping on and stumbling over reclining people whilst trying to find your space. She picked a spot at the end of the shelf near the little window so that she could look out at the distant flickering of lightning and stripped her outer clothes off. It was chilly in the dormitory so she pulled a track suit bottom and a warm T-shirt on before crawling under an extra layer of blankets. It was a rudimentary sleeping arrangement but Sarah quite liked the simplicity and no frills, basic nature of life in a mountain hut. It was a refreshing reversal to basic needs with the veneer of comfort and luxury of modern life stripped bare. She liked the sharp cool air in the darkness of the dormitory and the scent of the rough timber of the walls.

Finding some peace and contentment at last, after the confusion of the last days, she huddled down and tried to sleep. She knew, by experience, that it normally took her a long time to get off to sleep at high altitude so she lay awake for some time thinking. She thought long about the two men in her life whose differing agendas were seemingly poised to clash and it was no help to her in her quest for sleep. So she let her mind wander and its rambling brought her to the one thing that lulled her toward slumber. Before slipping off into fitful sleep her last thoughts were of Daniela Devin.

Chapter Twenty-Six

The thunderstorms of the night had refreshed the mountains and the air was cool and clean in the morning sunlight. Cumulus clouds formed high fluffy ranks; parading over the peaks and matching the great mountains in their majestic size, if not in their substance. Sarah awoke in fine humour, although that had little to do with the amount of sleep she had had. In fact she had slept poorly. This she had expected. Sleep at high altitude was often a somewhat fitful affair punctuated by strange dreams. This was so characteristic of life in high places that the German word for a nightmare, Alptraum, translated as Alp dream in English. Better sleep did come with acclimatisation, Sarah knew, but this was the first time this year she had slept high on a mountain and she had not yet re-adjusted. For all that, she felt fine for the crisp clear morning raised her spirits and made her eager to be out and about on the mountainside.

Bernhard was long gone and she had the hut to herself. Before leaving Bernhard had left the essentials of her breakfast out for her and she fell to it hungrily, for she had awoken with a keen appetite. The usual breakfast fare in these mountain huts consisted of thick crusty bread smeared with butter and jam and washed down with mugs of coffee. There was a residual English girl, still in Sarah's make up however, that left her feeling the inadequacies of that diet as a foundation for a day's hard labour in the mountains. She didn't exactly favour a full English breakfast of bacon, eggs, sausages, beans, grilled tomatoes, fried bread, mushrooms, tea, toast and marmalade but, nevertheless, Sarah liked something savoury with her morning repast. She was grateful to Bernhard, therefore, that he knew her tastes well and had left her a great half wheel of cheese to help herself to and a jar of mustard.

The cheese was special, as well, for it was an Appenzell cheese wrapped in a black label. A black label on an Appenzell cheese meant that it was the "extra" variety, aged for at least six months and usually longer to bring out the full strength of it. The cheese was golden in colour, hard, salty with the herbal brine in which it was cured and delicious with a powerful smell and a rich tart nuttiness which was complimented by the smear of strong mustard, Sarah applied to it. The butter was fresh and creamy; the bread chewy and wholesome. Sarah ate three thick slices of bread and cheese and another smeared thickly with jam.

She giggled to herself. If Daniela could see her now she must wonder if this girl ever stopped eating. It was a fair question for Sarah had always been possessed of a healthy appetite and she had never had to recourse to a diet in her life. Sarah just never put on extra weight. She could count her blessings in this regard for there was many a woman who would have cheerfully sold their soul to the devil for Sarah's apparently contradictory attributes of fine appetite and admirably slender frame. But then few women led such an active lifestyle as Sarah. She would burn off the calories of her breakfast by lunchtime.

Sarah finished her meal and tidied up; cleaning her dishes and stowing the components of her breakfast away. She took a last cup of coffee whilst writing a note for Bernhard before pulling on her boots and shouldering her rucksack. She had things to do today; pleasurable things and she was eager to be away. She took a slightly higher route than yesterday before dropping down through a zone on the flank of the mountains that separated the Schaffberg from the Altmann. This drop was an interesting place for it was a sunny flank of dry sub-alpine scrub which held an interesting flora and was dotted about with reclining stunted mountain pines, dwarf willows and alpenrose.

304

Sarah had picked out this route deliberately for there was something she much wanted to see that was possible here. For once, she ignored the alpine flowers and scoured the bushes and scrub with her binoculars for her target. She was looking for a bird and a rare one. The bushes were full of wrens and dunnocks which were common to these high-altitude scrub regions, a fact which often surprised people who more thought of them as garden birds at low altitude. There were also Lesser Whitethroats, another bird of surprisingly montane habits. There was also one spectacular avian resident in the region as evidenced by a dumpy finch like bird of startling orange red hue that flew by with a loud "jip". This was a relatively scarce bird locally but, in some years, the numbers of them increased explosively for it was a well-known irruptive migrant, a common Crossbill; a full plumaged male in this instance. It was a wonderful sight but not the bird she had come looking for.

She spent a long time looking for her target could be surprisingly elusive and skulking; keeping low to the ground and furtive. Sarah's efforts were rewarded for, after scouring the area assiduously, she finally spotted her target. It was being quite cooperative, in fact, for it was perched on a small rock singing with a curiously un-musical buzzing song. It was a handsomely plumaged male with a chestnut mantle, a rufous chest and belly and a strikingly marked pattern of black lines on its grey head. Sarah felt a thrill at the sight, for Rock Buntings were rare birds in the Toggenburg. They were more a bird of the warmer cantons in the south; the Ticino or the Valais but this sort of dry sunny slope suited them and this was one of the few places in the Toggenburg where you could hope to find one. Sarah grinned in delight, her day already crowned with triumph. Sarah was quite possibly the most knowledgeable naturalist in the Toggenburg. It is possible that only she, at this time, knew of this particular location for breeding Rock

Buntings. It never occurred to her that she was a repository of quite unique knowledge.

Sarah lingered long on the mountainside for she was in no hurry this day and felt inclined to simply enjoy her mountains. The day was growing warmer and the butterflies were already on the wing in all the variety that only the mountain pastures could provide; drab browns and ringlets, gaudy flamboyant fritillaries, little jewel-like blues and coppers, dashing clouded yellows and fluttering whites, striking Nymphalidae and the big spectacular Apollos; all dancing across the ludicrously rich carpets of flowers. It was a little piece of heaven.

Oddly, Sarah felt a sense of loneliness whilst watching the wondrous harmony of nature on her mountainside. For years she had enjoyed this rich tableau of life with Peter. Peter was the only person close to her who came close to her abiding love of the alpine environment. She had spent many days with him hiking these slopes and sharing their wonder with him. She knew she could never have that with Alan. Alan was the kind of man that took the car to go to the shop on the corner. He would walk a golf course but that was about as far as his rambling activity would take him. He would never share her joy in the mountains. It was a telling point against him. Must she lose her mountains for Alan? With Peter that problem didn't arise. Marriage to him might be poor but it would at least have the riches of the mountains. Would she sacrifice material wealth for a companion who understood her affinity to the high places? On that glorious morning on the mountainside, she rather thought she might.

Beauty is best shared after all. It gave her as great a pleasure to show somebody else the loveliness of the great symphony of nature she so adored as it did to see it for herself. A pleasure shared was a pleasure doubled. She longed to show Daniela these mountains. Sarah frowned. It was odd how often Daniela came to her mind unbidden. She had simply been thinking of sharing the mountains with Peter and suddenly the thought of showing them to Daniela had insinuated itself into her reflections. It was a powerful intrusion too for Sarah knew instinctively that Daniela was a person who would truly appreciate the natural beauty of the mountains. Daniela possessed a sense of wonder and a deeply romantic nature. She was a woman who would write songs in eulogy to the mountains. It would be an adventure to show her these places; it would be an extraordinary awakening. Daniela would fall in love with the mountains. For the moment she admired them from afar like some distant unobtainable lover. Sarah wanted to bring her into their embrace. In a sudden shock Sarah realised that the person she would most like to be next to on this wonderful day was Daniela.

With a snort she rose hastily to her feet and began to descend shaking her head as if that would drive the disturbing thoughts away. With grim visage, she took the steep track down as if a shadow had been cast across the mountainside; a shadow of social ostracism and the unspeakable unknown of questioning her very nature as a woman. Daniela was an alluring temptation to disaster; a promise and a threat. She didn't dare to think of her.

Before long Sarah found herself on the alp that led down to Gamplut. It was a sheltered grassy valley carpeted with wild flowers with multitudes of bees and other insects buzzing in the warm temperatures. A small herd of cattle was grazing placidly along the floor of the valley and one of Sarah's old friends was stood chewing the cud among them. Lucifer was an enormous great Swiss brown bull, massing well over 1,000 kilos, of menacing demeanour and possibly the worst named ruminant in all of Switzerland. Lucifer, or Lucy to his friends, was a disgrace to the fearsome reputation of the male of his breed for a more docile and dopey, empty headed example of bovine masculinity you would have been hard pushed to find. Sarah had known Lucifer since he had been a knock kneed, doe eyed, little calf nuzzling at her hand and bleating plaintively and she was forced to admit that maturing years had failed to instil in him any sense of greater adult responsibility. Even the matriarchs of the herd tended to push him around and Sarah had seen small children playing between his legs completely unafraid of his ominous bulk. Let it be said that Lucifer's male attributes in other respects were not in any question for he was a prize-winning bull and had sired enough offspring to fill half the barns in eastern Switzerland. It was just that he was as soft as a brush. He would wander up to you and put his head on one side the better to facilitate you scratching him behind the ear with all the air of a particularly daft dog. It took a certain degree of talent for over a thousand kilos of muscular bull to look goofy but Lucifer could manage the feat with alacrity. Sarah adored him.

From Lucifer's little patch of paradise, it was an easy stroll back down the alp to the restaurant at the top of the cable car at Gamplut. Sarah had dawdled along the route and it was lunchtime before she arrived at Gamplut so she took the time to take a light meal and a drink on the congenial terrace with the bulk of the Schaffberg mountain towering overhead. The Schaffberg was an interesting mountain to Sarah for, in her school holidays, she had occasionally worked on the mountain with the sheep; hiking up the mountain two times a week to see that all was well with the herd. Sarah was not fond of sheep. They had a perverse tendency to always be either at the highest point on the mountain they could reach or alternatively on the other side of the mountain from that which you were looking for them. Sheep were great believers in making their tenders work as hard as possible. A pair of Golden Eagles nested on the Schaffberg traditionally as well and, from her seat on the bench outside the Gamplut mountain restaurant, Sarah scoured the mountainside with her binoculars for the small herds of Chamois and Ibex that you could always find on the mountain.

She lingered long at Gamplut for she was in a lazy mood and had no real rush to be home. She told herself that the sun was over the yardarm, a nautical term of which she had not the slightest inclination of the meaning of, and used it to justify treating herself to a carafe of white wine. She eased her boots off and discarded her socks to take a little wander into the adjoining meadow, thinking of Daniela and how Daniela had told her that she loved the feel of the grass under her bare feet. As always, the thought of Daniela brought a certain languid sensuality to her thoughts and she stroked her hair tenderly before recovering herself briskly and banishing the thought almost guiltily from her mind. Daniela remained a dichotomous paradox in her consciousness.

So long did Sarah tarry at Gamplut, that it was well into the afternoon before she finally raised herself and set off back on the final descent to home. From Gamplut was a route that led across a broad meadow before plunging into thick forest that descended to Alpli; the little side alp where Sarah lived with her mercurial friend Nicole. Sarah had a mind to spend some time in the forest for she had another ornithological target on her day's list. The forest leading down to Alpli was a spruce forest but it was not a neat and orderly one for it had been extensively damaged by storms. This meant that there were many open areas, a good deal of fallen timber and lots of shattered broken trees; many dead and infested with rot and wood boring beetles and their larvae. Such infestations did not endear themselves to the valley's foresters for they regarded them as proliferations of vermin but it was an ideal place to look for woodpeckers.

309

There were seven different species of woodpecker in Switzerland (eight if you counted the problematical migratory Wryneck) and four of these species were resident in the high coniferous forests of the Toggenburg. Most common of all were the Greater Spotted Woodpecker and these handsome black and white barred birds were ubiquitous in the forests, probably outnumbering all the other three species put together. Then there were the flamboyant Green Woodpeckers with their green plumage and red crests and the far carrying laughing calls that always sounded to Sarah like maniacal cackling. The most spectacular species was the big Black Woodpecker, as big as a crow and extravagantly demonstrative as they flew around the forest uttering their piercing yelps and ringing calls. They were not a species you associated with quiet discretion. Even when they tapped on trees to dig out the insets within, it sounded like someone taking an axe to the tree. By far and away the real treasure to sight was the scarcest and most elusive of the alpine woodpeckers. It was a smaller but quite distinctive black and white species and notoriously hard to find. It was called a Three Toed Woodpecker and it was so retiring and scarce that Sarah reckoned that if she saw two a year it was notable.

This damaged woodland with its food reserves of insects in the dead timber was the place to find it however and Sarah spent the next hours combing the forest for it. It seemed as if she had expended her luck for the day with a sighting of a Rock Bunting, however, for the woodpecker eluded her. Several times she stalked a likely sounding tapping from the trees only to find that the cause was a Great Spotted Woodpecker or a Nuthatch, another bird with a propensity for boring holes in trees. Frustrated at last, she sat on a log to scribble notes in her field diary. The woodpecker might have evaded her grasp but as she sat writing she was awarded a fine compensation. A bird whistled in the dense under-shrub of the forest on the slope beneath her. She couldn't see the bird but she didn't need to in order to instantly identify that call. Only a Hazelhen sounded quite like that and it was another elusive species; a small game bird that was by no means common in the Toggenburg.

On that note of triumph, Sarah decided that she had achieved enough for the day and made her way leisurely down through the forest to Alpli. The day had one last pleasure to offer her. Along the forestry road in front of her a hare leaped out, scuttled some distance before her and jumped back into the undergrowth abutting the trail. It was an animal that was always a delight to see for it was a Mountain Hare. They were smaller than their cousins, the Brown Hare, and they turned pure white in the winter. In the summer they could be instantly recognised by their tails which remained pure white throughout the year. In pleasure Sarah noted the sighting down in her diary. She was conducting a survey of the observations of these animals with a view to determining their abundance and distribution within the Toggenburg. It was another project likely to be curtailed by her forthcoming marriage.

Out of the forest at last, Sarah devoted some time to examining the stone walls of the Alpli. She wasn't particularly interested in the walls themselves so much as the mosses that grew on them. In the last year she had developed an interest in mosses. Previously she had simply regarded them as attractive green growths that decorated such things as, well dry stone walls for instance. Latterly however she had decided that that was doing them less than justice. They were a fascinating branch of botany in their own right. She had read somewhere that there were over twenty thousand recognised species of moss in the world and that figure probably represented only a fraction of the true total. They were a sadly neglected and overlooked body of

311

plants. Sarah suspected that the reason for that was that they were, for want of a better word, so useless. Nobody ate mosses. They had virtually no industrial or medicinal purpose. They just grew on forest floors, on trees or, yes, stone walls. Mosses were unobtrusive, inoffensive, minded their own business and just got on with living. They were often hard to identify to species, as well, which made the study of them one for specialists. Sarah didn't know how many bryologists there were in the world but she guessed it was not an astronomical number. She hoped, at least, that some people loved the little velvety carpets of them and dedicated lifetimes to their study.

All in all, Sarah's lazy ramble down the mountain to her house in Alpli took her most of the day and it was early evening before she approached her house, a delay even further exacerbated by a long pause to pull off her boots and dangle her feet deliciously in the cold stream that ran through the alp. In spite of her troubled mind Sarah's short sojourn in the mountains had achieved its purpose for she was at ease with herself and tranquil as she approached the house. Her first clue that that tranquillity was about to be shattered came as she neared the house. Nicole's car was parked at the side of the house. Sarah frowned in concern. She had expected Nicole to be at work.

Chapter Twenty-Seven

Discarding her boots at the front door, Sarah strode into the house in puzzlement. Nicole was curled up on the sofa with an air of such abject misery that Sarah came to a grinding halt. "Nicky!" she expostulated. "What the hell is the matter?"

Nicole looked awful. She was huddled up gripping her knees and her eyes were red in the pale background of her pinched face. She held a tissue in one hand and snuffled miserably. "Where have you been?" she asked accusingly.

"I've been hiking. Didn't you see my note?"

"You went off and left me without a word! I didn't know where the hell you were. How could you do that to me?"

"Nicky I went hiking. I wrote you a note to say I'd be back today. What on earth's the matter with you? Why aren't you at work?"

Nicole dabbed her eyes. "They sent me home."

"Sent you home? Why?"

"I was poorly so the boss sent me home. I feel rotten."

"Poorly? What's the matter with you?"

"Oh nothing just PMS."

"PMS?" Sarah was astonished. She knew that Nicole sometimes suffered from menstrual cramps but this was the first time she had confessed to Premenstrual syndrome. "You've never had PMS before."

"How would you know? You're never here."

Sarah sat on the sofa beside Nicole and wrapped an arm around her. "Oh Nicky I'm sorry! I'd never have gone off hiking if I'd known you were poorly."

"Hmmph! As if I matter to you."

"Don't be silly Nicky! Of course you matter. Are you sure it's PMS?" Sarah held a hand to Nicole's brow. "You're not coming down with something are you?"

"Dunno. I just feel horrible."

Sarah hugged her. "Well let's get you to bed then. Have you eaten anything?" Nicole shook her head feebly. "Right then. Let's put you to bed and I'll make you something to eat."

"I don't know if I can manage anything."

"Nonsense Nicky. You must eat. I'll rustle up some spaghetti and a warm drink and you can eat in bed."

"Are you going out again?"

"No Nicky. I wasn't planning to."

"Stay in Sarah. Just tonight. Stay with me. I feel awful."

"Of course I'll stay with you. I'll make us both something to eat and then we'll cuddle up in bed together and watch a couple of DVDs on the telly. How's that sound?"

Nicole managed a watery smile. "Fine. Where did you go for the last two days anyway?"

"Just up to the Zwingli hut Nicky. I just wanted to take a little hike."

"Was *she* with you?"

"Was who with me? What are you talking about?"

"Daniela. Did she go with you?"

"Of course not. Why on earth would you think that Daniela would be with me?"

"Just wondered that's all."

"Nicky I left you a note saying I was going hiking for two days on my own. Surely you saw it."

"Yeah I saw it."

"Well then you know what I was doing."

"I suppose so."

Sarah looked at her friend critically. "You look terrible Nicole. You should be in bed. Come on now I want you in bed."

It took some cajoling but eventually Nicole allowed herself to be chivvied into bed with a mug of hot chocolate. Sarah went downstairs to prepare food. Nicole loved spaghetti Bolognaise and could have happily lived on little else. Sarah took a packet of fresh mincemeat from the fridge, a tin of tomato puree from the kitchen cupboard and set to dicing onions and garlic to make her sauce. She took a packet of grated Parmesan cheese from the cabinet and paused to run a hand in bewilderment through her hair. She had never heard Nicole complain of PMS before. She had certainly no inclination that Nicole suffered from it to such a severe degree that she would be sent home from work with it. Something was seriously wrong.

The telephone extension in the kitchen chimed loudly and Sarah picked up the receiver tentatively. "Hello?"

"Hello. Is that you Nicole?"

"No. No it's Sarah; Nicole's housemate."

"Oh Sarah! How wonderful to hear you again. It's Frau Wald from the Hotel Hirschen."

"Oh hello Frau Wald. Are you phoning about Nicole?"

"Yes. Yes I am. I was just worrying about her and if she got home all right."

"Yes she's here at home Frau Wald. I've put her to bed. She looks terrible. What on earth happened?"

"She broke down at work Sarah."

"*Broke down!*"

"Yes I'm afraid so. She completely came apart on us, collapsed in tears and we could do nothing to console her. She was in a hell of a state. Is she all right now?"

"Well she looks pretty miserable Frau Wald but I put her to bed a few minutes ago and she seems to be cheering up a little bit. She says she suffers from PMS."

"Yes that's what she told me. I have every sympathy. I know from personal experience what that's like. I do hope she's feeling better."

"I'm sorry Frau Wald. I do hope it hasn't left you short in the hotel."

"Oh we're all right tonight Sarah. I've got enough people on and we're not that busy. Do you think she'll be ok in the morning though?"

"I don't know Frau Wald but my instinct says she'd be better for a good night's sleep."

"Damn! It's just that she's on the rota to serve breakfast and I'm a bit short handed in the morning tomorrow."

Sarah thought for a second or two. "When is her breakfast shift Frau Wald?"

"From six to eleven in the morning Sarah. I could really do with her then if she's feeling up to it."

Sarah ran over timetables in her head. "I really think that she needs to get a good sleep Frau Wald. I'll tell you what I'll do however. If you're short in the morning I'll come in and do Nicole's shift for her. Would that be acceptable for you?"

"Oh Sarah there's no need to trouble yourself to that extent."

"It would be my pleasure Frau Wald. I've worked enough breakfasts in hotels before and, although I might have to learn some of the ropes at the Hirschen, I'm sure I'll soon pick it up. In any case, it's better than you going without anybody at all."

"Well if you're absolutely sure Sarah."

"Yes I am Frau Wald. There's only one thing though. I will have to leave at eleven prompt because I have to catch a train for Winterthur in the afternoon. Would that be a problem?"

"Not at all Sarah. In fact we might be able to let you get away early. Most of the breakfast is done by ten and then it's just a matter of cleaning up really and I'm sure we can handle that."

"Very well then I'll see you at six in the morning."

"Thank you very much Sarah. You've taken a weight off my mind. Tell Nicole I asked after her."

"I will do Frau Wald. Until tomorrow then."

Nicole was propped up in bed with a box of tissues when Sarah walked in with a tray containing two steaming plates of Spaghetti Bolognaise. She'd been crying again and Sarah's concern deepened. "Are you ok Nicky?"

Nicole nodded dismally. "I'll live."

Sarah looked at her worriedly. "I've cooked some spaghetti Nicky; your favourite. You must try to eat."

"Will you stay with me?"

Sarah smiled. "Of course Nicky. Look I put my pyjamas on so move up a bit and let me crawl in and let's get crumbs in the bed. I toasted some garlic bread as well and I've got a bottle of that Spanish Rioja out of the wine cabinet."

Nicole hung her head in misery. "Why are you being so nice to me?"

"Hmm! Difficult one that. Maybe it's something to do with the fact that you're my best friend in the whole world and I hate to see you so miserable. Just a suggestion of course. I'm sure it must have more obscure reasons behind it."

"Oh Sarah!"

"Stop weeping Nicky. Come on, move up and let me into bed before our dinner gets cold." Nicole shuffled aside to allow Sarah under the bedclothes and Sarah laid the tray down across their laps. "Oh by the way Nicky your boss phoned up."

"Oh hell! What did she want?"

"She just wanted to see that you're all right. She was a bit worried about the morning too."

"Oh shit! I'm supposed to be working the breakfast shift." Nicole buried her head in her hands. "I can't go in in the morning! I can't face it!"

"You don't have to. I've sorted it."

Nicole raised her head. "What do you mean?"

"I'm doing your shift in the morning. You can have a lie in."

"Are you crazy?"

"Not at all. I told Frau Wald that I'd cover for you tomorrow. She's fine about it. You might have to give me a quick briefing on things before we sleep tonight but I'm sure everything will be just fine."

"But Sarah..."

Sarah stilled her words with a finger to her lips. "Hush now. It's all sorted. Now eat before it gets cold."

Nicole ate in silence and Sarah noted with gratification that, despite her protests, there was little wrong with Nicole's appetite. They drank a glass of wine and put a silly girly DVD on the television to amuse themselves with. Nicole still seemed sad but at least her melancholy was not as deep and she began to recover her morale. Sarah's therapy was proving most efficacious. They placed the tray aside, replete and lay back in bed together. Nicole hugged Sarah and clung to her tenaciously, burying her head in Sarah's shoulder. Her acute depression was not yet past for Sarah could feel the dampness of her tears through her pyjamas. She gripped Nicole around the shoulders and held her tenderly. "Nicky what's wrong with you? It isn't PMS is it?"

Nicole shuddered and would not look her in the face. "You wouldn't understand Sarah."

"Try me!"

Nicole shook her head and gripped her tighter. "No! I can't."

Sarah sighed and stroked Nicole's hair. "All right Nicky but you'll have to tell me sometime."

318

"Maybe sometime."

They lay quietly in each other's arms for a long time and presently they fell asleep.

Chapter Twenty-Eight

Sarah stepped out of the railway station in Winterthur the following day, at a little before three o'clock. It had been a bit of a rushed day and, so far, a long one for Sarah had risen from bed at five in the morning to take Nicole's car to drive to Wildhaus to cover Nicole's shift at the Hotel Hirschen. Frau Wald had been pathetically grateful for Sarah's intervention and she'd treated Sarah like some long-lost prodigal daughter. She hadn't exactly killed the fatted calf, but she'd insisted that Sarah eat some breakfast before starting work and she'd been kind and considerate all morning. Sarah had donned an old waitress's uniform of black skirt, white blouse and pinafore, that was a legacy of her previous summer's work at the Hotel Toggenburg, and mucked in with the breakfast shift. She considered that Frau Wald was over dramatising the emergency of not having Nicole on duty, for breakfast hadn't been that busy.

The hotel laid on a self-service buffet for breakfast and the waiting duties consisted mainly of clearing away dirty dishes and producing pots of coffee and tea. It had been straightforward and Sarah privately thought that Frau Wald's other waitresses could easily have picked up the slack had they not been apparently allergic to anything resembling hard work. Frau Wald had been delighted however. Sarah was a hard-working conscientious girl and it did not elude Frau Wald's notice that she managed to do nearly twice as much work as either of the other two girls on duty, in spite of her never having worked in the hotel before.

Sarah, for her part, had been gratified to note that Frau Wald held Nicole in high esteem. Nicole, it has to be said, had a less than exemplary work record in her previous employments but, on the evidence of Frau

Wald's enthusiastic endorsement, she had applied herself diligently to her work in the hotel and become an important cog in the day to day running of the establishment. Frau Wald clearly liked Nicole. She was genuinely worried about the crisis that had overtaken her the previous day. She had plied Sarah with concerned questions and seemed comforted by Sarah's reassurances. Nicole it seemed was quite a favourite of hers, albeit one about whom she had no illusions of the temperamental nature of. Sarah noted a common characteristic of those people that liked Nicole. Their admiration was always tinged with amusement. Nicole was a loveable eccentric and, love her as you might, there was always that little part of you that refused to take her seriously. Nicole was Nicole; a character and an endless source of diverting anecdotes. It was impossible to think of her without a smile.

If Frau Wald liked Nicole, there was, furthermore, no doubt whatsoever that she adored Sarah. Sarah never really understood the roots of her popularity in the valley but it was very nearly universal. Frau Wald considered it typical of Sarah that she would instantly offer to cover for her sick friend's absence. It was just the kind of noble gesture that Sarah would perform. Frau Wald cursed the fortune that Sarah had come so late to the valley that summer, after she had filled her staff vacancies for the season. In Sarah, she would have had an altogether completely reliable young lady to serve in her hotel who was popular, of amicable nature and diligent in her duties. She would have been an enormous asset to the hotel. Staff of those qualities were hard to come by. Frau Wald even wondered if her staff budget would allow her to take on Sarah without the necessity of off-loading one of her current employees.

Before Sarah had left that morning therefore, Frau Wald had insisted on her sitting down with a cup of coffee and discerning Sarah's plans for the summer.

Sarah had reiterated the scenario she had discussed with Frau Fritzl at the Hotel Toggenburg and indicated that she would be available for temporary employment should the need arise and left Frau Wald her telephone number. Frau Wald had been enormously satisfied by the details of the arrangement for it gave her Sarah's outstanding services, as and when required, without the problematical obligation of placing her on a full-time contract. Sarah was finding a useful niche in the Toggenburg's tourist industry.

However, Sarah had had to rush to drive home at the end of the breakfast shift for she had more compelling priorities this day; to wit a crucial and perhaps life defining meeting with Peter in Winterthur, at three in the afternoon. Nicole, by now seemingly feeling much better, had greeted Sarah's return to the house effusively and, realising the importance of Sarah's mission that day, had enthusiastically launched herself into action on behalf of the cause. They'd only had an hour in terms of preparation but Nicole, shrugging off her lethargic depression of the night before, had addressed the question of Sarah's appearance for the forthcoming showdown with admirable energy. She had dressed Sarah to kill and, refusing to let her appearance suffer at the uncertain hands of the postal bus service, had driven her to the railway station in Nesslau all the while drilling her on the subject of suitably feminine wiles for the potential capture of her future mate. "Be sweet and demure!" she had warned Sarah, "And for fuck's sake try not to bore him to death with conversations about alpine eco-systems! He's after a girl not a fucking biologist."

Sarah had regarded Nicole vexedly. "I'm not a street tart out touting for business Nicky. Peter will have to take me as I come."

"A policy that hasn't exactly born fruit up until now Foxy. For God's sake try and forget that you know more about the life cycle of Lycaenidae butterflies than he'll ever know and bat your eyelashes seductively and try being a fucking woman for a change."

"Oh now *you're* doubting my female credentials are you?"

"I'm just telling you to flaunt it a bit. A man needs to see a suitably submissive little feminine thing and doesn't want the fact that she's three times cleverer than him rubbed in his face. Let him woo you and make him think he has to protect you and nurture you even if we know he couldn't be trusted to put a pair of matching socks on in the morning without supervision. Men have got fragile egos Sarah. They turn to so much mush without us telling them how wonderful they are regularly."

"God you make them sound like infants!"

"They *are* infants Sarah. By the time that a man is mature enough to be on equal terms with a woman he's generally too old to be attractive. Even then most men don't grow up at all. They're all just big kids when it all boils down to things."

"I'm trying to get married Nicky not take on maternal responsibilities."

"Amounts to the same thing. Look we're coming up to the station. Now have you got all the necessary cosmetics in your handbag?"

"Yes Nicky." Sarah told her, in some exasperation.

"Good because you'll need to correct your face in the train. Don't forget to spray a whiff of that perfume on you before you walk in the pub. Don't lose it either. That stuff cost me over seventy francs for the bottle."

Sarah sighed. "I shall endeavour to follow your instructions Nicole."

Sarah had taken the train to Wil with a certain amused exasperation but at least she was gratified that Nicole seemed to be bouncing back from her malaise admirably. Sarah had been worried about her and

Nicole's protestations that her malady was nothing more than pre-menstrual stress hadn't convinced her for a moment. Something deeper was going on with her normally ebullient house mate. Sarah was concerned and at a loss to explain it.

But Sarah had more pressing issues to address today than her friend's emotional fluctuations and she'd boarded the Inter-City train to Winterthur in a spirit of excitement, tinged with apprehension. Her nervousness had increased during the short journey to Winterthur and by the time the train had pulled into Winterthur station she'd been biting her lip with anxiety. Now, emerging from the station, she took a deep breath and steeled herself for the crucial meeting that lay ahead. Sarah had no illusions about the importance of the impending interview with Peter. In a real sense her entire future could hinge on the outcome of the serious talk Peter wished to conduct with her. She might have decisions to make whose consequences could determine the rest of her life. It was a pivotal day and her nervousness was understandable.

Chapter Twenty-Nine

Sarah crossed the road, outside the station, with trepidation, taking care to watch out closely for the trolley buses that pulled into the bus station outside the bahnhof. Sarah was very afraid of trolley buses. The electric buses that took their power from overhead lines in Winterthur were deathly quiet. Once, when she'd been a young girl, Sarah had nearly been run over by a trolley bus in Winterthur because she'd failed to hear its whispering approach as she skipped across the road. She'd been wary of them ever since. Even after three years at university in Bern Sarah was uncomfortable with the hazards of urban life.

Winterthur was not a big city but it was a busy one and, unusually for a Swiss town, it had virtually no tourist trade. Winterthur was a small industrial town of around 100,000 inhabitants and it had previously grown to prominence as a centre of the Swiss railway industry and heavy engineering. Much of that industry had largely disappeared, by now, but the city was still a transport hub and its engineering background was reflected in its large technology school and its science and technology museum. Although, in common with other Swiss cities, Winterthur had a strong banking and insurance sector there was still the feeling that this was a functional town; a place where things were made; whose commerce was greased with machine oil and not merely the nuances of high finance. Its elegant pedestrian shopping streets and fine restaurants could not conceal that this was a town where people were accustomed to getting their hands dirty.

It was perhaps this functionality that attracted Sarah to it for she had little understanding of the rarefied upper echelons of financial institutions. Alan might live in that world but it was alien territory to Sarah. She did, however, understand the basic principles of honest labour; that you made something and sold it for solid money and that the fruits of your labour were tangible and had a physical existence. It was not Sarah's nature to understand how a person might sit at a computer and generate millions of francs in revenue simply by juggling figures around. She was a person who liked to be able to have the solid evidence of her labour in her hands and not merely as an abstraction in numbers. Winterthur, therefore, had Sarah's sympathy. It was not the most beautiful and elegant of Swiss cities but it felt like an honest one.

Having negotiated the road safely, Sarah was surprised by the sound of a piercing wolf whistle. She glanced around curiously for the source of this sound and the possible motivation for it. A group of young lads were lounging by the bus station in the middle of the road and regarding her admiringly. With a blush, Sarah realised that the whistle had been directed at her. Feeling flustered she hurried on but, once on the long pedestrian shopping street that led away from the station, she paused to look at her reflection in the plate glass window of a boutique. Sarah was unused to such overt demonstrations of physical admiration on the street and she felt embarrassed, a touch irritable, prudishly outraged and secretly rather pleased. The reflection in the window told its own tale for Sarah blinked in surprise to see the lovely young lady that stared back out at her from its polished surface.

Nicole had done a fine job for Sarah looked radiant. Nicole had insisted that Sarah wear her hair loose. Men loved the stuff she'd explained. Long luxurious hair of the kind that Sarah was endowed with was a siren's call to the male libido. Let the gorgeous stuff flow she'd insisted. Don't tie it back like you usually do when you go to town. Let it hang out and shimmer in the sunlight and every warm-blooded male in town will want to stroke it or bury his face in it and make animal growling noises.

Sarah wore the third of the three new dresses she had bought in Buchs and, although it was the cheapest of the three, it was, in many ways, the most becoming on her. It was a simple white summer cotton dress, sleeveless and buttoned up the front and very short, exposing a generous length of Sarah's impeccably smooth legs atop the simple white shoes she wore. It was sexy' without being provocatively so, and of such soft cotton that it both clung to her frame and swished away from her at the slightest movement. Sarah looked angelic in it. Nicole had been delighted. It was just the thing to flaunt her feminine charms and yet retain a degree of virginal innocence. If Peter's animal lusts were not stirred by it then Nicole declared that they would have to declare him clinically dead and have him removed before the smell became offensive. Sarah took a lingering look at her own reflection and wondered what was becoming of her. For her to be seen in public wearing three new sexy dresses (not to mention a new bikini and beach wrap) within the space of a few days was unprecedented. But nevertheless Sarah was privately pleased. She was beginning to enjoy her blossoming femininity.

It was a short walk down the pedestrian street to the English pub where she was due to meet Peter. These "English" pubs were popular in Switzerland especially among younger people. They were for the most part, it must be admitted, pretty awful imitations of the English public house complete with brass fittings, phony brass and copper decorations, English style bars and garish mirrors. They'd often have pictures of John Bull and Lord Kitchener or other English icons decorating the walls. There were even yards of ale hanging over the bar, fake old English pub signs, advertisements for English beer and any other tacky artefact that their misguided designers considered to be the essential accoutrement to an English public house. They were usually characterised by loud juke boxes, gaming machines, dart boards and pool tables, as well, which frequently made them a poor choice for quiet conversation. The service tended to lower Swiss standards too for they had a policy of English service which meant you had to go to the bar for your drinks rather than have a waiter deliver them to your table. They were plastic, cheap parodies of a true English pub and most English people would have cringed in embarrassment at the thought that Swiss people considered this an Englishman's natural environment.

The English pub in Winterthur, although fairly wretched, was at least one of the less objectionable examples of its breed and it had been around long enough to begin to acquire the beginnings of a character that was the true mark of a traditional English pub. There was a small sunny terrace outside the pub on the side of the pedestrian precinct and Sarah hoped that Peter would have had the sense to take a table there in the open air and sunshine. Sadly the terrace was full of young people, all looking shockingly intoxicated given the early hour of the day, and Sarah resigned herself to the gloomy smoke-filled interior.

She saw Peter as soon as she entered the pub although for a moment she failed to recognise him. When she did register that the handsome well-dressed man leaning on the bar was the very same one with whom she was scheduled to hold an intimate and clandestine rendezvous with, she skidded to a halt, barely able to credit the evidence of her eyes. Peter was leaning over his beer glass lost in thought and he didn't notice Sarah's arrival for some seconds. This gave her time to peruse him at leisure and to hastily return her sagging jaw to its customary position. It was Peter but Peter as she had scarcely, if ever, seen him before. It was obvious that she was not the only person that had made an effort to dress up today for Peter was casually but smartly dressed in neatly creased trousers and a fine open-necked shirt under a smart, well fitted, blue grey blazer that suited him well. His shoes were new and polished while his normally, unruly hair was newly trimmed and styled. Sarah was so used to the image of Peter in his old clothes; his regrettable old green flannel or corduroy trousers and frayed shapeless shirts; his muddy mountain boots and thick polo necked pullovers with holes in the sleeves, that this image of him dressed in debonair city fashion left her at a loss. He looked devastatingly good-looking.

Sarah realised that she was standing there, foolishly staring at him, and made toward the bar. At the same time, Peter caught sight of her and turned toward her with a hesitant smile. He was looking, if anything, more nervous than she was. He embraced her warmly however and pecked her lightly on the cheek. At close quarters Sarah scented the aroma of a good quality after-shave on him and his face was smooth with no trace of stubble. Sarah approved. She liked her men clean shaven. For the brief moment that Peter folded her in his strong arms she felt a flickering twinge of arousal. She felt suddenly very girly indeed pressed against his firm body in her thin cotton dress. Sarah was not a small girl but Peter towered over her and his chest and arms were huge. She was aware of the blood rushing to her cheeks and the hardening of her nipples.

"It's good to see you Sarah." he said at last.

"And you too Peter." Sarah held his hand and took a step back to look at him. "My word you look just beautiful. Are those clothes new?"

Peter squirmed in embarrassment, "Yeah I just bought them yesterday. Er you look very nice too Sarah."

329

"Why thank you kind sir. Now are you going to buy me a drink?"

"Yes! Yes of course. What will you have? Beer?"

Sarah hesitated. It was warm out and she was thirsty. What she really wanted was a kubel of beer. She could almost feel Nicole jiggling her elbow. *"Be ladylike you twit! You've dressed up like a high-class tart now for fuck's sake don't go and spoil the effect by sitting there with a half litre mug of beer you halfwit!"* "Er I'd like a small sherry if I may Peter."

"Sherry?" Peter looked perplexed.

"Yes Peter. Sherry! It's a sort of fortified wine produced from white grapes from the town of Jerez in Spain I believe." Sarah could hear an imaginary Nicole groaning in the background. *"Shut up Sarah! Stop being a clever dick!"*

"Right er... sherry then." Peter turned to the barman. "Er a small sherry please."

"Cream, Fino or Amontillado sir?"

"Eh?"

Sarah hastened to the rescue. "An Amontillado if you please."

"Very well miss."

Once furnished with her drink Peter nodded to a corner of the pub. "It's a bit quieter over there. Shall we take a seat?"

Yes thank you. I'd like that."

They walked over to a free table. Sarah stood expectantly by a chair but Peter seemed oblivious to the fact that she was waiting for him to pull the chair out and offer to seat her gracefully. He flopped down opposite and regarded her in puzzlement. "Why are you still stood up?"

Sarah sighed resignedly. "Oh no reason." She took her seat.

Peter was pointing accusingly at the tiny glass in front of her. "Since when have you ever drunk sherry

Sarah? The only time I can remember you drinking sherry was that time you pinched a bottle out of your dad's drinks cabinet at Christmas when you were fourteen and we drank it at Steffi Gugelheim's party and you were as sick as a dog the next day."

Sarah raised an exasperated eyebrow indignantly. "You're really getting this conversation off to a good start aren't you Peter?"

Peter's expression of perplexity grew deeper. "What do you mean?"

"I'm just trying to point out a fairly unusual and obviously not particularly apparent fact Peter."

"Which is?"

"Well namely that, due to some mysterious and incomprehensible metamorphosis, I am actually no longer a spotty faced adolescent but in fact a grown woman."

Peter shook his head. "No that's not true. You were never spotty; a bit gangly and awkward perhaps but certainly not spotty."

Sarah issued a silent prayer for patience. "You're not really getting the point here are you Peter?"

"Well give me a few clues Sarah."

Sarah took a deep breath. "What I'm trying to say Peter is that I'm no longer fourteen years old but in fact a twenty-one-year-old woman who would rather not have the foolishness of her youth dragged up whilst she is attempting to convey the maturity appropriate to her years."

Peter frowned. "You've changed Sarah."

"Yes Peter. I know. It's called growing up."

Peter shook his head thoughtfully. "No I don't mean that. Well perhaps I do maybe. Oh I know you've grown up. Sometimes it's hard for me to recognise it because in my mind your always my little Sarah; almost my kid sister."

Sarah frowned. This was not a promising start. "Sister?"

"Yes I've always sort of thought of you like that. I was never close to my sister. You're the closest thing to thing to one I have."

Sarah stifled a groan. This was going to be hard work. She realised that she was not exactly following Nicole's instructions. She forced herself to soften her face and smile. "Peter people do grow up you know. I'm not your kid sister. I'm a grown woman. I'm a grown woman with her own prerogatives and her own...." Sarah allowed her eyes to lower suggestively, "her own needs."

Peter leaned back in his chair and took a swig of his beer thoughtfully. He didn't seem to be able to meet Sarah's eyes. "Yes Sarah." he said at last. "You've grown up. I'm sorry. I'm not an easy man with words. I didn't want to... well to demean your womanhood. I know you're a woman. I saw that the day you visited me up on the alp. You're not the young girl I used to know. You're a woman and that makes things difficult for me."

Sarah blinked in surprise. "Why should that make things difficult?"

Peter sighed heavily. "I don't know. I suppose I had some growing up to do as well. I've always thought of you as my little sister and then when you came up to the alp I saw that things were different; you'd changed into a woman. I see you now all dressed up and so very.... well so very female. I suppose I'm just having a hard time getting my head around it."

Sarah felt confused but she pressed on bravely. "I think you've grown up too Peter. You could have knocked me out with a feather when I walked in here today. I've never seen you look so handsome and so... so masculine." Sarah could hear Nicole's cheers in the background. *"Atta girl Foxy! Flatter his ego and the job's half done."*

332

Peter took a long deep breath and leaned forward over the table suddenly to take Sarah's hand. "Sarah I want you to know, whatever happens, what you mean to me. You've been my dearest friend for most of my life. I love you to pieces and I couldn't bear the thought of us being separated."

Sarah squeezed his hand gently. This was more like it. "Thank you Peter. That's a lovely thing to say. You mean a lot to me too. Perhaps we might not have to be separated." "*There now*" Sarah thought. "*I can't give you an opening better than that!*"

The gambit seemed to pass Peter by however for he looked troubled. "I don't know what to do Sarah. I'm frightened of losing you."

Sarah smiled and leaned across the table to touch Peter's face gently. "Why should you lose me Peter? I am here. I am still uncommitted. I'm still here to be won not lost."

Sarah was surprised at Peter's reaction for his discomfort increased by the second. "That's the problem Sarah."

"What *is* the problem for God's sake Peter?"

Peter disengaged his hand and took a moment to marshal his thoughts. Sarah waited holding her breath; the sounds of the pub seemed to recede into a distant buzz. Peter was squirming uncomfortably and agonising over his words. "I don't really know how to begin." He confessed at last.

Sarah urged tranquillity on herself. "You wanted to talk to me Peter." She reminded him. "You said that you had private things to discuss; things about me and my marriage and so forth. You've told me that you're frightened of losing me. Perhaps we can start with that."

Peter it has to be said was not the most articulate of men or the most comfortable in discussing private matters and Sarah saw that she was in for a long haul. "Sarah" he began finally with all the air of a man wading through treacle. "Why do you suppose I asked to see you today?"

"I don't know Peter. I gathered from the snippets of information that I managed to garner from your not particularly specific preamble that there were certain issues that you had with my upcoming marriage and that there were things that you needed to say before I made a commitment to that marriage. You told me on the telephone that you love me. I presumed that you wished to elaborate on that statement and, as a result, that it may or may not have some bearing on my future plans. Other than that Peter I'm fuddled. I could do with some more input here."

Peter grimaced in consternation. "Why have you come dressed like that Sarah?" he asked petulantly.

Sarah was taken aback and she blinked at him in surprise. "Is my choice of dress offensive to you Peter?"

"You look lovely Sarah; too lovely."

"*Too lovely?*"

"Yes! I mean look at you. I've never seen you dress up so well just to go for a couple of beers in the pub. You're wearing make-up and a dress for God's sake. When you walked in this pub half the men present couldn't take their eyes off you. A year ago you'd have come in an old pair of jeans and a shirt. Now you come flouncing in like a fashion model. This isn't you. It's not the Sarah I know."

Sarah blushed feeling foolish. "I'm sorry Peter." She mumbled sadly. "I thought you might like me to dress up nicely for a change. Maybe I wanted you to see that I'm a woman. I don't know. I'll put a pair of dungarees on next time if it makes you feel more comfortable." Sarah turned her eyes away feeling slightly hurt.

"You dressed like that to appear more attractive to me didn't you Sarah?" Peter asked her accusingly.

Sarah's face blushed crimson and she lowered her head. "Yes I did Peter. I... I didn't know it would offend you."

"Sarah! What about Alan?"

Sarah raised her head defiantly. "What about him?"

"You know what Sarah. You're practically engaged to the man and here you are flaunting yourself at me. I saw it the other day up on the alp too. You deliberately dressed up provocatively when you knew you were coming to see me. Am I right?"

Sarah felt the beginnings of anger and she flared at Peter. "Are you suggesting that I'm dressing up like a tart Peter?"

"I'm not suggesting anything of the sort Sarah. You can never be a tart. Nevertheless you are, by your own admission, deliberately dressing to attract me. Isn't that true?"

"Well what if it is? Why shouldn't I?"

"What would Alan say?"

"The devil with Alan! All he sees when he sees me are dollar signs. If I wanted to attract him I'd dress up as a blank cheque."

"That's unfair Sarah. Alan is a fine man and he thinks the world of you."

"Oh really? Is that why I receive such long eulogies of love, undying devotion and breathless prose concerning his inability to live without me?" Sarah's sarcasm was bitter. "I know and, if you had two brain cells to rub together, you'd know that this is an arranged marriage largely based upon financial advantage. I'm not a future wife to Alan Peter. I'm a sound career move."

"That's enough Sarah! I'll not hear you disparage him like this. You are doing him an injustice. Perhaps he's not the best at articulating his feelings but I know that he's devoted to you and that he wants to make you happy."

Sarah stared at Peter in shock. "Have you been discussing me with Alan?"

"Well yes a couple of times Sarah. In fact he phoned me up yesterday."

"I don't believe I'm hearing this!"

"Don't go loopy on me Sarah. He was worried about you is all. Apparently your mother has been in touch and told him that you're having second thoughts about the marriage and he says you were downright abrupt with him on the phone the other day."

"You mean the bastard has been consulting with other people behind my back and hasn't the balls to talk to me in person?"

"Enough Sarah! Of course Alan has talked to other people since you've hardly demonstrated a will to talk to him yourself. He's worried Sarah; worried sick. He expected that you'd be moving to the Ticino to prepare for your marriage as soon as you left uni and now he hears from your mother that you are stubbornly refusing to contemplate such a move on the grounds that you're not officially engaged. You've led him to believe that the engagement is a pure formality and now you're saying that it's anything but. Naturally he sought advice from people who know you. I admit he asked me to have a talk with you."

Sarah slumped back in her chair angrily. "So in fact this entire meeting is just a marriage guidance interview. Alan has enlisted your assistance in bringing me back into the fold has he? What are you supposed to do Peter; spank me for flaunting myself at other men whilst my fiancée's back is turned? Shall I throw away my new clothes and prostrate myself in sack cloth and ashes in church to beg forgiveness for my sins?"

"Sarah! That's enough."

"Don't talk to me like a child Peter. Do I have to keep pointing out I'm a grown woman?"

"Then start acting like one and listen to what I have to say Sarah."

"When will you talk to Alan again Peter?"

"I don't know. He said he'd call sometime this week."

"Excellent! Would you therefore do me the singular favour of informing the gentleman you are representing that he needn't bother to get measured up for his top hat and tails because I wouldn't marry him if he was the last bastard left on the planet possessed of XY chromosomes!"

Peter held up his hands. "Sarah! Please. Calm down. Just calm down and let me finish."

Sarah took a deep breath. "I'm listening Peter."

Peter collected his thoughts once more. "Very well Sarah for one thing I'm not just Alan's representative. I have my own reasons for wanting to see you; personal reasons. Secondly Alan has not solicited my assistance concerning you. He phoned me up on a completely unrelated issue and it was during the conversation that your name came up. It was understandable Sarah. Alan usually talks about you. After all you are the person he wants to marry. Naturally he thinks about you all the time and it is reflected in his conversation. I detected that all was not well and it was I that volunteered to have a word with you. He was grateful for that because, as I've already said, he's not a man that's easy with intimate words."

"So he handed the job over to the world's greatest orator then in the confident knowledge that your velvet prose and romantic poetry would make me see the error of my ways and rush back to his arms in contrite supplication."

"All right Sarah! There's no need for that. I know I'm not the best person with words either but I'm trying and this isn't easy for me."

"You don't need a lot of words to explain my position Peter. The simple phrase "please take your engagement ring and shove up it up your arse." will be amply sufficient."

Peter groaned comically and shook his head in exasperation. "This isn't like you Sarah. I expected at least that you would give me a chance to explain."

"I think I've got the picture Peter."

"No you haven't! That's the problem Sarah. You haven't even looked beyond the frame."

"Well then enlighten me."

Peter regarded his empty glass mournfully. "I need more beer first. This is going to be harder than I expected. Can I get you another sherry?"

"Yes please; a large one this time."

Once he had replenished their drinks Sarah felt almost sorry for Peter. He was obviously agonising over how to proceed. Eventually he drew breath and waded in manfully. "Look let's start over Sarah. When I took that job with the cows on the alp it wasn't particularly that I had a hankering to spend two weeks in a freezing cold hut, up to my arse in cow shit. I needed to get away from things for a while; to think things through. There have been things going on in my life that have unsettled me and I've had to face up to them. Up on that alp I took a good long look at my life and decided it was going nowhere. I'd been hiding from things for far too long and it was time to confront them and address them. I made some important decisions but not easy ones. There are things I have to do that might upset a lot of people. There was one thing, however, that gave me comfort and that was you."

"Me?"

"Yes Sarah. You were the one stable thing in my life; the one thing that remained constant. There was always Sarah. You were the one person I thought would understand. We've known each other all our lives near enough. Every time I wonder about some problem I ask myself what would Sarah do? Every time I see something beautiful I want to share it with you. You're the only person that's ever really understood me. I've loved you as long as I can remember. I even keep a picture of you in my bedroom and blow it a kiss every night. If I was the marrying type the only woman in the world I would marry is you."

Sarah scratched her head in bafflement. "Then why in the name of hell are you championing Alan's cause?"

"It's not that easy Sarah." Peter smiled slowly. "You know everybody at school and later always expected us two to get together sometime. Even my family thought it was only a matter of time before I popped the question to you. They were devastated when it turned out that you would be marrying Alan. They think the world of you and would have loved you for a daughter in-law. My mother's never forgiven me for not snatching you up when I had the chance. She's always saying I was a fool for letting you go."

Sarah was bewildered. "Forgive me Peter but I seem to be getting all sorts of mixed signals here."

Peter nodded sadly. "I know Sarah. I realise that what I'm saying sounds contradictory."

Sarah took a deep breath. It was a day for measured inhalation. "Why *did* you let me go Peter?"

"Not through any fault of yours believe me Sarah."

Sarah set her jaw realising she was close to tears. "You didn't have to Peter. I waited all those years to hear you tell me what you thought about me. Why did you wait until I'm nearly married to tell me you love me?"

"Oddly enough that was the best time to tell you Sarah. My love for you is pure. I won't stop loving you because you're married. I only want you to find happiness with Alan Sarah. He's a good man; better than you give him credit for. He's helped me a lot when other people would have turned me aside. If I thought for one moment that he wasn't good enough for my Sarah I would move heaven and hell to stop him from marrying you. If I ever thought he might hurt you I'd break his neck!"

"Peter forget Alan for a moment."

"I can't Sarah and neither should you. You've been his girlfriend for three years he surely deserves some respect. I know that Alan can come across somewhat materialistic and unemotional. That's just his way. He falls back on the familiar when his inability to express himself robs him of the appropriate words. Deep down though Sarah, Alan is a caring and understanding man. He is a true gentleman and there are few of that ilk nowadays."

"Peter I know of Alan's qualities. I've been his girlfriend and lover for three years and I'm not totally insensitive. I've put up with the many frustrations of our relationship because I recognise he's not a bad man. But just acknowledging his better qualities is not enough Peter. A good man or not I have to ask myself if I can live the rest of my life with him. That's a whole different question. I am not convinced that I can."

"But why Sarah?"

"For a number of reasons Peter."

"Such as?"

"Well *you* for instance you muppet!"

"Sarah listen..."

"No *you* listen! If you're going to beat around the bush we'll be here all day. I thought it was women that were supposed to fanny about."

"But Sarah..."

"Let me have my say Peter and then you can voice your opinion. Yes I did go up to the alp the other day to see you and yes I did wear some clothes that I hoped would do something to stir your apparently moribund libido. Fat chance! I would probably have done better to hang a bell around my neck and graze on the dandelions for all the notice you seemed to take."

"I did notice Sarah it's just that..."

"I haven't finished Peter. Ditto today. Yes, of course, I dressed up especially to see you. I wanted to look my best for you. I took pains over my appearance and what happens? I get told off like a naughty girl for dressing up saucily to see another man when I should be the very image of sober chastity in deference to my forthcoming status as a serious married woman. Well the hell with that Peter! Nobody's asked me to marry them yet. I repeat Peter that this is an arranged marriage. I'm being shepherded along to church without a single damn person having the common courtesy to ascertain my wishes in the matter. My parents, Alan's parents, Alan and even you, apparently, all seem to regard my marriage as an inevitability and take my submission to that inevitability for granted. Well maybe I'm old fashioned Peter but a girl likes to be asked. I'm not going to be bullied into a wedding dress for the bloody convenience of a nice cosy business deal between my family and Alan's."

"Oh Sarah it's not just that..."

"I'm still not finished Peter!"

"Sorry."

"Right then as far as I'm concerned I'm not officially affianced and I won't be until I give my consent and accept a suitable token of betrothal." Sarah held up her left hand. "See that Peter? That is a hand conspicuously lacking in any sign of the aforementioned token! There's no ring on my finger and until there is there is no ring in my nose either and I damned if I'm going to be led to church like the fatted cow until there is. Until such time as I grant my official consent to be married I reserve the right to keep my options open. You have always been one of those options. More than that you have been and, as far as I'm concerned still are, the major remaining option. I waited donkey's years for you to get off your arse and declare your intentions and I'm *still* waiting. You didn't have to let me go Peter. I always expected you to take me one day but when you never did I lost hope and then there was Alan and things weren't as simple anymore. But that doesn't mean that it's too late. When you phoned me to ask me to meet you I thought that finally you were waking up to the looming reality that I was about to marry someone else and, given that I'd expressed reservations about that marriage, you had realised that the window of opportunity to make amends for your earlier hesitation was closing fast and you had decided to act. I must have been barking mad. I honestly thought that today you were going to present a counter proposal to Alan's. That's why I dressed up for the occasion. I actually thought that this might be an important day."

Peter blinked. "You thought I was going to ask you to marry me?"

"Well in effect yes or at least lay some sort of proposal and ask me to reconsider my marriage to Alan. When I saw you so nicely dressed for the occasion I thought that you too had some cognisance of the momentousness of the forthcoming interview and had made an effort to look handsome for me. Then what happens? I get told off for my scandalous behaviour and you insinuate that I'm being as close as damn it to being unfaithful to my poor long-suffering fiancée while his back is turned."

"I didn't say you were being unfaithful..."

"And then you admonish me and extol Alan's virtues before then telling me that you've loved me all your life and that I'm the only woman that you would marry and wishing me well in my marriage to Alan and I don't know *what* to think any more. Either I'm losing the plot or you are."

"I had a feeling that this was what you had in mind Sarah. I'm so sorry!"

"What the hell for? Look Peter I've laid my cards on the table. I've told you that my marriage to Alan is not yet a done deal. I've told you that I'm still open to alternative suggestions. Furthermore I've indicated that you are the most important of those alternatives and that I'm likely to look favourably on any advance from your quarter. Now if that isn't plain enough for you then let me state that I love you too and that I am still waiting for you to declare your hand. Until you do I can't say anything more."

Peter buried his head in his hands. "Oh God! What's Alan going to say?"

"The hell with Alan Peter! Right now there's just you and me. You don't have to live a life of regrets and missed opportunity Peter. You don't have to see me married away in comfortable obscure suburbia and lament what might have been. You can still change it. I can't tell you any plainer than that. If you've got something important you want to say to me then say it now. Change the habit of a life time, stop pussying around and wringing your hands in guilt over Alan and say what you have to say. You're right. I've grown up. I'm a woman. Now for fuck's sake start being a man!"

"I'm so sorry Sarah. I can't marry you."

"Why? Because of Alan?"

Peter shook his head. "No. You don't understand."

"You're damn right I don't."

"Sarah why do you think I phoned Alan?"

"I have no idea."

"Well actually I've been conferring with him for some time now. He's been helping me."

"Good God! With what? Don't tell me you've taken up golf and he's advising you on your handicap."

"Don't be petty Sarah. It doesn't suit you. No he's been advising me on something else. Well he's been

343

advising me on a few things really. He's been giving me advice on personal things but more to the point he's been helping me with certain financial matters. I'm lousy about things like that but Alan's been very supportive and helpful."

"Financial matters? Your usual financial concerns consist in wondering if you've got enough beer money until payday."

"Not any more Sarah. I've come into an inheritance from my grandparents and I've been thinking how best to invest it. I'm dressed up smartly today because I've been visiting an estate agency."

"*What!*"

"That's right. I'm thinking about putting a deposit down on a mortgage for a little pub. It's nothing grand you understand but it's a lovely old place and I like it. I made the decision up in the alp. I knew I had to change my life around and settle down with my own place. I thought that I had everything covered and then you came along and told me that you were thinking of not marrying Alan but that you were interested in marrying me; a consideration that you've just repeated. That threw me into a quandary Sarah. You see I can't marry you Sarah. When I said I was frightened of losing you it wasn't because I was afraid of losing you to Alan it was because I was afraid that you'd never forgive me for not marrying you myself. You're precious to me Sarah. You're the one person whose support I need."

"What the hell's this got to do with you buying a house?" Sarah sat up straight and stared at him. "Wait a minute you're not telling me that Alan's helping you out financially and that that help is dependent on you withdrawing from the field as it were?"

"You're miles off base Sarah. Oh Alan has been a little wary of me previously because I think he worried about whether I was a rival or not but he has no further concerns. He knows my private considerations and he respects them. I certainly am not dependent on Alan for financial help. I haven't inherited a fortune but it's a tidy sum and I wouldn't take a penny off Alan. No he's just been giving me the benefit of his professional advice."

"So what has this got to do with it? Oh don't get me wrong, I think it's wonderful that you've come into some money and decided to buy your own place. But why does that preclude you from marrying me?"

"Sarah I didn't go to that estate agent alone."

Sarah stared at him with the blood draining from her face. Finally she understood. "Oh God! I've been such a fool! You... you've met someone else haven't you?"

Peter nodded seriously. "Yes Sarah. I have. In fact I'm thinking of getting married. The pub and the house will be for both of us."

Sarah buried her face in despair. "Oh God! How could I have been so stupid. You must think I'm a stupid little girl. Here I am thinking you're going to ask me to marry you and all the time you have someone else. I'm just an idiot! You didn't care about me at all. That's why you were encouraging me to not give Alan up. You were already spoken for and I was just a silly little girl with a childhood crush on you. Oh God! I'm stupid! I've made a complete fool of myself." Sarah raised a tear stained face. "I'd better go Peter. I'm sorry for embarrassing you."

"Stop it Sarah! You haven't embarrassed me. You're going nowhere. Here..." Peter produced a spotless white handkerchief. "Stop crying now, wipe your eyes and blow your nose. You look a mess."

Sarah took the handkerchief and glared at him. "How could you Peter? How could you sit there and tell me you loved me and tell me that you'd never marry any other woman and then drop this on me?"

"Sarah I meant every word. I do love you. I love you as the sister I never had; as the friend that I always did have; my own sweet Sarah, the dearest friend in my life. You will always be that to me Sarah. Nobody can take your place in my heart in that way. But I cannot be your husband."

Sarah renewed her tears. "I... I don't understand Peter."

"I'm sorry Sarah but this is the hardest thing I've ever done. I want you to meet my betrothed."

"What?"

"Please Sarah I need you on this."

"I... I can't!"

"Please Sarah. Of all the people in the world I need *you* to understand."

"Understand what?"

In reply Peter stood and walked to the bar. When he returned he was accompanied by a young man Sarah had never met before. The boy was extraordinarily handsome; almost beautiful with dark hair and soulful brown eyes. "Sarah I'd like you to meet Simon. Simon is my boyfriend."

Chapter Thirty

Nicole rapped sharply on Sarah's bedroom door and tried the handle for the tenth time. "Come on now Sarah." she pleaded "Stop being so silly! Open this door and let me in."

"Go away! Leave me alone!" the anguished sobbing squeak from the other side of the locked door was curiously muffled. Sarah evidently had her head buried in the bedclothes.

Nicole sighed heavily. The shared household was going through a stormy patch. No sooner had she recovered from her own emotional low point than had Sarah returned from Winterthur and precipitated this latest domestic crisis by storming into the house in a flood of tears and rushing upstairs to lock herself into her bedroom. "I will not leave you alone Sarah. I'm going to stand here and bang on this bloody door until you let me in. Now come on open this door and talk to me."

"I... I can't!" the refusal was accompanied by another storm of tears from the interior of the bedroom.

"Come on Sarah! You're trespassing on my prerogative here. I'm the one that's supposed to be the drama queen remember? You're supposed to be the sensible one. Now please open the door."

It took a good deal more pleading and cajoling but, sometime later, Sarah was sat on the sofa in the living room clutching Nicole's hand and holding a damp tissue in the other. There was a large box of paper tissues on her knee. It was taking some punishment. Sarah's eyes were red and swollen and she paused frequently in her account of the day's dismal events to dab tears from them. "I... I couldn't have made more of a prick of myself if I tried!" she lamented. "I bloody near as damn it proposed to him. He must have thought I was a complete berk! I even thought he'd dressed up nicely to talk to me and all the time it was just because he was visiting the estate agent with his bloody boyfriend."

Nicole shook her head in wonderment, "I just can't believe Peter is gay." She repeated for the twentieth time. "I'd have never have seen it."

"Well you can take it as gospel truth. He's not only gay but he's in love. He couldn't take his eyes off the sodding boyfriend! Talk about feeling like a spare fanny at a wedding." Sarah snatched another tissue from the box savagely.

"So what happened next; I mean after he'd introduced this Simon to you?"

"That was the worst part in some ways. They were really nice to me. Simon's actually a really nice guy... damn his eyes! He said he'd heard a lot about me and he'd been looking forward to meeting me. I bet he wouldn't have been so damn sympathetic if he'd realised that I'd just been trying to steal his boyfriend. They insisted on taking me out to dinner in this Italian restaurant. They kept holding hands under the table and talking about the new house they were taking together. I wanted to throw my penne all'arrabbiata all over them!"

"Oh God! Please don't tell me you made a scene in an Italian restaurant. It's almost a fucking cliché!"

"I did *not* make a scene. I just sat there with a sickly grin on my face murmuring platitudes about how pleased I was that they'd found someone to share a life with and wishing them the best for the future when all I wanted to do was crawl away somewhere and die."

Nicole groaned in sympathy. "Oh God you poor thing. It must have been horrible."

Sarah nodded miserably. "Yes especially when Peter explained how difficult it had been for him to come to terms with his homosexuality and how much he wanted me to understand and accept it. He was asking for my support and an hour earlier I'd been throwing myself at him like a cheap tart."

"Don't say that! You're not a cheap tart. It wasn't your fault that the one bloke in the world that you truly loved is a steaming great pouf! How were you to know? Anyway what has Alan got to do with all this?"

"Apparently Alan's known for ages that Peter is gay. He's never said a thing to me. Peter says it's because he asked Alan to be discreet and not to say anything to me because Peter wanted to tell me that himself."

Nicole shook her head. "Oh Christ!"

Sarah was racked by another bout of sobbing. "Peter says that Alan's been very noble and understanding. I'll bet he has! He's always been leery of Peter because of my fondness for him. He must have been delighted to learn that Peter was gay. Took the opposition right out of the picture."

"You say he's been helping them?"

Sarah nodded abjectly. "Oh yes! He's been giving them advice on their tax status if they make a formal legal union and he's been advising them on the financing and paperwork for their new house. Alan's come up smelling of roses in the whole bloody affair. He's been phoning from America and arranging all their legal and advisory meetings. He's damn near negotiated their mortgage himself and he's got them brilliant terms. He's the blue-eyed boy as far as they're concerned. Apparently his conduct has been exemplary; all noble sacrifice and throwing himself selflessly into the fray on their behalf. The bastard!"

"You might be doing him an injustice Sarah."

"Whose bloody side are you on?"

"Well I wasn't aware that we were drawing up battle lines Sarah but if we are then I'm solidly in your camp. You know that."

Sarah sniffed and wiped her eyes. "You might be right Nicky... bugger it! He's certainly come out of the affair looking better than me. According to Peter Alan has spared no effort striving to help them. They think he's an angel and all the time there was me trying to cheat on Alan with the very person he was going out of his way to help. I feel like a worm."

Nicole nodded sagely. "Yes and he'd be good at that sort of thing too. If there's one thing you can say about Alan it's that he knows how to cut through red tape and get things done. He'd be a handy man to have in your camp when you were wrestling with property deals and the like. I just hope that Peter is as discreet as he is when it comes to a discussion regarding your conduct. If Peter passes on the details of your conversation to Alan the shit will really hit the fan!"

"He says the subject is forgotten. He won't say a word to Alan. Damn him why should he? He *wants* me to marry Alan. He spent half the evening telling me what a wonderful man Alan is and how I should feel ashamed of myself for playing the field elsewhere. He made me promise to be nice to Alan the next time he calls and to reconsider my doubts about the marriage. He insists that Alan loves me and only wants to make me happy. What the hell am I supposed to do now Nicky?"

"I don't know Foxy. It's a mess. All the problems with Plan A are still in place and Plan B's gone tits up before it even got off the ground. I don't know what to advise."

"I could join a fucking nunnery!"

"Hmm difficult that. Most sisterhoods are Catholic in Switzerland. I think I've heard about Lutheran orders in Germany which is rich, when you think about it, since Luther railed against monastic life and married a runaway nun. There are Anglican sisterhoods certainly and there's an ecumenical establishment in Taize, France that might have you. Shop about a bit or otherwise think about changing denomination. If you decide to convert to Catholicism then there're endless possibilities. Not many women these days take up monastic vows. They'll be crying out for new blood. They'll probably bite your hand off."

"Shut up Nicky!"

"I'm just trying to lighten the mood Sarah. Anyway I've got news for you."

"What? It better be something good like the announcement of a new malignant ailment with a hundred percent fatality rate that only affects men."

"Frau Fritzl phoned up."

"Oh God what does she want?"

"You apparently. It seems that her waitress Magdalena has come down with beri, or yellow fever, or whatever infectious diseases are endemic to Portugal and taken to her bed. She wondered if you could come in to cover her shifts. She says she might need you the rest of the week. I can always phone her up and tell her that you're not feeling up to it."

Sarah shook her head. "No I'll do it. A bit of honest labour will do me good. When did she want me to come in?"

"Tomorrow. She asks if you can cover lunch and dinner in the restaurant."

"I'll phone her up."

"It's getting late Sarah. She said you can call in the morning."

"Ok. What about you? Are you going into work?"

Nicole nodded. "Yes. I'm feeling better." Nicole paused to stroke Sarah's hair fondly. "Listen honey you look a fright. Why don't you go run a hot bath and go and soak awhile and I'll make us some hot chocolate and dig out some biscuits."

Sarah nodded mournfully. "Yes ok. I could use a bath."

Nicole jumped to her feet and dragged Sarah off the couch to send her on the way with a playful slap on the rump. "Go on then! Go jump in the bath and I'll rustle up some supper."

With Sarah away to the bathroom Nicole busied herself in the kitchen. Her labours were interrupted by the telephone. She picked up the receiver. "Hello! Toggenburg infirmary for the clinically depressed here."

"I'm sorry?"

Nicole took a double take. She recognised instantly the warm soft voice on the end of the line. "Oh! I'm sorry. Is that you Daniela?"

"Yes. Yes it is. Is that Nicole?"

"Yes. Er did you want to talk to Sarah?"

"Well yes if it's convenient Nicole. I'm sorry for calling so late."

"Well I'm sorry Daniela but it's not a good time I'm afraid. We have an ongoing domestic crisis. Sarah's in bits. She's currently in the bathroom trying to re-assemble her component parts."

"Oh I'm sorry to hear that Nicole. Is she all right?" Daniela sounded concerned.

"Well, apart from the fact that she's just discovered that the boy she's loved all her life and was hoping to marry in preference to her current fiancée is gay, she's just dandy!"

"Oh the poor girl. She must be devastated."

"I've seen her in better form."

"Perhaps I'd better call another time then."

"I would advise it. She's not particularly coherent for the moment."

"Will you give her my regards and tell her I'll call her tomorrow?"

"Er I don't know when you'll catch her. She has to work tomorrow at the Hotel Toggenburg."

"I see. Well send her my love won't you. Oh and Nicole...."

"Yes?"

"Look after her won't you."

Nicole frowned and hesitated. "I'll do that Daniela."

"Thank you Nicole. I'll catch you later. Bye bye."

"Er goodbye Daniela." The line went dead and Nicole slammed the receiver down furiously. She leaned against the kitchen top her brow furrowed in concern. Plan A still didn't look good and Plan B had fallen to pieces. What she was really worried about though was Plan C.

Chapter Thirty-One

Sarah walked to work the next day. It was a long walk down through the Alpli and the descent to Unterwasser, before the long haul up the hill on the far side of the valley to Schwendi, but Sarah didn't mind. The physical effort was a balm to her melancholy. At least she was wearing sensible shoes to negotiate the route. They were black and quite plain but they were comfortable. Any girl that had ever worked as a waitress soon learned that, for a person who was destined to spend most of the day on her feet, comfort took precedence over elegance and vanity. It was a warm day again and Sarah carried her jacket loosely in her hand. She wore a simple black skirt and a pretty white blouse; the universal uniform of the female serving class. Her white pinafore was folded neatly in the plastic bag she carried and her long hair was tied back in a ribbon. She was a working girl on her way to a day of toil in the Swiss tourist industry.

Frau Fritzl smothered her in a great hug as she entered the hotel. "Sarah! Thank you for coming at such short notice. You're a sight for sore eyes girl. I was already a little shorthanded this week with Elsie away to see her mother and now Magdalena's poorly. I'd have been at my wit's end if you hadn't been able to come in."

Sarah smiled, liking the ebullient Frau Fritzl enormously. "It was my pleasure." She shook out her pinafore and donned it briskly in a business-like way. "So what's the situation? Are we going to be busy?"

Frau Fritzl bit her lip. "Hard to say Sarah. Lunchtime's been fairly quiet the last couple of days but you can never tell. We thought we were going to be quiet on Monday but we got murdered. We had a party of Japanese tourists in."

Sarah raised her head in surprise. "Japanese?" Switzerland took a lot of Japanese tourists during the summer but they tended to congregate around more famous resort areas such as the regions around Interlaken or Zermatt. The Toggenburg was well off the Japanese tourist itinerary map and Japanese tourists were very rare locally.

"Yes. God knows what they were doing here." Frau Fritzl paused in puzzlement. "You know Sarah I spent a few weeks in Kyoto when I was younger. I like the Japanese. They're clever, polite, civilised people so why do they all turn into myopic, camera clicking, morons as soon as they go on holiday?"

Sarah laughed. "I think tourist dumbness is universal Frau Fritzl. Whenever I've been to Germany I've never noticed that the people were boorish, uncouth and impolite. That's just the personae they reserve for foreign visits. And as for English tourists.... well!"

"Tell me about it. We've got a few in house at the moment. They were complaining about flies. I told them that they're in rural Switzerland. In rural Switzerland you get cows and where you get cows you get cow shit and where you get cow shit you get flies. Deal with it."

Sarah grinned. Frau Fritzl was just the person she needed to restore her morale. "So we might be busy then."

"As I say Sarah, I don't know. We've got a lot of people in house but most of them are going out for the day so I'm guessing that lunch will be quite quiet. Still I have to cover every possibility. It's a warm day so there might be a few people popping in to eat out on the terrace. Dinner's another problem. We've got forty-eight booked so far and that number's liable to increase so we could be rushed this evening. Are you all right doing a split?" Frau Fritzl meant a split shift; the bane of the hotel worker's life.

"I'm easy. What times do you want me?"

"Well if you work the lunch until say around two o'clock or half past and then come back in say around sixish for the dinner service. Would that be all right?"

"That's fine Frau Fritzl."

"I could do with you until the weekend at least Sarah. Would you be available?"

"Yes I'm ok with that. I've nothing else on."

Frau Fritzl regarded Sarah carefully. "Are you all right Sarah? You seem a little less chipper than usual. Is something bothering you?"

"Please Frau Fritzl I'm fine. Just boyfriend troubles; the usual."

"Hmmph! Most of the trouble in this world will be solved when we find a way for females to reproduce parthenogenetically and render males obsolete. I can't think of anything more useless than the average male."

"Some people find them quite useful Frau Fritzl."

"Well I suppose they're all right as long as you employ them in brute physical labour not requiring any brain power."

Sarah laughed. "You're just an old cynic. Shall I go and see if the restaurant's set up properly?"

"Go ahead. I'm afraid it'll be just you and Andrea for lunch but I'll get in to help out if we get busy."

Lunch in the event turned out to be quite busy. With the lovely warm weather inducing many people outdoors, the terrace of the hotel did a brisk business over the lunch hours. Sarah fell rapidly back into the familiar routine of working at the hotel and she enjoyed herself. Sarah liked waiting on tables. She took satisfaction from the smooth running of a restaurant and enjoyed contact with people. She found something fulfilling in feeding and catering to a wide diversity of people. She was good at it too. She rarely mixed up her orders and could keep tabs on whatever was happening out in the restaurant admirably. Like many an experienced waitress, Sarah could carry four plates simultaneously; two in her left hand, one balanced on her left wrist and the other in her right. She could clear a table of dirty dishes in sharp order and distribute drinks and menus with calm efficiency. Above all she was unfailingly friendly and cheerful and the customers loved her. Her co-worker Andrea was delighted with her new colleague for the half litre beer mug that was serving as a repository for their communal tips was filling up admirably.

Frau Fritzl had joined the service early when it appeared that there was a higher volume of service required then she had anticipated and she was quietly thrilled to have Sarah's services for the day. She had long maintained that Sarah was one of the best waitresses that she had ever had and Sarah's calm competence on this unexpectedly busy lunchtime had done nothing to change her opinion. She was in the kitchen when Sarah bustled in with an armful of dirty dishes. Sarah piled up the dishes for the kitchen porter to dispose of and took a slip of paper down from the kitchen situations board. "Ok! That's table five cleared and paid. How are those desserts coming along for table eight chef?"

"Two minutes."

"Good. Give me a shout. I have to get coffees for that German couple on fourteen."

"How is it going out there Sarah?" Frau Fritzl asked.

"It's slowing down Frau Fritzl. I think the rush is over. We've just got three tables waiting for desserts and what have you"

"Good. Well you go and get those coffees and I'll see to the desserts. After that you'd better get yourself off. It's nearly three o'clock. Andrea and I can manage from now. I want you bright eyed and bushy tailed for dinner tonight."

"Are you sure?"

"Of course I am. I didn't expect to keep you this long but then I didn't think it was going to be this busy. Be back at half past six all right."

"Thank you. I'll just see to those coffees."

Sarah was just placing coffee cups, cream and sugar onto a tray at the bar's espresso machine when Frau Fritzl approached her once more with a curiously enigmatic smile. "I'll take those Sarah. Could you just see to table two out on the terrace? There's somebody to see you."

Puzzled Sarah walked out into the bright sunshine of the terrace. She saw Daniela straight away. Daniela had eschewed the normal designer label dresses that Sarah was coming to associate her with and she was clad in a simple pair of stylish blue jeans and a simple white blouse. But her hair glowed in the sunlight and she looked radiantly beautiful. Sarah came to a halt in shock. "Danny!"

Daniela smiled mischievously and raised an eyebrow. "What do I have to do to get some service around here?"

"Er what can I get you?"

"A small orange juice will be just fine please."

Sarah grinned at her. "Straight away Miss."

"Just a moment Sarah. Are you working all day?"

"No. In fact I've got a break now until half past six."

"You got anything you have to do?"

"Nothing at all."

"Then perhaps you'd like to spend the time with me."

"I would love to."

"Good maybe we could go for a walk somewhere."

"Yes I'd like that. Look let me get you your drink and I'll tell my boss I'm getting away."

Daniela smiled and her smile was shaft of sun in Sarah's troubled mind. "Don't be long." She urged.

Frau Fritzl's face was a baffling mixture of amusement and smug satisfaction when Sarah reported back and asked if it was all right for her to leave as soon as she had delivered Daniela's drink. "Of course Sarah. I told you to get off. Now go get that drink, then smarten up in the ladies and don't keep your young lady waiting."

It was on the tip of Sarah's tongue to protest that Daniela was not her "young lady" but somehow she realised instinctively that her words would not be convincing. Sarah rushed out with Daniela's drink. "I'll be out in five minutes." She told her.

"Brilliant! How much do I owe you for the drink?"

"One eighty." Sarah leaned forward to whisper. "And if you dare to tip me I'll never speak to you again."

Daniela laughed merrily. "I wouldn't dream of it."

Chapter Thirty-Two

Sarah was back in an indecently short period of time, pausing only in transit to brush out her hair, refold her pinafore and pick up her handbag. Daniela rose to her feet as Sarah returned and picked up a largish shoulder bag. "What's in the bag?" Sarah asked inquisitively.

"A surprise."

"A surprise?"

"Yes I brought you a little present. Don't worry. It's only something small."

They were just passing off the terrace but Sarah came to a halt and regarded Daniela in puzzlement. "You've brought me a present?"

"I told you it's only something small."

"Yes but how did you know I was going to be here at all? I thought you'd just popped in for a drink coincidentally. Are you telling me that you knew I was working here today?"

It was Daniela's turn to look puzzled. "But of course. Nicole told me."

"Nicole told you?"

"Yes when I phoned up last night."

"You phoned me?"

"Yes. Nicole said you were indisposed and in the bathroom. Didn't she mention that I'd phoned?"

"No! No she didn't."

"So you didn't expect me to turn up at all today?"

"No of course not. How could I?"

"I just thought you might have done."

"Why?"

In answer Daniela lifted a finger to Sarah's neck. "Because you're wearing my necklace. I thought you must have put it on for me."

"Oh no! I just put it on today because I thought it would look nice with my waitress's blouse."

"Oh I see."

Suddenly Sarah laughed ruefully. "Oh no! I don't believe I said that."

"Said what?"

"Oh Danny I'm lying. I told you an absolute whopper and I don't even know why."

"Confessions will be accepted. I'll decide whether a spanking is in order or not depending on your level of contrition."

"I didn't just put it on today Danny. Actually I haven't taken it off since you hung it around my neck." It was true. She'd even worn it to Winterthur the previous day. Peter hadn't even noticed it.

Daniela smiled and took Sarah's hand to raise to her lips and kiss her fingers. "Your sins are forgiven. I'm touched."

They passed out of the hotel and onto the road. Sarah was still puzzled. "Why didn't Nicole tell me you'd phoned while I was in the bathroom?"

Daniela's face was neutral and unreadable. "Perhaps she forgot to mention it." She said diplomatically. "She sounded very worried about you. She said you'd had some er... problems yesterday and you were upset."

"I was being bloody hysterical. I'm not proud of myself."

"Well perhaps Nicole thought you had enough on your plate and didn't need any other distractions."

Sarah shook her head disbelievingly "Hmm perhaps." She paused in the road. "Where's your car?"

"At home Sarah. I walked over here."

"You walked?"

"Don't look so surprised Sarah. I do have two legs you know and it's not *that* far from Oberdorf."

Sarah grinned wickedly. "Well I'm just surprised that's all. I thought rock and roll superstars never walked anywhere."

Daniela looked at her sideways. "Shall we find somewhere quiet Sarah? Somewhere quiet in the bushes where I can put you over my knee, lift up your skirt and give you that spanking you've wriggled out of once today?"

Sarah pulled a face of mock contrition. "Sorry ma-am."

"Get on with you. Let's go for a walk shall we?"

"Yes. Let's take a turn around the Schwendiseen."

The idea met Daniela's approval and soon they were on the path that led around the two little lakes. Daniela took Sarah's hand as they walked and Sarah found herself in a dilemma over the small intimacy. In truth, she was not at all used to holding somebody's hand in public. Alan was uncomfortable with public displays of intimacy and rarely touched her out of doors. Even with Nicole, Sarah had very rarely grasped hands. In fact Sarah hadn't really walked hand in hand with anybody for any distance since she was a young girl and that most usually with her parents or older sister. So Sarah felt somewhat awkward and shy to begin with.

Daniela had no such inhibitions. She was unabashedly tactile and she held Sarah's hand so naturally it seemed as if she could scarcely contemplate the idea of walking without its comforting reassurance. Indeed, she appeared reluctant to relinquish it and when she required the use of her right hand she simply transferred Sarah's to her other hand rather than let go of her. There were a number of people walking along the path around the lakes and Sarah felt timid whenever they passed someone else although Daniela scarcely seemed to notice and would greet their fellow walkers politely and show, neither the slightest embarrassment over her

362

affectionate embrace of Sarah's hand, nor any inclination to abandon it.

As she grew used to the feel of Daniela's slim hand in hers, Sarah's inhibitions began to fade and she was forced to admit that she liked it very much. There was something precious and sisterly about the intimacy; a togetherness that felt enormously satisfying. They didn't just hold hands carelessly either for Daniela's hands were expressive and, as they talked as they walked, she would punctuate her words with little squeezes and barely perceptible caresses with her fingertips. Sarah found herself responding in kind and if Daniela were to say something kind and complimentary to her, which was often, she would reward it with a little squeeze of her own. Their hands became almost a little secret form of physical communication between them. There was another thing too. Sarah became aware of a growing feeling of pride; a pride that, if only for today, she possessed the hand of this beautiful and extraordinary woman.

As they reached the little copse of trees that separated the two lakes Daniela suddenly pulled Sarah to one side into the trees away from the path. For a moment Sarah was alarmed but once out of sight from the path Daniela released her hand and dropped her bag to the ground to rummage in it. Sarah felt strange to be parted from Daniela's hand as if some umbilical cord had been cut but Daniela looked animated and excited as if by some secret conspiracy. "Look I brought you this." She announced. With that she withdrew a lovely sleeveless summer dress in a rich floral print of pinks, yellows and blues, with a deep neckline and plunging back and held it up for Sarah's perusal. "What do you think?"

"Danny! You're crazy. I can't accept this."

"Of course you can. It's not new Sarah. It's one of my own. I thought you'd look nice in it."

Sarah reached out to touch the material. "It's silk Danny." she noted accusingly. "This is an expensive dress."

"And one that's going to look absolutely gorgeous on you."

"Why have you brought me a dress Danny?"

"Well to be honest I thought you might welcome a change of clothes for your free hours. I've seen some of the awful uniforms waitresses are obliged to endure. Having said that, I must confess that you look very smart in yours." Daniela giggled suddenly. "Mind you I wish you'd left that little pinny on. You looked cute in that."

Sarah placed her hand on her hips. "*Now* who's asking for a spanking?"

Daniela grinned. "Come on then try it on."

Sarah was appalled. "What? You mean here?"

"No I thought we'd wait until we reached the pub by the roadside. Of course I mean here. Come on Sarah. Don't be shy. Nobody can see you in these trees."

"*You* can see me."

Daniela placed her tongue in her cheek and tried to look serious. "Well if that's what's bothering you I'll turn my back."

"You won't peep?"

Daniela lifted three fingers "Guide's honour."

"Well all right but turn around."

With a grin Daniela complied. "Well get on with it then."

Feeling hunted Sarah quickly stripped out of her skirt and blouse and picked up the dress. There was another problem. "My bra will show with this dress Danny." she protested to the back of Daniela's head.

"Well take it off then you do-nut! The dress is perfectly well structured in the bosom. You won't flop about."

Timidly Sarah reached behind her back to unfasten her bra. Once divested on the garment she picked up the dress once more. Daniela took advantage of the moment to turn around and look at her. Sarah squeaked in outrage and held the dress in front of her to cover her nakedness. "You said you wouldn't peep!"

"Oh didn't I mention that they threw me out of the Girl Guides following my scandalous behaviour at summer camp? They formed a hollow square under the flagpole, tore off my merit badges, confiscated my toggle and drummed me out in disgrace. I've kept the uniform though. I like to dress up in it every time I feel like singing a rousing chorus of Ging Gang Gooly Gooly Wotsit!

Sarah grinned in spite of herself. "You're a scandal Daniela Devin. Baden Powell would turn in his grave."

"Put the bloody dress on Sarah."

"You're watching!"

Daniela grinned. "I'd hurry up if I was you Sarah. I think I can hear somebody coming." With a muffled squeak Sarah hastily pulled the dress over her head. Daniela regarded her in satisfaction. "You look gorgeous."

Sarah smoothed the material of the dress over herself enjoying the sensation of the silk against her skin. She looked down and frowned. "These shoes don't really match it though."

"Hah! Did you really think I'd overlook that?" With the air of a magician pulling a rabbit from a hat, Daniela produced a pair of gold coloured sandals from her bag.

Sarah regarded them uncertainly. "What if they don't fit me?"

"They will do. Oddly enough you take almost exactly the same size shoe as me."

"How can you possibly know that?"

"I'm an observant person Sarah especially where you're concerned. I can even tell you more or less your bra band and cup size. I can tell you your waist measurement, your height, your hip size and even hazard a good guess at your weight. I can tell you things about your complexion and hair you don't even know yourself and your facial features are so familiar to me I can draw your face from memory."

"That's impossible."

"Let's just say I've studied you."

Sarah stared at her in bewilderment and she felt an uncanny tingling in the hairs on the back of her neck. If Daniela spoke truth, then she must have made an intense examination of her. Sarah doubted if even her own mother could remember her bra size. It was almost unnerving that someone had conducted such a meticulous visual study of you. It bordered on intrusion into your privacy and it bespoke of an almost obsessive fascination. Sarah once again recognised that intensity to her new friend; that sense that even the most trivial of words and gestures were charged with meaning and significance.

"Come along." Daniela told her. "Sit on that stump and try these sandals on." Sarah obeyed and sat bemused as Daniela squatted to ease her shoes off. Before fitting the sandals to her feet however Daniela took the time to hold Sarah's feet and stroke them gently. "You have good feet." She said at last. "Not the most elegant and dainty although they're pretty. They're just honest good healthy feet. They're a little hard in places but then you walk a lot. I'll give you some moisturising cream for them to soften them." Sarah felt oddly touched by Daniela's concern for her feet. Daniela frowned before reaching up and stroking a finger down Sarah's calf. "What happened here?" she asked.

Sarah leaned down to look. There was a thin almost imperceptible white scar on her leg; faint and hardly noticeable against her skin. "Oh God! I'd forgotten I even had that. I did it when I was twelve or thirteen. I slipped on some sharp rocks on the Santis and cut my leg open quite badly. Is it that noticeable?"

366

"Oh no. You can hardly see it. I love it though."

"You love it?"

"Of course. It's part of Sarah. Without it these would just be a perfect set of legs but that little scar makes them *your* legs. There's a little girl in that scar that climbed in the mountains one day. That scar is a mark of a lifetime being uniquely you. The mountains have marked you; put their brand on you to remind you that ultimately you belong to them. You should treasure it." With that Daniela leaned forward and kissed the scar quickly.

Sarah felt a jolt of sensation from the brief kiss and swallowed. "You're quite somebody Daniela. I never met anybody like you before." she croaked hoarsely.

Daniela chuckled softly. "Oh take no notice of me Sarah. I'm just a hopeless romantic. Come on let's try these sandals on you." The sandals fitted perfectly and Daniela looked smugly pleased. "She took Sarah's hand and pulled her to her feet. "Let's walk Sarah. Come on I'll carry your uniform in my bag. There are some pretty flowers around the back of the little lake I want you to tell me the name of."

And so they ambled on, closer than ever now that Sarah had undressed before Daniela. The dress was cool and light; its touch soft and sensuous on Sarah's body as she walked. She experienced once again the worrying imminence of losing control of her senses in Daniela's presence; the knife edge upon which her resistance teetered above the abyss of surrender. Daniela was too strong; too overwhelming in the sensual assault of her charisma. Just to be close to her was a siren's call of danger; to touch her a vertiginous faltering on the cliff face of disaster.

Sarah cleared her throat as they walked and resumed an earlier conversation that at least promised a degree of mundanity. "So why did you come home so early?" she asked.

Daniela shrugged her shoulders. "Oh I wasn't needed in the studio really. It was just a bunch of techies fiddling with mixing levels, audio enhancement, sound processing and all sorts of other mysterious black magic terms that you really need a goatee beard, an unshakeable faith in binaural recording systems and the absence of a meaningful life to comprehend. After listening to two days of endless discussions about pulse-code modulation, level fluctuation compression and multi instrument digital interface, I sort of lost the will to live and told the band I had pressing business to attend to back in the Toggenburg."

"And did you?"

In answer Daniela raised Sarah's hand to her lips to bestow a kiss on her knuckles. "But of course."

"Danny!" Sarah tried to sound shocked.

Daniela laughed gaily. "Come on here are those flowers I want you to identify for me." Daniela indicated a damp meadow at the back of the smaller of the two lakes. "There. Those funny looking round yellow flowers."

Sarah smiled. "They're common enough Danny. They're Globeflowers; *Trollius europaeus* if you want the Latin name."

"I thought they were some weird kind of buttercup."

"Well you're close Danny. They belong to the same family; the *Ranunculaceae* which is the buttercup family but they're not the same genus which is *Ranunculus*."

"Does your head ever hurt with all this stuff in it Sarah?"

Sarah laughed. "Oh I was brought up on this stuff Danny. I won't say I absorbed it with my mother's milk because my mother wouldn't know a rose from a Stinking Hellebore but I grew up loving the flowers that grow on the mountains here."

"I think you're fantastic."

"Nothing special Danny. You could have looked this up in the book I gave you."

Daniela stopped and rummaged in her bag. To Sarah's surprise, she pulled out the copy of the Collins guide to Alpine flowers that Sarah had sent her. Sarah felt pleased and moved that Daniela carried it with her. Sarah watched in amusement as Daniela opened the book biting her lip in concentration. "Buttercup family you said." she murmured.

"You'll find it on pages thirty-eight and nine."

Daniela looked at her sharply, in wonderment. "Do you actually know this entire book by heart?"

Sarah blushed sheepishly. "Well yes more or less."

"My God! That's a hell of a brain you're carrying behind that pretty face of yours Sarah."

"Are you trying to tell me I'm sad?"

"Sad is not an adjective that comes to mind when I think of you." Daniela started suddenly and pointed a finger in excitement. "Look at that butterfly! Is it a Swallowtail? I'm sure it's a Swallowtail. I've seen pictures of them."

Sarah nodded enjoying Daniela's enthusiastic wonder immensely. "Yes it's a Swallowtail." She said to confirm Daniela's spot diagnosis of the large gaudy insect, resplendent in yellow and black with blue and red highlights to its extended hind wings. "There's a colony of them around the lakes here."

Daniela's eyes danced in delight. "I'll bet a bucket of gold to a barrel of cow shit you know the Latin name for it."

"*Papilio machaon* Danny."

Daniela squeezed Sarah's hand in pleasure. "I knew it! You're a phenomenon Sarah."

"Stop it Danny. I just have a brain full of useless facts. It's nothing special."

"Oh Sarah. You have no idea just how special you are." Daniela smiled as Sarah blushed crimson. Daniela was entranced by Sarah's innate shyness. She nodded to a little dry corner of the meadow by an old stone wall. "Come on Sarah let's sit awhile in the sun." Daniela picked out a patch of short grass by the side of the wall and, once again, reached into her shoulder bag to remove a small blanket which she spread on the ground. Kicking her shoes off in pleasure she sat down on the blanket and patted the material beside her in invitation. Sarah hesitated, for the blanket was very small and they'd be crowded sharing it, but it wouldn't do, she decided, to soil Daniela's dress by sitting on the grass and so she took the proffered seat timidly. They were close enough to be touching on the blanket and Sarah swallowed nervously as Daniela took her hand once more.

But Daniela seemed lost in rapture. She held Sarah's hand loosely but her eyes were fixed on the vista before them, with the two little lakes like mirrors in the green hollow of the alp and with the blue and grey bulk of the Santis massif shimmering hazily in the heat of the afternoon in the distance beyond. Sarah glanced at Daniela's eyes. They were as misty as the distant peaks, as if the soul that owned them was absent and dancing away somewhere on the slopes of the mountains at the edge of vision. To Sarah's surprise a small tear appeared at the corner of Daniela's eye. Daniela uttered a great sigh of pleasure. "God it's good to be alive!" she said at last. "If I were to die now I would still thank God for the beauty of this moment. No wonder you are so special Sarah. Nobody could live their life in this land and not be touched by its magic."

Sarah shook her head with a smile. "You say the weirdest things Danny."

Daniela laughed breaking the spell. "I usually write them down in a song Sarah. That's how I make my living."

"Well don't be writing any songs about me."

"Too late! I already have done."

370

"*What?*"

Daniela giggled and leaned forward to peck Sarah on the cheek with her lips. "Don't worry. It won't be on the next album. Look are you thirsty? I brought a bottle of Fanta."

Sarah grinned caught up in fascination. She was caught continuously by surprise at Daniela's mood changes. One moment she could be as serene and serious as a goddess and in a second change to a simple girl as merry as any lass that wore daisies in her hair. The spark of life danced incessantly in her as if she were bound by a fairy's blessing to take every last second of her life and extract the maximum joy and meaning from it. Here was a woman that would regret not an instant of her life and greet every sparkling moment of it as if she could not believe her luck that she was so blessed by it. It made her irresistible.

Daniela produced a litre bottle of the fizzy orange beverage and they shared pulls at it drinking straight from the bottle. Sarah was normally fastidious about sharing a bottle with someone but since she had already tasted Daniela's lips then hygienic concerns seemed rather a case of shutting the barn door after the horse had bolted. Daniela it seemed could charge any mundane act with significance; even the sharing of a bottle of cheap pop could become an intimacy. The Fanta was too warm and sweet but it tasted like liquidised ambrosia when passed from Daniela's lips to your own.

Daniela laid the bottle to one side. "Sarah," she began more seriously, "I don't want to intrude into your personal business but Nicole told me that you had a bad day yesterday and I was worried about you. She said you were very upset. If you'd like to talk about it you may trust me to keep it to myself. Of course if you don't then I'll respect that too."

Sarah blew a soft sigh. "Yes I had a bad day Danny. But that was yesterday. I thought the world was coming apart. I thought that everything was dark and doomed. Now it just seems like a bad dream you can barely remember any more. I don't even know why!"

Daniela gripped her hand. "Tell me about it."

And Sarah did. She had noticed before what a good listener Daniela was; one who rarely interrupted except to ask for clarification or to murmur in understanding. Sarah told her all about Peter and all her dreams and thoughts of him; how she had wondered about being his wife and how he had compared to Alan. She told her of her lifelong friendship and her secret wishes and how they had all been cast into a blasted wasteland of lost dreams by the accident of biology or socio-sexual orientation or whatever you wished to call it. She told her how forlorn she had been that the only man who she had truly felt an empathy with was denied to her because he did not desire her. And she told her how the marriage she feared now loomed ever closer because the only alternative was now taken away. It was odd for Sarah to tell the story for, in this moment, sharing a blanket with Daniela in the sunshine in the meadow, all her troubles seemed so trivial and pointless and it was hard for her to convey the full sadness of her disappointment whilst she felt so liberated and content.

Daniela seemed to understand however for she was gently sympathetic and non-judgemental. She had sympathy for Peter it seemed as well for when Sarah had finished her story she nodded sagely. "I think your friend Peter was very brave Sarah. I don't know the man but, from what you say, it sounds as if him telling you that he was gay must have been very hard for him. I think it's a measure of his esteem for you that he both trusted you enough to reveal that to you and also that he knew that he had to tell you. It sounds as if it is very important to him that you accept his sexual orientation and that he doesn't lose his friendship with you as a result. I'd say you are a very important part of his life."

Sarah shrugged helplessly. "I never even guessed it Danny. I mean you know a person all your life and you think you know all there is to know about them and then suddenly you realise you didn't know them at all. Seeing Peter with his boyfriend was so weird. He was suddenly a stranger to me."

"Sexual preference is not necessarily an identity Sarah. The Peter you knew is still there. He's just decided he likes boys better; that's all. I mean he doesn't sound like a mincing queen as if he's making a conscious effort to be gay. You might find that he's spent most of his life secretly admiring boys and he's only just resigned himself to the fact. I know it's hard on you but you should respect it. There's nothing to stop you still being a dear friend to him. Perhaps you haven't got all you wished for but those things that were sweet are still there. He's according you an enormous privilege by openly declaring himself to you Sarah. That takes courage. You should think the better of him for it."

Sarah conceded the justice of Daniela's remarks ruefully. "Yes I suppose so. I was upset at the time though. Perhaps it was wounded ego. I mean I thought he was going to propose to me and it turned out he wasn't in the slightest bit interested in me."

"Oh I think he's interested in you Sarah. He just doesn't want to sleep with you."

"Well it's back to the original plan anyway."

"Which is?"

"That I marry Alan."

"Do you love him?"

Sarah sighed. "I don't know. I thought I did once. When I was first with him he always seemed so decisive and clever. I'd never known that before. I suppose at school I was always the clever one and I privately thought that most of the boys I knew were... well a bit slow. Alan was the first man that could match me in brains. He was so handsome too. He still is! Most girls turn to jelly when he talks to them. He can be very charming too. I suppose most girls would think I'm crazy for wondering if I ought to marry him; good looks, brains, charm and money as well. I suppose I ought to feel lucky."

"But you don't."

"I don't know. You know last winter he visited me in Bern and we drove through to Burgdorf where there's a lovely French restaurant and he treated me to dinner. Now that was nice of him but in the restaurant he picked up the menus and ordered for both of us without even consulting me. It was as if he didn't expect me to be able to read a French menu or know what might be on it. I even speak better French than he does! I saw then that Alan takes over your life. He expects to be the dominant partner and what he says is law. I don't have any say about where we'd live or what career I might have. Everything I do is supposed to be subservient to his ambitions. I'm just the decorative housewife waiting for him at home and to entertain his boss when he comes for dinner. He's even started talking about my household budget. I told him once that I'd like to go on to post graduate study; a Master's degree or even a PhD and his eyes just glazed over as if I'd just told him that I fancied taking up needlework or some other girly hobby. He sees me as a potential wife not a person."

"So why are you going to marry him?"

"Well I don't have any other option now do I?"

"Er you could just *not* marry him. That's still an option isn't it?"

"My family would never forgive me Daniela. It would have been bad enough if I turned Alan down to marry Peter but at least they might have come around to that in time. But just to reject Alan because of some nebulous doubts I have about him..... well they'd go nuts with me. The truth is that I don't even know myself why I'm suddenly questioning my marriage with Alan. He hasn't done anything particularly wrong. He's kept up his side of the bargain I suppose. All I've got is a sort of numbing dread about the thought of being married to him; as if it was a sort of suicide. I can't explain it."

"You don't have to explain it Sarah. Your rational mind might tell you that there's nothing at all wrong but your heart is telling you that there's something far wrong. You should listen to your heart."

"Nicole says the same thing in a different way."

"Well perhaps you should take her advice. I think you sometimes underestimate your friend Nicole. I think she's a lot deeper and more complex a character than you give her credit for."

"What makes you say that?"

"Just a hunch."

Sarah smiled resignedly. "Well I won't argue with you Danny. On recent form I'm hardly the best judge of character it seems. I didn't even manage to spot the fact that my best friend who I've known most of my life is gay."

"People don't always come with labels attached Sarah."

Sarah took a deep breath and turned to look at Daniela. "And you Danny?"

"What are you asking Sarah?"

"Well I mean... are you... well do you... I mean..."

"Are you asking if *I'm* gay; lesbian whatever you want to call it?"

Sarah blushed and lowered her eyes. "I'm sorry Danny. That was a very intrusive thing to ask. It's none of my business."

"I'd say it was very much your business Sarah." Daniela reached up to lay a hand on Sarah's face. "Would it worry you if I was?"

"I... I don't know."

Daniela's voice lowered to a soft seductive whisper. "Well would it worry you if I told you that my dearest wish right now is to take you in my arms, peel that dress from your body and lay you naked down among those flowers? Would it worry you if I told you that I want to tease your naked body with soft kisses, run my tongue over your nipples and stroke your thighs with my fingertips until you beg for release? Would it worry you if I said I wanted to take you and make love to you right here, right now under this blue sky and bury my lips between your legs until you cried out in joy? Would it worry you?"

Sarah felt herself trembling under Daniela's hand on her face. Her voice didn't seem to be working. "Yes," she croaked at last. "Yes I think it would."

Daniela sat up straight with a delighted laugh. "Oh well, in that case, I won't mention it!"

"Aww Danny! You're awful!" Sarah pushed her in exasperation and Daniela fell sideways giggling helplessly. "Stop teasing me." Sarah demanded with a laugh.

Daniela lay on her side; her eyes sparkling with amusement. "Oh Sarah it's so much fun being with you." Suddenly she sprang to her feet and grasped Sarah's hand to lift her. "Come along Miss Fuchs. Since your rejection of my base intentions precludes your public violation as part of the day's itinerary I suggest we go along to the restaurant and have a drink before you have to get back to the treadmill."

Sarah grinned, disarmed by Daniela's humour. "A drink sounds fine to me."

They walked slowly back along the path on the far side of the lakes and, in a new escalation of the bonding between them, they linked arms and took gentle satisfaction in the close physical contact between them. Sarah was quiet as they walked; strange thoughts in her head. Daniela looked at her quizzically and with soft amusement on her face. "A penny for your thoughts Sarah."

"I don't know if they're worth that much."

"Well tell me what they are and we can negotiate their value."

Sarah smiled but then she realised that she had been smiling all afternoon. "I'm sorry Danny. I'm just thinking." She paused in troubled concern. "Did you mean it? I mean did you mean what you said back then or were you just teasing me?"

"I said a lot of things back then Sarah. I could do with some specifics here!"

"Stop evading Danny. You know what I mean. I mean about what... I mean what you.... well wanted..." Sarah groaned agonisingly. "Oh God! However I say this it's going to sound horrible."

"'You mean about wanting to make love to you; about wanting to strip you naked and ravage you to my hearts' content?" Daniela asked in mock seriousness.

"Well yes I suppose so." Sarah regarded Daniela disapprovingly. Her friend had dissolved in giggles. "Stop laughing at me!"

Daniela recovered her composure with an effort and squeezed Sarah's arm. "Sarah my sweet. I'm not laughing at you. Seriously I'm not." She paused to stifle another giggle. "Well I am just a little bit, but for all the right reasons. I'm laughing because you are such a joy. I'm laughing just because it is so good to be with you."

"You're being evasive again."

"Not at all. I'm just taking my own sweet time to answer you. A woman never gives a straight answer Sarah until it is important and she absolutely has to. It's the basis of our feminine mystique and it drives men mad."

"I'm not a man Danny."

"Oh I know sweetheart. You're a beautiful and captivating woman."

"One that you'd like to ravage?" Sarah persisted.

Daniela dropped her frivolity and regarded Sarah seriously. "Sarah. Trust me when I say that I would never make you do anything that you didn't want to."

"There's a hole in that I could throw a cow through!"

"Why so?"

"Because you might make me *want* to do something; want to do something that maybe I shouldn't."

"Shouldn't, wouldn't or couldn't Sarah?"

"Stop clouding the issue."

Daniela smiled easily but her words were serious. "Sarah all I'm trying to say is that I respect you and I respect your wishes completely. Please disregard my wishes if you find them uncomfortable. I'm not trying to seduce you. I'm not trying to do anything other than simply enjoy your presence. Yes I have feelings for you but I will not impose them upon you. If all I have is your sweet company then that is sufficient for me. I'm sorry if I teased you."

"You never answered my question."

"I thought I was doing my best."

"I mean you never answered my question when I asked you if you were lesbian. You don't have to of course. Your private life is your own affair."

"I am not a lesbian Sarah."

Sarah blinked. "Oh!"

"No. I just happen to like girls."

Sarah shook her head in confusion. "*What*?"

Daniela laughed merrily. "Oh you should see your face. It's precious."

"Stop it Danny! What on earth do you mean?"

Daniela grasped Sarah's arm. "I mean Sarah that I don't follow the dictates of sexuality. I am what I am and I follow my heart. I don't see a person according to their gender Sarah. I see a person who I love and it is love that ultimately rules me. I don't classify myself according to my sexual orientation. I follow my heart not my gonads.

I'm looking for someone to love Sarah not someone to bed. Do you understand me?"

"I... I'm not sure. I... I thought perhaps you wanted to bed me."

"I want to love you Sarah; nothing more and certainly nothing less than that. If you came to my bed in love I would be the happiest woman in all this valley but I do not demand it. I will love you anyway; love you if all I ever have are just some sweet moments of your time, the touch of your hand in mine; the sound of your lovely voice or the sight of your treasured face. It is enough for me that you have touched my life with happiness and that I am a richer person for having known you. Anything else would be a blessing beyond that which I deserve to be granted. You are Sarah and my world is a better place for your having graced it with your presence."

Sarah choked and gripped Daniela's arm. "Nobody ever said anything like that to me before."

"Well it's time they did." Daniela brushed her hair from her face with a laugh that seemed to encompass the beauty around them in its merriment. "Come now! Let's not be so serious. Let's go and get a drink and treat ourselves to a big slab of Apfelstrudel with cream."

They shared the Apfelstrudel and Daniela teased Sarah by taking a blob of whipped cream on the end of her finger, holding it meaningfully aloft for a few seconds and then licking it from her finger seductively; her eyes never leaving Sarah. Sarah threw her napkin at her and Daniela giggled helplessly. It was frivolous and fun. Daniela was an incorrigible tease and in the serious and conservative Sarah she had found the perfect foil for her mischievousness. Sarah had seldom enjoyed a few hours company more.

At last, however, it was time for Sarah to return to work and Daniela insisted on accompanying her for the short walk back to the hotel. "How are you getting home tonight Sarah?" Daniela asked.

"Oh I'll probably walk if the weather stays nice."

"What? All the way back over to the other side of the valley? It's bloody miles!"

"I'm used to it Danny."

"What time does your shift finish?"

"About ten or maybe half past I suppose. Frau Fritzl just wants me for dinner service so I don't have to stay on for serving drinks after we stop serving food."

"It'll be dark by the time you get home. You can't walk home alone in the dark."

"Danny this is the Toggenburg. We've got a crime rate lower than the average nunnery. I'm not going to get mugged or raped or anything. The worst that can happen to me is that I step on a frog or something."

"What if it rains?"

"I've got a jacket with me or, if it's really bad, I'll just phone Nicky to come and pick me up."

Daniela shook her head firmly. "*I'll* pick you up! I'll drive around about tennish and drive you home."

"Oh Danny you don't have to do that."

"It will be my pleasure."

"But...." Sarah began.

Daniela raised a finger and placed it on Sarah's lips. "Hush now! Don't argue. I'll pick you up at ten. If you're not finished by then I'll just have a coffee and wait. I don't want you to walk home on your own in the dark. If it's not too late by the time you finish maybe we can stop off in Unterwasser for a nightcap somewhere."

Sarah grinned. "Ok! You've sold me."

They came to the front of the hotel and stopped. "Well until later then." Sarah ventured hesitantly.

Daniela laughed and reached into her bag. "I think you'd better take your uniform Sarah. You look lovely in that dress but it's not exactly what the well-dressed serving wench is wearing in Switzerland this season."

"Oh Christ!" Sarah had quite forgotten that she'd changed clothes. Hastily she draped her skirt and blouse over one arm and took her working shoes in her hand.

Daniela grinned wickedly and held Sarah's bra up on one finger. "Better not forget this honey." Blushing furiously Sarah snatched the offending item out of Daniela's hand affording more amusement to Daniela's impish sense of humour. Daniela raised her face expectantly. "Kiss?" she asked hopefully. Sarah glanced around hauntedly but the road was empty and they were alone. Quickly she pecked Daniela on the cheek. Daniela pouted. "That was rubbish Sarah! You'll have to do better than that! Kiss me properly!" Sarah groaned in exasperation but she did lean forward to kiss Daniela on the lips. Daniela took the opportunity to raise a hand to the back of Sarah's head; to hold her there and let this kiss linger. After a few seconds Sarah broke the embrace nervously glancing around again to reassure herself that there was nobody in view. Daniela was of course entirely unfazed. Daniela would have been perfectly at ease kissing her in a manner liable to cause public outrage in the middle of a crowded shopping mall. "Until later then Sarah." she whispered and with a toss of her long blond hair she turned to walk away pausing only to turn back and blow a kiss from a distance looking very pleased with herself.

Hastily Sarah dashed into the hotel. The first thing she saw was Frau Fritzl sat at a window seat in the foyer with her papers and correspondence laid out on the table in front of her along with a coffee cup. In despair Sarah realised that she must have had a panoramic view of everything that had just passed on the street outside from her vantage point in the window. She lifted her head from her paperwork to smile. "Hello Sarah."

"Oh hello Frau Fritzl. I... I'll just be a moment. I have to get changed."

Frau Fritzl lifted an amused eyebrow. "Nice dress Sarah. It looks lovely on you. Did Miss Devin give you it?"

"Oh er she just lent me it Frau Fritzl. We went for a walk and I didn't want to get my uniform dirty." It didn't sound at all convincing. Sarah was a terrible liar.

"I see. Well did you have a nice afternoon?"

"Yes thank you. Er Frau Fritzl may I ask when we'll be finished this evening. It's just that I'm getting a lift home."

"Really? Well I should think we can let you get away early Sarah. We're not going to be as busy as I thought. We've had a group cancel. What time's your lift?"

"Er about ten o'clock I think."

"Oh you'll be finished by then I should think. I'll see to it that you get away."

"Thank you. Er I'd better go and get changed."

Sarah rushed away. Frau Fritzl pushed her paperwork to one side and leaned back in her chair with a smile. "Well, well, well!" she thought to herself. "Sarah Fuchs and Daniela Devin! Now this *is* going to be interesting."

Chapter Thirty-Three

In the event, Sarah ended up working for the next three weeks at the Hotel Toggenburg. Sarah was slightly puzzled by this since Magdalena, Frau Fritzl's Portuguese waitress, was fit enough to return to duty after only three days and there seemed no great extra volume of trade in the hotel to justify Frau Fritzl retaining Sarah's services once Magdalena was fit. Frau Fritzl, however, insisted that Sarah's contribution was invaluable even while Sarah thought privately that there were more than sufficient staff members to cover the work without her. Sarah certainly did not object to the extension of the short-term agreement. On the contrary she was delighted. It wasn't just that she enjoyed working at the hotel although, of course, she did. Neither was it a case of Sarah really needing the money, although a girl of her prudent sense of financial management would always welcome a little extra income. No, the real reason she was delighted by the situation was because of the hotel's close proximity to Oberdorf and the opportunity it afforded her to spend her afternoons in the company of Daniela Devin; a situation, it must be said, that had Sarah been of less naive nature and thus able to see more clearly into the devious mind of Frau Fritzl, she would have realised was the *true* reason for her extended employment.

For multiple and complex reasons Frau Fritzl became the active champion of the developing relationship between Sarah and Daniela. This is not to say that she overtly advocated the relationship for she was far too subtle and discreet for that. It was more a case of quiet endorsement and encouragement. In effect she granted Sarah a safe haven from which to tentatively explore her strange new relationship and the occasional gentle guiding hand or word of advice. She sympathetically allowed Sarah a good deal of flexibility in her work to permit her to spend quality time with Daniela and she watched developments with growing satisfaction.

Frau Fritzl's motives for doing this were complicated. Certainly there were immediate benefits to her from a crassly commercial point of view. Frau Fritzl was a shrewd business woman and it had not escaped her notice that Sarah's presence among the working staff meant the daily accompanying presence of the Toggenburg's most glamorous and currently famous celebrity. Daniela was there every day towards the end of the lunchtime service to pick Sarah up and to spend the afternoon in her company. Frau Fritzl, to her credit, was always careful to shield Daniela from the intrusive attentions of inquisitive celebrity watchers but she was not above taking satisfaction in the prestige and accompanying upsurge in income afforded by her having a famous young star among her regular clientele. The lunchtime trade had increased noticeably once Daniela's visits had become a visibly recognisable daily routine although Daniela remained apparently serenely untroubled by the interest in her displayed by other clients in the hotel.

It would be unfair, however, to append a label of pure financial interest to Frau Fritzl's motives. The truth was that she *enjoyed* watching the relationship develop. In fact she thoroughly approved of Sarah and Daniela's interest in each other and considered it to be an affiliation to be nurtured and encouraged. Frau Fritzl almost saw herself in a mother's role concerning Sarah, who was a great favourite of hers. She had little time for Sarah's mother, considering her, unjustly, to be trivial and shallow and not the best maternal figure for the sweetly serious Sarah, who had inherited her great good looks but little of her character. Frau Fritzl had long harboured her own doubts about Sarah's marriage to

Alan and the conversation she had had with Sarah concerning it had done nothing to alleviate those doubts. It is also true that Frau Fritzl herself, after many years of unsatisfactory marriage and her subsequent happiness with another woman, was inclined to view a relationship between the two young women with sympathy.

Mostly however Frau Fritzl just gloried in the burgeoning happiness of her young protégé. Even Sarah herself did not realise just how much she was starting to blossom as a result of her daily contact with Daniela. She was not a girl who could easily hide her emotions however and her growing excitement each day, at the approach of the hour when Daniela would arrive to take her off for the afternoon, bordered on an almost childlike level of exuberance. To Frau Fritzl's eyes, Sarah had never seemed happier or more beautiful. She seemed almost radiant with joy and she sparkled like a jewel in her newfound joy. Frau Fritzl saw that Sarah was in love even before Sarah knew it herself.

The daily routine became swiftly established. Each day, Daniela would arrive at the hotel between half past one and two o'clock in the afternoon and take a quiet seat on the corner of the terrace with a good book. Sarah would serve her a cold drink or pot of tea and leave her with a smile or perhaps a daring wink. Frau Fritzl, eager to avoid any whiff of scandal attaching itself to Sarah, would, at a discreet moment, a little later, approach Daniela and inform her that Sarah would be finished in five minutes. Calmly Daniela would pay her bill, leaving a generous tip for one of Sarah's less obstinately proud colleagues, and then make her way around to the side of the hotel to meet Sarah at the staff entrance by the kitchen door. Daniela had firm ideas about the protocols of greeting and would always insist on a kiss. Sarah was slowly losing her inhibitions concerning Daniela's fixed notions of affectionate propriety and she came to look forward to these moments of tenderness when they could embrace briefly in the discreet concealment by the kitchen door. The embraces were by necessity very short (although they lingered more dangerously as time went by) but they were sweet and, if they stopped well short of erotic, Sarah nevertheless enjoyed the brief contact of Daniela's warm body and the taste of her lips.

Once the conventions of courtesy had been satisfied, the two young women were free to enjoy themselves for the afternoon. The Toggenburg sweltered under an unseasonal heat wave and they were days of bliss indeed. There was rarely any plan to their afternoons although Sarah, by now, made a habit of bringing a change of clothes with her to work to free herself from the constraints that would otherwise be placed on their activities by her working uniform.

There was another reason for Sarah bringing a change of clothes too. By doing so she hoped it would preclude Daniela from the necessity of providing Sarah with clothes from her own wardrobe. This was a largely unfulfilled hope however. Daniela proved to be incorrigible when it came to furnishing Sarah with gifts from the apparently inexhaustible resources of her boudoir and it was a rare day when she did not have some present for Sarah. This became one of the few minor points of contention between them for Daniela overruled all of Sarah's objections to her largesse and pressed her gifts on her with such childlike enthusiasm that Sarah was forced to capitulate.

Sarah was uncomfortable with her friend's generosity however and it did not help her discomfort that Frau Fritzl so obviously regarded with amusement the fact that she would disappear from the hotel dressed in one set of clothes at two o'clock only to return dressed entirely differently at half past six. Daniela's protestations that the gifts she pressed on Sarah were merely extraneous items from her own wardrobe were starting to wear thin as well and Sarah caught her red handed in the lie one day, when she pointed accusingly at the shop label, on a clearly expensive and beautiful silk blouse, that Daniela had negligently forgotten to remove when she had bought it that very morning in a shop in Buchs. Daniela seemed to regard Sarah as her own personal Barbie doll however and she so enjoyed dressing Sarah up for her own pleasure that Sarah found her remonstrances useless. Oddly enough Sarah's mother would have approved of this particular influence of Daniela's for Daniela succeeded in cajoling Sarah into more feminine items of clothing in just a few weeks of acquaintance than she had managed to bully her into in the last three years.

In order to offset Daniela's unceasing generosity, Sarah tried to reciprocate. That however was no easy matter. There was nothing that Sarah could think of in her possessions that she could gift to Daniela. What could you possibly give to someone who was rich enough to buy whatever their heart desired? Almost by accident Sarah discovered the truth that there are some things that not all the money in the world can buy. One day she gave Daniela a piece of mountain crystal; a six-sided prism of quartz perhaps three inches long that she and her brother and father had excavated during a mineral hunting expedition in the Bergell some years before. Daniela was enraptured by the gift and listened in pleasure as Sarah told her how her brother and she had extracted the crystal along with others in a day of hot labour high on a mountain in Southern Switzerland. Daniela took the crystal and wrapped it in a tissue with such reverence that Sarah realised that she could have gifted Daniela with a pair of her old hiking socks and Daniela would have treasured them as if they were one of the choicer items from one of King Solomon's mines.

Thereafter it became a game to Sarah to find among her collections small items that she could give as presents to Daniela. Of course they had little intrinsic value, for Sarah was not a rich girl, but they were presents of love and it delighted Sarah to see how much genuine pleasure they afforded her friend. One day for instance Sarah gave Daniela a traditional cowherd's belt, in black leather, decorated with brass cows and cowherds, depicting the annual herding of the cattle up on to the alps. Daniela was enormously pleased but devastated that she couldn't wear it straight away for it was a hardly suitable accessory to the soft pleated blue dress she wore. Sarah was wearing a pair of jeans and an old shirt and so Daniela solved the problem by insisting that they swap clothes so she could wear Sarah's gift. It meant a moment of embarrassment and rather puerile girlish giggling in a small copse of trees by the roadside but eventually they emerged dressed in the other's clothes. Daniela was slightly shorter than Sarah but otherwise the two girls were uncannily similar in proportions and Sarah was forced to admit, ruefully, that Daniela managed to look far more glamorous in her checked shirt and old faded jeans than she had ever done.

The only time that this giving of gifts ever really threatened to become seriously contentious was the day that Daniela gave Sarah a pair of earrings. Sarah had had her ears pierced two years earlier at her mother's insistence but she rarely wore earrings. Instead she maintained her piercings with small gold studs or little studs with gold cows on them as was traditional among the rural classes in Eastern Switzerland. Daniela was a great respecter of tradition but, nevertheless, it pained her that her beloved Sarah was walking about with a pair of cows in her ears. As a result, therefore, she determined to furnish Sarah with a proper pair of earrings. The result very nearly led to a row between them for, as Sarah opened the little box that Daniela presented her with, she gasped. Reclining inside were two beautifully elegant tear-drop earrings, silvery of sheen and each containing a dazzling, large clear gemstone. Sarah had never seen such brilliant gems. They danced with fire; sparkling with iridescence and flashing every colour of the spectrum.

"Danny!" Sarah protested heatedly. "This time you've gone too far. I can't possibly accept these. You can't give me diamond earrings. Look at the size of these stones. They must be worth a fortune."

Daniela waved her hands dramatically. "Whoa slow down! They're not diamonds."

"Nonsense! What else could they be?"

"Honestly Sarah they're not diamonds."

Sarah squinted at Daniela intensely. "Are you telling me that these are fake?"

"Er... they're not diamonds."

"You hesitated! You're telling me fibs."

"They're not. Really they're not."

"Are you sure?"

"Guide's honour!"

Sarah glared at her. "I think we've already established your lack of honourable credentials as a girl guide before Danny!"

Daniela laughed "All right. Just don't tell Brown Owl." She grew serious. "Honestly though Sarah they are not diamonds."

"Do you swear?"

"Look if I swear by all I hold holy that they are not diamonds will you wear them?"

Sarah regarded the jewels suspiciously. "They're awfully beautiful for fakes."

"I just thought they'd look nice on you. Do try them on Sarah. I promise you that they're not diamonds." Reluctantly Sarah allowed herself to be persuaded to don the earrings. They glittered sharply on her ears and Daniela clapped her hands in pleasure. "Gorgeous!" she declared and after that there was no alternative but for Sarah to wear them for the rest of the afternoon.

Sarah did not realise the depth of Daniela's perfidy until she returned to the hotel for her evening shift. Frau Fritzl was sitting once again in the window of the foyer overlooking the road and Sarah was beginning to suspect that Frau Fritzl was deliberately placing herself strategically there in order to observe Sarah's return with Daniela. Sarah had come out without a handbag and it gave her a problem. She took her earrings off in the foyer. It was, of course, not acceptable for her to wear earrings while serving. "Do you have somewhere I could put these Frau Fritzl?" she asked. "It's just that I don't have a handbag. Daniela gave them to me and I don't want to lose them."

Frau Fritzl rose and took the earrings. She looked at them closely and issued a small whistle. "Yes well we'd better find somewhere safe for these Sarah."

Sarah frowned uncertainly. "Daniela told me they were only fakes."

"Oh did she?"

"Please don't tell me that they're real."

Frau Fritzl smiled. "Real what?"

"I beg your pardon."

Frau Fritzl raised an eyebrow. "Come with me Sarah." She led Sarah to her office behind reception and rummaged in a drawer to pull out a small box. "You know I used to be a jeweller before I took up the hotel trade Sarah. I like to keep my eye in though. Let me have a look at your "fakes". Frau Fritzl opened the box and withdrew a small jeweller's eye loupe from the midst of a collection of tools of the jeweller's trade. She screwed the instrument into her eye and examined Sarah's earrings meticulously. "Hmm I thought so. Your young lady is very generous with you Sarah. These are not fakes."

Sarah slapped her hand on the table in exasperation. "I knew it! She was being deceitful with me. She swore that they weren't diamonds. She promised me. Why did she lie to me?"

Frau Fritzl laughed. "Sarah there is lying and there is lying. Poor liars just tell you whoppers. Clever liars on the other hand tell you the truth. They just don't tell you the whole truth. So Daniela told you that these weren't diamonds did she?"

"Yes."

"Well then she told you the truth. They're not diamonds."

"But you just said they weren't fakes."

"They're not. What Daniela didn't tell you is that they're moissanite."

"Moissanite?"

"Yes Moissanite isn't fake diamond because it's a gemstone in its own right. Its silicon carbide actually and it is a very rare mineral indeed. In fact, until recently, the only Moissanite known in the world was extra-terrestrial in nature because it was found in a meteorite that crashed in Arizona around fifty thousand years ago. It was discovered by a bloke called Henri Moisson in 1893. It's a remarkable mineral Sarah. It has a hardness of 9.25 on the Moh's scale which makes it the second hardest mineral known after diamond and much harder than sapphire. These are synthetic stones of course. Moissanite doesn't occur in gem stone sizes naturally. There's only one real manufacturer of moissanite gems in the world I believe and these earrings are by them; Charles and Colvard. Moissanite is more brilliant and lustrous than diamond. It has a refractive index of 2.65 to 2.69 as opposed to diamond's 2.42 and the lustre index is 20.4% compared with diamond's 17.2%. It also has better dispersion, what jeweller's call "fire", due to the faceting in the crystal structure. That's measured at 0.104 as compared to diamond's 0.044. That's what makes moissanite so brilliant and dazzling. Some aficionados even regard it as a more beautiful gemstone than diamond. It's certainly more spectacular in some respects and it's even more durable than diamond is."

Sarah was always fascinated by listening to an expert on their pet subject. She closed her mouth and took a breath. "Yes but is it valuable?"

"Oh yes Sarah. Of course it's not as valuable as diamond but it's a high-quality gemstone in its own right and these are good sized stones, probably one and a quarter carats and set in platinum to boot. Look after these Sarah. I doubt very much if these little trinkets cost your young lady a penny under two grand."

Sarah placed her hands on her hips in vexation. "I'll slap her! I swear I will!"

Frau Fritzl laughed. "I think your young lady has been a bit clever with you Sarah. She wanted to give you something special but she knew you wouldn't accept diamonds so she foisted these on you instead. Quite romantic really; a jewel that we only found out about when it fell to earth from the stars. She's quite a dreamer your young lady. She's taken a little bit of starlight and hung it on your ears. She must think a great deal about you Sarah."

Once Frau Fritzl had put it that way it was impossible for Sarah to remain angry with Daniela and, in truth, that was the only friction between them. Otherwise the days were truly bliss. They had only a few hours each day but they spent them well and if they did little else of great endeavour then it was sufficient simply to bask in each other's company amid the splendour of the summer Toggenburg. The path around the Schwendiseen was a favourite of theirs and the two girls linking hands or arms became a familiar sight in the long hot afternoons. They would sometimes have a picnic in the meadows abutting the lakes and talk incessantly about their lives, their hopes and dreams all the while with the unspoken awareness that these were somehow merging together.

Sometimes, as they sat together in the meadow, one would lie down and rest her head in the other's lap. On the first occasion that this happened, it was Daniela who, replete with food from their picnic, lay her head in Sarah's lap. Sarah was talking although the subject she was discussing could not have been of arresting interest for after a short while she realised she was talking to herself. Daniela, lulled by the droning of the bees among the floral beauty of the meadow, had fallen fast asleep. Sarah felt curiously touched by the sight of Daniela asleep in her lap, with her great cascade of golden locks draped across her knees. She fell silent not wishing to waken her and, in the relative safety of Daniela's slumber, she dared to succumb to the temptation to stroke that glorious hair. Daniela slept for nearly an hour and Sarah was content for her to do so.

On another occasion the roles were reversed. Sarah was learning new things about her friend all the while and one of the things she learned was that Daniela was a lover of poetry. She had an anthology of some of her favourite poets in her bag and as Sarah lay in her lap she read them to her. Sarah knew little about poetry and could not appreciate the finer points of poetry but she could, and did, appreciate the rich timbre of Daniela's beautifully modulated voice as she spoke the words that touched her heart. Daniela it seemed had a particular affinity for the great English poets of the romantic movement of the late eighteenth and early nineteenth centuries; Blake, Wordsworth, Shelley, Keats, Byron and Coleridge; but she also retained an affection for the later poets in the nineteenth century such as Tennyson, Browning, Arnold and Hopkins. What many of her favourite poems seemed to have in common was a deep romanticism sometimes bordering on the mythic. Daniela was a dreamer. Sarah could have listened to her all day.

Even better was the day when Daniela brought a guitar and sang some songs for her. It was a rare treat to be granted a private concert from an artist of such rich talent and acclaim. Sarah watched in fascination as Daniela plucked at the strings of the guitar; the fingers of her left hand moving in liquid motion over the fret-board teasing melodies out of the steel stringed, acoustic instrument to harmonise with the glorious tones of her voice. Sarah had hitherto only heard that voice in its full majesty on record accompanied by full instrumentation; embedded in a rich tapestry of complimentary sound. It was easier, Sarah realised, to sound so wonderful with all the technical assistance of the recording studio and with such accomplished backing as was afforded by the skills of talented musicians. Hearing Daniela singing purely, with only her own prowess on a guitar as accompaniment, Sarah began to fully understand the virtuosity of Daniela's genius.

It was remarkable that voice; almost an orchestra in its own right, soaring from spine-tingling heights to soft and sultry whispers with scarcely a hesitation. The vocal range was extraordinary for Daniela could handle comfortably the ranges of soprano to mezzo-soprano although some voice experts have classified her in the dramatic soprano category. She could lower her range into the contralto however and still retain power and timbre. Without doubt hers was one of the most flexible, widely ranging voices in contemporary music. Had fate or inclination determined otherwise she would have made an extraordinary opera singer. One critic described her as the best voice never to have performed "Carmen", a mezzo-soprano role, and one which, ironically, was Daniela's favourite opera. Daniela nevertheless brought a highly trained and virtuoso singing voice to the medium of popular music and enriched it beyond measure. Hers was a voice that transcended the often mediocre vocalisations of many pop artists and even the most unlearned of her fans in terms of technical knowledge could recognise that they were hearing something remarkable. There was magic in Daniela's voice. Sarah could only sit and listen in wonder.

Daniela did not simply serenade Sarah with her brilliance however. Sarah herself had a sweet singing voice and Daniela encouraged her to utilise it; teaching Sarah a simple song and urging her to sing the harmonies. In this way Sarah would always associate Daniela's voice with the beautiful surroundings of the meadows by the Schwendiseen. She would, in years to come, hear Daniela stun audiences in concert or admire her prowess in a recording studio but, for Sarah, the purest Daniela was just a beautiful woman sitting cross-legged, plucking at her guitar and beguiling the landscape with her luxurious melodies as if the very insects of the sunny hollow were stopping to listen to her or the very flowers of the meadow turning their heads toward the sunlight of her music.

On that day they ended up at the little restaurant at overlooking the lakes as was their habit and some guests and staff members prevailed upon Daniela to sing them a song. Daniela, always conscious of the debt she owed to her admiring fans, obliged and sang them a hauntingly beautiful love song. Her audience was enraptured but her eyes never left Sarah as she sang and Sarah knew, with a thrill that was both enchantment and apprehension, that Daniela sang the song for her.

Daniela was a consummate artist and her artistic talents did not stop at her musical abilities. One day she brought her sketch pad to their daily meeting. Sarah was astonished at Daniela's expertise. In a few quick strokes with a pencil or crayons she could capture the lines of the landscape or the essence of a flower in the meadows. She had a true artist's eye and her slim hands were as deft on paper as they were on the fingerboard of her guitar. She saw things with the eyes of a romantic and there was a freshness and yet a deep affinity to her visual depictions. She insisted on drawing a portrait of Sarah and Sarah sat uncomfortably as she worked. The drawing however was astonishing when Daniela finally permitted her to see it. It was instantly recognisable as Sarah but Sarah thought it made her far too beautiful and interpreted in some fashion that was elusive in nature. It was Sarah as Sarah had never seen herself before. It was Sarah through the eyes of Daniela; eyes helplessly tinted with love.

They did not spend all their time by the Schwendiseen for Frau Fritzl occasionally allowed Sarah a little more time in the afternoon for more ambitious endeavours. One day they walked up the hill to Iltios and, from there, took the cable car to the summit of the Chaserrugg, there to spend a pair of hours exploring the broad shoulder of the mountain. Sarah discovered that Daniela was frightened of heights. It was not a fear born of irrationality; not a disarming phobia of vertigo but rather just the fear of a person unfamiliar with the precipitous abysses of the high mountains. She did not display any discomfort in the cable car on the ride up the mountain, for she felt secure in the confines of the gondola, but, on the summit, she was afraid to approach the edge of the mountain overlooking the vista to the south. On their northern flanks the mountains of the Churfirsten were relatively benign slopes flowing down to the Upper Toggenburg. To the south however they fell away in a series of awesome cliffs straight down into the waters of the Walensee, reputedly one of the deepest lakes in Switzerland, some one thousand nine hundred metres below. Daniela would only approach the edge of this dizzying chasm with Sarah's arms clutched firmly around her waist and when Sarah nonchalantly stepped onto a rock perched precariously high above this terrifying vertical space Daniela covered her eyes and pleaded with her to return to safer ground.

Otherwise they spent their time looking at the high alpine flora on the mountain summit or throwing bread from their sandwiches high into the air to test the aerobatic prowess of the Alpine Choughs that wheeled in the air around the mountain. Daniela became fascinated by the little black crows with their bright yellow beaks and red legs and became obsessed in her quest to throw the most difficult catch to them she could. The choughs picked every effort of hers out of the air with effortless alacrity and she clapped her hands in gleeful applause at their flying skill. "How do they do it?" she asked in wonder.

Sarah observed her childlike enthusiasm with pleasure. "They're just masters of the air." She told her.

"You're not kidding. Forget Jonathon Livingstone Seagull. These babes could teach any seagull a few lessons in aerodynamics."

Sarah laughed. "For heaven's sake give me one of those sandwiches before you feed *all* of them to the bloody choughs."

On another day they walked over to Oberdorf and took the chair lift up to Gamsalp. Sarah had been looking forward to showing Daniela the Gamsalp for it was a favourite of hers. The lovely alpenrose scrub zone between the tree-line and the higher alpine meadows captivated Daniela and she wandered with Sarah among the outcroppings of rock, potholes, dwarf mountain pines, reclining willow shrubs and patches of velvety green short grass studded with alpine flowers in enraptured amazement. She kicked off the trainers she had donned for the afternoon's excursion and luxuriated in the feel of the short grass beneath her bare feet. Sarah showed her the beautiful Spring Gentians of iridescent blue tinged with purple and their larger cousins the Trumpet Gentians. She hunted for some time before she found another related bloom; the tiny and delicate Snow Gentians which were a speciality in this region.

She became caught up in the game of displaying her beloved Gamsalp to Daniela and in so doing precipitated one of those cusp moments that would forever define their relationship. She was kneeling on a grassy patch, so immaculate it seemed as if it had been mowed and tended to a perfection by a loving lawn keeper, and examining carefully some of the precious and tiny blooms that grew in profusion among it when she became aware that Daniela had grown silent. She glanced up to see that Daniela was sat on a rock watching her. Daniela's eyes were shining unfathomably and she seemed to be holding her breath.

"What are you looking at?" asked Sarah nervously.

"You! I'm looking at you in your garden," Daniela swept out a hand to encompass the loveliness of the alp. "This is your natural habitat Sarah. You have no idea how beautiful you look just kneeling there among your flowers and your butterflies. This is Sarah's garden. I feel privileged to be allowed to share it with you."

"It's not my garden Danny. I didn't make it."

"You make it perfect with your presence Sarah." In a fluid movement Daniela rose from her rock and crossed the distance between them. She kneeled down and took Sarah's hands. "Will you grant me a kiss my lady Sarah; the benediction of a kiss to tell me that I'm blessed in this, your garden?"

Sarah flushed. "Oh Danny...."

"Ever such a little kiss Sarah. It would mean so much to me."

So Sarah kissed her but with her heart beating wildly she dare not let the kiss linger and she caught her voice to say. "We'd better be getting back to the chairlift soon Danny. I don't want to be late."

Daniela smiled and helped her to her feet. "Of course." Sarah wondered why her knees felt weak and why the moment seemed charged with destiny. "Sarah's Garden" would become Daniela's most beloved and popular ballad, birthed on a sunny, early summer day in the Gamsalp.

Chapter Thirty-Four

That poignant moment on the Gamsalp was characteristic of the slowly growing intimacy between them. There were limits; definable boundaries across which they did not cross and Sarah was aware that it was she that determined the parameters of those boundaries. Put simply, there were physical limits to their intimacy that Sarah dared not transgress. Daniela of course had no such limits but she respected Sarah's placement of the boundary stones and kept firmly to them even while she chipped away, with relentless patience, at Sarah's perception of those boundaries. For the boundaries moved inexorably in the direction of growing physical intimacy by the day. A caress, touch or contact that might be rejected on one day would be tentatively accepted by the second and regarded as acceptable by the third. Daniela was an infinitely patient young woman and content to allow their intimacy to develop by such tiny increments.

They had started by holding hands on their walks and by now that was the most natural thing in the world. From there it was an easy step to linking arms and, from that point, not an enormous gulf to wrapping an arm around each other's waist as they strolled among the natural beauty which so complimented the growing ease between them. Daniela was always more tactile than Sarah and far more likely to touch Sarah with perhaps the palm of her hand against Sarah's face or reach out and finger Sarah's hair, curling it around her fingers. She loved to stroke Sarah's hands as they sat together and she would examine them with her fingers for protracted periods or rub the palms with her thumbs, pausing occasionally to lift them to her lips and kiss them. She had a habit, when in a particularly languorous mood, of coming up behind Sarah and wrapping both her hands around her waist and placing her head affectionately upon her shoulder. She would hold the position for a second or two before bestowing a gentle kiss to the side of Sarah's neck and then releasing her. Sarah always found herself breathless after such a contact and her heart would be loud in her chest. In a more playful or teasing mode, Daniela would slap Sarah quite sharply on the rump, making her jump, and then giggle helplessly at Sarah's outraged indignation and blushes.

They were not, in the most base of definitions, lovers for their intimacy never extended into overt sexuality but even Sarah realised that they were growing ever closer toward that Rubicon and that she was fighting a rear-guard action on that watershed of no return. Sarah herself was forced to admit that if anyone should chance to observe them in the precious moments that they were alone they would come to the inescapable conclusion that the two young women were lovers. In fact, even in public, the close contact between them was sufficient to suggest something more than mere sisterly affection but, so subtly incremental had Daniela's campaign of patient seduction been, Sarah remained almost unaware of just how demonstrative the gestures of intimacy between them had escalated.

Apart from Daniela's startling suggestion on their first afternoon together the subject of sexual intimacy only arose one more time between them and that in a somewhat oblique fashion. They were sat in the Schwendi restaurant shortly before Sarah was due to leave and present herself back at work. Daniela was asking Sarah at what time she needed to be picked up that evening after work for it had also become a habit that every night, when Sarah's shift was finished, Daniela would come for her in the car to drive her home to the Alpli. They were also moments of sweetness for Sarah for they would drive home slowly as Sarah wound down from work and perhaps take a nightcap at the Post or the Sternen in Unterwasser before Daniela drove Sarah up the hill to the Alpli. Occasionally they would sit in the car close to Sarah's home to chat awhile, before parting with a last kiss, although Sarah, fearing Nicole's disapproval, never invited Daniela in. Daniela however had another thought. "You know Sarah," she said, "If you'd bring a change of clothes you could stop at my place tomorrow night. It would save you that long walk in the morning and you could put your working clothes in my washer to be ready for work."

Sarah hesitated long. "I think Nicole would worry about me Danny."

"So just give her a call and tell her that you're stopping over at the hotel or something. I'm sure that she'd understand."

"I... I still don't think it's a good idea Daniela."

"Why?"

"You know why!"

Daniela smiled gently. "Listen Sarah I'm not trying to coerce you into bed or something. I don't mind driving you home at all. On the contrary I want to. I'd just like to save you such a long walk in the morning."

"We... we'd end up in bed Danny. I... I can't do that!"

"Sarah! I have a big house with plenty of bedrooms. You'd have your own room; quite separate. You can even lock the door if you're that worried. Please trust me."

"I *do* trust you Danny."

"Then what's the problem? I'm not going to *do* anything."

"I know you're not. It's *me* I'm worried about Danny. I don't trust *myself*!"

Daniela nodded with a soft smile. "Ok Sarah. I understand. Look you'd better get going. I'll pick you up after ten." And so they left it but that tension of imminent explosion remained.

The days with Daniela were an escape however and Sarah was honest enough to understand that she was living in a cloud cuckoo land of unreal fantasy. The problems that beset her would not vanish simply because she enjoyed a few hours of enchantment with her new friend. Indeed the problems were exacerbated the longer she spent under Daniela's spell. In spite of Daniela's protestations to the contrary it was obvious that Daniela had hopes for their relationship that went far beyond that which Sarah was prepared to surrender to. Sarah, alone in her bed at night, would often wonder about that. To her, Daniela was such a glittering star that she could not believe truly that Daniela was so enraptured by her.

Sarah was modest; too modest in fact for she was frequently the last person to realise just how remarkable she was. Sarah considered herself to be down to earth, possessed of a realistic appreciation of her own worth and that worth, while not without merit, to be, nevertheless, of fairly mundane characteristics. She took so much interest in the world about her it never occurred to her to really take an interest in herself. It is often a trait of authentically extraordinary people that they believe themselves to be very ordinary when of course they are anything but. Nearly everybody who knew Sarah believed otherwise. She thought she had friends. She had more than that. She was very nearly universally loved. Her influence among the people who knew her extended far beyond her comprehension and she would have blinked in bafflement had anyone tried to tell her that. Nearly everybody recognised some beauty in Sarah's spirit. Few people however would find the words to articulate it or be able to so capture it in understanding. It took a rare talent and sensitivity; perhaps an artist's feel for the wondrous and magical to gaze into Sarah' soul and comprehend the true nature of the light within, that others would merely have a glimpse of, as it shined through the cracks in the armour of outward persona that

Sarah presented to the world; the armour so rigidly erected that Sarah herself had come to believe was her real character. It took a mind of extraordinary perception to discern the true Sarah. It took in fact a Daniela.

At this point only Frau Fritzl had seen it. Only she had seen the instantaneous contact that was inevitable between the two young women. Sarah and Daniela were, to her, made for each other; kindred spirits forged in some favourite mold of the creator and brought gently together so that the sum total of their combined spirits would blaze forth in dazzling spectacle. She might have reflected, however, that if you slap two pieces of uranium 235 together you may well create a blast of light to rival the sun but you will leave devastation in its wake.

Dancing like a doomed moth around the flame of Daniela, Sarah was forever on the edge of catastrophe. The world outside the dream days she spent with Daniela was slowly beginning to impinge itself. There were testy messages from her mother reminding her of her forthcoming marriage and her social and logistical obligations in preparation for that. There was a particularly wrenching call from her father to ask when she was planning on coming home. Her father considered her home to be with her family. Sarah's patient explanation that she already *was* home seemed to be falling on deaf ears. Then there was a phone call from America from Alan. Alan seemed to have learned his lesson from his earlier call for he was kind and understanding and he was careful to tell her how much he cared about her and how much he was looking forward to seeing her again. Sarah suspected that he had been forewarned by her parents or, even more possibly, by Peter, that she was being difficult and to be sure to treat her nicely, for she had never had such a pleasantly warming telephone call from Alan. Sarah found herself racked with guilt. Peter himself called briefly one morning to inquire how she was and it was a difficult few minutes before she could insist that she had to be on her way to work.

Sarah was living for the moment however even while she didn't quite understand what the moment was. The only matter of immediate concern to her; the one that couldn't be placed on a back burner was Nicole. In fact Nicole and Sarah saw little of each other in the days when Sarah worked at the Toggenburg hotel. Nicole was working long hours at the Hirschen in Wildhaus and away early in the morning for the breakfast shift. She'd work until lunch then take a few hours off before working the evening shift in the restaurant. During her few hours in the afternoon Sarah of course was spending her free time with Daniela. Sarah would often return home late and find Nicole already in bed in preparation for another early start. Thus, although occupying the same house they had only the briefest glimpses of each other.

In honesty, Sarah was quite relieved that her contacts with Nicole were so brief for she was curiously reluctant to have to explain to Nicole that she was spending her time with Daniela. Somehow Sarah's relationship with Daniela was driving a subtle wedge between Sarah and Nicole. Sarah didn't understand why but she sensed that Nicole disapproved of the relationship. It was becoming obvious, however, that, in spite of the fact that Sarah didn't mention that she was seeing Daniela, Nicole was nevertheless aware of it. Nicole after all was not an unobservant girl and, considering that Sarah was the worst person imaginable at concealment and the fact that Nicole had known her most of her life, she was bound to know that something was going on. For one thing Sarah was careless on one occasion by placing a new dress that Daniela had given her in the wash. Nicole knew Sarah's wardrobe as well as she did herself and the presence of an expensive new item in it would have instantly alerted her. That Sarah's wardrobe was starting to fill out with items of clothing and jewellery would have sounded all Nicole's alarm bells and Sarah found herself discreetly hiding her new acquisitions at the back of her closet. Another signal was that Daniela drove Sarah home each night. Sarah never invited Daniela in, although she knew that would have been the civil thing to do, but, instead, traded a last kiss in the car before dashing indoors. Nicole was not always asleep when she came home and Sarah knew that she must have heard the car. The engine in Daniela's Ferrari was distinctive and an unmistakable klaxon in the quiet of the Alpli.

It was always a nervous moment when Sarah came home to find Nicole not in bed. She continuously expected Nicole to confront her with the evidence of her dallying with Daniela. Oddly enough, it never happened. Nicole seemed to be deliberately avoiding the subject. She never even raised Daniela's name as if the topic were taboo in the house. She pointedly never suggested that Sarah and she meet up in the afternoon when they were both, free as if tacitly acknowledging that Sarah would have other plans for her free time. On top of this she seemed a little spiritless for the moment and reluctant to talk. She looked tired Sarah thought. Perhaps she was working too many hours. Sarah mentioned Nicole's mood in passing to Daniela one day and she was surprised when Daniela grew a little quiet and melancholy. "Poor girl." she said.

"What do you mean?"

"Oh nothing Sarah. It's just from what you've said that I think she might be having a bad time for the moment. Be kind to her won't you."

"What makes you say that?"

Daniela shook her head. "Nothing much. I like Nicole though and I don't like to think of her being sad. Take care of her Sarah." Then Daniela had changed the subject and Sarah had the feeling that she had said less than she could have done.

In fact, despite the underlying tension in the house, Sarah and Nicole only had one minor row during this period which, on the face of it, had absolutely nothing to do with Daniela. Sarah arrived home one night to see that the light was on in Nicole's bedroom and that she was clearly still up. Sarah liked a mug of hot chocolate before retiring and set out to make herself one in the kitchen. Nicole called from the upstairs landing. "That you Sarah? Are you making a drink?"

"Yes I'm just putting some cocoa on. Do you want a mug?"

"Please."

So Sarah had made a mug of cocoa for Nicole and carried it up to her bedroom. Nicole was squatting on a chair by her computer console. She had evidently just switched it on for she had the start-up screen showing on the monitor. Sarah came to a shocked halt. Nicole's background image on her start up screen showed a young woman dressed in a pink bikini lounging by the side of the Schwendisee; herself. Sarah pointed at the image accusingly. "What," she inquired indignantly "Is *that* doing on your computer?"

Nicole looked at the screen in puzzlement. "What are you talking about?"

"You know bloody well what I'm talking about. That picture."

"It's the photo I took of you the other day at Schwendi. I downloaded it from my camera to my computer."

"I know bloody well what it is! What I want to know is why you thought fit to blazon it across the front of your computer screen."

"Why not? It's a nice photo."

"I think you might have asked my permission before putting it on your computer screen."

"Oh come on Sarah. Why can't I have a picture of my best friend on my computer? You've got pictures of me in your picture collection on *your* computer. I've seen them. You've even got a picture of me hanging on your wall for heaven's sake."

"Not ones with no bloody clothes on I haven't."

"Don't be such a prude Sarah. You're perfectly decent with a bikini on. Anyway it's not as if I'm showing it to the whole world. There's only me that sees it and I've seen you without your clothes on before!"

"I think you ought to remove it."

"Well I don't. It's a lovely photograph of you and I like it. It's doing no harm whatsoever as wallpaper on my computer console and I refuse to delete it just in deference to your outmoded bloody Victorian sense of propriety. I've hardly got any decent photos of you and that one stays."

"I wouldn't display a half-naked photo of *you* Nicky."

"No. You're right. You wouldn't!"

Sarah frowned. "What are you trying to say?"

"Only this. I have a nice photo of my best friend and I love it. It is not in the public domain but merely a private image for my own personal pleasure. You can't deny me the simple pleasure of your photograph for my own private enjoyment. Anyway I see so little of you these days I have to have a photograph to remind me what you look like."

The last statement came perilously close to dangerous waters and Sarah bit back her retort. "Well all right then." she conceded reluctantly. "Just don't be sending it to anyone else."

It was, in truth, the only real moment of overt friction between them but it disturbed Sarah not least because of her guilt over her neglect of Nicole. It was one more reminder that her friendship with Daniela was fraught with danger. Daniela was an irresistible siren luring her with sweet promise toward the shoals of jagged rocks upon which her life could flounder. Frau Fritzl might have phrased it differently. She was not insensible to the risks involved in Sarah's flirtation with disaster. She was also concerned that Sarah's inbuilt caution could promise even more danger; that she could yet miss the opportunity she might regret the rest of her days through pusillanimous caution. Yes there was a precipice but sometimes in life you had to take life by the horns, grasp your chance and the devil take the hindmost. Sometimes you had to throw yourself off the precipice. But, before you could jump off the precipice, you had to climb the mountain. In Frau Fritzl's opinion Sarah and Daniela had a mountain to climb. Three weeks after Sarah starting to work in the hotel, she and Daniela set off for the mountain.

(to be continued)

Postscript

Although the people in this story are completely fictional and bear no resemblance to anybody alive or dead, the Toggenburg is a real place and I have done my best to depict it as accurately as possible. It is a truly lovely valley in the mountains of Eastern Switzerland set between the bulk of the Santis Massif to the north and the Churfirsten chain of mountains to the south. The cover picture of this volume shows the Upper Toggenburg looking eastwards. The mountain in the centre of the picture is the Schaffberg and one can just see the ridge rising from it, to the left, toward the summit of Mt Santis. The village in the middle distance is Nesslau and the village of Unterwasser is just around the curve in the valley. The side valley immediately below the Schaffberg is the Alpli; the little hanging valley where Sarah and her irrepressible friend Nicole share their little cottage.